Critical Praise for *All or Nothing* by Preston L. Allen

"As with Frederick and Steven Barthelme's disarming gambling memoir, *Double Down*, the chief virtue of *All or Nothing* is its facility in enlightening nonbelievers, showing how this addiction follows recognizable patterns of rush and crash, but with a twist—the buzz is in the process, not the result . . . As a cartographer of autodegradation, Allen takes his place on a continuum that begins, perhaps, with Dostoyevsky's *Gambler*, courses through Malcolm Lowry's *Under the Volcano*, William S. Burroughs's *Junky*, the collected works of Charles Bukowski and Hubert Selby Jr., and persists in countless novels and (occasionally fabricated) memoirs of our puritanical, therapized present. Like Dostoyevsky, Allen colorfully evokes the gambling milieu—the chained (mis)fortunes of the players, their vanities and grotesqueries, their quasi-philosophical ruminations on chance. Like Burroughs, he is a dispassionate chronicler of the addict's daily ritual, neither glorifying nor vilifying the matter at hand." **—New York Times Book Review**

"Dark and insightful . . . The well-written novel takes the reader on a chaotic ride as . . . Allen reveals how addiction annihilates its victims and shows that winning isn't always so different from losing." **—Publishers Weekly**

"A gambler's hands and heart perpetually tremble in this raw story of addiction. 'We gamble to gamble. We play to play. We don't play to win.' Right there, P, desperado narrator of this crash-'n'-burn novella, sums up the madness . . . Allen's brilliant at conveying the hothouse atmosphere of hell-bent gaming. Fun time in the Inferno." **—Kirkus Reviews**

"Allen's new novel poignantly depicts the life of P, a likable guy who drives a school bus and lives with his wife and four sons in a pleasant house; a guy with brains but no discipline . . . Told without preaching or moralizing, the facts of P's life express volumes on the destructive power of gambling. This is strongly recommended and deserves a wide audience; an excellent choice for book discussion groups." **—Library Journal**

"*All or Nothing* is funny, relentless, haunting, and highly readable. P's inner dialogues illuminate the grubby tragedy of addiction, and his actions speak for the train wreck that is gambling." — *ForeWord Magazine*

"By turns harrowing, illuminating, and endearing, Preston L. Allen's *All or Nothing* is more than a gut punch, it's a damn good book."
—**Maggie Estep, author of** *Alice Fantastic*

"*All or Nothing* is a breathless tour through the mind of P, a gambling junkie who divines lucky numbers everywhere, even in the mumblings of his severely asthmatic son as he comes out of anaphylactic shock. Winning the bet is the only thing. And money has little value except as a means to place the next one. Preston L. Allen's writing is as tight as a high wire. Out of the hyper-kitsch world of gamblers and the casinos they inhabit, Allen creates a novel that is frightening and sad and thrilling." —**Gonzalo Barr, author of** *The Last Flight of Jose Luis Balboa*

"Allen has done for gambling what William S. Burroughs did for narcotic addiction. He's gotten into the heart of the darkness and shown us what it feels like to be trapped, to be haunted, to live without choice. Allen is relentless and unsparing in his depiction of the life of a gambling addict, from the magical thinking to the visceral thrill of risking it all. And now the world will know what we in Miami have known for a long time: he is such a good a writer it's scary."
—**John Dufresne, author of** *Johnny Too Bad*

"*All or Nothing* is a smart, riveting novel of obsession; an in-depth character study rendered in tight, sparkling prose. This is a moving story of love and addiction that will hook the reader from the first word."
—**Ivonne Lamazares, author of** *The Sugar Island*

Jesus Boy

Jesus Boy

Preston L. Allen

Published by Akashic Books
©2010 Preston L. Allen

ISBN-13: 978-1-936070-04-6
Library of Congress Control Number: 2009938473

Printed in Canada
First printing

Akashic Books
PO Box 1456
New York, NY 10009
info@akashicbooks.com
www.akashicbooks.com

To Dawn, thanks for choosing love

Acknowledgments

Many thanks to my brothers: Cameron Allen, Edgar Allen, Sherwin Allen; and to my brothers-from-a-different-mother: Jason Murray, Kevin Eady, Gene Durnell, Geoffrey Philp, Leejay Kline; and to the greatest teachers a young writer could ever hope to have: Les Standiford, Lynne Barrett, John Dufresne, Meri-Jane Rochelson, and James Hall—thanks for being there at the birth of this baby.

I give my thanks as well to those who gave generously of their time to read the parts or the whole, or who listened attentively while I read it to them: Lou Skellings, Ken Boos, Andrea Selch, Janell Walden Agyeman, Joseph McNair, Josett Peat, Elena Perez, Ivonne Lamazares, Robin Steinmetz, Joseph Steinmetz, Lisa Shaw, Tiina Lombard, Ellen Milmed, Edward Glenn (your comments on the "Pinkeye" section were great—sorry that passage didn't make the final cut, LOL), Ariel Gonzalez, Sally Naylor, Jesse Milner, Ellen Wehle, Elizabeth Cox, Gonzalo Barr, David Beatty, Marlene Naylor, Anthony Thomas. Your patience and your wise words are much appreciated. I listened . . . most of the time.

To Johnny Temple, words cannot express my gratitude, but all I have are words. Thanks, Johnny. You make writing books fun again.

I. Testament of Innocence

Thirty Fingers

I never really wanted to play the piano, but it seemed that even before I touched my first key I could.

When the old kindergarten teacher left to go have her baby, the new teacher made us sing: "Row, row, row your boat, gently down the stream . . ."

"Elwyn," said the new teacher whose long name I could never remember, "why aren't you singing with us? Don't you know the words?"

Yes, I knew the words—just like I knew the words to "Mary Had a Little Lamb" and "Twinkle, Twinkle, Little Star"—I had memorized them as soon as the old teacher, Mrs. Jones, had sung them to us the first time. But I could not sing the words. Mrs. Jones knew why I could not sing the words but not this new teacher.

"Elwyn, why won't you sing with us?"

I could not lie, but neither was I strong enough in the Lord to tell the teacher with the long name that singing secular music was a sin. So I evaded. I pointed to the piano and said, "Mrs. Jones plays the piano when we sing."

"But I can't play the piano," said the new teacher. "Won't you sing without the piano?"

I had assumed all adults could do a simple thing like play the piano, so this amazed me. "I'll show you how to play it," I said, crossing the room with jubilant feet.

"Can you play the piano, Elwyn?"

"Yes," I said. Though I had never touched a piano key before in my life, I had observed Mrs. Jones at school and the ministers of music at church and had developed a theory about playing I was anxious to test: high notes go up and low notes go down.

After a few tries, I was playing the melody with one finger. "See? Like this," I said. My theory was correct.

The other kids squealed with excitement. "Let me play, let me play," each cried.

What's the big deal? I wondered. High notes go up, low notes down. It only made sense.

But the new teacher had to give each one a turn and I directed them: "Up, up, now down, down. No. Up, up more."

When it came to be my turn again, I played "Mary Had a Little Lamb." The new teacher got the others to sing the tune as I played. I had but a child's understanding of God's Grace. I reasoned that if I sang secular words, I'd go to hell, but I had no qualms about playing the music while others sang.

I was young.

That day should have been the last time I played the piano because in truth my fascination with the instrument did not extend further than my theory of high and low tones, which I had sufficiently proven. No, I did not seek to be a piano player. I assumed, most innocently, that I already was one. Should I ever be called upon to play a tune, I would simply "pick it out" one note at a time. This was not to say, however, that I was not interested in music.

On the contrary, music was extremely important.

Demons, I was certain, frolicked in my room after the lights were turned off. At night, I watched, stricken with fear, as the headlights of passing automobiles cast animated shadows on the walls of my room. Only God, who I believed loved my singing voice, could protect me from the wickedness lurking in the dark. Thus, I sang all of God's favorite tunes—hummed when I didn't know the words—in order to earn His protection. When I ran out of hymns to sing, I made up my own.

I am Your child, God. I am Your child—
It is real, real dark, but I am Your child.

God, I believed, was partial to high-pitched, mournful tunes with simple, direct messages. God was a brooder.

What did I know about His Grace?

What did I know about anything?

Ambition. Envy. Lust. Which was my sin?

I did not want my neighbor's wife. I did not want his servant. I did not want his ass. There was, however, a girl. Peachie. Brother and Sister Gregory's eldest daughter.

I had known her all of my life, but when she walked to the front of the church that Easter Sunday, sat down at the piano, and played "Were You There When They Crucified My Lord?"—my third-grade heart began to know envy and desire.

Peachie Gregory did not pick out tunes on the piano. No, she played with all of her fingers—those on her left hand too. Such virtuosity for a girl no older than I. And the applause!

That was what I wanted. I wanted to go before the congregation and lead them in song, but all I could do was play with one finger. I had to learn to play like Peachie.

An earnest desire to serve the church as a minister of music, then, did not compel me to press my parents—a maid and a school bus driver—for piano lessons, though that is what I claimed. When they said they could not afford piano lessons, much less a piano, I told them a necessary fiction.

"Angels flew down from heaven playing harps. They pointed to this great big giant piano. They wanted me to join them. I trembled because I knew I couldn't play the piano." I opened my eyes as wide as possible so as to seem more scared and innocent. "I have never taken any lessons."

"Were you asleep?" my father asked, one large hand clutching my shoulder, the other pushing his blue cap further up on his head, exposing the bald spot. "Was it a dream?"

Before I could answer, my mother jumped in: "He already told you he was wide awake. It was a vision. God is speaking to the child."

"You know how kids are," said my father, from out of whose pocket the money would come. He chuckled. "Elwyn's been wanting to play piano so bad, he begins to hear God and see visions. It could be a trick of the devil."

My mother shook a finger at him. "Elwyn should have been taking piano lessons a long time ago. He is special. God speaks to animals and children. Elwyn doesn't lie."

My father peered down at me with a look that said, Tell the truth boy, but I kept my eyes wide and innocent, still struck by the wondrous and glorious vision I had seen. My father said to my mother, "But we can't be so literal with everything. If it's a dream, maybe we need to interpret it."

"Interpret nothing!" shot back Isadore the maid, who pursued Roscoe the school bus driver to the far side of the room; he fell into his overstuffed recliner where it was customary for him to accept defeat. "You call yourself a Christian," she shouted, raising holy hands, "but you'd rather spend money at the track than on your own boy! Some Christian you are."

My father hung his head in shame. He was beaten.

He did, however, achieve a small measure of revenge. Instead of giving up his day at the track, he told my grandmother, that great old-time saint, about my "visions," and my grandmother, weeping and raising holy hands, told Pastor, and Pastor wrote my name on the prayer sheet.

How I cringed each week as Pastor read to the congregation, "And pray that God send Brother Elwyn a piano to practice on."

I believed that God would send one indeed—plummeting from heaven like a meteor to crash through the roof of the Church of Our Blessed Redeemer Who Walked Upon the Waters and land right on my head.

I had lied and liars shall have their part in the lake of fire.

I prayed, "Heavenly Father, I lied to them, but I am just a child. Cast me not into the pit where the worm dieth not."

Thank God for Brother Morrisohn and his ultrawhite false teeth. If he hadn't stood up and bought that piano for me, I would have surely died just like Ananias and Sapphira—struck down before the doors of the church for telling lies.

Brother Morrisohn was a great saint, a retired attorney who gave copiously of his time and energy—as well as his money—to the Church of Our Blessed Redeemer Who Walked Upon the Waters. It was his money that erected the five great walls of the church, his money through the Grace of God that brought us warmth in the winter and coolness in the hot Miami summer. It was his money that paid Pastor's salary in the '60s when the Holy Rollers built a church practically on our back lot and lured the weaker members of the flock away. After a fire destroyed the Rollers' chapel, it was Brother Morrisohn's money that purchased the property back from the bank, putting the Rollers out of business for good.

"I can't sit by and watch God's work go undone," he always said.

On the day they delivered the secondhand upright piano, he told me, "You're going to be a great man of God, Elwyn," and he extended his forefingers like pistols and rattled a few keys.

He was already in his seventies by then, but lean and healthy and proud of his looks. His full head of gray hair, which he parted stylishly down the middle, was a contrast to his dark, handsome complexion. He always wore a jacket and tie and carried a gold-tipped cane. Grinning, he showed his much-too-white false teeth. "I love music, but I never learned to play. Maybe someday you'll teach me."

"I will," I said. I had just turned eight.

"I wish you would teach him, Elwyn," said Sister Morrisohn, the wife who was about half Brother Morrisohn's age. From a distance she could be mistaken for a white woman with her fair skin and her long black hair cascading down her back. She was the prettiest woman at church, everyone always said, though she had her ways, whatever that meant. She removed her shawl and draped it lovingly over his shoulders. "We have that big piano at home no one ever plays."

"I'm not cold," Brother Morrisohn protested, frowning, but he did not remove the lacy shawl. He rattled the keys again.

"I'll teach you piano, Brother Morrisohn," I said.

He reached down and patted my head. "Thank you, Elwyn."

I was so happy. I hadn't had my first lesson yet, but I sat down on the wobbly stool and made some kind of music on that piano.

A little after midnight, my father emerged from the bedroom and drove me to bed.

"Goodnight, goodnight, goodnight," he sang, accentuating each beat with a playful open-palm slap to my rump. It was a victory for him too. Just that weekend he had won $300 at the track. It didn't seem to bother him that my mother had demanded half the money and set it aside for my piano lessons.

Every night I offered a prayer of thanksgiving, certain God had forgiven me.

Peachie Gregory was another thing entirely.

Peachie Gregory—with those spidery limbs and those bushy brows that met in the center of her forehead and that pouting mouth full of silver braces—I didn't completely understand it when I first saw her play the piano, but I wanted her almost as much as I envied her talent.

She dominated my thoughts when I was awake, and in time I began seeing her in my progressively worsening dreams—real dreams, not made-up visions—dreams of limbs brushing limbs, and lips whispering into lips in a parody of holy prayer. Then I began manipulating my thoughts to ensure that my dreams would include her. At my lowest, I dreamt about her without benefit of sleep.

By age thirteen, when I began to use my hands, I knew I was bound for hell.

I couldn't turn to my parents, so one Sunday I went to the restroom to speak with Brother Morrisohn.

He said, "Have you prayed over the matter?"

"Yes," I answered, "but the Lord hasn't answered yet."

He smiled, showing those incredible teeth. "Maybe He has and you just don't understand His answer. I'm sure He's leaving it up to you."

"Leaving it up to me?"

We stood inside the combination men's washroom and lounge his money had built. Four stand-up stalls and four sit-down stalls lined one wall. A row of sinks lined another. In the center of the room, five plush chairs formed a semicircle around a floor-model color television. We were between services, so a football game was airing. Otherwise, the television would have picked up the closed-circuit feed and broadcast the service to the Faithful who found it necessary to be near the facilities. These days Brother Morrisohn, pushing close to his promised four score, attended most services by way of this floor-model television. His Bible, hymnal, and gold-tipped cane rested in one of the chairs.

"I don't care what anyone tells you, God gets upset when we turn to Him for everything. Sometimes we've got to take responsibility. Elwyn, it's your mind and your hand, and you must learn to control them. Otherwise, why don't you just blame God for every sin you commit? God made you kill. God made you steal. God made you play with yourself."

Brother Morrisohn was so close I could smell his cologne. His teeth made a ticking sound each time his jaw moved. Suddenly, he began to tremble and coughed a reddish glob into his hands. He moved quickly to the faucet and washed it down, sighing, "Age. Old age." Then he turned off the faucet and looked down at me with an embarrassed smile.

I said to him, "What about the dreams?"

"Dreams?"

"The nasty dreams about . . . Peachie."

"God controls the dreams," Brother Morrisohn explained. "They're not your fault."

"Okay."

"Control your hands."

"I will."

Brother Morrisohn was himself again. In his black suit and tie, he stood tall and handsome. All signs of weakness had vanished. Old age would not get the victory. God would get the victory.

He mused, "Peachie Gregory, huh?" The old saint pointed with his chin to the television. "That was Peachie last Sunday backing up Sister McGowan's boy, wasn't it? She's a talented girl. She and that Barry McGowan make a great team. He can really sing."

Now Barry was not my favorite brother in the Lord. Barry was a show-off, and he had flirted with Peachie in the past even though he was much too old for her. He was a high school senior. But now I smiled because soon he would be out of the way. "Barry just got a scholarship to Bible College," I announced.

"Good for him. He's truly blessed. But that Peachie is a cute girl, isn't she?" Brother Morrisohn chuckled mischievously. "If you're dreaming about *her*, Elwyn, by all means enjoy the dreams."

I handed him his cane. He patted me on the head.

He was a great saint.

Praise be to God, as I grew in age, I grew in wisdom and in grace. With His righteous sword I was able to control my carnal side.

While she lived often in my waking thoughts, it was only occasionally that I dreamt about Peachie anymore, and even less frequently were the dreams indecent. Awake, I marveled at how through the Grace of God I was able to control my mind and my hand.

At sixteen, I counted Peachie as my best friend and sister in the Lord. We both served as youth ministers. Together, we went out into the field to witness to lost souls. As a pianist, she demonstrated a style that reflected her classical training. Disdaining my own classical training (we both had Sister McGowan for piano teacher), I relied on my ear to interpret music. Thus, on first and third Sundays of every month, she was minister of music for the stately adult choir; on second and fourth Sundays, I played for the more upbeat youth choir. As different as our tastes were, we emulated each other's style. I'd steal a chord change from her. She'd borrow one of my riffs. We practiced together often.

By the Grace of God, genuine affection, however guarded, had replaced the envy and lust I felt for Peachie as a child.

Thus, when Brother Morrisohn passed in the late summer of '79, it was my best friend Peachie whom I called for support.

"They want me to play," I said.

"You should. He was very close to you."

"But my style may not be appropriate. When I get emotional, my music becomes too raucous."

"Do you think it really matters?"

I tried to read Peachie's words. For the past few weeks she had grown cranky and I had chastised her more than once for her sarcasm, which bordered on meanness.

"Yes," I said. "I think it matters. It's the funeral of a man I loved dearly."

"Well don't look to me to bail you out. Play what's in the book."

"I hate playing that way."

"Then play like you know how to play. Play for the widow. Play for Brother Morrisohn. Play like you have thirty fingers."

"Okay. I just hope the choir can keep up."

"We can," Peachie assured.

Then we talked about what songs I would play and in what order and some other mundane things, and then somehow Peachie ended up saying, "Don't worry, Elwyn. The Lord will see that you do fine. And I'll be there watching you too."

"Bless His name," I said.

"Glory be to God," she said.

So it was a funeral, but you wouldn't know it from my playing.

Keep up, choir, I thought. I'm syncopating. Keep up!

I played for the stout old ladies of the Missionary Society, who sat as Brother Morrisohn's next of kin because at seventy-eight he had out-lived most of his near relations. All that was left were his wife Elaine and a daughter from his first marriage, Beverly, who was a few years older than her stepmother. In their black dresses and big, black church hats with silk ribbons tied into bows, the twenty or so women of the Missionary Society took up the first two rows. My grandmother stood among them, raising holy hands. Back in the old days, when the church was just getting started, Brother Morrisohn and my grandmother, my mother's mother, had founded the group, which later became the ful-crum of the church's social activity.

Sister Elaine Morrisohn, his fair-skinned widow, sat weeping among her dark sisters. She was the youngest member of the Missionary Society and that was mostly because she had been his wife. It was rumored that Sister Morrisohn had lived a life of singular wickedness before meeting and marrying Brother Morrisohn.

Beverly Morrisohn, his daughter, was not in attendance—although I had spotted her briefly at the final night of his wake. She wasn't much to look at, a round-faced woman with her hair done up in an ugly bun.

A nonbeliever, Beverly had worn pants to her own father's wake. No wonder she and Sister Morrisohn hadn't been on speaking terms for longer than the sixteen years I had been alive.

I played to comfort his widow.

Watch out, ushers, I'm going to make them shake today. I'm going to make them faint. Watch out!

I played so that they would remember Brother Morrisohn, benefactor and friend—Brother Morrisohn, the great saint, who had put the Church of Our Blessed Redeemer Who Walked Upon the Waters on the map.

My fingers burned over the keys. Remember him for the pews and the stained glass windows! Remember him for the nursery!

Remember him for the piano he bought me!

Now the tilting hats of the women of the Missionary Society were my target. I aimed my cannon, fired. Musical shrapnel exploded in the air. They jerked back and forth, euphoric. They raised their sodden handkerchiefs toward heaven and praised the Holy Spirit, but it was I who lured them into shouts of dominant seventh—Hear That Old-Time Gospel Roar Like a Lion! It was I who made them slap their ample breasts through black lace.

Remember Brother Morrisohn. Remember!

The choir was swaying like grass in a measured breeze as I caught the eye of Peachie Gregory, my secret love, singing lead soprano. Though I seldom dreamt about her anymore, I would marry her one day. Peachie winked at me and then hammered the air with her fist. It was a signal. Play like you know how to play!

I did. I hit notes that were loud. I hit notes that didn't fit. Then I pulled the musical rug out from under them. No piano. No piano—except a strident chord on the third beat of each measure backed by whatever bass cluster I pounded with my left hand.

Peachie gave me a thumbs-up. I had them really going now.

Laying into that final chorus like I had thirty fingers, I joined them again. I was playing for Peachie now. She kept hammering the air. I kept touching glory on the keys. The celestial echo reverberated. The whole church moved in organized frenzy—the Holy Spirit moving throughout the earth.

I was so good that day. Even Peachie had to admit it.

Was that my sin? Pride?

At graveside, I hurled a white rose into the hole. The flower of my re-membrance slid off the smooth surface of the casket and disappeared into the space between the casket and the red and black walls of earth. Suddenly, the widow collapsed beside me. I caught hold of her before she hit the ground. My skinny arms and the meaty black arms of the Missionary Society steadied Sister Morrisohn on her feet again. She was not a heavy woman. She smelled of blossoms sweeter than the rose in her hand.

"I don't want him to go," she wailed.

"The Lord taketh the best, sister," my grandmother said. "He lived way beyond his threescore and ten."

"Amen" and "Yes, Lord" went up from the assemblage.

"His life was a blessing to all," said Pastor, just beyond the circle of Missionary Society women that surrounded Sister Morrisohn.

"Yes, but I don't want him to go," wailed the widow.

My grandmother, that great old-time saint, had one arm across the widow's back, massaging her. "Throw the rose, child," my grandmother urged.

My own arm had somehow gotten trapped around the widow's waist and I couldn't snake it out of there without causing a disturbance as my grandmother's bell of a stomach had pressed the hand flat against Sister Morrisohn's ribs. Peachie Gregory watched it all from the other side of the hole.

"Throw the rose."

Sister Morrisohn clutched the flower to her chest. "Can I see him one more time?"

"You shouldn't, child," replied my grandmother.

Sister Morrisohn said, "Please," and the August wind blew aside her veil revealing her ears, each of which was twice pierced—before she had accepted the Lord, of course. "Please."

My grandmother finally gave in and pulled away, muttering to herself, "Lord, Lord." She crunched through the gravel in her flat-soled funeral slippers to Pastor and commanded him in a loud conspiratorial whisper to open the casket one more time.

"Amen" and "Yes, Lord" went up from the assemblage again.

When the groundskeeper, a burly man with a patch over one eye, leaned in to pull the levers that raised the coffin up from the hole, Sister Morrisohn took my hand and walked me over to the edge of the shiny box in which Brother Morrisohn lay.

His hair was neatly parted. His lips were fixed in a taut line. He had an expression on his face like a man dreaming about childhood. Sister Morrisohn fixed her husband's dead fingers around the white rose. When she stepped back from the box, I stepped with her.

"Tha's all?" said the man with the patch over his eye. A hand in a dirty work glove rested against the controls. "Y'all finish?"

"Yes," said my grandmother. "You may lower it again."

The man snorted, "Church folk." As he set to work lowering the casket, he mouthed what may have been obscene words but we couldn't hear him for the singing:

We are marching to Zion, beautiful, beautiful Zion,
We are marching upward to Zion, that beautiful city of God

I ushered Sister Morrisohn into the hearse already loaded with sisters from the Missionary Society. The widow squeezed my hand. "Thank you, Elwyn. He really cared about you. Your music meant so much to him."

"Thank you. I'm glad."

I remained by the door of the hearse because Sister Morrisohn yet held my hand. Should I tell her that Peachie Gregory was waiting for me, that we had planned to stop off at Char-Hut to finish our grieving over french fries and milkshakes? How does one break away from the recently bereaved?

I averted my eyes and in a sudden move wrenched my hand from her grasp. When I dared look again, the hand that had held mine was brushing at tears.

"Don't forget about me, Elwyn."

Strange music began to play in my head. Was my light-headedness a result of her flowery perfume? The memory of the shape and feel of her waist? God forgive me, I silently prayed, this is Brother Morrisohn's widow. Brother Morrisohn, a man I loved.

"I won't forget you," I said.

When I got to my car, where Peachie awaited, I was breathing as though I'd just run a great distance.

"The church is going to be a sadder place without Brother Morrisohn," I said as we drove to Char-Hut.

"Poorer," Peachie answered distantly. Her forehead was beaded in perspiration despite the wind from the open window that animated her long braids. It was hot and my old Mazda didn't have air-conditioning. "No more free rides for the Faithful. The candyman is gone."

"At any rate," I said, "I think we presented him a great tribute."

"Especially your playing, Brother Elwyn. It brought tears."

I ignored her sarcasm. "He was a great saint. He'll be missed. I for one am going to miss him."

"You and the widow both."

"What?"

"Nothing." Peachie continued to stare out her window. "I said nothing."

She was not telling the truth—she had indeed said something, a something that unabashedly implied impropriety: *You and the widow both.* I may have been in love with Peachie, but I was not going to suffer her insolence. I had never been anything but a gentleman with any of the sisters at the church, Peachie and Sister Morrisohn included. How dare she intimate such a vile idea! Such a rude side of Peachie I had never encountered.

Was she jealous?

Just as I was about to chastise her for her un-Christlike behavior, my Mazda stalled.

"This old car," she grumbled.

"God will give us grace," I said, cranking the engine to no avail as the vehicle rolled to a stop in the middle of traffic. Other cars began blowing their horns, whizzing around us.

I got out. Peachie crawled into the driver's seat. I popped the hood and jiggled the wire connecting the alternator to the battery. Peachie clicked the ignition at regular intervals. When her click matched my jiggle, the frayed end of the wire sparked in my hand and the engine came to life. I closed the hood and got back into the car, rubbing my hands. "That takes care of that."

Peachie stared out the open window again. "I'm not hungry. Take me home."

"Peachie—"

"Please, just take me home."

I passed to the center lane to make a U-turn. The traffic light caught me. I floored the clutch and the gas pedals so that the car wouldn't stall while we waited for the green. "You could at least tell me what I did to upset you."

"Who said you upset me? I have serious things on my mind."

Serious things I had little doubt. She was jealous.

"Ever since you got into the car, you've been answering me curtly or ignoring me altogether. I thought we were friends." The light changed. I made the U-turn. "See there," I said, "you can't even look at me."

"Says who?" She turned on me with angry eyes.

"Are you jealous of Sister Morrisohn?"

"Jealous of the fragile widow?"

"Are you jealous?"

"Now you're being silly." Peachie laughed. "Wait. Are *you* in love with Sister Morrisohn? You certainly seemed concerned about her at the funeral. And what—do you think she's in love with you? She's only about ten times your age."

"You don't have to be so mean to me. I just thought that maybe you felt threatened."

Peachie stared at me with eyes that mocked. "And what—how can I feel threatened? Do you think, my dear brother in the Lord, that I possess any feelings for you other than the sincerest and purest friendship?" If she had been standing, Peachie's hands would have been akimbo. "Did I forget to share with you that Barry McGowan has written to me several times from Bible College?"

"Barry McGowan?" Why didn't he just leave her alone? He was too old for her. "What does Barry have to do with this?"

"He graduates in December. He's building a church up there in Lakeland. He already has the land and everything. He wants me to direct the choir." Then she added with finality: "He wants me to marry him."

"What? Well you won't," I said. "At least you won't marry him now. You still have school to finish. And your mom and dad—"

"They're all for it. They love Barry. I can finish school up in Lakeland, and then go to Bible College."

"But they'll just let you go like that? You're so young."

"Lots of sisters get married young," she said, as though I should know this, and well I should, having played at many of their weddings. But Peachie didn't have to go that way. She was virtuous, I was sure. "Don't worry, Elwyn, Barry can take care of me. He's a great man of God."

I had trouble focusing on the road. "This is so sudden."

"I've been thinking about it for four months."

"Four months! You never told me. We're best friends. You tell me everything."

"Everything but this." Her features softened, and she lowered her eyes. "I didn't tell you this, Elwyn—because, I guess, I didn't want you to hold it against me. You're so perfect, so holy."

"I'm not that holy. I told you that I deceived my parents in order to take piano lessons."

"That's small, Elwyn. Everyone does little things like that," she said. "I took piano lessons with Sister McGowan in order to be around Barry."

I shook my head. "You never told me that. You're making this all up."

"Elwyn, you're so innocent, you wouldn't understand how these things happen. If I had told you about Barry and me, you'd have held it against me."

"I'd never hold anything against you." I said a silent prayer for courage, and the Lord sent me courage. "How can I hold anything against you, Peachie? I love you."

"Don't say that."

"But I do. I love you—"

"Elwyn, do you?"

"—and I think you love me too, Peachie."

"Why didn't you tell me this before?"

"You knew. We both knew."

"Oh, Elwyn."

I let go of the gearshift and found her hand. "Don't go to Lakeland with Barry. Stay here with me. You are the love of my life. You are the only girl I will ever love."

She squeezed my hand in both of hers for one hope-filled moment. Then she pushed it away.

"Stay, Peachie."

She shook her head. "I can't."

"You can," I said.

Peachie patted her stomach. I had to look twice before I understood. Now it made sense, but impossible sense.

"You and Barry?"

"Four months."

"But that's a sin. Fornication. The Bible says—"

"It is better to marry than to burn."

"But you have defiled your body—the Temple of God."

"God forgives seventy times seven. Will you forgive just once, Elwyn?"

How could she smile such a cruel smile? She was mocking me. And the church. Where was her shame? I wanted to cry, really cry. My Peachie, whom I had never kissed. Gone. Out of the ark of safety.

"Christ is married to the backslider. Barry and I went before God on our knees. We repented of our sin. But you, Elwyn, will you forgive us?"

"I'm not God. It's not for me to forgive."

"It's important to me. You are my true friend."

"I'm not God."

She made a sound somewhere between a gasp and a sigh. My Mazda stalled again. I got out, walked around to the front, and popped the hood. I jiggled as Peachie clicked. Oh God, I prayed, give me grace.

I didn't feel so holy as I waited for the last remnants of the Missionary Society to leave Sister Morrisohn's house.

My grandmother, of course, was the last to go. She stood on the porch with her heavy arm draped over Sister Morrisohn's shoulder telling the grieving widow a last important something. As my grandmother talked, she scanned the surroundings. East to west. What was she looking for? Did she think I would make my move with everyone watching? She should have known that I would park down the street behind a neighbor's overgrown shrubbery where I could see and not be seen.

My grandmother embraced Sister Morrisohn and kissed her good-bye on the cheek. At last, she lumbered down the short steps with the help of Sister McGowan (the mother of Barry!), who often gave her rides now that she was too old to drive. As Sister McGowan's car pulled off the property, I fired up my engine.

I left my black funeral jacket and tie in the car. I prayed for courage. I rang her doorbell.

"Elwyn. Come in."

"Yes, ma'am."

"Sit down. Would you like something to drink? There's some fruit punch left."

"Okay."

I was sucked into the plush red-velvet couch. Mounted on the wall across from me was a large oil painting of them on their wedding day. She was chubbier as a young woman. He looked about the same. She had only been twenty-six the day they married. He had been sixty-two. Beneath the painting was the grand piano he had bid me play every time I visited his house. I remembered that two years prior, the youth choir had performed the Christmas cantata right here in their living room. I had played "O Holy Night," while Barry, on Christmas break from Bible College, had sung. I had foolishly thought that Peachie's enthusiastic applause was meant for me.

Sister Morrisohn, still wearing black, returned with a glass of fruit punch and a napkin. I took it from her and she sat down on the couch a few inches away from me. Limb brushed against limb. I drank the better part of my punch in one swallow.

She cupped her stomach. "I don't know when my appetite will return. I haven't eaten but a mouthful of food since I woke up and found him. I knew it would come one day, but I still wasn't ready for it. We're never ready for it, are we?"

"Well," I said, because I didn't know what else to say. "Well."

"If it weren't for the church, I don't know how I would have made it. Everyone has been so nice to me."

In a voice that flaked from my throat, I said, "You must have loved him."

"Yes. I was a very different person when we met. He saved me from myself. He led me to the Lord."

She was different when he met her. I prayed, Lord forgive me, as I glanced at her doubly pierced ears. What was she like before? Could she be that different person again?

"Before you met him, what kind of sins did you commit?"

"Sins? I don't think about them anymore." She raised holy hands. "Praise God, I'm free."

"Praise God," I said, raising holy hands, careful not to spill the remainder of my drink. "But are you ever tempted?"

"All are tempted, Elwyn, but only the yielding is sin." She clapped her hands. "Hallelujah."

"Hallelujah" died on my lips as my eyes followed her neckline down to the top button of her funeral dress. Bright flesh showed through black lace like a beacon. All the signs were there: her smell, her touch, her plea that I not forget her. Limb against limb. I would not let her get away as Peachie had. "But do you ever feel like yielding?"

"What?"

I folded my napkin under my glass of punch and with trembling hand set the glass on the octagonal coffee table before the couch. I turned and reached for her hand.

"Elwyn, what are you doing?"

I kissed her on the mouth. I pressed her hands up against my chest.

She tore away from me and sprang to her feet. "Elwyn—help me, Jesus!—what are you doing?"

"You're a beautiful woman," I squeaked, but it was no use. She was not to be seduced.

"Elwyn!"

I buried my head in my hands.

"You need prayer, Elwyn," she said sadly. "You need the Lord."

"Yes," I replied, without looking up. "Yes."

Now there was a soothing hand on my neck like a mother's. I wept and I wept.

"Serving the Lord at your age is not easy, Elwyn. Don't give up." Sister Morrisohn rubbed my neck and prayed. "Christ is married to the backslider. Confess your secret sins."

And confess I did.

And then I wept some more because the more she rubbed my neck, the more forgiveness I needed. For when she got down on her knees beside me and began to pray against my face, the very scent of her expanded my lungs like a bellows, and her breathing—her warm breath against my cheeks, my ear, into my eyes burning hot with tears—was everything I imagined a lover's kiss might be.

My Father's Business

At sixteen, I met my first great temptation, and I yielded with surprisingly little resistance, I who had proclaimed myself strong in the Lord. There had been, it seems, a chink in my armor, through which Satan had thrust his wicked sword.

As I wondered how I could have felt so strong and yet been so weak, I labored mightily to get back into the ark of safety.

I took a more active role in the Lord's work. On Sundays, I rose early and joined the maintenance brethren in preparing the main hall for morning service; I stayed late to help them clean up afterward. Brother Al and Brother Suggs were surprised but happy to work with me. Often, we discussed music.

"Elwyn, I really like when you do that dum-dum-da-dum thing at the end of service," said Brother Suggs, a retired seaman of about seventy who had both a stoop and a limp. When he pushed a broom, he resembled a man perpetually playing shuffleboard.

Brother Al, a squat man with a massive chest and arms like telephone poles, shouted down from the ladder upon which he stood replacing a cylinder of fluorescent light: "I was first trumpet in my high school band."

Unemployed and in his late twenties, Brother Al spent his days lifting weights or visiting the three children he had sired out of wedlock with a Nicaraguan seamstress named Bettie. This was, of course, before he had accepted the Lord.

"Maybe you and me'll do a duet one Sunday," Brother Al suggested.

"Maybe we will, Brother," I answered, scraping chewing gum from the underside of a pew with a putty knife.

Now on those Sundays when it was not my turn to play piano for the youth choir, I stood as usher at the entrance to the church: I'd rather be an usher in the house of the Lord than a prince in the palace of hell. My legs, standing motionless for the better part of the hour, were diligent for the Lord, my knees strong and true.

I stopped the children from talking or fighting, tapped them awake when they fell asleep. "Suffer the little children to come unto Me," Christ said. When babies cried, I was quick to pull them from their grateful mothers' arms and take them outside into the calming sunlight, or lead some other mother—a visitor—to the restroom at the back where she could change a soiled diaper, or perhaps nurse her baby.

When the Holy Spirit descended, I waited for Him to touch one of His favorites—Sisters Davis, Breedlove, Naylor, or Hutchinson—and set her to trembling, to move upon her so powerfully, in fact, that she would collapse. I would rush to the fallen sister and drape the velvet shawl over her spasming legs, hiding what would otherwise be revealed—the usher is the guardian of decency—and then with the help of another usher, I would carry the fallen sister to the nursery where she could rest on a cot until the Spirit had passed.

Scripture says it is not through our works that we are saved, but only through His Grace, and Scripture can't be challenged. I reasoned, however, that if I were indeed going to work, then let it be in the service of the Lord.

* * *

It struck me that part of my problem was that I didn't pray enough; yes, morning, noon, and evening found me on my knees, head bowed, but what about the times in between? Scripture admonishes us to pray without ceasing, so I increased my standard prayers to five times a day and began a campaign of fasting on the weekends.

One Sunday afternoon, during the lull between morning service and youth hour, I sat in my bedroom reading from the Book of Daniel, searching perhaps for my own handwriting on the wall.

I heard my grandmother say: "Elwyn's not eating today?"

As was customary, we had guests over for Sunday dinner—my grandmother and Sister McGowan, my old piano teacher.

My mother answered, "Elwyn's fasting."

"Fasting? Every time I come over here he's fasting."

My mother said, "All of us Christians should be fasting along with Elwyn. There is so much trouble in the world."

"Especially the way them Arabs have shot up the gas prices," said my father.

"Please pass the salt," said Sister McGowan.

"Here it is, Sister," said my father. "Over there in the Middle East, there's sure to be a war. Armageddon."

"We are living in the last days," said my mother.

"Watch and see if the Lord doesn't return soon," said my grandmother. "Watch and see." There was a chorus of Amens, and then she continued, "I still think he's been too serious lately. Something's bothering him."

My mother said: "'Wist ye not that I must be about My Father's business?' The Lord was only twelve when He said that."

My grandmother's voice boomed, "Don't quote Scripture with me, girl."

"Mother," said my mom timidly.

"I know my grandson. And I know—"

"So much salt?" I heard my father say.

Sister McGowan answered, "I know it's bad for my blood pressure, but I've had more of a taste for it since Barry and Peachie announced they're getting married."

Oh Peachie. My foggy eyes could not read the prophet. I found my ear moving closer to the open door. Why did I want to hear what I already knew?

"Peachie and Barry make a nice couple," said my father. "I pray their children don't witness Armageddon.

"They're so talented," added my mother.

Then there was awkward laughter as they attempted to maintain the pleasant air.

"Humph," snorted my grandmother, "all this time I thought she was Elwyn's girl."

"Mother," said my mom, "Elwyn doesn't have a girl."

"At sixteen?" said my grandmother.

"But he likes girls, I can tell you." My father laughed without vigor. "He's my son."

"I-thought-Elwyn-liked-Peachie," my grandmother said, punching each word.

It became quiet.

I pictured my grandmother, her large arms folded across her chest, her head tilted at a defiant angle, and everyone else seeming to eat but only just touching their lips with empty forks, or filling their mouths with drink they did not swallow. My grandmother was an old-time saint. She wielded the truth like the double-edged sword Saint Paul says it is. She was noted for rebuking the women of the Church of Our Blessed

Redeemer Who Walked Upon the Waters when in the late '50s they thought it was acceptable to straighten their hair. Later when the skirt-like *gauchos* became popular, my grandmother exhorted the women not to wear them because skirtlike or not, *gauchos* are pants, and women aren't supposed to wear pants.

And chastity? My grandmother's chastity was legendary among the Faithful. She had kept her virginity until age thirty-four, "and would have kept it longer," she always said confidently, "if the right man hadn't come along."

The right man was Private Cooper.

None of us except for the real old-timers had ever met my mother Isa-dore's father, but from what Gran'ma had revealed about him over the years, we knew Private Cooper had been a migrant laborer and a country preacher.

Private Cooper was foreign born, she told us, a Jamaican, but when Gran'ma met him, he had been living in America for several years and spoke American English with only a slight accent. Upon hearing him speak for the first time, Gran'ma (who was known as Sister Mamie Cul-pepper back then, or Sister Mamie because she was still a maiden) had guessed incorrectly that he was from the Bahamas, where folks were known to talk funny. There were lots of Bahamians around South Flor-ida back in those days working the agricultural circuit for the big fruit and vegetable farmers alongside the Mexicans and the regular Ameri-can black folk. In fact, the small wooden houses with the slanted roofs and the porches out front that you see in places like Overtown, Coco-nut Grove, and Goulds to this very day are Bahamian-style houses.

My grandmother Mamie Cooper (née Culpepper) herself was the offspring of field laborers. She was born in Tifton, Georgia, but didn't remember much about the place (or her own father who had stayed behind) because her mother had brought her to Florida when she was too young for it to stick. Her earliest memories were the series of small wooden shack homes in South Florida as they followed the crops through the yearly cycle of picking oranges and grapefruit and lemons and limes and tomatoes and peppers and onions, and chopping sugar cane with her mother and her aunti (who had no name that I ever heard of other than "Aunti").

When she first met Cooper, Gran'ma knew right away he had come from somewhere else. It was not just the hint of accent. He wore his suit too tight, and he let too much cuff show. When he ran—and often he did run in his fervor on the pulpit at tent meetings—his knees didn't bend enough, and his arms, with the Bible tucked tight under one of them, hung straight down at his sides. Some of the boys, the other cutters and pickers, joked: "He's a big man, but he runs like a girl."

"He does not run like a girl," Sister Mamie would say in his defense. She knew the other boys were just being mean out of jealousy. He was a good preacher, a fast fruit picker, and he was not afraid to court Mamie, who was on fire for the Lord and had already dismissed a goodly number of the same jacklegged suitors who were poking fun at Cooper.

"He's so young for you, Mamie. He's got to be ten years younger than you, if not more. You know that means trouble," some of the ladies would warn. But she knew where that was coming from too. These lady friends of hers believed that if a woman waited so long to marry she deserved only the slimmest of the pickings, but Cooper was handsomer and more gentlemanly than all of their ugly, old dried-up men.

She first saw him in the orange groves near Goulds, shirtless, swinging a machete. He cut quite a figure. When she found she couldn't get him off her mind, she prayed and asked the Lord if he was the one. The

Lord told her yes. They met formally at the tent meeting he was running with the permission of the local preacher, none other than Brother Buford Morrisohn, who had come from up north to build the Faithful flock down here in South Florida, where Catholics, AMEs, Holy Rollers, atheists, and Baptists were in abundance. Sister Mamie and her family had been mostly Holy Rollers and "jump up" Baptists until Brother Morrisohn arrived, but they had been among the first to convert and they were strong in their faith and brought many into the fold.

Their hands first touched as Gran'ma, the blushing Mamie Culpepper, dropped her coins in the collection plate.

It was around the time of the war, and there was a training camp set up down there. It was common to see men in jeeps or armored vehicles rolling through the old dirt roads. A lot of the boys back then were joining up. It was a great opportunity for black men to make some good money to support their families. It was a great opportunity for black women who were looking for husbands who could take care of them properly.

But Mamie was thirty-four, and she had just found love and she didn't want her man leaving to go fight some war no matter how much money he might send back home. She warned Cooper that she would not marry him if he planned on joining the war. He told her he would not join because he was in love. Their two-and-a-half-week courtship was chaste and pleasant. Brother Morrisohn officiated the small ceremony, attended by a few friends plus Aunti and Brother Morrisohn's first wife, Mother Glovine. Gran'ma's mother, whom she called Momma, had passed away a few years earlier so she was not there to see her holy daughter finally marry. Shortly after the wedding, my mother Isadore was conceived. It was the perfect love.

Cooper was also a good cook, Gran'ma would tell us.

"He could cook a duck and make it taste like pork!" she would boast, as her tongue lolled in her mouth and her dentures clicked. "You should taste his curry goat!"

In the grainy black-and-white photograph of him that she kept in a locket she always carried in her purse—never on a chain around her neck, for jewelry is jewelry, and jewelry is sin—he was wearing a polka-dot jacket and a striped ascot. He was a smiling, fair-skinned man with sleepy, wide-spaced eyes and his hair was slicked back and parted at a jaunty angle. He looked a little bit like the secular singer Cab Calloway. Neither my mother nor I bore any resemblance to Cooper. We were dark like Gran'ma, with close-set eyes and a rougher texture of hair.

Then one day Cooper suddenly up and joined the war. Times were very hard and patriotism was high. Gran'ma did not want him to go. She told him killing was a sin. Even the killing of Nazis.

He told her volunteering was his duty to his adopted country. It was a righteous war. And besides, the Lord would protect him. The Lord would protect them all.

The way Gran'ma explained it, "We fought. We were in love, we loved the Lord, but we were husband and wife, so we fought. That happens in a marriage sometimes. Even now I'm ashamed of myself. What Cooper wanted to do was good. It was a noble thing. I didn't see it like that back then. I just wanted my man." Gran'ma would admit sadly, "The devil got ahold of me. A woman should submit herself to her husband. Cooper was so mad. I'm sure if I hadn't been pregnant, he would have hit me. I would have deserved it too."

My mother Isadore was born three months after Private Cooper was shipped off to Europe with the other young men. Aunti was the midwife. Private Cooper sent his wife a letter reaffirming their love, in spite of it all. Gran'ma mailed him a photograph of their child. A month or so later, she received a letter from the government telling her how she should be proud to be married to a dead man who had served his country so bravely.

"What hurt most," Gran'ma always said, "was that the letter I had sent him with the photograph of Isadore in it was returned unopened. Private Cooper had never seen his child."

My grandmother, Sister Mamie Cooper, that great old-time saint, never remarried, but she still wore her wedding band or carried it in her bosom when her arthritis was acting up. It was the only piece of jewelry she owned.

"Jewelry is jewelry, and jewelry is a sin, but the wedding band is sanctified by God," she would explain. "It shows a woman's submission to her husband, who is the head of her house, as Christ is the head of the Church."

It was about a half minute before my grandmother's voice broke the silence: "But now I guess Peachie and Barry have to do what's right."

"I've seen them . . . they do love each other," said Sister McGowan tentatively.

I felt a useless anger well up in me. This anger was an emotion I, the meek and forgiving Christian, was unused to. Anger obscured the obvious: Peachie was lost; and the other one, the one I had offended, the widow, should never be mine. I prayed for a clear head.

"It's probably Elwyn's fault," my grandmother said. "He's too serious for these modern girls, that's what."

"He tries to be a good Christian," my mother said.

"I guess you can't blame him," said my grandmother. "But he could at least give me a hug. He played so nice today."

"Yes, he did," my mother said.

"Lord, I'm proud of that boy," my grandmother said. "He's going to do great things for the Lord. He just has to wait upon the Lord."

"He was always my best student," Sister McGowan said.

"The actual city of Armageddon," said my father, "is somewhere in the Middle East, isn't it?"

Fasting left me numb, light-headed, closer to God. Fasting was good. But as I heard the sound of forks clinking against the good china again, my stomach growled. I sipped from my glass of water, which was the only thing the Faithful were allowed to consume on a fast.

Lord, give me strength, I prayed, to fast and to forgive. Give me a clean heart, Lord, that I may follow Thee.

Then I headed out to the dining room and greeted Sister McGowan and gave my grandmother her hug.

At my high school, I did not speak to my acquaintances except to witness to them.

Admittedly, a large number of students fled at the sight of me. Others hungrily accepted the tracts and Bibles I handed out. There was always a crowd at the prayer meetings I held in the back of the cafeteria during lunch. Many came to laugh and deride, but others came to bow their heads and utter their first timid words to their Creator. More than a few shed tears of repentance.

I skipped classes in order to confront those of my fellows who were themselves skipping to smoke marijuana cigarettes and vent their carnality in the dark dressing chambers between the band room and the auditorium. These last were not happy to see me, but as God was on my side, they came to respect, both spiritually and literally, the power of the light I brought. None could escape the Faithful servant of God.

I was on the battlefield for my Lord.

In fact, I increased my evangelistic efforts so much so that I found myself barely paying attention at school.

I was busy saving lost souls—John Feinstein, Eldridge Pomerantz, Marco Japonte, Marigold Hendricks, the bubbly Anderson twins, Tina and Sabina, and many more to whom I was spiritual leader. What did I care about trigonometry?

I ended up sitting on a backless chair in the principal's office.

Mr. Byrd was a short man with a voice that thundered. His office was dominated by a large wooden desk overflowing with pink and yellow sheets of paper. In a picture frame nailed to the wall directly behind the desk there was a color photograph of Mr. Byrd and a plump woman wearing a pair of riding pants and riding boots. The woman stood a few inches taller than Mr. Byrd, who had his arm around her waist.

"Just stop it," Mr. Byrd said. He sat on the edge of his desk, an unlit pipe hanging out of his mouth. "Stop it."

"I am a child of God," I said.

"Amen. I'm a deacon. A Baptist," he said. "But I'll expel you if you don't stop it."

"Then you understand, Brother Deacon. I've got to do my Father's business."

"Just stop it." The short man's heavy voice seemed to shake the very walls.

"No, sir."

"Would you like me to call your parents?"

"They support my evangelism."

He nodded. "That's right. You're all fanatics. That whole Church of the Blessed Christ Walking Whatever-you-call-its."

I was prepared for such as he, and I said, "The Faithful is what we are called. Feel free to make fun of us because we don't drink, don't smoke, and our women don't wear pants."

"Pants?" Cupping the bowl of his pipe in his hand, Mr. Byrd glanced back at the picture on the wall of him and the woman in the riding pants. He eyed me. "What's wrong with pants?"

"Pants," I informed, "Deuteronomy 22:5. The woman shall not wear that which pertaineth unto a man."

"And you don't danceth or weareth jewelry either?" he mocked.

"We do not."

"King David danced. He wore a good deal of jewelry too," he offered.

"David was before Christ's time. That's Old Testament."

"Deuteronomy is Old Testament too."

"Well, Christ didn't do away with everything under the old law."

"Not those things which pleaseth your church, at any rate," said Mr. Byrd slyly as he hopped off the desk. He raised the volume of his already powerful voice. "They didn't even have pants in the Old Testament!"

I was undaunted, but my time was too precious to argue with such as Mr. Byrd. I should be out serving the Lord saving lost souls. I said to him, just as slyly, "I guess Baptists can do just about any old thing they please."

Mr. Byrd let out a dry laugh, pointing at me. "Oh, no. Don't mistake us for you." As Mr. Byrd cackled, the unlit pipe in his mouth whistled. He lifted a folder filled with pink sheets of paper from his desk and read from it in an officious and mocking tone: "Elwyn James Parker, six un-excused absences, seven tardies, failing English, failing health, a warning in trigonometry—do you plan to go to college, young man?"

"Bible College."

The grin left Mr. Byrd's face and he sighed, as though I, a child of the King, were the lost cause. "Do you plan to graduate high school?"

"Of course."

"Then stop it. Get back to being the student you were."

"God's will."

Mr. Byrd closed the folder. He tried a friendlier approach—"I don't want to expel you, Elwyn. You're not the worst kid we have here"—but I wasn't buying it.

At last, he put the folder down and signaled with his hand for me to leave. I stood.

"Just stop it."

I shook my head. "No, sir."

"The Bible is a book about life here on earth, Elwyn. For your own sake, start living life."

"I am living, Deacon. But perhaps you'd rather I smoked a marijuana cigarette or got someone's daughter in trouble."

"You wouldn't know where to start," he fired back drily.

I opened the door and stepped out of his office. I shouted, "Praise the Lord!"

Mr. Byrd's door slammed behind me.

I was gracious with Barry McGowan. I even shook his hand in brotherhood during one of his trips home from Bible College to preach a sermon on humility. Barry proved a charismatic speaker. That and the two songs he performed evoked thunderclaps of "Amen" and "Yes, Lord" from the congregation in spite of what he had done. I wished Barry well and meant it.

I also wished Peachie well, now that her condition had become obvious and the congregation was reacting to her as it always did to those who had strayed. Pastor had removed her from the choir and relieved her of her duties as minister of music. She no longer led prayers at youth hour, though she continued to give a cautionary testimony that moved all of us teenagers to avoid lasciviousness. Like me, Peachie was determined to regain that special relationship with God that she had lost.

As a further show of forgiveness, I asked Peachie and Barry after service that night if there were anything at all I could do.

"Play the organ at our wedding," said Peachie.

"I'd be honored to, Peachie." I embraced her, careful not to disturb the unborn child, who seemed to kick, she said, especially hard when I was around.

Barry said, "Remember, Elwyn, this is a wedding. None of that boogie-woogie stuff you like to play." Barry was a tall man, broad with thick limbs, whose little head seemed wrong for his Goliath body. When Barry shook his head back and forth, it reminded me of those wobble-headed dogs people decorate their dashboards with.

"Don't be silly, Barry," said Peachie, standing between us, holding one of my hands, one of his. "Elwyn's always done a fine job at weddings."

"I'm just making sure. Things are bad enough as it is without the musician going boogie-woogie on us."

"Things aren't that bad," responded Peachie, who was five months pregnant.

"I'm just making sure," Barry said, looking straight at me. "I'm not flexible on this point."

"I promise I won't play boogie-woogie at your wedding, Brother Mc-Gowan," I said, smiling up at him. "Especially since I don't play boogie-woogie. It's called gospel."

Peachie shot me a warning look, but Barry didn't seem to take notice or offense.

"Well that's settled," he said, nodding his little head. "Now how much is it going to cost? You know we're on a tight budget with me try-ing to build the church up in Lakeland and all."

Before I could even answer, the groom-to-be added, "And we'll pay you $20. If you want more than that, my mother will get one of her other students to play." He glared at me with his little eyes. "I'm not flexible on this point, Elwyn."

The nerve of him. Sister McGowan, his own mother, wouldn't play at a wedding for less than $350. My usual fee was $100. There was no musician in the whole church who would take $20 to play at a wedding. But—Praise God—the Holy Spirit bridled my tongue. Twenty dollars? I did him one better.

"Barry, there's no charge. Think of my music as a wedding gift."

As the bright college boy Barry McGowan struggled to figure out how I was getting over on him, his eyes grew large in his little head. "A gift?"

"Thanks, Elwyn," Peachie said quickly. She gave me another hug and then flinched. "Ugh. The baby just kicked. Isn't that funny? Every time you're around, Elwyn."

Barry stuck out his hand to seal the deal. We shook.

"Thanks a lot, Brother Elwyn. And no boogie-woogie, right? I'm still the groom."

"Anything you say, Barry. Praise the Lord."

I had asked God for grace, wisdom, humility, and strength. And He had given them to me. A little more than a month after my trans-gression and already I had gotten over Peachie. I had stomached Barry, even Barry. My faith was stronger than it had ever been. I was well on my way to becoming a great man of God, a beacon unto the Faithful.

There was but one thing I had left undone—my confession—and with my renewed faith I was willing to do even that.

Of late, I had ceased avoiding the widow's eyes. I had greeted her quite pleasantly last Sunday as I stood usher and she passed through the doorway amid a trio of Missionary Society sisters. I had addressed her by her name, Sister Morrisohn, and cast a friendly smile her way. She had seemed surprised, but smiled back, waving with her fingers. Is this the same Elwyn who had offended me so foul?

Yes, I was he, that vile, weak creature, but now I had thrown off my mantle of iniquity and had been reborn. Christ lived in me.

Yes, if the widow so desired, I would even confess my secret sin.

Peachie married Barry the second Saturday in October, and the entire congregation was there.

The members of the bridal party were Peachie's thirteen-year-old sister Gwen, who stood as maid of honor; Ricardo, Brother Al's four-year-old Nicaraguan son, who was cute and precocious as the ring bearer (we all laughed when he loudly echoed the "I do's" of the bride and groom); and Brother Philip, Barry's roommate from Bible College, who stood as best man.

Peachie wore a powder blue dress that was tailored to hide the obvious. Oh, she was beautiful, my Peachie, despite the somewhat desolate expression she wore throughout the ceremony. Then again, who could be truly happy marrying Barry?

At his own wedding, he sang a solo, "O Perfect Love," which drew tremendous applause. He sang on his knees, troubadour style, earnestly peering up at Peachie. His mother accompanied him on piano while I sat at my silent organ musing. They hadn't told me about the solo and it wasn't in the program, so I didn't play it.

I suppose I could have played it by ear, but I didn't want to.

Barry and Peachie's reception was the first gathering held in the church's dining hall since we had renamed it the Buford Morrisohn Dining Tabernacle three Sundays earlier in honor of our late benefactor and founding member.

The Faithful ate home-baked pastries and drank grape juice beneath pink and blue wedding streamers and Brother Morrisohn memorabilia: photographs of him from childhood to adulthood, the plaques we had given him over the years, his degrees from Tuskegee and Oberlin, even his birth certificate, dated February 1, 1901.

He had been our greatest saint.

He had been my friend. It was he who had purchased the old upright that stood in the hallway of our home, the piano upon which I had learned to play. It was he who had bought the used Mazda for me to drive when I turned sixteen. It was he who had taught me what it meant to be a good Christian man.

I had no appetite. In my mind, the Buford Morrisohn Dining Tabernacle that afternoon was divided into three zones. Peachie and Barry controlled the middle zone, surrounded by food, drink, well-wishers, levity. I occupied the zone at a far end, away from the commotion. At the other remote zone sat the widow. She seemed more interested in the pictures of her late husband than the overflowing joy of the newlyweds. She still grieved, as did I, for Brother Morrisohn.

Passing through the throng of well-wishers gathered around the bride and groom—"Congratulations, Peachie. Good luck, Barry, though I know you won't need it, ha, ha, ha"—I made my way to Sister Morrisohn's side of the room.

"Hello."

"Elwyn!"

I got right to the point. I bowed my head and said, "I have to tell you how sorry I am."

"For what?" She closed her eyes, then opened them slowly, remembering. "For that? Don't let it worry you."

"What I did to you . . . what I assumed about you was horrible."

An eyebrow lifted. "Did I strike you as that kind of a woman?"

"It was all my fault. I was confused."

She smiled. "I forgive you."

"Thanks for forgiving me."

"God, I'm sure, has already forgiven you, and that's what really counts."

"Praise His name."

"I hear," she said, "about all the things you're doing around the church and at school. You're amazing."

"Praise His name," I said.

She opened her hands. "And this. I don't think I could have played at Barry's wedding if I were in your place."

I shrugged. "It's just a wedding. I've played at lots of them."

"Don't deceive yourself, Elwyn." She extended her hand and I took it. She was wearing a sky-blue dress that was a cascade of fine lace. The hat on her head, tilted at a stylish angle, had the same lace pattern on it. Her hair was braided into a single long black tail. She uncrossed her legs as I helped her out of her seat. "All liars, even those who deceive but themselves, shall have their part in the lake of fire."

I took my hands away from hers and shoved them in my pockets. A few feet away, Barry guided Peachie's hand in the ceremonial cutting of the cake. A camera flashed. There was applause. It all seemed very far away, as if happening in another country but being broadcast on TV.

I turned back to Sister Morrisohn. "Peachie and I never promised each other anything."

"Deception, deception," she sang in a voice that tinkled. "You can't fool me. It must have really hurt you." She reached up and touched the side of my face near my mouth. "Poor boy, love is often cruel."

I considered Sister Morrisohn's own mouth, the way the bottom lip poked out when she pronounced a word with an open vowel sound: "you," "poor," "boy."

The devil was causing me to focus on the pink on that pulsating bottom lip and urging the physical manifestations of lust to take place within me. I reminded myself that I was strong in the Lord. The Lord reminded me that I was still in control of my feet.

"Sister Morrisohn, I've got to go," I said hurriedly.

I left her and walked straight to my car. In a blur of confusion and emotion, I sped down familiar streets made unfamiliar by my anger at my shameful weakness. Fearing what I might do to myself, I pulled over to the side of the road, clasped my hands, and bowed my head before the steering wheel.

Lord, I prayed, give me a sign. Show me what to do.

My vision cleared. I looked up and saw that I had parked beside a canal. A large turtle rested in the grass on the shoulder of the water. I got out of my car. I picked up a long branch that still had some leaves on it and prodded the turtle until it retreated into its shell. I put down the branch and pondered the large animal safe inside its shell and at length concluded that if this were, in fact, a sign, then I certainly had no idea what it meant.

At about 6 p.m., when I figured the reception had ended, I drove back to church to help Brother Al and Brother Suggs clean up.

I would work for the Lord. I would be strong. Praise Ye the Lord!

I was the last one to leave the church that night. And when I left, not a scrap of dirt remained behind.

The next day was Sunday, and I fasted.

That night, I received a call. It was Peachie, but she was crying so much that it took me a few minutes to figure out what exactly she was saying: "I made a mistake and now everyone hates me."

"No one hates you, Peachie. And you know God loves you. His greatest gift is that He forgives us our sins."

"It's not that, Elwyn. It's just that everyone thinks I deceived you."

I sat up in my bed. "What?"

"Your grandmother makes it sound like I—"

"My grandmother?" Of course. The truth is like a two-edged sword. It cuts going and coming.

"Sister Morrisohn too, and that whole Missionary Society. They make it sound as though I—"

"Sister Morrisohn?"

"Yes, she wouldn't even talk to me at my own wedding."

Peachie deteriorated into sobs and it was awhile before I could understand her again.

"Sister Morrisohn is the one who pressured Pastor to kick me off the choir."

"But you're pregnant," I said. "What did you expect?"

Peachie shouted, "It has nothing to do with my pregnancy! There've been pregnant girls up there before and you know it. You said yourself God has forgiven me. They wouldn't even let me have a regular wedding. That ugly blue dress! The real problem is I offended their pet. You."

"Me?"

"With all the witnessing and stuff you're doing at school, you make the Church of Our Blessed Redeemer Who Walked Upon the Waters look good. All of those new converts. And me, your perfect mate, big and pregnant for another man."

"That's not how it is."

"That's what it looks like."

I felt a great sadness for Peachie and her plight, but in many ways this turn of events served her right. These were the wages of her sin, the fact that she had wronged me notwithstanding. I could not tell her this, so I tried to change the subject.

"Where's Barry?"

"He's right here. He told me to call. He's afraid they won't ordain him if I don't apologize to you."

"Peachie, this is ridiculous. You don't owe me any apologies."

"Yes, I do."

"No, Peachie."

"I'm sorry, Elwyn. I am so very, very sorry," she said. "I hope that satisfies you, you arrogant knucklehead."

"Oh, Peachie, don't be that way."

The second day after Peachie married Barry was a Monday, but I did not drive directly home from school.

I stopped by Mr. Byrd's office. I was a conqueror come to claim new lands for the Lord.

With an exasperated expression on his face, Mr. Byrd looked up from his cluttered desk. "What now, young evangelist?"

"I feel I'm being persecuted for my religious beliefs."

"How so?"

"Security broke up my prayer meeting today."

"Good," he said. "I sent them." He put his pen down and came around the desk. "The cafeteria, I believe, is a place for eating. Many of the students complain that your activities upset their stomachs so much that they can't eat their meals."

"I don't believe you. What students have complained, sir?"

"Don't press me, boy."

I had him where I wanted him. I opened my book bag and pulled out five sheets of paper. "I have a petition here signed by over a hundred students and staff who feel that we should be allowed to form a Jesus Club at this school—"

He snatched the papers from my grasp. "I don't see my signature," he said. He tore the petition in half two times and dropped it in the wastepaper basket.

"I have a photocopy."

"Who cares? The real issue is not your prayer meeting but your grades. This is a school, not a church!" Mr. Byrd roared.

We stood toe-to-toe now, and he proved to be about an inch shorter than I (and I was no giant), but I was suddenly afraid of him. I shrank at the sound of his angry growl.

"I know Christians, but you're not one, Elwyn. You're weak. And you use your religion to shield your weakness. You can't make it on the football team, so you lure the best players away to your Bible studies."

"I'm not an athlete. They come freely."

"You can't get a girl, so you preach about adultery and fornication."

"Fornication is ruining our women."

"Not my woman. And I got a woman." He pointed to the photograph behind his desk. "A big, happy, sexy woman. Look at her smile."

"I'm happy for you."

"You should try passing your classes instead of passing out Bibles."

"I can pass if I want to. I'm an honors student."

"You *were* an honors student."

"I'm smart."

"Smart enough for Bible College at any rate. What SAT scores does Bible College require?"

"What is that supposed to mean?" I was on the verge of tears, and I didn't know why. "You're persecuting me."

He grabbed me by the shoulders. "Don't use God as an excuse for failure and unhappiness, Elwyn. Don't think that your misery on earth is a free ticket to heaven. Have fun. Be young. Pass your classes."

"No!" I could not prevent the tears from rolling down my cheeks. Satan was winning. Then Mr. Byrd slapped me three times hard in the face.

Whack. Whack. Whack.

It stung like a revelation. I tested my lip, which had begun to swell, and I stared without anger at Mr. Byrd.

"Now you'll probably sue me for assault," he said as he ushered me out of his office, with the hand that had smote me holding the door open against its strong spring.

I did not drive directly home after getting slapped by my principal. I visited Sister Morrisohn. A Christian must be valiant, brave. A Christian who has sinned must confess.

"I am saved."

"By the Grace of God."

"How, then, did I let go of His unfailing hand?"

She forced my palms together. "Pray, Elwyn."

I bowed my head and closed my eyes. A sobering thought prevented me from praying, and I opened my eyes. "You never told anyone what I did that day."

"There was no point in ruining your reputation."

"I would have lost my position in the church, like Peachie."

"You didn't really sin," Sister Morrisohn said. "Peachie sinned."

"I did sin."

"But you prayed for forgiveness."

"So did Peachie. And she confessed openly. I didn't so much as do that. Open confession is good for the soul."

"God knows the heart. That's enough, don't you think? Let your little transgression be a secret between me, you, and God."

"But the secret is driving me crazy." I was at a crossroads of faith. I had to either do what the Bible said was right, or not do what was right at all. It was now 4:15. Sister Morrisohn wore a red sundress. A half hour ago she had removed her shoes. I had been there almost an hour. I had told her the devil had got ahold of me and made me love her. She had raised her eyebrows and then removed her shoes. Another revelation. She had beautiful feet.

"There are many secrets in the church. Those who confess are no worse than the rest, but they suffer for their forthrightness."

"The Bible says open confession is good for the soul."

"Everyone will treat you like a backslider. You don't want that." She closed her eyes. "Some will even laugh at you."

"Laugh?"

"You're so much younger than me. They would find that amusing."

"Did they find it amusing," I asked, "when you married Brother Morrisohn?"

This seemed to catch her off guard. Her face underwent a series of quiet transformations, from disbelief to anger to resignation, before she spoke again: "How old are you, Elwyn? Sixteen?"

"Almost seventeen."

"I'm twenty-six years older than you." She rose from the couch where she had been sitting for the last half hour and walked in her stockinged feet to the other side of the room and stood beneath the portrait in oil of her and Brother Morrisohn on their wedding day. It was a painting in broad strokes and drab colors: black, gray, a rusty brown, a pasty yellow where there should have been white. "I was married for nearly twenty years to a man close to forty years my senior, and I loved him every second of that marriage."

"You're saying it doesn't really matter, then, the age difference."

"It matters a little. Oh, there are times when it matters." She laughed suddenly into her hands. "I'm so flattered. I just can't believe that at your age—well, just look at me." Sister Morrisohn lifted her arms like wings and spun in gay circles, revealing herself from all sides.

I gazed unabashedly. She had dancer's calves, a slender waist, arms that were thin as a young girl's.

"I see nothing wrong with you."

"Look at me again." Now she grabbed her hem with both hands and raised it above her dimpled knees. "All of these imperfections that come with age." She spun. Her sundress spread out like an umbrella, exposing thigh-high garters and the black silk panties of mourning.

I saw no imperfections.

When I looked at my watch, it was 8:00 p.m.

"Elwyn, this is a secret you'd better keep." Sister Morrisohn rolled over and hid her face in my chest. She laughed out loud and then she cried, soaking my chest with her tears.

I ran my fingers through her beautiful hair.

After that, we scrambled to end it, to get back to our lives. What pieces of our clothes we could find, we put back on, and then we knelt at the foot of the bed to pray for the forgiveness of our sins. But she was too close to me, and Satan won the battle again. My hand went under her dress and touched her.

"Oh God," I said.

"Lord," she said.

And then we sinned again—me and the woman who smelled like spring blossoms, whose slender waist fit so pleasingly into my palm, the woman who did not weigh much when she fell. Me and the wife of my deceased benefactor and friend.

Afterward, she said, her cheek against my neck, "How are we going to do this, Elwyn? People may begin to wonder."

"I could be giving you piano lessons twice a week," I suggested.

"Good," she said. Then: "Only twice a week?"

I called home once more. "I'm still at the mall," I told my mother. "Witnessing."

"Don't forget that dinner is waiting for you," she said. "Or are you fasting again?"

"I'll be home in a little while. I'm hungry. My fast is over." I looked at Sister Morrisohn. She turned her head away.

My mother said, "Well, I'll keep your plate warm. Bye, Elwyn."

"Bye, Mom." I hung my head in shame.

Father, forgive me.

His All-Seeing Eye

Peachie should have been happy.

She was married now, Praise the Lord, so the baby would have a name. In time the Faithful would forgive her too.

She had a husband, Praise the Lord, so they did not have to sneak around to do it anymore. They could do it anytime they wanted, and they certainly did. This was the honeymoon period, the best part of being married everyone had always told her.

Praise the Lord.

So why was happiness eluding her?

Barry snored beside her contentedly. Peachie touched his shoulder, but he did not awaken.

It was still early, barely past midnight, but Barry would not awaken until morning. In the old days when they were sneaking around, she and Barry would talk on the phone until 3 or 4 in the morning. But now he was an early sleeper, she had come to learn, especially after sex.

During this first week of marriage, she had come to learn many things about Barry, many of which she did not like. For instance, he was a bit on the sloppy side. He only showered every other day. And he had a way of being very condescending when he became angry, and he seemed to get angry for such stupid little things and so often. And he expected her to cook for him, even though his mother was perfectly willing to do it and Peachie was perfectly uncomfortable cooking in a strange kitchen.

"Well, I have a wife now, or don't I? I sure do remember marrying her," he said one evening, and Peachie did not like the tone he used at all, or the fact that he had addressed the comment to his mother when she, Peachie, was standing right there beside him in the kitchen.

But she still loved him, of this she was sure. It should not matter so much that he was at times insensitive. There was a lot of pressure on him as a young preacher in a situation like this. But he should not make her feel as though she had ruined his life. They were in this together. They were a team. A husband should protect his wife from bad feelings, and if he didn't, then what did that mean?

Tomorrow they would be moving to Lakeland to begin their new life together. She would not have her parents around anymore to protect her. Could she trust Barry to be there for her? She needed to talk to someone. She shook him again and said his name, but her husband continued to snore. She said to the darkness, "Barry, I love you. Do you love me? Barry? Barry? Barry!"

The snoring was replaced by a low, grumbling sigh. "What is it now, Peachie, honey, sweetie, dear wife of mine?"

There was that tone again, which she ignored.

"Do you love me, Barry?"

"I married you, didn't I?" he quipped. "And I am sleepy. We have a long drive ahead of us tomorrow."

"It's only 12." She shifted her abdomen carefully so as not to hurt the baby and stretched her arms across his bare chest. She put her face against his neck. "I think," she said, "that we could love each other more. I think there are things we could do so that our love would be the perfect love that King Solomon wrote about in the Song of Solomon. Our love could be a shining example to the Faithful."

"Example," he snorted. "We sure started out on the wrong foot."

"Is it wrong to fall in love?"

"It's wrong to fornicate."

"Is that all it was to you?"

He snorted again, dismissing her. "A woman should remain a virgin for her husband. It's in the Bible. Read it. Now I'm sleepy, Peachie, honey, sweetie, dear wife of mine."

"Then go to sleep, knucklehead." She pushed away from him and got up from the bed.

"Where are you going? Come back to bed. Peachie!" he called, but he did not even bother to get up to attempt to follow her as she left the room. He put the pillow over his head and rolled over, grumbling, "A wife. This is some wife. I need this, right? Heavenly Father, what did I get myself into?"

She did not slam the door because Brother Philip, Barry's college roommate, was sleeping on the couch in the living room. He was there to help with the move in the morning. She walked quietly through the living room past the packed boxes stacked in twos, the large, polished-marble coffee table, the upright piano she had been trained on, and knocked lightly on her mother-in-law's door.

"Sister McGowan," Peachie whispered. The tears were already falling. She felt so alone in the darkness. She had to talk to somebody. She just had to. "Sister McGowan!"

Sister McGowan opened the door in a housecoat she held closed with one hand.

"I'm not going to Lakeland. I can't."

Sister McGowan took the girl's hand and drew her into the room.

Peachie continued to blubber: "I'm sorry I messed everything up for everybody. I'm sorry I ruined Barry's life. I can't go up there to Lakeland. I have to stay right here in Miami."

Sister McGowan let her talk it out. Only once did she let go of the girl's hand and that was to get tissue from the nightstand to wipe her eyes. Sister McGowan felt like crying too, for the girl, for Barry, for herself.

She had known Peachie Gregory since she was only one of many little girls with ponytails reciting Bible verses in the beginner's Sunday school class she taught. At eight, Peachie came right here to this house and became her piano student. She lacked natural talent, but she was a hard worker who eventually became one of the most reliable ministers of music at the church.

Sister McGowan had always liked Peachie, and perhaps that was the problem. She had missed Peachie's sneaky side. The girl had seemed to like Sister Parker's boy, Elwyn. Perhaps she had only pretended so that Sister McGowan would let her guard down and leave her alone with Barry. And she had left them alone together too often. Barry had denied it, but she believed they had enacted their carnal union a few times right here in this house behind her back.

What a shame it was for her to lose a son this way, especially after her own experience with Barry's father, Dr. Leibnitz, her choir director at the University of Miami, who used her for his own pleasure and then abandoned her. Dr. Leibnitz had had that same sneaky look, as he praised her for being the first black girl to sing lead soprano in the school's world-famous chorus, as he held her hand, as he touched the small of her back. It was right on his face all the time, but she had missed it back then too. It was the late '50s. She chided herself for always being too easy, too trusting—and now her son was stuck with this girl. Sister McGowan felt like crying, but she held up.

When the girl's rambling quieted, Sister McGowan said, "You're such a pretty girl. I see why Barry fell in love with you. I was worried you were too young, but I see you're smart. Barry needs a smart woman to watch over him. He can't do it without you. You must help him build his ministry. You go up there, Peachie, and you play that piano just like I taught you. In time, you'll come to love him."

"But I do love him," Peachie replied. "I don't think he's happy. I thought we would be happy if we did the right thing."

"But did you do the right thing? Girls nowadays are so smart. They do it, and they never get pregnant. So when they get pregnant, you have to wonder why they didn't do something *not* to get pregnant."

"What could I have done?"

"You don't know?"

"Well, after we would do it, then I would stand up and shake . . . you know—"

"My Lord, you're just like I was. They never teach us anything. We have to learn the hard way." Sister McGowan dabbed at the girl's tears with the tissue and started to hate her a little less. "You're married and you should be happy. You deserve to be happy, you poor thing."

Peachie sobbed, "My husband doesn't love me."

"He loves you, I'm sure, but he's angry too because you got pregnant and made him look bad in front of the others. He's a good boy. He's always done the right thing. He wouldn't be with you if he didn't love you." She brushed back a strand of the girl's hair, which had fallen across her face. She really was a pretty girl. At least their children would be pretty. "Stand behind your husband. Show him that you are a good wife. You go up there to Lakeland and help our boy build that church and everything will work out just fine, okay?"

"I will."

There was a sound from outside.

Sister McGowan whispered, "I'll bet you it's Barry and Brother Philip with their ears pressed to the door." A mischievous twinkle came into her eyes. "Let's give them something to talk about. You put on one of my housecoats and you and me'll go have some fun."

"To eat?"

"Yes."

"Egg salad."

"You like my special egg salad."

"There's still some left in the fridge," said Peachie, warming to the idea. "And we need some ice cream."

"We have vanilla."

"What about licorice-flavored?"

"I don't have that," Sister McGowan said, adjusting the sash on her housecoat, "but we could go get some. The Dairy Queen is open all night."

So Peachie and her mother-in-law, decked out in housecoats and slippers, opened the bedroom door and strode without a word through the living room to the front door, past Barry and Brother Philip, who could only sit quietly mystified as the car engine fired up outside.

When they returned home an hour later, Peachie found Barry awake with the lights on. She removed his mother's housecoat and sat on the bed. He was ready to listen to her now. She said, "I know you're scared. I'm scared too. We need to be there for each other. If we're there for each other, no one can come between us."

"I'll be there for you."

"I'll be there for you, Barry."

He took her in his arms.

She said, "These are real vows this time."

"I was ashamed."

"I had no bridesmaids."

"Your dress was ugly. I hated it."

"It didn't hide my stomach at all. I never want to see those ugly old pictures."

"One day, after you have the baby, we'll have another ceremony and we'll take better pictures," he said, passing his hand through the arm holes of her full slip. He caressed her fat breasts, which used to be such little things. "You will wear white," he said, moving his hand down over the rise of her abdomen and into her panties.

"Only virgins wear white."

"You'll always be a virgin to me."

"Mmmm. It feels good in there, baby. You always know how to make me feel good."

"Shhh, baby. Don't talk dirty."

"It is such a pleasure to be married to you. It is like the Song of Solomon being with you."

Peachie shifted out of her clothes. They made sweet love this time and Peachie slept contentedly.

In the morning, as soon as Sister McGowan could get Barry alone, she scolded, "You'd better watch that girl, you hear me? I don't know why you took up with her in the first place. I don't trust her one bit. She's a skinny, little nothing."

Barry nodded.

I Need Thee Every Hour

He read from the Book of Daniel, then got down on his knees to pray, but there was a knock on his bedroom door and he looked up as his mother stuck her head in: Sister Morrisohn's on the line.

Elwyn unclasped his hands and picked up the phone. He took a deep breath. He was still kneeling.

Sister Morrisohn said, Can you talk?

No, he answered.

Can you listen? You can at least listen.

He rested his head on the bed and said to himself, Heavenly Father, what did I get myself into?

You missed church. You never miss church, she said. I'm putting myself in your place now. I see that you're not ready for this.

He said: I'm not ready. I really am not. This is bad what we're doing.

I'm not making excuses for what I did. I was flattered by your attentions. I wanted you to like me. I should have known better. You're young. Are you still there?

I'm here.

I just want you to understand me, is all. Who I really am.

I'm listening, he said. He was still on his knees.

I'm a mountain girl, she said. I come from a PO Box settlement about seven miles outside of Asheville, North Carolina. We didn't go to church when I was growing up. My father didn't allow it. We didn't go to school either. We were homeschooled. But my mother was a very religious woman. Some kind of Pentecostal, I believe. We read the Bible every morning when we got up and every night before we went to bed. My mother brought me and my little brother up believing that there was a God in heaven who loved us. She told us we must be good if we wanted to meet her in heaven. She was much older than my father and sickly. She knew she wouldn't live to see us grow up. She died when I was fourteen.

She paused for a long moment and then he heard her cough and do something else that sounded like clearing her throat before she continued. She was so much older than him, twenty-six years, which made her older than his mother.

His room was dark now because his blinds were drawn and he hadn't turned on the lights. Outside his room he could hear his parents talking with Deacon Miron and his wife, who was pregnant, and he heard them say his name occasionally, not calling him, but mentioning it as they often did because they were proud of him and remembered him every time the words *child* or *son* or *young people today* were mentioned. He was the perfect example of a good Christian son. Oh, if every child could be like Elwyn, they would say.

What I'm saying, Elwyn, is that I grew up without my mother, so I had but a skewed understanding of how a woman is supposed to behave. My mother had three sisters who would come up the mountain and visit us. Maybe I could be like them; these were wild, beautiful women. Mulattos, every one of them, just like my mother, their sickly baby sister, who would die and leave her children to an uncertain fate in this dark and sinful world.

She paused again, but this time he believed she might be crying. He could not hear her crying. There was something covering the phone, perhaps her hand.

From elsewhere in the house there came the sound of piano music. It was Deacon Miron's wife playing "I Need Thee Every Hour" with that heavy left hand of hers. Elwyn suspected she had the book propped open in front of her. Sister Miron was good when she had a book open in front of her, but she could not play by ear no matter how hard he tried to teach her. Sister Miron was a very fat, very pretty girl only about three years older than Elwyn. He used to call her Ginny Parker before she got married. Now she insisted that everyone call her Sister Miron, even Elwyn, who was her first cousin. Deacon Miron, a widower, was in his forties. He was Elwyn's godfather. He heard them say they would name the baby Elwyn if it were a boy because Elwyn was such a model Christian. He could not hear what they would name the baby if it were a girl because Sister Miron was putting that heavy left hand into her music and Sister Morrisohn was speaking again.

You asked me once what kind of sins I committed before I met Buford. I tried to be a mother to my brother in my mother's absence—cooking, cleaning, keeping the house for my lazy father—but once my innocence was lost, it became easier to behave like my aunts, who were a very bad example. Drinking. Smoking. Riding into town every Friday night in some strange man's pickup truck. Not coming back till Sunday morning. I was a woman, but I didn't really know what a woman was. I understood sex, but I hated the man I was sleeping with. He was the worst brute. At eighteen, I became pregnant. I lost the baby, which was probably the best thing—God forgive me for saying that—but now I could not live at home anymore. I had to leave. I tried to take my brother with me, but my father would not let me.

Someone out there said, Where is Elwyn?

It was Ginny—Sister Miron.

Someone answered, He's still on the phone with Sister Morrisohn, I think.

It was his mother.

Elwyn got up from his knees and went to the door and closed it. Then he went back to his bed and lay crossways on it with his legs hanging over the side.

Sister Morrisohn said, I came down and lived with my cousin and her husband until that became a problem. He made me feel I owed something more than the $35-a-month rent I was paying. When I wouldn't give him what he wanted, he got rough. When I told my cousin, she believed her husband. Never mind that I had a torn dress and a busted lip. I was out on the streets. I got fired from my counter job at Woolworth's. For the first time in my life, I lost contact with my little brother Harrison. I hooked up with an ugly crowd. Sex, drugs, stealing to eat. I smoked marijuana. I shoplifted. I had lots of boyfriends, though I hated and feared men . . . Then I met Buford and Mother Glovine. They were ministering at the Dade County jail, where I was being held.

The church was bailing everyone out who would allow Buford and Mother Glovine to preach to them. Buford was such a good man. Not only did he bail us out, he also acted as our legal counsel pro bono. He seemed to be very impressed with me. I guess because I was articulate and perhaps pretty. We debated often, with me usually getting the better of him. He found me a job at the library downtown. He helped me get a little apartment in Overtown. Most importantly, he helped me get my brother away from my father. Brought him down to Miami and then paid for him to go to college up at Tuskegee when he finished high school. Harrison is now an accountant up in Boston.

Elwyn said to her: When I was a kid, I think I remember he used to sit with you and Brother Morrisohn and Beverly.

Beverly *never* sat with us. She absolutely refused.

I was too young. I remember it wrong.

Yes, you do. You were too young . . . you are too young. You are a child.

I didn't mean to make you . . . mad, Sister Morrisohn.

I am mad. I am nutso.

I need Thee, O I need Thee, he heard his mother singing to Sister Miron's accompaniment. It sounded good—it would sound better if Ginny would ease up on the bass.

Sister Morrisohn said, I fell in love with Buford immediately. How could I not? He was such a good man. Intelligent. Handsome too. Though nothing happened between us while Mother Glovine was alive. Buford wouldn't allow it. But she was gravely ill. We married a month after she passed. Maybe that was the problem. Maybe that's what started the gossip. But we were in love. What did they expect us to do? This caused the rift between me and Beverly, my loving stepdaughter, who is actually older than me, ha-ha-ha. She's become a real problem for me with Buford's inheritance. There were vicious rumors about me tricking a senile old man into marriage to get his money. Your grandmother, Elwyn, I'm sorry to inform you, was chief among my accusers. But I loved Glovine . . . Mother Glovine. She was a mother to me . . . Our love overcame it all. I had found what I wanted in Buford, a man who would love me in spite of my past. A man who would not abuse me. A man who looked at me every day and said, *I am so glad I met you. My life is complete.*

She continued through sobs, Isn't that what we all want? Not once while I was with Buford did I ever think of any other man. Not once while I was with him did he ever remind me of my past.

Elwyn said, Sister Morrisohn, don't cry.

I loved him at first sight. And you remind me of him so much! It's just that our situation—our ages, I don't know what I feel for you or why. With him it was easy. I felt so old when he died. I thought I'd just hide up on a shelf for the rest of my life and gather dust. That day when you came over, you made me feel beautiful again. You made me feel young again. I didn't fear you or hate you as I had other men, because I knew you were good. I had watched you grow up . . . You're still growing up. You're still a child. Oh God.

Sister Morrisohn, he said, Mondays, Wednesdays, and Fridays at 4:30 sharp are best for me.

Yes. You're so sweet to . . . teach me the piano three times a week.

And I won't take money from you.

You must take the money. Piano lessons don't come cheap.

I will not take money from you.

You must, or they will know.

But it's weird.

We're weird. We have weird love, me and you.

Me and you. It sounds so . . . yeah, weird.

But so right.

So . . . weird.

I wish you were here right now so I could kiss you, my darling. I want to kiss you all night. I want to wake up in your arms. Do you mind that I said that?

I don't mind.

Outside his room was quiet. He wondered if Deacon and Sister Miron had left. It was rude not to have gone out and greeted them, especially since they planned on naming their son after him. He would make it up to them. He would apologize and say something flattering about Ginny's—Sister Miron's—heavy-left-hand music. He was, after all, the model Christian son.

Sister Morrisohn said, I bet when I told you I wanted to kiss you, you blushed.

Elwyn said, Maybe it would be safer if we didn't call each other so often. We'll see each other on Mondays, Wednesdays, and Fridays.

You don't understand how unpredictable this thing can be. Sometimes only your lover's voice will do.

I'm blushing now, I think.

I wish you were here so I could kiss you.

I'm definitely blushing, Sister Morrisohn.

I wish you were here so I could make love to you, my darling.

Long after her lover had hung up, she kept the phone to her ear like an embrace.

When she pulled away, finally, she went into the kitchen to pour herself a drink. The music from her record player in the living room switched from Tammy Wynette to Chester Harbaugh and His Old-Time Fiddle Band to the Louvin Brothers to Jim Reeves. She kept time nodding her head. She liked old-time country music, the kind she had grown up listening to back home in North Carolina. In her father's house. She liked the heartbreak songs, because she was a heartbreak girl. She liked the twanging and the whining in the music as a complement to the clever, sometimes depressing lyrics. She was a girl who was often depressed. Well, she used to be, but not anymore. Things, she told herself, were going to change. She opened the cabinet and took out the bottle. The wine was the good kind, a little tart with a sharp bouquet. She had kept the bottle hidden from Buford, who like all of the Faithful had disapproved of strong drink. But the Faithful are too strict in their rules concerning alcohol, Sister Morrisohn thought to herself. The Faithful are too strict about many things. Wine is good for the spirit, the Bible says so. Noah invented wine. Jesus turned water into wine. The Faithful are a bunch of tight a**es. She put the wine to her lips. Her spirit soared. There is warmth in the wine. There is warmth in him too. Her mind had gone back to Elwyn. There is warmth even in his voice, she said out loud.

She'd always had a problem finding warmth.

After her mother died, she had sought refuge from the cold fury in her father's house. She was most unsuccessful in that endeavor. *Now that your mother is in the ground, don't act like you don't know what we're doing.*

Now he didn't have to waste all that energy beating her to get her pants down. There was no one to protect her now that her mother was dead. She got pregnant by him again. This time the baby died, thank God. And after that, she grew stronger. When he tried to put his arm around her, she had the knife. He was laughing at her, calling her skinny red ugly. She stabbed him, trying to dig out his ribs. Sent him to the hospital at death's door. But still laughing: skinny red ugly, and got spirit just like your momma, ha-ha-ha.

She grew into a beautiful woman and had no shortage of men. Though some of them were kind, they never gave a thought to her needs. She hated them, she loathed them, she was dead scared of them—they all hit harder than her father, and they all hit, even the kind ones. Then Buford came. He offered to protect her for no reason other than she needed protecting. This was a different kind of love.

Christian love, he called it, which she thought she knew about because he was not the first married preacher who had fancied her. But Buford's love was about loving your neighbor as yourself.

Who is my neighbor, Daddyo?

Anyone in need.

You don't even know me, Daddyo.

I know that you are in need.

You're just like the rest of them—what you want from me is between my legs.

I have a wife, thank you, and I'm quite happy with her.

That's what you say now. That's what you say until you get me alone and show your wild side.

I'm a wealthy man, I don't need to cruise the jails to find women to sleep with, little girl. I'm Holy Ghost filled. I'm washed in the blood of the lamb. The only high I get is on Jesus. The only wild side I got is I'm on fire for the Lord.

Is that right?

That is right.

We'll see about that, Daddyo.

She smiled, remembering being with him in bed, free at last, after Mother Glovine had died. Wild side? Well, Buford did have his wild side. You could hardly call that Christian. But what he had felt for her, she decided, that brand of love was generous, kind, brave, warm. He had saved her and her brother (her son) Harrison with his warmth.

And here it was again, coming from the most unexpected of sources. Here was a boy, a man, a young man, who was generous, kind, brave, and warm just like Buford. They were about the same height too: 5'9". They had the penetrating gaze of Sidney Poitier. They shared that beautiful ebony complexion. Out in the living room, Jim Reeves sang "Four Walls." And Sister Morrisohn lost it.

She beat her chest and cried, Oh, Buford, what am I doing with this little boy? She collapsed on the kitchen floor. She washed the tiles with her tears.

In a little while, the last of the country songs stacked on the record player had played, and there was only the annoying clicking of the needle against the stereo housing. She got up, capped the wine, and put it away. She went into the living room and turned off the record player. In her bedroom, she stretched out on her lonely bed, where she immediately fell asleep. She dreamt of Elwyn's penis. How slender it was in her dream, so much less threatening than the sturdy lance he wielded in real life. How warm it made her feel, even in a dream.

She awoke at precisely 5:01, just enough time to prepare herself for night service at 6:00. At night service, Pastor preached a sermon on divine healing, which she found dull, but she said her perfunctory Amens and Yes Lords along with the rest of them. Then Pastor turned it over to the minister of music, Brother Elwyn, who would lead the testimony meeting that would end the night's service.

Excitement soared through every fiber of her being as her *man* moved to the piano. She was so proud of him. He was so handsome. She sat up straighter in her seat, which was in the second pew between Mother Naylor and Sister Spann as usual. She approved of Brother Elwyn's choice of testimony chant for tonight, "I Need Thee Every Hour." She sang with especial enthusiasm whenever the chorus came, *I NEED THEE, O, I NEED THEE, EVERY HOUR I NEED THEE,* because she really did need him every hour, but Brother Elwyn kept his eyes lowered. Perhaps he was not sending her a message with his marvelous playing.

When it came to be her turn to testify, Sister Morrisohn arose and said, I thank the Lord for being here. I thank the Lord for being saved and sanctified. I thank Him for giving me the strength to go on after Brother Morrisohn passed. Saints, you don't know how hard it has been. But the Lord just keeps on providing and providing and providing and providing and providing and providing!

She ended with a shout. A short, robust bark of a shout.

There were cries of "Amen" and "Praise the Lord" from the others. But Brother Elwyn just kept on playing, with his eyes focused hard on his fingers, as though he hadn't heard.

As she sat down with a satisfied smile on her face, she knew she was being naughty. She shouldn't have shouted like that, but she was trying to send him a message by shouting like she did during orgasm because that's how he made her feel every time she was with him. She just wanted to rip off her clothes and fly to him. He was so tight and so fresh and so full of juice. His skin was smooth as a baby's bottom, his stomach was flat, his arms and legs were lean and strong—he was a lean, strong, fresh-tasting black boy—he looked good enough to eat. She wanted to eat her fill of him, but she knew that was impossible. She could never get enough of him no matter how much he gave her. No matter how much she took—even if he came over more than three times a week she could never suck it all out of him. He had so much. It was spilling over. She wanted to lick his clean, black skin. She wanted to bite him. She wanted to crunch him between her teeth like an apple. There had to be a way to eat him all up.

She shook her head. Three days a week. Not enough, Lord. Not enough.

He kept on playing.

Again she shouted her orgasm shout, which went unnoticed by the congregation among their holiness shouts, Amens, and Hallelujahs. But she kept her eyes on Elwyn.

There it was! A flinch. He had heard her.

And he was definitely blushing.

HERE ENDETH THE TESTAMENT OF INNOCENCE

II. Testament of Innocence Lost

Book of Genesis 3:6
*And when the woman saw that the tree was good for food,
and that it was pleasant to the eyes, and a tree to be desired
to make one wise, she took of the fruit thereof, and did eat,
and gave also unto her husband with her; and he did eat.*

Epistles I

1.

Dear Elwyn,

    Now that I'm married, I can forgive you. I see things differently now. I forgive you, my dear friend, my dear brother in the Lord.

Yours,
Peachie McGowan

2.

From Elwyn James Parker to the Lord, then torn up into tiny little bits and discarded:

Make me not to want it. Make me to look at it and laugh. Take it away from me. Hide it from me in the cleft of a rock. Cover it from mine eyes. Harden my heart against it. Give me the victory over it. Make me pure again. How can I enter Your house in my vileness and shame? How can she? She is the devil. "Such is the way of an adulterous woman; she eateth, and wipeth her mouth, and saith, I have done no wickedness." Proverbs 30:20. Take her away from me. Hide her from mine eyes, O Lord. Amen.

3.

I forgive you, Elwyn. Marriage has doused the fire of my anger and given me time to reflect. I now have a clearer perspective on things. I forgive you, Elwyn, as well as Sister Cooper and Sister Morrisohn, for the part you played in ruining my wedding.

Sister Cooper turned the Faithful against me. She's your grandmother and I mean no disrespect. She's the one who started calling me "skinny nothing." Someone that you know real well told me that she even called me "an harlot" in missionary meeting. She is just so much more perfect than me. Lucky her. With perspective, I see that she and her generation were able to live a perfect Christian life because they lived in an easier time. Work and then school and then church. They did not have TV. They were allowed to marry at 14 and 15 without a stigma. They were expected to marry young. I mean no disrespect, but Sister Cooper should ask herself why she got married so late. Was she too ugly? Or was she a miserable cow like she is now? Christians shouldn't be miserable. In other words, don't mess up my wedding just because you got married like twenty years later than everyone around you. No offense, Elwyn, but is she jealous because I'm light-skinned? Someone told me that she is very skin conscious. I'm not giving you any names, but you can trust my sources (you know who my mother-in-law is). I don't have a *problem with skin. I would have been just as happy marrying a dark-skinned man like you. If I had been in love with you, I mean. I'm not saying I didn't like you at one time, but Barry is the man for me. You just have to learn to deal with it.*

And Sister Morrisohn. Let me tell you about Sister Morrisohn. She has the nerve to pull rank on anybody? Do you know the woman was in jail? Do you know she stole Brother Morrisohn from his wife? I hear they used to do it right in the bedroom while Sister Glovine was there hanging on for her last days. She's a sex maniac. That's why Beverly Morrisohn hates her and is going to take her to court to win that fancy house she lives in. You'll see. And she'll win too. Sister Morrisohn is a jailbird. She's well-dressed-up now with Brother Morrisohn's money, but she's still a tramp. I hear she's a heavy drinker too. I have good sources. They're people you know. She had the nerve—she and her Missionary Society sisters—to meet me and my mother at the bridal shop. She played up to my mother saying, "Oh, I was not a virgin either when I married Buford. If you're not a virgin, you can't wear white. Here's a nice blue one. Blue is nice." We already had a nice dress picked out, but my mother trying to do what's right got all caught up and confused and I ended up with that blue dress. I hate my wedding pictures. I hate my wedding pictures, Elwyn, but I love my husband. How do you like that?

And you, dear friend. You were my best friend. I'm going to admit something secret here, so I trust you will destroy this letter after you've read it. I did love you at one time. I think around fourth grade. I thought you were cute. And again around eighth grade. Remember when we went to the youth prayer retreat at Camp Dilmore? Or was it up here in Lakeland that year? At any rate, it was the year our team came in second to the Jacksonville Fifth Street Faithful in the volleyball competition. Remember we beat the Orlando-Evans Faithful by two points in the tiebreak for second? I don't even like sports that much, but I remember everything so clearly. I thought you were so cute in your white shorts. I prayed for you each time you went up to serve. You were the best server on the team that year and I believe my prayers had something to do with it. On the bus back to Miami, I wanted you to kiss me. I even held your hand while we talked. About music, I'm sure. BORING, and you did not kiss me. I don't know what I would have done if you had kissed me. I was deep into you that night. I went to sleep with my head on your shoulder. You didn't even put your arm around me. You were stronger than me as always. You didn't feel it burning like I did, or you felt it but fought it off. But that was fine. I was talking to Barry at the time, so it turned out for the best.

After all the feelings and friendship we shared for all those years, Elwyn, you betrayed me. You insulted my husband at his own wedding. I knew you were jealous of him, but I didn't think you'd go so far. You played boogie-woogie at our wedding. I know it's called gospel. I know what gospel is, knucklehead. But you were just showing off as usual. Oh, everybody just loved it. You're such a fine musician! But it was Barry's wedding, not yours. You had no right. You had made a deal with him, remember? He was so upset. I tried to defend you. I said, "He meant nothing by it." Barry said, "Yes, he did. He hates us. I bet he doesn't give us a wedding gift." Elwyn, I checked every gift. None from you. Barry was right. It hurt me so.

But I'm married now and happy and I forgive you. I always considered you so strong in the Lord. I envied your strength. What your childish, selfish performance at the wedding shows is that none of us is perfect.

Love,
Peachie

The Little Preacher

My father and I were eating chicken cacciatore at a restaurant called Mama Louisa's near the TWA departures inside the Miami International Airport. A hundred languages chattered around us as travelers from every part of the civilized world hauled their luggage through one of the busiest and most culturally diverse hubs in America.

My father and I didn't know it, but we were being watched.

I had just come from college out of state and I would only be in town for about a week. He had insisted on picking me up, though I was perfectly willing to cab it home. He rarely got to see me, he said. He really missed me sometimes, he said. We could eat dinner together at the airport and bond a little. I figured it was some kind of religious thing he was going through. I said, Okay.

The restaurant was loud with Italian music, but not too busy, and the chicken was good. My father, not one to waste food, was wolfing his down. We talked about things small and large, skyrocketing gas prices, trouble in the Middles East, the fierce look of young black men's attire. We laughed loud even when our jokes weren't all that funny. He kept his head down, mostly looking at his plate, so I was afforded a good view of his head and found myself wondering if I would go bald that way, receding from the front and then thinning in a perfect circle on top.

I was also wondering what his game was.

I certainly liked his company. We got along just fine—the few times we saw each other. The problem was that lately he had been doing a lot of things like this restaurant deal. Bonding things.

I looked hard at his full face and hoped he wasn't dying or anything like that. What could it be? Well, I'm only human, so I allowed myself to hope. I allowed myself to hope for the best possibility of all—that my father was here to come clean about me with his family.

I was so excited that I couldn't eat.

My father took notice of this and set his fork down at the side of his plate on the folded napkin. For a few moments neither of us said anything. Finally, I set my fork down too and said, "This is cool, man, but what's it all about?"

"I guess I'm nervous."

"Don't be, man." Now his nervousness made me even more nervous. But he had let me down so many times that I had learned to let my natural cool take over. I leaned back in my chair and opened my hands, palms up. "It's just a thing. Say what you got to say."

He pushed back, stood up from the table, and straightened his tie. He always wore a tie. All of them wore ties at that church. "You're right. Lemme go take a leak. And I'll set everything straight when I get back."

"Is it going to be good?" I said after him.

He glanced over his shoulder. "I'll let you be the judge."

My nervousness was completely under control now as I watched my father go through the swinging doors of the bathroom, for I had remembered who he was.

How weak he was.

He couldn't go through with it, whatever he had come here originally planning to do. He could not.

I understood then that his little trip to the bathroom was a way for him to stall and come up with a new story to tell me. He would come back and say, "I'm thinking about taking a night class and I want your opinion," or, "I'm thinking of changing jobs." We would talk about it and laugh, and we would both know that this was not what he had planned to say. We had been through this before.

But today was different.

Today we were being watched.

And the person who had been watching us from another table spotted the opportunity. I was alone. The person crept up behind me. I felt two hands on my shoulders. Before I could shake away, a sweet kiss was planted on the back of my neck.

I whirled around and there before me stood the most beautiful woman I had ever seen.

She was about 5'7". What curves this honey had. Her face was as fair as some lightly tanned white people, but with the striking angles and prominence of a Nubian beauty. Her hair was pulled back tight and roped down to her waist in a magnificent, lustrous braid of black. My heart left me to go buy a plane ticket to wherever she lived, though she was kind of old for my taste. I figured she was at least in her thirties. Maybe older.

I maintained my cool and spoke to her, but already the expression on her face was broadcasting that it had been a mistake. She was as surprised as I was. You see, the kiss had not been intended for me, but for another.

Just my luck.

We exchanged embarrassed laughter.

"You look like someone I know," she explained.

"At least from behind . . . hmmm."

"Well, yes. You're right. But the man you were eating with, he looks like someone I know also. So when I saw you two together, I assumed you were this other person I know. His son."

I chuckled. "You kissed the back of my neck. Hmmm."

"I sincerely apologize. What was I thinking?" She blushed. "But that man looked so much like my friend Roscoe, and so I assumed you were his son."

"That is Roscoe," said I. "And I am his son."

"Roscoe Parker?"

"You know my dad?"

"Oh my God," she said.

In that moment, the beautiful woman and I suddenly understood the manner in which we were connected. The revelation brought a mischievous smile to my face.

But she said, "Oh my God," and then fled.

She had no other choice but to flee before my father came out of the bathroom and learned the truth about her and his son. Not me, but his other son. My brother. For it was my father's face that had drawn her to this table and her lips to the back of my neck. But I was the wrong son.

I was Benny Willett, a college student with a 4.0 GPA and a stomach full of Italian chicken and broken promises. I was nobody special.

As I watched the woman's bouncing backside flee the airport restaurant, I was filled with the wonder and mystery of my brother, the little preacher for whom the kiss had been intended, my little brother Elwyn Parker, whom I had never met.

The Boy from Opa-Locka

When I got up the next morning, I heard voices in the house and not just my mom's. They were already here.

I went into the bathroom and brushed and flossed my teeth and took care of some other urgent business. Someone pushed on the door, which had no lock. I didn't want to be seen in the middle of my business, so I hurriedly yelled, "I'm in here!"

"Oh, Benny! College boy. I didn't know."

It was Character Pierre, my mom's sometime boyfriend.

"How was the trip down from the university of the state of Massachusetts? You think the team has a chance to win the national title this year?"

"I'm not going to talk through the bathroom door."

"I'll give you your space. Good to see you."

"You haven't seen me yet. Jeez."

I was still angry with my mother for dating him of all people. The neighbor from around the corner. What happened to the cop who was supposedly flirting with her? Now *there* was a good father figure and role model.

Outside the bathroom, Character was waiting and he gave me a hug, which I returned weakly. It was a strong hug, like a test of strength. It always surprised me how strong Character was, compared to how frail he looked. He was a small Haitian man, maybe 5'3", but tough like braided wire. He could handle himself. He claimed to have killed a man back in Haiti who had offended his mother. But that was a long time ago, Character assured us, before he had fled the island to make a better life here in America. He was a man of peace now. He wore a khaki, four-pocket work shirt, a pair of oversized jeans rolled up at the cuff, and my old kick-about slippers, which I had lost track of some months ago.

"So that's where they are," I said, without explaining.

"What?" asked Character.

"Nothing."

"Benny. Benny. Good to have you home."

Home. Yeah, right.

In the kitchen, breakfast was already waiting on the big table. The children, Character's daughters Marie, Amoneeze, and Sabine—fifteen, fourteen, thirteen—were there too. They were eating cereal, toast, and eggs scrambled with tomatoes. I shot the oldest girl, Marie, a frown in greeting. She frowned right back. Stuck out her tongue. Mom drank coffee, black with no sugar, and Character picked up a smoky glass filled with something no doubt alcoholic and drained it. He was a man of peace who liked his liquor first thing in the morning. I didn't appreciate that sometimes he raised his voice at my mom when he had drunk too much. To his credit, he had never raised his hand.

The two younger girls lifted their heads from their plates long enough to say good morning. There was a place set for me at the table, but I didn't sit down.

"You're not going to eat?" my mom Patsy asked, looking up from her coffee.

She was a smiling bright-skinned woman with large boobies and a small waist. I'm not bragging just because she's my mom, but she was very good looking, and she could do better than this little Haitian guy from around the neighborhood. I had waited all of my life for her to settle down with a man I could sort of look up to as a father figure, and she picked a guy who didn't even understand football.

My mom said to me, "Sit down and eat."

"I've got a paper to do." I showed her the folder in my hand. "I'm going to the library."

Marie lifted her eyebrows and shook her head pathetically.

My mom said, "You're home for a few days. Relax. Sit and eat breakfast with your family."

I winced inwardly at the word "family." They were not my family, not yet, not until my mom married Character, which I hoped would never happen. The oldest girl, Marie, said something in Creole, and everybody including Patsy laughed at it, but not me. I deliberately did not speak Creole.

Patsy translated for me: "*Pa etidye twop paske ou kapab aveg.* Marie said to you, Don't study too much or you'll go blind."

"I won't," I assured them, and then I went out the door.

Now why didn't she just say it in English? Marie spoke perfectly good English. They did these things to upset me.

The bus ride from Opa-Locka, where we lived, to the North Dade Regional Library was long enough to make me regret not eating breakfast. I looked over the notes for the paper on international monetary exchanges, but I was distracted and kept rereading the same few lines. When I got off the bus, I went to a vending machine and bought a granola bar and a small bag of peanuts. I gobbled the granola bar and stuck the peanuts in my pocket for later.

Everybody in the library said hi or waved at me. They all knew me. I had been coming here since a kid. I got in the elevator. At the second-floor stacks, I found myself distracted again.

Character was a good plumber, but he drank too much and was perhaps dangerous. One minute he was trying to bond with me, the next he was trying to prove he was a stronger man. The girls spoke Creole to deliberately exclude me. I had talked to Mom about it, and she encouraged me to learn Creole as she had. I could have if I'd wanted. Mom worked as a certified Spanish, French, and Creole translator at the immigration building on 79th Street—she was so talented and yet so unmotivated it killed me. She could be anything she wanted, marry anyone she wanted. Every good-looking, well-put-together brother who had ever seen her had made a play. And she still lived in Opa-Locka. Jeez.

Maybe if she had played her cards right with Roscoe, Elwyn would have been the outside child, and I would have been numbered among the Faithful. Both Mom and Isadore were pregnant at the same time. In fact, I'm three months older than the little preacher, so that means Mom had had the first shot at Roscoe and, of course, she blew it because she was waiting for her Haitian in shining armor to come along. Ah Patsy.

But being her son was not all bad. I inherited from her a gift for languages, and I was good enough in Spanish and Portuguese to win the *Miami Herald's* Silver Knight Award in languages, which helped pay my way to Boston University, where I was majoring in international business. Yes, I was smart. I had graduated high school at fifteen. I was currently on an accelerated timeline to be done with college just one month shy of my seventeenth birthday. I would complete my master's by nineteen, having already been accepted into the graduate program at Yale.

I'd done well for a boy raised by a single mother in a poor neighborhood. Unlike my mom, from whom I had inherited my gifts, I was motivated. When I wanted something, I went out and got it. I made a plan and I stuck to it. My motto was, *He who fails to plan, plans to fail.*

My ambition was to retire as a millionaire from my various successful business ventures before the age of thirty-five and accept from a grateful president the U.S. ambassadorship to Brazil, where all the girls were perfect tens like in the movie *Black Orpheus*.

There was movement on the other side of the stacks. It was Marie, who giggled and came around to my side.

"What took you so long?"

"They were watching me."

"What did you tell them?"

"I'm at Nicki's house. I'm having so much fun. We're playing with dolls."

"You're too old for dolls."

"We're braiding hair and talking about boys." When Marie got next to me, she smelled literally good enough to eat, but it was the brown paper bag in her hand. She passed it to me and I looked inside. Egg sandwich. Bacon. A carton of orange juice.

"You brought me breakfast."

"I knew my baby was hungry."

"Hungry for you," I said, smacking her on the backside.

"Fresh," Marie said, pecking me on the lips.

We rode down on the elevator and left the library holding hands. As we waited on the bus bench, I ate my breakfast and Marie chattered on about some little party that she had been invited to that her friends were having tonight. I knew she was hinting that she wanted me to come. I kept quiet about it. I did not want to go to some kiddie party.

But for Marie I might do it.

Marie was my first crush. My first kiss. Back when we were in fourth grade. We were the two smartest kids in the class before I got double-promoted out and up to sixth grade. After that, there were some other girls, some other kisses, but they were getting older and stupider. Now they were too old, and saw me as too young. At college, they were all in their late teens or early twenties. They saw me as a kid, which left me kind of lonely. But it was okay. It gave me time to study. Then my mom had to go and start dating Marie's father. Marie was at my house a lot. My Marie. It was weird the first time I saw her in my house, my own house. Jeez. We started liking each other again. But like Marie said: "We never actually broke up. I wondered where you went."

So we picked up where we had left off in the fourth grade. Of course, we were careful not to let on. We hadn't had sex yet. We were both virgins. We were saving it until we got married. Or until I became ambassador to Brazil.

When I finished my yummy meal, the bus still hadn't arrived. I punched Marie in the shoulder. She punched me in the shoulder. We rolled off the bench and into the grass and ended up smooching under a palm tree.

When we got off the bus, Marie said, "This is a church."

"Good observation."

"You said we were going to meet your brother."

"Your Benny keeps his promises. Roscoe said he would be here."

"But it's Saturday."

It was a large church, with five walls that came together in a steeple topped off with a large crucifix. The name was really long: The Church of Our Blessed Redeemer Who Walked Upon the Waters.

We went inside giggling at the church's grandiose title. Inside was huge. There was a pulpit, an altar, and stained glass windows as in most churches. There were three columns, each containing about about thirty wooden pews. It was a Saturday afternoon, but Roscoe was right. There was a service of some kind going on. We seated ourselves in the furthest pews back. There was music being played on the piano, and dirgelike singing. I was disappointed when I saw it wasn't Elwyn at the piano. There was an elderly woman up there playing as they sang.

> *Is your all on the altar of sacrifice laid?*
> *Your heart, does the spirit control?*
> *You can only be blessed,*
> *And have peace and sweet rest,*
> *As you yield Him your body and soul.*

When I looked around trying to get a glimpse of my brother, I began to realize this service they were having was unlike any I'd ever seen before. Marie and I were the only ones seated in the back pews. Everyone else was crowded to the front seven or eight. Something was happening up there that I could not make out too clearly. Some of them were standing. Some were seated. Others, I discovered after watching awhile, were kneeling before those who were seated. The kneeling ones seemed to be doing something to the feet of the seated ones.

I sighted Roscoe, who was one of the standing people, but before that he had been seated. Roscoe had no shoes on his feet. Someone brought him a small white pail and a towel. Roscoe took the pail and the towel and knelt before someone who was seated. I craned my neck to see. The seated person, a man, was wearing no shoes. Roscoe dipped the towel in the bucket of water and proceeded to wash the man's feet.

"Okay. That was weird," I said to Marie. "My father is not only a bus driver, but he washes feet too."

The church continued to sing their dirgelike hymn.

You can only be blessed,
And have peace and sweet rest,
As you yield Him your body and soul.

Marie said, "This do in remembrance of me."

The men were washing the feet of the men. The women were washing the feet of the women.

"What do you mean, This do in remembrance of me?"

"It's in the Bible. Jesus made the disciples do it."

"Do what?" I asked. Then I said: "That's him. That's Elwyn." I squeezed Marie's hand and pointed. "That's him."

"Where?" She looked to where I was pointing. "That's your brother?"

"That's the little preacher."

"I should have known. He looks like you."

"He's short."

"He's not that short."

"He's shorter than me."

"He's taller than you. At least an inch."

"Thou poor blind Haitian child. Let me lay my hands on your eyes so that you might see."

"He's cute."

"Let me lay these holy hands on your eyes and give you back your sight."

"You say he's musically talented too? He's the full package."

"Duh. I'm in my senior year in college and I'm sixteen."

"Show-off."

"And I'm not washing anybody's feet like some slave."

"Shhh. Before they throw us out."

Then Elwyn rose up, fresh from washing another man's feet, and made his way to the piano on the platform. He was wearing a white shirt, a black tie, and pin-striped black pants. There were no shoes or socks on his feet, as they had just been washed.

He got behind the elderly pianist and reached around her to place his hand on the piano keys. Smoothly and without missing a beat in the song, he replaced her at the piano.

Your heart, does the spirit control?

As Elwyn continued the music, the elderly pianist went to one of the pews, took off her shoes, and another lady knelt before her and began to wash her feet.

"It's so cool you have a brother."

"Yep."

"Who is taller than you."

"Shut up."

"And a foot washer."

"Shut up."

"This do in remembrance of me."

"Never heard of it. Explain, smart lady."

"Foot washing, you heathen. It's in the Bible. Jesus washed the disciples' feet the night He was betrayed. They had the Last Supper and then they washed feet. Then they went out and Judas betrayed Him. You should try going to church once in a while."

"But I don't need my feet washed."

"I'll wash your feet," Marie teased.

"I'll leave them extra crusty for you."

"Gross."

Then the woman washing the elderly pianist's feet lifted her head and I saw her face. And she saw mine.

It was the woman who had kissed me at the airport.

"Uh oh." I grabbed Marie's hand.

"What?"

We got up and quickly left the church.

Epistles II

i.

I keep telling him I don't think they'll ever come, but he's stubborn.

These factory workers, these farm hands, these citrus pickers, these smiling shopkeepers, these whistling front-yard mechanics, these fix-anything-that's-broken-for-whatever-you-can-spare silver-haired men in overalls crisply pressed and dusty Brogan shoes (they call it BROW-GINE, Elwyn), and, of course, their dour wives who dislike me because, first of all, they think I'm too young to be the mother of a church, and second—"How old did you say that baby was?"

They will not come, these Faithful of Lakeland, for Lakeland, they argue, already has a church, the Fourth Street Church of Our Blessed Redeemer Who Walked Upon the Waters. Why worship in an empty barn?

Our one-bedroom apartment is at the back of our church, that empty barn. It was freezing cold in Lakeland last week, and the heat went out. We slept bundled in blankets with the baby between us.

I get up every Sunday and play piano for fifteen to twenty people, including myself, the baby, Barry, Barry's loyal Brother Philip, and our choir of six. There is no night service.

The Faithful of Lakeland have rejected us.

I tell him to forget them. Let's fill our church with new people. Let's go out and witness like we did in Miami. I was so mad I slipped up and used your name. "Let's witness like Elwyn does." He didn't talk to me for a week.

I love my husband.

I have a part-time job at Eckerd Pharmacy.

Love,

Peachie, a preacher's wife

2.

Sometimes I go to Fourth Street Church. The Big Church, we called it when we were kids.

You remember how beautiful it is. Its five walls of white polished marble slope nonchalantly up from the grass, so gradually you can climb them like a hill. Up they go, these holy walls, until they come together in a point, up where they put that huge crucifix you can see from five miles away in daylight and even further away when it's lit up by floodlights that bathe it in white one minute (Behold, the lamb of God) and red the next (His blood was shed for you).

Inside are the arched ceilings, the floating balconies in three layers, the silver organ pipes rising up and out of the southern wall, the oak pews upholstered in royal purple velvet; the hewn-stone altar and pulpit, the orchestra pit, the white grand piano that me and you played three years ago at Convention. I outplayed you, knucklehead. The sacrament pots and candles of gold. The stained glass windows that depict great moments in the life of Christ. Do you remember the small gold plates in each pew where the names and dates of the great saints are inscribed? Elwyn James the Younger, 1780–1831, Elder Cuthbert Rogers, 177?–1840, Elder (Colonel) Hanes Culpeppar, 1801–1869, Bishop Curtis Rogers, 1809–1901, Rev. Jeroboam Montgomery, 1844–1918, Rev. D.L. Kirkaby Jr., 1859–1903, Kinew, 182?–1891, Mother Dorothy "Missy" Beecher, 185?–1941, and so on.

Three thousand members. The Big Church. For $125 a month, I, a preacher's wife, a mother of the church, vacuum and dust and polish at the Big Church. It is humiliating, but I have to do it. We are so broke, but he refuses to take a job at the factory. He's a minister, he says. He's writing songs for an album, he says. Poor dreamer. Last month the church collections brought in $200 and half of that was money we put in the plate ourselves. I still have my job at Eckerd. The manager gets fresh. I want to quit, but we need the money. It's hard right now, Elwyn, but we manage with the help of the Lord. Brother Philip floats us each month, bless him. His parents have money.

Love,
Peachie, as we pray for victory over Satan and temptation

3.

He called me "an harlot," then said he didn't mean it.

We were arguing—fighting about why we have so few members (it's up to thirty-three now, thanks to me evangelizing at work and at the daycare and not thanks to his stupid songwriting). I was trying to explain how you have to go out in the community and witness, and he was whining about how the Faithful of Lakeland will eventually come around because of how popular he was at Bible College, and Junior was crying because he was sick with the cold all week, and I said to Barry, "We need medicine for the baby." And he said to me, "So?" And I said, "Well, go buy some. And while you're at it, buy some Pampers and wipes and Similac." And he said something about babies being so expensive. And my tone was not exactly nice when I said, "Not if you have a job." And this hurt him and he said in a real nasty way, "There didn't have to be a baby." And I said, "You wanted it just as much as I did. I didn't rape you." And he said, "I'm not the one who's the harlot." And I said, "Who are you calling an harlot?" And he said he was sorry, he didn't mean it, but it was too late—I had heard him.

He'd been lying all this time. He was just like everybody else. Everybody believed that everything was my fault. The baby. The wedding. His low membership. All my fault.

I thought a husband was supposed to stand by your side in sickness and in health, not just make you sick.

Peachie

4.

Another fight. A big one this time. But with a happy ending.

It was my fault. He found out about my manager at work, about what he had done a few months ago. Remember I told you how he locked me in the bathroom and kissed me and I kicked him in the groin?

I was telling the story to Momma again and he was listening in on the kitchen line. I didn't realize just how jealous he was until he came in the room yelling and screaming so loud he woke the baby and I had to hang up with Momma right away because he was The Man In His House. I explained to him what had happened, but he didn't believe me and I begged him not to go to Eckerd, but he and Brother Philip went, and there was trouble. He hit the manager—a man of God, a preacher, walking into Eckerd in a robe and slippers and punching the manager in the mouth. I had to bail him out of jail with what little money we had. I should have left him there.

He gets out of jail, and everything is my fault again. It's my fault men are after me. They can smell my scent, he says. I'm in heat all the time. They know I'm easy.

He said much worse than that, and we fought, and he hit me.

And then we made love.

Now I know this may sound strange to you, Elwyn, especially since you're a virgin and don't know very much about sexual matters, but this was *the best sex we had had in a long time. In fact, I don't think I fully understand why it worked out like that. I was very angry with him for hitting me and then denying that he had. "I didn't hit you, baby. I put my hand in your face. I was being demonstrative."*

"You hit me."

"Why would I hit you? I love you. Don't you know that?"

"No. Not anymore."

"I'm just afraid that you don't love me, is all. You're so beautiful and smart and you're right about the way the church should be built up. I'm afraid you're going to run away with someone better than me."

"Baby, there's no one better than you."

"I love you, Peachie." We kissed and he had my clothes off and had his face buried in my you-know-where before I even knew what was happening.

I lost my job at Eckerd. Surprise. I'm pregnant again. Pregnant and I can't even afford milk for this first baby. And guess what? You'll never guess. Brother Philip made a pass at me. "I loved you from the first time I set eyes on you," he said. "And you don't have to leave Barry. The Lord will see to your financial needs through me. I can take care of you."

He's one of the rich guys, remember, and he knows it. The way he dresses. His fancy apartment. Always floating us. But I have more sense than that. The devil comes in many forms. And I love my husband. My husband will take care of me.

Eventually. (ha ha)

Burn this letter, Elwyn. And pray for Brother Philip.

Yours truly,
Mrs. Barry Sebastian-Bach McGowan, as she struggles onward and upward for the Lord

5.

Regarding your last letter to me, I am speechless. I need you to call me so that we can talk about this. If I have read your letter correctly, and have correctly interpreted the implications to mean things of a serious sexual nature concerning you and a certain elder member of the church, I need seriously to talk to you. There are things that should not be put into print for fear of who might read them and so I urge you to call me on Saturday at work so that we may speak without fear of being overheard by uninvited parties. Let me just say that I am amazed at the implications. I am in disbelief. I cannot imagine that a coming together of such unequally yoked oxen would be permitted by the Lord, nor even attempted to be undertaken by one of His greatest servants.

Understand that I am your friend and shall ever be. Understand that your secret is safe with me as all of mine I am certain are with you. Nevertheless, I am quite hurt and highly offended by the situation as I am reading it to be. I am wroth with you, Elwyn, and I need to discuss this matter with you right away. Please call me on Saturday.

Your friend Peachie

Our Father

I was scared of him drunk.
I was scared of his enormous size, his roaring voice, his falling down. I was scared of his alcohol, pee, and Aqua Velva smell. I was scared of his razor stubble when he held me against his face and called me his man-child. I was scared of how he took me out of the bed some nights and put me to sleep on the couch so he could be alone in the room with my mother. I was scared of how he made my mother cry out from behind the closed door, how he made her laugh and shout. How he made my holy mother say swear words.

I had the worst father in the whole world. Why couldn't he be more like one of the Faithful brethren? All the brothers at church were quiet and clean. They took their children to the park on Saturdays to play. When I drove around with my father, he made me carry a crayon to write down his numbers for him. They appeared everywhere. On the big truck in front of us, on the billboard over the liquor store, large and glittery on somebody's mailbox: 6-5-4, 4-5-3, 4-5-9, 5-4-5. He claimed he was helping me with my arithmetic. This was when we lived in the ghetto in Overtown. My father was a gambler and a sinner. This was before he got saved.

I would confess to my mother that I was having trouble loving him the way Jesus commanded us to do, and she would say, You must love him. Honor thy mother and thy father that thy days may be long upon the earth.

And I would say to my mother, But he's an evil sinner. He's going to burn in hellfire.

Actually, I only said that to my mother once, and she slapped me a hard one right across the lips.

Watch your mouth, boy! He's your father!

And I ran into the closet to weep and pray.

Lord, don't make my burden heavier than I can bear.

But the Lord is a miracle worker.

One day somebody pounded on the door.

My mother dropped the laundry she was folding. I turned away from the picture Bible I was reading. A knock like that usually meant an emergency. In the ghetto where we were living at the time it usually meant someone had been shot, or the police were looking for someone.

My mother went to the barred window next to the door and pushed back the blinds, and a man pressed his ugly face against the glass.

I remember he was dressed in a suit like some of the men at church wear, except he didn't have on a tie and his jacket was all rumpled up and his hair was nappy looking, and in his fist he had a gun.

He saw my mother and growled angrily, Open the door, whore!

My mother answered, Who are you?

You know who I am, the man demanded. Open this door I said!

The man began hitting the glass with the butt end of the gun.

I ran to my mother and she held me. She said to the man, Sir, I think you got the wrong door. We're Christians in here!

The man took the gun and pounded the glass hard, shattering it. My mother pushed me to the floor and covered me with her body as the man reached his hand through the broken glass and started rattling the iron bars with the gun.

He kept shouting, Open the door! Open the door! And he kept calling my mother bad names.

I was scared and crying.

My mother said to me, Don't worry, Elwyn. The Lord will protect us.

But that man, I said, he's going to shoot you. I don't want you to die.

Don't worry, Elwyn. The Lord will protect us.

And my mother began to pray.

Though I was still afraid of dying, I began to feel stronger in my faith when my mother prayed. I was still sobbing, but I joined her by reciting my memory verse for Sunday school: *In my distress I cried unto the Lord, and He heard me. Deliver my soul, O Lord, from lying lips and a deceitful tongue.*

And then the miracle came: my father got home.

He appeared behind the man, the old monster of my dreams, my father, but this time he was my savior.

He turned the man around with a punch to the face. He punched him again and the man fell.

There were more punches after that, but I couldn't see because it was happening down below the window ledge. There was a lot of shouting and groaning and the sound of heavy bodies rolling around.

When the police came and wrestled my father off the man, we were all standing outside with half the neighborhood. I remember the man in handcuffs, with a black eye and a bleeding mouth, explaining to the police about being drunk and knocking on the wrong door because of some girl who had stolen his money.

Checking the flight above ours, the police found the prostitute the man had been looking for crouching behind a garbage can. As they marched her past our apartment, the woman said to my mother: Ma'am, y'all got any aspirin?

She was dressed in hot pants and she had an Afro so huge that it flopped over her eyebrows and her ears.

Now the police were laughing with my father, calling him a hero, and he went to put his arm around my mother, who pushed him away.

She said to him, The blood of the innocents is on your hands.

But baby, my father said, I got here in time.

She said to him, Where were you, Roscoe? Where are you when you're not home? Where are you when your family is in danger? I know where you were. Don't even try to lie to me. It's that woman—

As my parents fought, one of the police officers started laughing: Uh oh. Trouble in paradise.

I can't live like this anymore. You're going to have to make a choice.

Isa, my father said. Isa.

He went to touch her and she pushed him away.

You smell like her, she hissed.

My father was quiet for days after that. My mother was quiet too. Every time I got a chance, I would smell my father to see who he smelled like. My mom had said my father smelled like *her*. I didn't know anybody else who smelled like that.

We slept quietly in our room, my mother holding me, my father holding her, both of us pretending he wasn't there. My father didn't put me out even once during that time to sleep on the couch so he could be alone in the room with her.

One morning, I awoke and found them on their knees, my father weeping.

Lord, I want to thank You, he was saying. I almost lost my precious family. You have given me a second chance. Thank You, Lord. Thank You.

My mother had her arms around his back as he prayed and shouted. As he lifted holy hands. She was weeping too. My grandmother came over. Pastor and the elders came over. My father had gotten saved. My father had accepted the Lord.

O what a rejoicing.

On Sunday, my father was baptized. On Monday, he went with the Faithful to the home of the drunkard who had knocked on our door and witnessed to him. My parents dropped all charges against him and the drunkard became Brother Pendergast, the church mechanic, Praise the Lord.

Then they went to the jail and witnessed to the prostitute and paid the bail for her. She became Sister Winslow, the best singer in the choir.

On Tuesday, my father passed his chauffeur's license exam, became a school bus driver, and we moved out of Overtown to a better home with three bedrooms and two bathrooms.

In the new house, I got my own room. On the wall behind my bed, we hung a picture of the Last Supper. I had my own bureau and a little reading table, where I could study the Bible. We painted the walls blue like the heavens above.

This was back when I was five.

He's been a good father ever since then.

Good things come to those who wait upon the Lord.

The Brothers

The traffic to the airport was easy, like an omen. Sister Morrisohn found a curbside space big enough for the Cadillac just as he appeared.

She honked the horn, waving and shouting his name, though the windows were up. "Harrison! Harrison!"

Her brother.

Her son.

He carried a small valise in one hand and an overcoat under his arm. He stood out from everyone around him because he was tall, well over six-four, and he wore a hat—not a cap, but a hat, an elegant, black felt thing that hid his balding head. "The same old Harrison," she lamented. "I have such a long way to go with him."

Harrison had spotted her too, but did not return her wave as he strode to the car.

Sister Morrisohn dabbed her wet eyes with a kerchief and noticed the other man with him. He was short and red-faced with animated eyes. An older man, in his forties at least, he wore a thin mustache that made her think of a cartoon mouse. A mat of brown hair lay across his head. He had no hat and no luggage, but he wore a coat buttoned up to the neck that matched the one Harrison carried. She said a small prayer as Harrison opened the back door for the other man to get in.

"Elaine," he said, "this is Otto. Otto, this is Elaine, my sister."

They exchanged mumbled hellos, the man reaching over the seat, shaking her hand, as Harrison got in the back beside him, and Sister Morrisohn, who had not been hugged by this brother she hadn't seen in three years, felt every bit like a cabbie driving home through traffic that was difficult, like an omen.

When they got to the house in Coral Gables, Otto was the first out of the car. He strolled the yard touching and smelling the flowers. He removed his shoes and socks and spread his toes in the grass, which Elwyn had mowed just yesterday. He sat down and stretched his stubby arms behind his head. "This is just beautiful," he said. "I can see why she wants this. Isn't this just beautiful, Harrison?"

"You should see the inside," said Harrison, grinning. "It's huge."

"I feel like a kid again. I want to skip and jump," said Otto, rolling in the grass.

"You look like a kid," said Harrison, grinning at the dumbfounded expression on Sister Morrisohn's face as she watched Otto frolicking in her grass.

She clutched her keys. "Let's go inside. Let me show you inside, Otto."

Otto sprang to his feet. "Boy oh boy. I can't wait."

She opened the door to the house and Otto, a first-time visitor, a stranger carrying his shoes in his hands, was the first one in. He shouted from inside: "This is awesome! I can see why she wants this."

She whispered to Harrison, "I don't think this is going to work."

Harrison pushed his hat back on his head. "Believe me, Elaine. He's a very good attorney. He's never lost a case. Beverly doesn't stand a chance against Otto Windmere, Esquire."

"He acts like a child."

"Don't you lecture anybody about acting like a child," he warned as they went inside.

The food, which she had prepared beforehand, took only a few minutes to heat. It was broiled chicken with Harrison's favorite. Collard greens, heavy on the ham. Harrison, complaining of a lack of appetite, picked through his meal. Otto ate everything voraciously, chewing noisily, and unabashedly though politely asked for more. When Sister Morrisohn returned from the kitchen with a second helping for him, Harrison was feeding Otto from his plate. They were like two kids at camp.

She told them, smiling cheerfully, "That's not necessary. I brought you lots more, Otto. There's more in the kitchen too."

Otto and Harrison laughed. At her? At what?

She held out the tray, and Otto scooped a healthy helping onto his plate, wolfed a mouthful, and then began to discuss the case. He spoke while twirling the fork in the air. It was an easy case, he assured them, one they were certain to win. Beverly Morrisohn didn't have a leg to stand on. Brother Morrisohn's will was crystal clear and airtight. All his heirs had received what he had willed. Sister Morrisohn had gotten the car, half the money, and the house. Beverly had gotten the property in Atlanta, the vacation place in the Hamptons, her late mother's collection of African American art, and the other half of the money. In short, Beverly had no case. She was just a nuisance. Tomorrow in court would be a cinch.

But Harrison had to put in his two cents: "What she is, is disgusted to see the tart who spit on her mother's grave living in the house she grew up in."

Sister Morrisohn, who had been expecting something like this, fired back, "I did not spit on Glovine's grave. Beverly has her own personal axe to grind. I'm so tired of beating this dead horse—" But their family quarrel was interrupted by the stranger.

"Harrison," warned Otto.

Harrison pouted. "Don't let her fool you. She's one hot momma, Otto. When she wants a man, there isn't too much that will stand in her way."

Otto patted him on the hand. "Now, Harrison. Be nice to your big sister."

They watched each other then. Harrison watched Sister Morrisohn. Otto watched Harrison. Sister Morrisohn watched Otto watching Harrison and patting that hand. It was worse than she thought.

Harrison slept in his old room that night. Otto slept in the upstairs guest room, the tryst room. Sister Morrisohn did not sleep, and then at three minutes to 2 she heard the door to the upstairs guest room open. She was already positioned in a place where she could see Otto, who wore no shirt, skip lightly down the stairs to Harrison's room. She told herself that she should have expected this. There had been signs.

At two minutes past 5, when a shirtless Otto left Harrison's room, Sister Morrisohn met him at the foot of the stairs.

"Elaine!" he said, covering with his hands the red marks on his chest. He had a pink, hairless body, and was fleshy like a cherub.

"Come with me, Mr. Windmere."

"I know what this looks like."

"Just come."

He followed her to the veranda outside the upstairs guest room. He sat in one of the chairs set up out there without being asked. She pulled out a cigarette and leaned against the rail with her back to him and smoked. He made delicate clearing sounds with his throat while she smoked. When she finished her cigarette, she was ready to pounce, but he held up his hands.

"You got me where you want me. I'm a married man. I've got two children. I'm well respected in my community. A *straight* community. I'm begging you not to make a big deal out of this."

"I'm very angry with you, Mr. Windmere."

"Oh try to be modern about this. It's not like I pursued him."

"Last year he was telling me about some girl he was planning to marry. Wendy Mira. There would be children and everything. Now this."

"Wendy Mira? Or do you mean *Wind-e-mere?*" Otto chuckled. "That Harrison is such a kidder."

She closed and opened her fists. "God. God. God."

She put another cigarette in her mouth and moved to the chair across from his and sank into it.

Otto's face was pink and cheeky. Reaching up, he brushed his flop of hair back into place over the receding area. "All I ask is that you consider all the parties that could get hurt by this."

"I am considering them," she said, exhaling smoke.

Otto pleaded. "Be modern about this. We all find love wherever we can regardless of what custom or the law tells us we should do."

"Don't lecture me."

"All I'm saying is that homosexuality is not a crime. Statutory *rape* is."

Her mouth fell open when she heard that. She shot a hateful look at the mousy Otto Windmere and he stared right back at her with his beady eyes. He looked like a rat. He was a rat. And Harrison was a rat too. She mashed out her cigarette and went inside.

Otto Windmere was right about one thing.

The case was a cinch. After the judge threw it out of court, a joyful Sister Morrisohn shook Otto Windmere's hand. She went to hug Harrison, but he would only give her his hand. Then he went over to Beverly Morrisohn, looking ugly as ever in her old-fashioned bun, a man's overcoat, and a pair of outdated slacks, and he separated her from her attorney. Harrison and Beverly spoke for close to five minutes, with much head nodding, and then shook hands in parting while she and Otto looked on.

Otto hummed uncomfortably. "Fraternization with the enemy."

"Amen," Sister Morrisohn said.

"But I guess it is to be understood. Isn't he, like, her uncle? You're her stepmother, and he's your brother, so—"

"Don't go there," she warned. "Are you kidding me? You're kidding me, right?"

Otto sat up front on the ride to the airport while Harrison sat in the back with his hat pressed down to his ears. She watched him in the rearview mirror. He looked just like he did when he was a kid. Otto was very chatty. He knew about art. He knew about music. He complimented her again and again about how beautifully she kept the house and implied that he would love to come back and visit sometime. When they got to the airport, she tried to hug Harrison goodbye, but again he offered his hand. She would not let go of him.

"What are you doing, Elaine? I'll miss my plane."

"We're going to have this out, you and me," she said.

"Stay out of my business."

"I should slap you right in your mouth! You had no right to tell your little friend my private business. You're my brother. You're the only family I got left. You're trying to send me to jail or something? Is that what you want?"

"Ah, so now you see how it feels to be judged!"

"That was between us. You don't see me telling everybody about your activities, though what you're doing is shameful. It's a sin."

"A sin? You're practically a child molester. You're a frickin pedophile."

"You're a frickin sodomite!"

He pulled away from her hand. "Go ahead. Shout it to the world. That's what you want. You want everyone at the airport to know. Harrison's here and he's queer!"

"If you would just shut your big mouth and listen to what I'm trying to tell you, Harrison—I love this boy. It's different for me—I love this boy—"

"He's a boy, he's a boy, he's a boy, you goddamned hypocrite."

"If you would just listen—"

"Listen to yourself." He broke from her and strode off angrily, catching up to Otto at the checkpoint.

Elaine shouted after him, "I didn't mean to hurt you, Harrison! Please believe me. I'm trying to understand."

But he was already gone.

"Harrison, oh Harrison. You're all I got left," she said to no one.

She went into the bathroom to cry and pray. When she came out she was in no condition to drive. She felt like a drink to get her head together. It was Friday night and the airport restaurants were crowded. She did not want to be seen crying into her wine. But she wanted wine, and she wanted to cry into it. She found an Italian place, took a table in a dark corner, ordered the house wine. Red or white, she didn't care. Just bring it fast. "Harrison's problem," she said to no one, "is that I spoiled him. I was too easy on him. Buford and I gave him too much. If he'd had my life growing up, he would understand how special it is to have someone who will stand by you no matter what—"

She spotted a familiar face. It was Brother Parker.

She hid the bottle under the table and drank from the glass. And the boy sitting with Brother Parker, it was Elwyn.

Had they seen her? She didn't think so. As she watched them, they continued to talk. Their laughter winged across the room. They seemed to be enjoying each other's company. That's what family was all about. Why couldn't it be that way with Harrison and her? Why did they have to fight all the time? Why couldn't he see that she only wanted to help?

Elwyn's back was to her. That strong back, she mused. Strong enough to ride. Is my baby ready to go for a ride? That's what she needed right now, a good strong ride from her strong young man to get Harrison off her mind. It was Friday and she'd had to cancel a piano lesson because of Harrison's visit. She would signal her baby and set something up. She just had to wait for the right opportunity. He looked so delicious even from behind. That back, that strong back—mmmmmm.

He was wearing a shirt she was unfamiliar with, but his voice, coming from the far table, sounded deeper, more soulful. Sexier.

Perhaps it was the wine.

Certainly if Elwyn had seen her, he would have signaled. She waved the waiter over and told him to take the wine bottle away. She paid her bill and popped a few mints in her mouth to kill the smell of alcohol.

When Brother Parker got up and went to the restroom, she saw her opportunity.

She went over and kissed her sweet lover on the back of the neck, and a strange boy turned in his chair to face her!

The look of surprise on the boy's face was quickly replaced by delight. Imagine that such a vision of womanly beauty would kiss him on the back of the neck in an airport restaurant.

"I am so sorry. I thought you were someone else."

"Wow." The boy's face was radiant.

"From behind, you look like someone else."

He grinned. "Would you mind turning around so I can see who you look like from behind?"

"Are you getting fresh, young man?"

"I'm trying."

The boy, who was about the same age as Elwyn, wore a mustache and goatee that looked so handsome and mature on him that she decided right then and there she would make clean-shaven Elwyn grow a mustache and goatee. They resembled each other. The boy's forehead was slightly pointed where Elwyn's was broad, his cheeks less lean. Still, there was enough of a resemblance to justify an honest mistake. When he grinned, she saw that two of his teeth were gold. Yuck.

She explained, "I saw you sitting there with that man I thought I knew. I thought you were the son of this man I know."

He extended his hand for a shake. "My name's Benny, and you can just kiss me on the back of the neck any old time you like, ma'am. Ha-ha-ha. I love your perfume."

She took his hand. "Elaine Morrisohn. Mind your manners. Ha-ha-ha."

"I apologize, Miss Morrisohn, but this is too funny. Nothing like this has ever happened to me in my whole life. Wait'll Roscoe gets back. This'll crack him up."

"Roscoe? That man *is* Roscoe Parker?"

"You know my dad?" said the boy named Benny.

"Your dad?"

"What a lucky guy he is knowing a beautiful woman like you." He flashed his gold teeth. "Are you like his girlfriend or something?" His eyes twinkled and he passed her a sly smile.

"Wait! Are you like Elwyn's girlfriend? The little preacher? Ha-ha!" The boy's smile widened.

"Oh my God, Benny Franklin," Sister Morrisohn said, with her hand over her mouth. "Oh my God." She ran out of the restaurant.

Benny turned in his seat to watch the pretty lady go.

"The little preacher," he mused, brushing his adolescent goatee with a finger. "Wait'll Roscoe hears about this."

But then Benny thought about it. Really thought about it.

So when Roscoe came out of the bathroom a minute later, Benny Willet did not tell him about the woman who had kissed him on the back of the neck and then run out of the restaurant. He let Roscoe eat a few more mouthfuls of his chicken cacciatore while he thought it through. As much as it pained him to ruin a good story, Benny realized he would have to give his biological father an edited version. He had never met his little brother—"the little preacher," Roscoe had called him—but brothers had to stick together nevertheless.

"So what were you going to tell me, Roscoe?"

His father smiled nervously. "Well, I'm thinking of getting out of the bus-driving thing. I'm thinking of taking classes at the community college."

Benny, lost in his own disappointment, did not answer.

Roscoe said, "So . . . what do you think?"

"I don't want to hear about your community college classes. I'm not playing anymore, Roscoe. I want to see him."

"But—"

"It's not fair. I want to see my brother," said Benjamin Franklin Willet, Sister Morrisohn's godson.

HERE ENDETH THE TESTAMENT OF INNOCENCE LOST

III. Testament of Apostasy

Gospel of Matthew 10:34
Think not that I am come to send peace on earth:
I came not to send peace, but a sword.

Apostate

In two weeks I would be leaving Miami for Gainesville to enroll as a freshman at the University of Florida. I was eighteen and eager to get away from the widow and end our shameful affair. I would go away and, with God's help, come back a new man and a better Christian.

My father wanted me to study engineering because he had heard there was good money in it—even though engineers didn't get a chance to actually drive the train. My mother, disappointed that I had chosen not to go into the ministry, wanted me to endeavor toward a degree in social work, which she felt was the next best way to use my education in the service of the Lord. My grandmother, too, was saddened when I turned down my scholarship to Bible College.

"Be a teacher, Elwyn," my grandmother suggested. "Then when you come back, you can be superintendent of the Sunday school program.

Many of our Sunday school teachers just don't know how to reach our kids. We're losing them to the streets."

"I don't want to teach," I protested. Teachers were not my favorite people.

Just a few months earlier, I had attended the senior awards program at my high school and suffered my greatest humiliation. The principal, Mr. Byrd, in announcing the winners of the Grand Gopher Awards, deliberately stuttered: "El-El—"

I rose to my feet thinking he was about to say my name, Elwyn Parker, which was not a haughty presumption, for he was nearing the P's and I had been, at least during my junior and senior years, an outstanding gopher. Over the final two years, no one had achieved a higher grade point average with as rigorous a courseload as I carried—all Advanced Placement classes, all A's. No one had been better known around campus than I, by students and faculty alike, and no one more feared. For I had been exact and courageous in doing all that my Lord commanded. My confrontations with the secular school administration had become famous. I had been interviewed by the local newspaper too many times to count, so even the surrounding community was aware of me.

Finally, no one had presided over a school club with as many members, or as much influence, as the one I founded and headed, the Jesus Club. At our largest, we numbered 150; and it was through our efforts that the administration was forced to change the school's nickname, which had been around since the school opened thirty years before, from Red Devils to Golden Gophers.

Thus, I stood when Mr. Byrd said "El-El" because I deserved a Grand Gopher, deserved to have my senior picture hang permanently in the Gopher Hall of Fame.

"El-El-Eldridge Pomerantz," Mr. Byrd said.

I sat down quickly, but the damage was done. All around me, people were chuckling.

As Eldridge Pomerantz, a second-string football player who had been a regular at our prayer meetings until he made first string, took his place on the stage next to the other Grand Gophers, Mr. Byrd's eyes met mine, and I recall that he smiled. Another battle won by Satan.

But he was wrong. While the administration did not bestow upon me one single popularity prize that gloomy awards night, I did march to the stage four times to collect awards that had stipends attached to them: the National Merit Award, $2,000; the Young Musicians Award, $800; the National Christian Scholarship, $500; and from the Jesus Club, the Blessed Gopher Award, of which I was the first recipient, $298.

In truth, I didn't know what I wanted to study in college—music, medicine, anthropology all interested me—but if Mr. Byrd were an example of what a teacher is, petty, mean, vengeful, then no, I didn't want to be a teacher.

There was one more thing I didn't want to be, an attorney. Sister Morrisohn's late husband, Buford, had been an attorney, so she pushed for me to study law.

"Then when we marry," she explained, "it'll be like it used to be."

Sister Morrisohn had to be kidding, of course. I was eighteen. She was forty-four. Marriage was ludicrous. But as the time of my departure for college grew nearer, she had been kidding in that manner much too frequently to suit me. Her strange taste in humor gave me headaches.

Was it but a week ago that we visited the mall where she bought my going away gift, the expensive leather briefcase with dual combination locks and a hidden compartment for toothbrush and floss?

As always, Sister Morrisohn and I behaved in public as mother and son. While "mother" paid for the briefcase, "son" witnessed to a sixteen-year-old girl who had wandered into the store.

Yes, the girl attended church. A Methodist.

Yes, she knew about Jesus. Who didn't?

No, she hadn't accepted Him as personal savior, but she would when she was older, she said. Too much living to do now.

Take a look at this, I said to the girl, and I made to reach into my jacket pocket for a tract ("We Know Not the Hour When Death Shall Appear") but found my hand detained by Sister Morrisohn.

She kissed me on the mouth. "Let's go, hubby."

I jerked my hand out of her grasp but followed her out of the store, forgetting to give the confused sixteen-year-old the tract which might have led to her salvation.

I was so shaken, I didn't say a word until we reached her house.

"Why would you do a thing like that?"

"I was just kidding," she said.

"Someone from the church could've been passing by."

"No one saw. I checked first."

"It's dangerous. Crazy."

"You liked it though, didn't you?"

"No. It made me very nervous."

"You liked that girl, didn't you?" she said.

"I was just doing the Lord's work."

She grew silent. My devotion to the Lord always seemed to surprise her. It was true I had sinned—and would perhaps continue sinning until I put some distance between us—but I was not the great hypocrite Sister Morrisohn was. I had not hardened my heart against God.

While I prayed every night for forgiveness, she had gradually, if however discreetly, become a backslider. Once again she took pleasure in the things of the world—cigarettes, which she admitted she had never truly given up; wine, which she insisted helped her forget that she was a poor widow spending all too much time with a lover a third her age; and those melancholy Chester Harbaugh and His Old-Time Fiddle Band records. Not his hymns, mind you! But those monotonous two-step odes to heartbreak and unrequited love. How I grew to dread that brooding baritone. Those screaming fiddles. She often played her favorite, "Going Away Soon, Love," as a prelude to our sordid communion:

I'm going away (going away)
Soon my love (soooon my love)
I'm going away (going away)
Where you can't come
(yooou can't come)

I'm going away (going away)
And that you know (thaaat you know)
My heart will stay (stay-yay-yay)
I love you so
(I looove you so)

She asked me to teach her how to play "Going Away Soon, Love" on the piano, but I refused. At least she could not get me to do that.

So there we were after she had kissed me in the mall.

"I'm not interested in the girl. I was just doing the Lord's work," I repeated.

Sister Morrisohn seemed on the verge of either laughter or tears. "Do you love me, Elwyn?"

"Let's not get into this—"

"I'm nothing to you," she said. "You're just using me. All I am is your harlot."

"Don't say that."

"I'm a fallen woman. You could never love me."

"That's not true."

"I wish Buford were here. You don't love me."

"That's not true."

"Then say it," she said. "Say it, Elwyn."

She had that kind of power over me. She must have known I didn't love her. She certainly knew I couldn't risk losing her. I cried, "I love you! I love you!"

She smiled. "I don't believe you."

We were alone in her house. She moved close to me. She loosened her clothes. I should have turned my head. I should have prayed for God to deliver me. But no matter how many times I drank from the fountain, I found myself yet thirsting.

"Touch me when you say you love me," she said.

I touched her. I became aroused—this for a woman who had posed as my mother but a few hours before. "I love you."

We were on the bed. Our clothes were piled on top of the new leather briefcase on the floor. "Say it with feeling," she said.

As we moved, I felt many things, and I used some of these things to say it the way she wanted me to say it. "I love you."

It was, of course, a complete lie. Sister Morrisohn didn't seem to notice or to care. She hummed, but no matter—I still heard the words.

My heart will stay (stay-yay-yay)

I love you so
(I looove you so)

The wages of sin, it turns out, is not always death: sometimes it's a life of Chester Harbaugh records.

My grandmother said, "So what's wrong with being a teacher?" She spoke to my back; I watched her in the mirror. She had gotten so large that she had to use her hands to lift her legs, one at a time, up onto my bed, where, at last, she stretched out, exhausted. She fanned herself with a hand, breathed through her mouth. "He made some preachers; He made some teachers."

"I just don't think He's calling me to teach, Gran'ma."

"Well, your students say you're a better piano teacher than Sister Mc-Gowan, and nobody, not even Pastor, can explain Scripture like you."

"Well, Gran'ma, I don't know." My mother handed me a black tie. I slipped it around my collar and began the first loop of a double Windsor. I liked a thick knot.

"No. Wear your good white shirt," my mother fussed. "This one makes the tie fit funny." She turned and began searching.

"I like this shirt, Mom." But already I was beginning to unfasten the tie.

"Turn around," my father said. There he was with his new camera. "I want to take a picture."

I turned. "But I'm not wearing any pants."

"So? Now hold the tie like you're fixing it. No, don't smile. Act natural," he said. The camera flashed. "It's a work of art. Young Man Dressing."

"He's not going to wear that tie either," my mother said. She just couldn't make up her mind. Now she held the new blue one in her hand. "The church valedictorian's got to look his best."

I took the good white shirt and the new blue tie from my mother.

My father snapped a shot before I could put them on—just me in my Fruit of the Loom. "This one's even better. I'm going to put this one in the church yearbook."

"No you won't," said my grandmother. As she lay, propped up on her side, she might have been a Peter Paul Rubens woman—in print dress, and with ankles swollen by diabetes. "People won't know what to make of this family." She trembled with laughter, two fingers covering her mouth.

My father grinned. "He's not just smart and talented and a great warrior for the Lord, he's the flower of manhood." My father posed in accordance with the Marquess of Queensberry and when I blocked right, he landed one with a left. It hurt only a little. "Feel that. Solid!"

"Stop it. Stop it." My grandmother, slapping her thighs now, laughed until she coughed. "You two. Oh, what a blessing."

I put on my shirt, buttoned it, slipped the new tie around my collar.

"Take a picture," said my father. He handed the camera to my mother and put an arm around my shoulder. One more inch and I'd be as tall as he was.

"Let me at least put on my pants," I said.

My father laughed. "No." He wasn't holding me so firmly that I couldn't break away. We were having a good time.

"Take off your hat," said my mother behind the camera.

My father protested: "The bald spot."

"They already know," said my grandmother and mother in unison.

We all laughed at that, even my father doffing his school bus driver's cap. It amused us when we said the same thing at the same time. We were a family.

"Snap the picture," my father said.

"Something's wrong," my mother said. "Your collar's too large. That's not your good white shirt."

I looked down at my shirt. She was right. It was Brother Morrisohn's good white shirt.

"Where did you get that?" my mother asked.

"Sister Morrisohn gave it to me," I said in an offhand way, like don't you remember when she gave it to me, Mom? You were there. You were definitely there, so don't ask any more questions. I only have two more weeks in Miami, and when I return, I promise I'll be your son again. "A gift," I said.

My father tested the sleeve with thumb and forefinger. "That's very nice of her. This is good material."

"Rich. But why would she give you a white shirt?" asked my mother. "Pink, green, blue, I could understand."

"I don't know," I said. "She's old-fashioned."

"Graduation gift?" suggested my grandmother.

"No," said my mother, "I've seen this shirt in the laundry more than a few times and meant to ask you about it. When did she give it to you?"

"I'm not sure," I replied. I had to remain calm, nonchalant. I had to derail her instinctive suspicion. "I think she gave it to me after I taught her to play 'In Love Abiding Jesus Came.' That was Brother Morrisohn's favorite hymn. It's a dopey gift."

"Don't call a gift dopey, Elwyn," warned my grandmother. "All gifts come from God."

"Sorry, Gran'ma."

"Bridle your tongue, Elwyn. Buford, rest his soul, and Elaine Morrisohn are very dear friends of mine. They have always been fond of you." My grandmother pulled herself to a sitting position. "Buford, if you recall, bought that piano for you. You didn't think the piano was such a dopey gift, did you?"

"No, Gran'ma."

"Elaine was your first piano student. It's not so dopey when she puts ten dollars in your hand for a half hour's work, is it?"

"No, Gran'ma."

"With all the blessings God has given you, I should think you'd be the last to bite the hand that feeds you. Here you are on the eve of manhood, getting dressed to go to church and pick up a scholarship funded by the same woman who gave you a dopey gift."

The Buford Morrisohn Scholarship for the Outstanding College-Bound Christian, $4,000, of which I was the first recipient.

"Sorry, Gran'ma."

"Don't let me hear such rubbish again." My grandmother signaled for her four-pronged walker. I passed it to her. My father and I helped her to her feet. "I love you, Elwyn, but you'd better pray that God never takes back any of your dopey gifts."

My grandmother lumbered out of the room. My mother and father, shaking their heads, soon followed. I finished dressing alone.

It worked.

My mother had left without asking the one question I could little answer: by the way, Elwyn, where is *your* good white shirt?

I certainly couldn't tell her that on that night more than a year ago when Sister Morrisohn finally mastered the chord changes of "In Love Abiding Jesus Came," there had been a dinner set on the floor in the fashion of the Chinese with all the romantic trappings, and afterward someone's happy foot knocked over a candle and destroyed the sleeve of a good white shirt, which by all means had to be replaced.

I couldn't just walk into our house with a charred sleeve.

Oh, that? As the widow Morrisohn and I were making love . . .

And I certainly couldn't have entered our home barebacked.

Yes, Dad, it is a solid chest, isn't it? Quite manly! Those aren't birthmarks. Tonight during climax the widow used her teeth.

So instead, I accepted Sister Morrisohn's gift of one of Brother Morrisohn's shirts.

"They look the same," she had said. "I never noticed it before, but you're about his size."

And that's when she started with the Elwyn-marry-me jokes.

Not even John on the Isle of Patmos had such hellish visions of the future.

Two o'clock in the afternoon on a Saturday in August, the Church of Our Blessed Redeemer Who Walked Upon the Waters was packed for the awards ceremony.

I got up from the piano when they told me to get up and marched across the pulpit and stood where they told me to stand, at the head of a line of about thirty recently graduated high-schoolers. I could neither see the pews nor the floor, just three hundred brown faces floating above a sea of sharp suits and pretty dresses. Body heat negated the effects of the air conditioner. Sweat poured down my brow.

In my valedictory address, I said what they wanted me to say—The future is for the children of God. Satan's days are numbered, for with Christ in our vessel, we can smile at the storm—and so on, and so on, to thunderous applause.

Then I collected my Buford Morrisohn Scholarship for the Outstanding College-Bound Christian and sat back at the piano to close the service.

When it was all over, I mingled with my fellows and our parents (and grandparents), congratulating those who had received lesser scholarships, and receiving congratulations for my own award.

Then the larger crowd descended upon us. From every mouth there came the same questions:

"Where are you going to college?"

(As though you don't already know.)

"When are you leaving?"

(Not soon enough.)

"Are you excited?"

(Relieved.)

Everyone seemed to want to shake my hand, and I politely acquiesced, though I was eager to get away from the church grounds. I hoped to avoid Sister Morrisohn, who had been giving me the eye all through service.

Besides, my parents were throwing an afterparty for me at home where I could celebrate in safety.

Outside, small children dressed in their best clothes played with reckless energy, running and hitting and screaming and falling and getting up again. I ducked out of the way of a running one pursued by an angry one waving a hymnal over his head like the two tablets of stone. Another one said a naughty word, and I chastised her.

"It slipped out," she said.

Where were our children picking up such terrible language?

I scolded, "You want to grow up good so Jesus can take you to heaven, okay?"

The child was absolutely precious. Pigtails and ribbons and black patent-leather shoes. "When will I go to heaven?"

"When you die," I answered.

"Oh," said the girl, whom I recognized as Brother and Sister Naylor's youngest. "So can I go play now?"

"Yes."

"Thank-you-Jesus," she said and skipped away.

I opened the door to my old Mazda, slipped inside, slammed the door, and started the car.

Sister Morrisohn, appearing out of nowhere, knocked on my windshield. "Hey."

I rolled down the window. Up close, under her perfume, I smelled alcohol. She had been drinking wine again. She wore a blue church dress with a modest collar, but when she leaned against the car, almost passing her head through the window, the modest collar hung loose around her neck revealing that she was wearing no brassiere.

She had never behaved this way on church grounds before.

I pulled away when she made a sudden move, thinking she was trying to kiss me as she had in the mall.

"Hey," she said, passing me a greeting card. "Congratulations on your graduation."

"Thanks."

Raising her head, she checked to see that no one was near enough to hear. "We haven't been together in a week. Why are you avoiding me?"

"We'll talk later."

"Was it the mall?" she whispered.

"Yes. The mall."

She made a silly face. "That was a joke. No one saw. I swear."

"It's too risky. And it's so wrong. We're Christians. We're the light of the world."

"You don't plan to see me anymore."

"I don't."

"This is the end."

"Yes."

"When you said you loved me, did you mean it, Christian?"

I did a quick scan myself to see if we were being observed. "Could we talk later?"

Her eyes blinked rapidly. "Tell me now. Did you mean it?"

"No."

"Yes you did. Yes you did," she said, nodding her head vigorously.

"Sister Morrisohn, we have to get on with our lives. We have to wake up. What we did can lead to nowhere good."

She set her face. "Look, Elwyn, we're not going to get married. That's impossible. You're just a kid. I'm . . . mature. Too bad. But you can't tell me you don't love me because no matter where you go or what you do, I'll always love you." She put her hands together as in prayer. "And I know you love me."

"I'm sorry."

"You're not sorry. You're scared. What we did may seem wicked in the eyes of the church, but it is real. You know it's real."

"I want to go to heaven when I die."

Her eyes blazed. "So that makes it okay to step on my feelings? To use me?"

"I didn't use you."

"Then you loved me?"

I didn't answer. I wasn't sure anymore that I knew the answer. Why did I feel it necessary to go to another city? Why hadn't I broken it off before?

"Love is never a sin."

"Bye, Sister Morrisohn."

"Come by tonight. Let me prove your love."

"Sister Morri—"

"Just one last time," she cooed, "and then it's over forever. Go on with your life, pretend you don't love me."

"No." Help me, Lord. "No, I won't."

"Just one last time." She smoothed the hairs on my arm. "Then I'll let you go."

"Okay." Already I had become aroused. "One last time."

"You won't be sorry."

"Okay." I shifted in my pants. I had yielded one last time. I put the Mazda in reverse. "Bye."

"See you later," Sister Morrisohn said. And then: "You look very good in his shirt."

The party that took place afterward was a lot like the awards ceremony, except that there weren't so many people—just my parents, my grandmother, my best friends from church, and several members of the Jesus Club from school. The Reverend James Cleveland boomed "Lord, Do It" from the record player. There was turkey and ham and collard greens on the table. Hugs, congratulations, and the unavoidable questions abounded: "So where are you going to college?"; "Excited, aren't you?"; "Can we get together before you leave?"

My mother said, "It's your party, Elwyn. You say grace."

I said a quick one: "Lord, bless this food that it may give us the strength to do Your will."

"Amen," we all said.

My father said, "Dig in."

We ate, we laughed, we cried. After I straighten out my problems

with Sister Morrisohn, I thought, I shall be able to take genuine pleasure from such fellowship divine. As it was, I was eager for the party to
be over. The devil yet had full control of my hormones.

I was not the only one eager for the party to end. Eldridge Pomerantz, the Grand Gopher himself, was there. He had avoided me all afternoon, still fearing the power of God.

Now he sat at my piano with Sabina, the less bubbly half of the
Anderson twins. Sabina played the right hand of "Old Rugged Cross,"
Eldridge the left. She had already begun taking classes at Miami-Dade
Junior College, where she was a powerful witness for the Lord. He was
leaving in two weeks for Pennsylvania to play football and study archi-
tecture at the University of Pittsburgh.

I approached them.

"Elwyn," they said.

"Eldridge. Sabina," I said. "I see you're making lovely music together."

"I'm teaching him," Sabina said. "Praise the Lord."

"Praise the Lord," I said back.

Eldridge smiled. He was a nice guy, though a backslider. He wouldn't
have come to my party had Sabina not been there. They had been in
love for about a year.

Accidentally, Eldridge hit an augmented chord. "OOPS," he said.
"What was that?"

"Sounds good. Play it again," I commanded.

They played the chorus again, using the augmented chord instead
of the plain F chord.

"Wow," said Sabina. "We sound like experts."

"The augmented adds another dimension to the song," I observed.

And Sabina caught my cue. "Just as Christ adds another dimension
to our lives," she said.

Eldridge's spine lost an inch.

"We miss you at Bible study," I said, setting my hands on his wide shoulders.

Eldridge mumbled, "Football practice, you know?"

"I've been telling him," Sabina said, "that football won't get him into heaven."

"Neither will being a nice guy," I added. "And you're one of the nicest people I know."

"Neither will being married to a Christian," Sabina said. "You've got to seek the Lord for yourself."

"Neither will having your picture hang in your school's hall of fame," I said. "It is only through the Grace of God that ye shall enter the kingdom of heaven."

"Momma can't save you."

"Daddy can't save you."

"You've got to seek the Lord for yourself."

"Well," said Eldridge Pomerantz, a boy with thighs like fire hydrants, "I should know better. I'm just waiting—"

"Waiting? Jesus didn't wait to die for your sins!"

Eldridge's eyes darted from me to Sabina to the crowd that had begun to gather. I moved away and watched as the Christians, led by my grandmother—that great old-time saint—descended upon the only unsaved person in the room:

"Seek ye first the kingdom of God."

"Serve the Lord while ye are yet young."

"Tomorrow's day may never dawn."

"Do you want to lift up your eyes in hell?"

"Jesus died for you."

The Christians devoured the lion.

After a while, Eldridge fell to his knees and cried out, "Help me! Help me, Jesus!"

When the party ended, there were shouts of jubilation. A lost sheep had returned to the fold. No one was more delighted by Eldridge's conversion than I was.

"You must write to me when you get to Pennsylvania," I said.

"Yes, Elwyn," he said, brushing back tears.

"Are you happy?" I said.

"Yes." We moved out of the way so that the new offensive lineman for the Lord could shout and jump for joy. "Hallelujah! I'm going to heaven."

Now Eldridge was a truly Grand Gopher.

I helped my parents clean up, and then I headed for the door, on my way to the final trial.

My mother stopped me. "Where are you going?"

"To visit an old friend."

"You sure?" said my father.

"What?" I froze. I felt a small prick of worry. They never questioned where I went. I was their good Christian son. Did they suspect? Impossible. With Eldridge still on their mind, how could they?

"A friend. Are you sure?" said my mother. In her hands, she held the platter with the remains of the turkey on it.

"Yes. A friend."

My father was the first to come clean. He said, with an embarrassed laugh, "I know. We hear you, son. It's just that your grandmother thinks—"

My mother interrupted him. "No! I believe Elwyn. Let him go."

"Good," I said, still playing it cool. "I'll be back in a little while. Save me the leg."

But they knew. Somehow they knew.

"Where were you?"

I walked into her house, turned, scanned the street, then closed the door. "I think they know."

"Don't be ridiculous. No one saw us in the mall," she said.

"Not the mall. I think—" I couldn't finish my sentence. All I could do was stare at Sister Morrisohn.

"What?" she said, smiling innocently as though she didn't know what had left me temporarily bereft of speech. As though I should not be at all moved by the vision of her before my eyes—the see-through nightgown that stopped above her waist; the brassiere underneath that thrust her breasts forward but did not cover the nipples; the panties below that were but a cross-section of strings running through her private parts; and everything, her rouge, her lipstick, even the rubies in her earrings, red like the fires of hell. "What?"

"Blessed Jesus."

"Before I married Buford, I was a young woman. I loved him, so I surrendered my youth." She pirouetted. "But many say that at forty-four, I am still striking."

"You are," I said, stricken.

"Of course, the church doesn't allow me to dress as I like." She touched her earrings. "So even those closest to me may not notice my appeal."

"I see," I said.

She took my hand and led me into her bedroom. She sat down on the bed. I sat down beside her. I stared at her like an idiot. I reminded myself that I had seen it all before—not like this, but we had been together over two years. I should have more control.

"Would you like me to stand up again?" she asked.

"Please."

She stood up. She did a silly dance. I drank her in with my eyes. What did it matter? She was mine.

"A relationship should be built on more than physical attraction," she said. She walked over to her stereo and set the needle on the record. "But when your man goes away, the physical must be foremost on his mind or he will forget."

I'm going away (going away)
And that you know (thaaat you know)

The music did not upset me this time. In fact, I shouted, "Turn it up!" She did.

Holding her in my arms, I sang along with Chester Harbaugh and knew that I was no longer a Christian.

My heart will stay (stay-yay-yay)
I love you so
(I looove you so)

"Do you want to have sex with me?" she asked. It was the first time either of us had called it that. Sex.

"Yes," I said, and we did. And it was good.

Later she said, "Would you like to make love?" It was the first time either of us had called it that. Making love.

"Yes," I said. "I would like to make love with you, Sister Morrisohn."

"Elaine," she corrected.

"Elaine," I said, and then I made love with her. We made love.

And it was good.

We scrambled for our clothes when we heard the knock at the door.

The knocking did not surprise me as much as it did Elaine. I had been expecting it.

"Sit there at the piano," she told me. She wore her blue church dress and house slippers. She was naked underneath except for the strange brassiere. "We'll say piano lessons, okay?"

I sat at the piano as she commanded, though I knew it was useless. We had taken too long to answer the door. Elaine's face was still rouged.

My grandmother walked in behind her four-pronged walker. "Give me a firm seat," she said to Elaine. "If I sit in that fluffy couch of yours, I'll never get up."

When Elaine hurried to the kitchen on her errand, my grandmother stared at me but spoke to someone standing behind her outside on the porch: "You go wait in the car. I have to talk to Sister Morrisohn about something in private."

Who was it? Sister McGowan? Sister Jones? Because of her advanced age and poor health, my grandmother no longer drove. I heard the diminishing footfalls of whoever had dropped her off, as my grandmother closed the door. Thus, it was by her design that I did not see the unseen person and, especially, that the unseen person did not see me. Her heart was wroth, but she was still protecting me. It gave me hope.

"Elwyn, Elwyn," my grandmother said.

I looked down at the piano keys.

"You were His best, Elwyn. His best."

* * *

Sister Morrisohn placed the firm-backed chair in the middle of the living room, and my grandmother sat down heavily. She leaned forward, one hand on the walker for support.

Sister Morrisohn rubbed her hands together nervously. She said, "Can I get you something to drink?"

"Drink!" My grandmother shook her head in disbelief. "There'll be scarce little to drink where you're going."

Sister Morrisohn sank down heavily in the couch and bowed her head.

"I can't believe that a woman of your age would take advantage of a poor, innocent child of God. Aren't there enough slack-leg Johnnies with whom you can satisfy your vile, pagan lust? When it burns down there, why don't you just run to the nursery and throw yourself on the infant with the fattest diaper?"

Sister Morrisohn sobbed.

My grandmother said, "Thou thankless apostate, thou creeping Jezebel. The stink of thine iniquity rises to the nostrils of God."

Sister Morrisohn wrapped her arms around herself.

My grandmother said, "You should be flung from the highest tower. And when you burst open, the dogs should pick your rotting flesh from your putrid bones."

Sister Morrisohn cried out, "Oh God, what have I done? What have I done?"

This went on for many minutes, this exhorting, this lamenting. I trembled not only because my turn would come soon, but because Sister Morrisohn's pain was my pain. I wanted to put a hand over my grandmother's mouth.

My grandmother said, "You are lucky that Christ is faithful and able to forgive us our sins. If it were me . . . But Christ the redeemer died on the cross. Confess your sin, O daughter of Babylon. Confess before this humble servant of God."

And Sister Morrisohn confessed.

And confessed and confessed the entire two and a half years of our affair. Her memory was astonishing. It brought tears to my grandmother's eyes and set her old, gray head to shaking from side to side. But for me, each moment that had become part of the dull amalgam in my mind was reclaimed whole, distinct, and golden. I wanted to shout: *Yes, I remember the Fort Lauderdale Holiday Inn on Sunday between services. I remember the sun on your face at the pool, how your beautiful toes stirred water, then splashed, and every drop for me! Happy Birthday. Happy Birthday, each said. And I was happy. I held you too long and only just made it back in time for Youth Hour.*

Sister Morrisohn confessed and then collapsed onto the floor, hugging her waist, weeping and wailing.

My grandmother turned to me: "Elwyn, Elwyn, why did you turn your back on God?"

The tears flowed easily, though I didn't feel much like weeping. I wanted to jump and shout. I wanted to hold Sister Morrisohn, Elaine, and tell her not to cry. I wanted to tell her that I remembered.

"Elwyn, you were His greatest servant. You can be His servant again. Confess, confess here before me," my grandmother said. "I'll see to it that no one ever finds out about this, but you must confess. Jesus calls you to confess."

"Yes, Gran'ma."

"He is faithful and just to forgive us. Confess, my child. Confess!"

"Yes, Gran'ma."

And so I confessed on that evening two weeks before I drove my Mazda up the Florida Turnpike to Gainesville. I confessed to appease my grandmother. I confessed so that Elaine would know I remembered.

There was but one thing I left unsaid. I could have told my grandmother that as I sat confessing, my mind's eye wandered over the fallen body of Sister Elaine Morrisohn, and I began planning how in a few weeks when I returned from college to visit, I would arrive one day earlier than I would tell everyone else, and I would spend the night right here in this house with the beautiful forty-four-year-old woman I loved.

Chester Harbaugh and His Old-Time Fiddle Band, of course, would be on the stereo.

HERE ENDETH THE TESTAMENT OF APOSTASY

IV. Testament of the Apocrypha

For the Glory of the Lord

It was a feel-good filler about the National Merit Scholarship Program, and how a few of its most recent recipients planned to use their brains and talent to change the world.

He almost missed the article, because there were no photographs of the winners, but a chance glimpse of the word *Faithful* in boldface, all caps, drew his attention just as he was about to set the *Times* out with the rest of the recyclables. A more thorough perusal and he had spotted and then drawn a pencil line under the name of his brother, *Elwyn Parker*.

Benny Willet smiled and said, "Good for you. You made the big papers, little brother." His finger traced the page until he came to the beginning of the article, which was entitled, *National Merit, Meritorious Goals*, and he read his brother's section:

Elwyn J. Parker, 18, Miami, Florida. University of Florida, Expected graduation date, June 1986. SATs: 1330. Religion: FAITHFUL. Major: undecided. Hobbies: playing the piano and reading the Bible. How I will change the world: "One day I would like to open a free music school and teach every person who enrolls to play at least one hymn by ear. I think it would be great if everyone in the world could play at least one hymn for the Glory of the Lord."

The other winners were all going to become businessmen and attorneys and engineers, Benny mused. One had even planned to become a doctor and open a free clinic in Ethiopia. But his brother was going to give praise to God through song—and Benny believed that he would do it too. Already Elwyn had gotten his high school mascot changed from a devil to a gopher. He had run a successful campaign to get the blasphemous novel *The Last Temptation of Christ* removed from Miami-Dade County public school libraries. And in his drawer of Elwyn Things, Benny had a photograph from a *Miami Herald* article about high school sports, in which Elwyn and some other members of the Miami Gardens High School Jesus Club could be seen laying holy hands on and praying for an injured player on the sidelines of a football game. Clearly, little brother Elwyn could accomplish anything he set his mind to.

Thus, Benny, convinced that his brother was well on his way, got out his scissors and clipped the newest article, pasted it in the scrapbook, and put it away in the drawer with his other Elwyn Things.

Benny hummed joyfully as he clipped. He was humming "Jesus Loves the Little Children," the only song he knew how to play on the piano.

My Father

My Dearest Brother,

    I hope this letter finds you in the best of health and under the blessings and Grace of our Lord and Savior Jesus Christ.

    Please believe me when I tell you that I am trying my very hardest to understand and to accept the way you are. I know that it is the fashion these days for people to do their own thing. I firmly believe that no one should judge another for what he does in the privacy of his own home as long as he does not hurt anybody else. There was a time not too long ago when a black man was forbidden, by law, to show his love for a white woman. How ridiculous was that, right?

    I have done some reading into the matter and have learned that there are still laws on the books in this very same state of Florida, as well as many other states, that forbid people, even those who are lawfully married, to engage in certain sex practices that you and I both know are very common. We are talking about such common things as what people who are in love would do in the natural course of events. Do you know that there are some laws still on the books here in Florida that forbid a man to have relations with his wife in any position other than man on top? If these laws were enforced, that would make loving your husband very boring indeed.

    I have come to realize that the reason for the existence of such laws is that back in the olden days, religion played a greater part in people's everyday *lives. People were more religious back then and tried to live holier lives and the law reflected that. I am not so much a fool as to think that back in the olden days people only had sex in that one boring position, nor do I think that back then a man and a woman were holy enough to abstain from at least trying once in a while to do some of that special loving that we do with our mouths on each other down there.*

These laws on the books, since they could not be enforced, were guidelines for how we should perfectly live our sex lives if this were a perfect world. In bed, we should not do those things that hurt or offend each other. We should strive only to please in our lovemaking, not hurt. Finally, and most importantly, there should be an emphasis on the creation of new life as the end result of all of it. In other words, God created Adam and Eve to bring new life into the world through their love for each other. To encourage them to engage in lovemaking that would produce new life, he made them strongly attracted to each other's bodies. He also made lovemaking the most enjoyable experience two people can ever have by giving them the capacity to achieve orgasm through it.

Now I am going to put my personal feelings aside. I am not going to tell you how sick I get when I see you with that man and start to think about what you two do when you are alone. I am not going to tell you that I find it disgusting and upsetting to my stomach. I am not going to tell you that I am ashamed of you for yielding to carnal desires. I am not going to tell you the old cliché that God created Adam and Eve, not Adam and Steve. I am not going to quote the Bible, Leviticus 20:13. "If a man also lie with mankind, as he lieth with a woman, both of them have committed an abomination."

I am not going to do any of that because I am not a hypocrite. You know my life and you know what I have been through. Now take heart, I am not trying to make you feel guilty so that you will yield to my will. O my brother, I am only telling you the truth as it is. I know about the homosexual perver-

sion because of the evil that was visited upon me as a child. I know that your mind can be seduced into following the ways of the devil. God makes you a certain way, but then because of all the evil in the world you end up becoming something else. What that man did to me when I was just a child is an evil too great to be set down with pen, but I will do it because I fear that it has rubbed off on you by no fault of your own.

Through all of the suffering I endured, I was able to survive because of the hate I felt for him. Some girls I have read about say that love is what saved them. Because they refused to hate him, it was easier for them to heal. They were able to forgive him later on in life for doing that to them and thus they were able to heal themselves. But I used hate as my shield. Every time he came at me, I hated him more. I prayed at night for God to kill him. I used to fantasize every day about killing him. You know that I eventually went after him with the knife, but what you don't know is that I had been planning that every day from the first time he touched me. I hated him the day you were born. I hated him the day our mother died. I hated him. I retreated into my hate. I was all hate. Hate was my downfall.

He knew I hated him, but you see, there was this part of me that I could not shield with my hate. That part of me was the carnal side. He made my body respond to his evil touches, and then he would throw it in my face. He knew that I was trying to remain cold at his touch, but my body would respond some-times and he would laugh at me. He would say, "How can you hate me and like what I'm doing to you at the same time? You want this as much as I do."

To prove to me that I wanted it as much as he did, he would go days, weeks, without doing anything to me, without touching me or even leering. Those were the worst days for me. Those were the days when I hated myself. Those were the days when I contemplated taking my own life. It's killing me to write this. I did desire him sometimes. He made my body want him. Yet I still hated him. But how could I hate him, then?

The other girls, the ones who survived through love, they survived because the love they felt made them feel sorry for their monster. It made them pity him. In their minds they were saying, "He is in such pain that he is forced to hurt me like this. He is forced to do this evil thing to me, this wickedness." They never blamed him for it. They never blamed themselves for it. They were turning the other cheek even at that age. Thus, they never ever saw it as their fault. Unlike me, they never ever had to consider that maybe they were the cause of their own father's evil against them.

I stabbed him finally, not because I hated him, but because I hated myself, and he knew that. As they were taking him to the hospital he was looking at me, smiling. He knew. I knew. It would be even worse after he came back from the hospital. He would own me forever. And that smile said that he knew that I knew it. I hated him, but I loved him too. That's why we had to leave. That's why all of those men. That's why Brother Morrisohn. That's why, maybe, even Elwyn. Maybe you're right about that one. I'm still trying to find my way. I just need you to understand that what you are feeling for this man is not natural. I have been there. I know where it comes from. We can talk frankly about this. It is not you doing your own thing. It is not harmless. It is not a choice. It is evil. You have been seduced by the devil, and it is very likely my fault because I should have been more careful around you. I set a bad example. I passed on my weakness of the flesh.

I won't be a hypocrite anymore, my dear brother, and I promise I won't lie to you anymore. But you must be honest with me too. I must know this. You must tell me the truth about this.

Did our father ever touch you?

With Love Always,
Elaine

Mamie Girl

Mamie met him after Sunday service, as she sometimes did, down in Old Man Harbaugh's orange groves, which were in bloom.

It was a very warm day and a good long walk through the dirt streets of Goulds, at least two miles from the tent where they'd had the church meeting, during which he had signaled to her. When she got there she was so worn out from the walk that she sat down in the shade on a small wooden bench one of the hands had left. Mamie had her Bible with her, but she was too ill at ease to open it while she waited for him to show. She sat fanning herself from the heat, worrying and waiting.

Mamie didn't hear him come up behind her. She felt a tender hand on the side of her face and his heady shaving tonic smell mixing in with the pollen of the orange blossoms all around them, and then his lips were on hers. She kissed him hungrily, though she was nervous still. He must have felt it in her because his hands stopped roving over her dress and his lips broke away from the kiss.

She said, "I need to tell you—"

"Shusssshhh." He pressed a finger to her lips.

She heard it then, the rumble of an engine. Somebody was driving up the lane. He backed away from her four giant steps and turned to one of the orange trees like he was inspecting it, like that was his business there, as though anyone would believe that a black man in a sharp suit and tie in 1942 would have any business inspecting orange trees.

They thought maybe it was an army truck because the soldiers, who were stationed at the base just outside Goulds, Florida, liked to use the fruit trails to practice their maneuvers—and, of course, to steal and eat the fruit straight from the branches. But the rumble turned out to belong to the engine of someone's old beat-up Ford, and the someone turned out to be Chet Harbaugh, the owner's oldest boy, who oversaw this section of the grove during picking time.

Chet Harbaugh slowed when he saw them and an ugly grin spread across his face as he approached. You couldn't fool Chet about a thing like this. There was no point in even trying. He may not have had the brain power to keep up with his schooling, but he sure understood the ways of black folk, he claimed. He was all of sixteen with a lean, hairless face dusted with freckles and a dark olive-colored army cap on his head that he got from one of the soldiers. In the back of the truck, the long neck of the bass fiddle he played at the local dances could be seen sticking up. Chet leaned out of the open window of the slow-moving Ford and tipped his army hat. "Top of the mornin to you there, Sister Mamie. I see you're catchin a good shade in my trees. There'll be plenty of oranges enough for you to pick when the season comes. Don't you worry none about it."

Mamie shook her head at him. "Mornin to you, Mr. Chet."

Chet cackled and called to the man in the sharp suit, "Top of the mornin to you too there, Rev. I see you're out here smellin all the pretty flowers and whatnot. Turn around so I can talk to you."

Chet further engaged the brakes on his old Ford and it groaned to a stop.

Buford Morrisohn turned around to face him.

"My, my, my, that's one fine suit you got on there. Then again, that's one fine gal you got there too. Prettiest one I ever seen you with, am I right, Rev?"

"Yes, Mr. Chet," Buford said.

"How's the wife?" asked Chet, his blue-gray eyes twinkling with mischief.

"She's just fine."

"That's good. She at home, I suppose?"

"I believe so, Mr. Chet."

"And you're out here with this one. Ain't this that preacher lady?" Chet nodded his head, like my, oh my, you black people are something else. "Well, I'll be pushing off now, Rev. Don't you all go messin with my trees, now hear? If I find any of my buds missing, I'm gonna know who to come after."

Chet drove off slowly down the dirt track and when they couldn't hear his engine anymore, Buford came and put his arms around her and kissed away her tears, which had begun to fall. As he held her, she knew that she would love him forever. He took her further into the grove where it was safe, and he lay her down on a bedding of leaves. He was tender and generous in his lovemaking, as he always was, but she wanted him to know how she felt, so she urged him with her hips for more. He cried out when he came with open-mouth joy.

She was quite happy now, the nervousness gone, as she got back into her dress and patted her thick mat of hair back into place under her kerchief. He lay stretched out on the ground, propped up on his elbows looking at her, chewing a blade of grass, and she felt loved. She leaned down to his face and kissed him. Then she kissed his neck and his strong shoulders. He spit out the blade of grass and pulled her down as though they might do it again in the shade of the trees. She felt so full of love that she just had to tell him.

"I love you, Buford," she told him through a mouth stuffed with his kisses. "I will always love you."

His hands were roving again. It felt so good. There had to be a way out of their problem. There just had to be. She did not hate Glovine, but she knew that Glovine was not his true love. This, this here, was true love. There had to be a way for them to be together. He kissed her lips. His hands went under her dress. She spread her knees for him. He knew just how to touch her so that she lost control. He was biting her neck. He was pinching the flesh between her thighs. The flesh between her thighs began to twitch.

It was at that moment that she said to him, "Buford, I am carrying your child."

He stopped kissing her. Her world stopped spinning.

"Buford."

"You better go," he told her with an icy stare. Then he stopped looking at her altogether.

He broke away from her and stood up. He still didn't have his clothes on. He had a broad chest and a narrow waist and long, lean, muscular legs. His body was hard from working the fields and fruit picking and it glistened with the sweat from their loving. She took in as much of him as she could without embarrassment and then averted her eyes. She was thirty-four, yet shy as a maiden, for she had only recently been introduced to the mysteries of the body. He was forty, well respected, college educated, and married to her cousin Glovine, the daughter of her aunti.

Why had she done it? Oh Lord, why? To get this far up in years so pure and safe from sin only to make such a mistake as this.

Well, the truth is, she had always loved him. She had loved him from the day he showed up ten years ago. She hadn't been so old back then and she made a vow to herself as soon as she saw him: if this one comes to court me, I will accept. His passion for the Lord equals mine.

But this thing between them—this illicit but so wonderful love—they had been sharing it now for three months. It started right after the cane season ended. It had come on the night of fire and brimstone when Buford had preached the house down and Mamie, who had no professional musical training but had been blessed with a musical ear from the Lord, had been mashing the piano keys like she had thirty fingers. It was the mightiest tent meeting ever in these parts. Close to fifty had been saved, plus four white people. The Holy Spirit was going to and fro throughout the earth. But the devil was too.

Their hands touched as they were rejoicing outside the tent at the end of the service, which had gone way beyond midnight. Their hands touched and they knew. Well, Mamie had always known. She had been carrying Buford in her heart for ten years, but he hadn't even noticed her. How could he? How could any man notice her with her beautiful, bright-skinned cousin Glovine around? Yet that night when their hands touched, Buford knew it too. They kissed as brother and sister in the Lord, but that first kiss let the devil in. They fled the tent and the presence of the Lord for a place where they could be alone. When they kissed again it was in the murky, midnight darkness in the field of harvested cane. When they kissed again, Mamie began to know the mysteries of love between a man and a woman that had been kept from her all of her life. They were Adam and Eve in the Garden of Eden. They were the songs in Song of Solomon. They were fornicators and adulterers in a field of cane.

Oh why, Lord, why?

How could the Lord allow this to happen to them of all people?

She blamed it on the devil and on her music, and she never played an instrument again. Buford, for his part, did not pass blame. He refused to give what they were doing a name. He preferred to refer to it as *this thing*.

Now he was dismissing her: "Get on up from here and go, woman. Leave me alone."

"I love you," said Mamie, looking up at him desperately.

He was hauling on his underwear, which was bright white and starched. His sharp dark suit that he had folded so neatly and set in the branches of one of the trees, he now pulled down angrily. He stepped into his pants. He put on and buttoned his white shirt and then fastened his tie with quick, nimble fingers. He said, "All I sacrifice for this church. I don't have to live down here and take this. Had the Klan come to my house. Had white men box me on the face because I have an education. But I stay—I don't run away—I stay. Because things have got to change, and this is the thanks I get. I thought you were different, Mamie girl. I believed in you, but you're just like the rest of them. I can't believe you would do this to me."

"Buford, what did I do? I only told you that I am pregnant. I would never hurt you. I know it is my fault. I know it," she said, climbing to her feet. She tried to put her arms around him, but he pushed her away. He was so angry he was shedding tears.

"Trying to trap me."

"No, Buford. I love you."

"Messing up my marriage. Messing up my good name."

"I would never."

He put up his hands. "I've got to go, Mamie. If you, of all people, are going to stab me in the back like this, then I've got to go."

"I'm not stabbing you. I love you."

He studied her face, then. Was she telling the truth? He said, "The truth is, I love you too." He seemed weak. He groaned from somewhere deep in his soul. He went and held onto a tree with one hand for support. "But Glovine—oh, poor Glovine."

She was crying now too. "I had never been with a man before. I had never been with anybody but you. The devil got ahold of me."

He said, "What are you going to do? What are you going to do to me, Mamie, now that I am at your complete mercy?"

She put her hand in his. "I won't hurt you."

She had no other choice because she loved him. She opened her arms, and he let her hold him. She led him away from the tree, and they sat down upon the bed of leaves where she found her Bible. She set the Bible in her lap and they read it together, and he promised to love her, and she, of course, would always love only him, and they confessed their sins to each other, and they promised to sin no more.

Afterward, she felt better, though she was afraid of what it was going to be like to go it alone. Of course, he could not leave his wife. That would be a sin. Of course, he could not leave South Florida—he had to be here to fight the fight for the Faithful. Of course, he could not leave—she would never see him again if he left, and she did not want that to happen. These are the wages of her sin. She would have to raise the child alone and never name the father, for she loved this great man of God.

And if there should ever come a day when, God forbid, Sister Glovine should die, then he would marry her, his true love, he promised. This is what he told her sitting in the shade of the orange grove in bloom, and she believed him.

It was going to be hard. But she would do it, because she loved him and she believed him.

She would be a scorned woman because she had made so many enemies in the church through her fervent evangelism for the Lord. Now her enemies would punish her indeed—but only for a while, the Lord only lets His children suffer for a while. It was going to be hard, but Mamie would bear it for the God she served and the man she loved. Furthermore, she would have a child to love her and to remind her of their covenant.

She would wait, then, upon the Lord to fix the things that her own sinful nature had messed up. She would suffer as she deserved to, and she would wait. Good things come to those who wait upon the Lord. And Mamie loved Buford more than anything in the world. He was her good thing.

Thus, Mamie Culpepper sat talking with Buford Morrisohn on their bed of leaves in the grove in Goulds until the sun had moved to the west and their shadows were growing long. They had been talking for more than two hours. They had to leave soon or risk being missed. She did not want to let go of his hand. But she knew that she must. She looked into his handsome face and she saw the hope for her future. She looked into his handsome face and she saw love. His face made a slight movement and she thought that he was leaning toward her for a kiss, and so she leaned into him, hoping to be kissed one last time until the Lord shed His Grace upon them.

But Buford was not about to kiss her—he had just come up with an idea that he wanted to share with her.

So Mamie leaned in to receive what was not a kiss, but an open mouth from out of which Buford said, "I got a poem for you, Mamie girl. It just came into my head for you."

And he spoke the poem to her.

The words were King David beautiful as she listened to them but not too easy to figure out. There were parts in it that made her think it was about the hardness of hearts that have turned away from God, and something about a long journey on a narrow and twisting road in eternal darkness, and one part about love between hellfire and gentle rain. She did not quite understand it completely, but it made her very sad.

He said to her, "What do you think?"

She said, "It's beautiful."

And he took her in his arms and kissed her.

Though they had already been away from their people for too long, he undressed her and made love to her tenderly once again. This time his loving did not make her cry out in joy, but filled her with a sadness that was more perplexing than even his poetic words.

Covenant of the Lord

When Mamie got home, the Holy Spirit hit her with a heavy, vengeful hand and knocked her down to the floor where she received a vision from the Lord, which was the interpretation of Buford's poem.

They were two angels so bright and fair that she had to shield her eyes with her hand. One held up a sacred scroll, the other a golden sword. She thought the one with the sword would strike her, for there was wrath on his countenance, but when she looked again she saw that behind the first two angels was another, the Angel Beautiful, and his face calmed her soul. He came and stood between the first two and he spoke these words of truth: "His heart is hard. Your journey is long. The Lord will not suffer the fire to consume the rain."

With that, the three angels ascended into the heavens and disappeared from sight.

Mamie cried out, "Praise the Lord! Praise ye the Lord!"

The next day, bright and early, just as the Lord had promised, there came a knock on the door and Mamie met Private Cooper.

And she was ready for him because she had understood the vision to mean: the Lord will provide a father for the child.

The fire (the ministry) was Buford's passion.

The rain (tears from the pain of childbearing) was her passion.

The father for the child was this good-looking man at the door (with his hat in his hand).

He was handsome in the way that other women found men to be handsome—big, husky, tall, much taller than Buford, and with pretty skin—though Mamie, to be honest, had been expecting something else.

It was his age. He was so young. She figured maybe twenty-five, and here she was in her midthirties. But there he was at her aunti's door with the early-morning sun coming up behind him (the sun being the symbol of the Angel Beautiful), and not asking to see her aunti, but to see her, Mamie Culpepper.

He had his hat in his hands and his head was bowed in gentlemanly greeting. His reddish-brown hair was slicked back on his head in the style of the day, but she saw no signs of pomade in it—his hair was natu-rally fine-textured. He was one of those mixed boys. When he lifted his head again, it was done slowly, deliberately, so that he could take in the full measure of her. Mamie felt only a slight embarrassment at his in-spection of her because she had been expecting the Lord to deliver and thus put on her best dress, the yellow one, and best shoes, the ones with the unbroken straps. She had combed her lustrous hair into submission and tied her prettiest kerchief over it (the yellow one). The young man smiled in approval and then set his face for serious courting.

He said to her, "You are a vision of loveliness this fine morning, Sis-ter Culpepper, I must say, and it behooves a good Christian man such as myself to inform you of how happy I am to serve a Lord and Savior who blesses the world with flowers and birds and pretty smiles such as yours."

Mamie couldn't help but blush. Nevertheless she said to him, "Thank you, kind sir. Now it behooves a good Christian woman such as myself who has many important errands to run on this fine day, which the Lord has given us, to ask the young man to state his business plain out so that she might get to her appointed tasks."

He responded with nervous gestures, as his confidence was slightly shaken by her directness—he bit his bottom lip and folded and unfolded the brim of his hat, which was still in his two hands in front of him. "Well," he said, "My name is—"

"I know who you are, Jefferson Cooper. You're from one of them islands down there."

"Yes. Jamaica," he stammered.

"You've got two last names for a name."

"Well, my middle name is Thomas."

"That's a last name too."

"But you can call me Jeff," he said with a wink. "Well, as you know I work as a—"

"I know what you do. I've seen you pick fruit. You're fast."

He beamed. "Thank you."

"The rest of us can't hardly make a living you're so fast."

He lowered his eyes to his spit-polished shoes and stylized spats. "Sorry," he mumbled.

"I've seen you at the tent, and I've heard you preach."

"You've heard me preach," he said, lifting his eyes again. His chest swelled with pride. He said to her confidently, because he knew he was a good preacher—all of the girls who were trying to get their hooks in him loved his preaching: "So you like my preaching, huh?"

"I've heard better."

Cooper stumbled backward, then regained his stance and his composure. He said, smiling—O but she did love his smile: "Well, kind lady, my business is with you, if you must know. Now if I could have a glass of cold water on this good morning—"

"You came to my house so early in the morning for water, Cooper? Is that your business?"

"Well, ma'am, no. But I could sure use a glass of cold water to wet my throat, then I'll set down and state to you my business plain. Would you be so kind, ma'am? And call me Jeff. Or Jefferson, if you prefer."

Mamie was beginning to doubt the Lord. This is the one, this fidgeting boy? He had on a dark jacket and a white shirt, but no tie. He had a red rose pinned to the lapel of his jacket. She said to the young Jefferson Cooper, "Boy, what are you doing here all dressed up for? What do you want from me?"

From behind her she heard Aunti, coughing her harsh morning cough and asking, "Mamie, what's all that racket so early in the morning? Who you talking to outside?"

Mamie turned and shouted back, "Nobody. Go back to sleep, Aunti."

Aunti coughed again. "What man you out there talking to, Mamie? That the insurance man? That Reverend Morrisohn?"

Now she could hear the squeaking of springs as Aunti was getting out of bed to come see what all was going on. Mamie stepped outside the door and closed it behind her, and then she took the young Jefferson Cooper by the hand and hurried him away from the small wooden box she called a house. No way was she ready for gossips like her aunti to start piecing together rumors about her and Jefferson Cooper until she was sure that he was the one the Lord had sent.

She had his hand and she was pulling him down the dirt road to the Piggly Wiggly's, which had a porch, which she avoided because it was too public.

Not us on the porch, no way. Not yet. There will come a time for porches if he is indeed the one.

She took him to the alley behind the Piggly Wiggly's. When she got there, she backed him up against the wall and got right up in his face. He smelled good too, like two whole bouquets of flowers. "Now, Cooper, you know I'm not a young woman, so I've got no time for games. I'm tired of asking you why you came to my house this morning and you beating around the bush. So let's just get down to it. You tell me if the Lord sent you. You tell me if you—" but she could not finish.

Now it was she who was losing her confidence.

Here she was in the alley behind the Piggly Wiggly's with this handsome, well-dressed, fine-smelling young man and about to ask him if he loved her and they hadn't said but maybe a dozen words to each other since he came to town about a year ago and started preaching and picking and she was pregnant for a married man and soon to be found out and the Lord had to help her out of this mess—He just had to, He just had to. But how could she ask a man who was practically a stranger whether he loved her when she still loved Buford?

Feeling guilt ridden and dishonest as the lyingest liar, she backed away from Cooper with her head bowed.

"If I what?" he said to her.

"If nothing."

When she looked up, he had that beautiful smile on his face again. He still had his hat in his hands. He was such a big, humble, good-looking young gentleman. She wouldn't mind having a son like him, but a husband? He said to her, "If I what, Sister Culpepper?"

She sighed. This was not going to work. She waved him off. "It was just something I had in my head is all, Cooper. Go your way." She made a move as if to leave the alley.

He cleared his throat and stood up straighter and blocked her exit with his big body. "Well," he said, "I do know that you're the only woman around here who's worth anything."

She narrowed her eyes. "What do you mean?"

"Well, I'm on fire for the Lord. These girls around here, they're looking for husbands. They'll tell a man anything. But I've been watching you since I came." He smiled his handsome smile. "I must tell you, kind lady, I think you're beautiful." Then he quickly added, "And you are on fire for the Lord."

Mamie put her hands on her stout hips. "Beautiful?" At the entrance to the alley, she could see that the small town of Goulds was waking up now. There were cars and bicycles bustling about. She saw an open-top army car roll past with two white soldiers in it. An old brown and black lop-eared mutt entered the alley and trotted up to them, his tail wagging, his mouth open, begging food. Mamie shushed him away and the old mutt trotted off with his tail between his legs. She said to Cooper's sparkling eyes, "We need to go somewhere to talk, young man," and she took his hand and led him out of the alley.

Aunti was on the porch of their house, leaning over the wooden rail talking to Old Black Spensser, the milkman and all-purpose fix-it man. Aunti spotted Mamie and Cooper and waved them over, but Mamie waved back at her—no—and led Cooper down the road in the opposite direction, to Main Street, which was the only partially paved road in town.

There was a filling station and a general merchandise store owned by the Andersons, who were first cousins of the Harbaughs. The Andersons had a little sweet shop set up in the back, where they served breakfast to the colored soldiers and to the colored and Mexican laborers who worked the groves. It was out of sight from the main road, which offered the privacy Mamie sought, and it was cozy, so she led Cooper there.

He pulled out one of the wooden chairs for her, and she sat down, then he sat down. Manners too, she thought, smiling despite herself.

She said, batting her eyes like a coquet, "Now what is this I hear about you being in love with me, Cooper?"

His mouth fell open. "In love?"

"Yes."

He set his hat on the table. She watched as he struggled to regain his composure, through musing and a great deal of eyebrow furrowing. The young man was clearly thinking it through. Much to her surprise and satisfaction, he said, "Well, I must say that you are a direct one. But it is interesting. You do have all the qualities that I desire in a Christian woman. You are beautiful, you are close to God, and you've been watching me since I got here."

"No such thing, Cooper!" she retorted, attempting to trip him up again as she had at her door earlier. She enjoyed watching him stumble. She found it endearing, a man so off-balance in her presence. It made her feel beautiful. Maybe he was the one. At any rate, she was having her fun with him. She was enjoying his attention. She discovered that she quite enjoyed being spiteful. This flirting business, it was so against her nature, but she took right to it.

"Well now," Cooper said, clearing his throat. He had beautiful hands, except for a scab on his right one from some field-related injury which he picked at absentmindedly with his left thumbnail. "Well now. I heard that you have been watching me with interest."

"Who would tell you such a thing, sir?" She shook her head, tut-tutting.

"You haven't been watching me?"

"No. I am on fire for the Lord, sir. I don't have time to be watching men," Mamie said with a pout. She had seen other women pout when flirting with men, and so she pouted now because she had always secretly wanted to. But when Cooper gave her a strange look, she figured that it was the pout that was inappropriate at this point and so she stopped doing it. She regretted that she had such little experience in these matters, such little experience as a flirt.

"It's interesting," Cooper mused. "You are well spoken of. You are well admired. You do the Lord's will. You are beautiful—"

"You said that one already."

He kept picking at the scab as he counted off her attributes, each of which she smugly agreed with. "You are beautiful. You are sensible. You are virtuous. You are chaste—I have never seen you in the company of any man, and everyone speaks highly of your character." He nodded at her.

She continued to eye him, but with less coquettish fervor and less high-mindedness. Chaste. Too late for that one, she thought sadly. "Go on, Cooper. State your case. I am listening."

"I know that some say I am too young to be seeking a wife—there, I've said it—I am seeking a wife, and I don't have time for games either, Sister Culpepper." He stopped talking as he lifted a white silk handkerchief from an inside coat pocket and dabbed at his forehead, drying the beads of sweat that had appeared there. He replaced the handkerchief and went back to speaking and agitating the horrible little scab. "I came by your house this morning to begin a proper courtship of you, if you will have me, in a manner that is pleasing to the Lord. The Lord is calling me to build a church, and I need an help meet to be at my side. Someone with the courage to do what the Lord asketh us to do."

"An help meet," she said.

So there it was. There was the offer. She would be an help meet. She would be his wife. It sounded like the Lord, but was it?

She looked him over. He looked to be twenty-five. Twenty-six? That wasn't too bad. She asked him straight out, "Just how old are you, Cooper?"

"I'll be twenty in December."

Mamie rose in high-minded outrage from her seat. She would not be made a fool of. Oh the gossips of Goulds would love that one. Old Mamie done took up with a little, bitty boy. "Mr. Cooper," she announced, "it was good talking to you, but I do believe that this attempt at courtship is over. You're just too young."

He put up a finger. "Don't let my age fool you, Sister Mamie. I've lived many lifetimes in my twenty years."

"Nineteen," she corrected.

Cooper was unperturbed. He did not rise from his seat. He said, "Sarah was ninety when she got pregnant for Abraham."

Mamie said, "I'm not old as Sarah. What, you think I'm ninety? Shame on you to talk like that to a lady." Pouting. Prettily.

Cooper gave her his handsome smile in honor of the appropriateness of her pout. Despite herself, she was pleased to have pouted appropriately at last.

He said, "I serve the Lord today because He saved me from a life of shame and degradation. If it wasn't for the Lord, I'd be dead. There are nine of us in our family. I am the oldest child. I left home and joined the merchant marines at the age of thirteen so that I could send money back to my mother. We never lived good back home because Daddy is a drunkard and a gambler, who begged more bread in his life than he ever earned. He has seven more outside children that we know of. At fourteen, I was a mess boy on an oil tanker running the sea-lanes to England and France and Italy. The pay was good. I had enough money to send home to my blessed mother and enough to keep me in much drink and mischief. I got to see the world. It's a pretty big place. It's a pretty beautiful place, Praise God. But life is hard for a seaman, especially when you're colored. The sea is unforgiving and so are the white men you work with. I learned to defend myself. At the age of seventeen, I killed a man."

Mamie was aghast, but intrigued. A murderer.

Cooper urged gently, "Sit down, Sister Mamie," and it seemed to her that the presence of the Lord was upon him and she did as she was told. She sat down and she listened as he completed his narrative.

"From the moment he set eyes on me, this fellow, a big bearded Swedish man, he hated me. He rode me night and day attacking the quality of my work, calling me ugly black bastard, calling me shiftless and lazy. I took it all from him. I took it all, because I didn't want any trouble. I even stayed away from the card games that we would have at night. I took to drinking more. One night, the Swede seemed to have had a change of heart. He stuck his head in the cabin, which I was sharing with two other colored boys, and he invited me to the game that night. He said they were short a player and he'd heard I was a good card player and a good fellow. Well, this surprised me as well as the two fellows I was rooming with because he used to ride them as much as he rode me. So I went into his cabin, where they were supposedly having the game, but nobody was there yet. So he and I were just sitting around when he started to ask these questions about my accent, where I was from, what life was like for me growing up in the islands. Things like that. So I answered him and we talked like that for a while. Next thing I knew, the Swede had gotten up and attempted to perform an abominable act on me. I pushed him off. He got angry and began calling me names that challenged my manhood. The devil got ahold of me and I took a swing at him. He swung back. We went at it then, grappling in the room, knocking over the card table that was set up for the game. He outweighed me by at least fifty pounds, but I was younger and quicker. I soon got the better of him. Instead of surrendering, he pulled out a knife and lunged at me, cutting me right here."

Cooper opened his coat and lifted out the tail of his shirt to reveal the long scar that ran from his third rib down into his pants, like black railroad tracks on his apple cider skin.

He explained, "It goes down almost to my knee. He got me good. But I had a knife too. Before he could lunge again, I had pulled out my knife and gutted him like a fish. There's nothing else to say about it. He fell back on his bed and died. It was that easy. Then his cabin door opened and the other seven players showed up and caught me with my knife in this guy's guts. I tried to explain what had happened. I showed them where he had cut me. It didn't matter to them how badly hurt I was. The important thing in their mind was that I had killed this white guy. They beat me up pretty bad. They took me up on deck, and one of them proposed that they shoot me and throw my body into the water. The rest of them agreed. If I ever needed the Lord, I needed Him right then."

Mamie was listening with rapt attention and watching his handsome features as he spoke.

Cooper said, "The Lord is a miracle worker. Praise God! Before they could shoot me, there was a mighty explosion. Our tanker had been struck by a torpedo from a German U-boat. The ship was crippled. Furthermore, we were transporting oil. The exploded fuel was burning so hot the hair on my body was cooking. We were on fire. We were going to burn or blow up before rescue got to us. There was no way out of this. To make matters worse, the Germans hit us again with two more torpedoes. Finally, there was another tremendous explosion and the ship split in half. I was flung into the sea. As I was fighting for my life against the searing flames and the mighty currents trying to drag me under, I remembered the name of my God and I called out to Him and He heard me. It was a black night, but the flames were bright and I soon spotted something floating on top of the water. It was a lifeboat. I swam to it and got in. The Lord's mighty hand was on that lifeboat and He steered it away from the deadly pull of the sinking ship. Everything else floating was being sucked down into the black water by the whirling pool created by the sinking ship. Everything but the little lifeboat that I was on disappeared in seconds. Then it was very quiet. There is nothing more terrifying than the infinite quietness when you are alone in the middle of the ocean at night. There were not even stars in the sky. I kept my eyes open, but there was nothing to see. Everyone else was gone. All night I kept my eyes open, looking for survivors, but there was no one. In the morning when the sun came up, there was much debris in the water and two floating bodies among the wreckage. I recognized the Swede's body. The other was the body of the man who had come up with the idea to shoot me. I took their bodies as a sign from the Lord. It was a warning of what should have justly been my fate. There were other things floating in the ocean. A wooden crate with a canteen of water in it, four tins of salted pork, and a blanket. Another crate floated near and when I opened it, it was empty except for a Bible. I made that water and that salted pork last for three weeks. I covered myself by day in the blanket to protect from the sun, and at night I slept in it to protect from the cold. I read my Bible every waking hour. The Psalms were of a special comfort to me. The Gospels gave me hope that the same Jesus of Nazareth who had died on the cross for me was keeping me alive now and would eventually save me. But why? Why should a sinner like me be allowed to live? To serve Him, that's why, Praise the Lord! There were no oars in the boat, so I floated until I was picked up. I floated for twenty-two days and was picked up by a Spanish freighter on the day my last drop of water ran out. It was another sign from the Lord. If all hope is gone, trust in the Lord."

When he had finished, Mamie looked at him indeed as a man who had lived many lifetimes in his nineteen years. She looked at him as a man she could love, given time. She saw herself as the man adrift at sea with no hope, but then a crate floats by with fresh water and food and a Bible. She was adrift and Cooper was the crate floating by. He was fresh water. He was food. He was the Bible.

But there was a problem. When she looked at Buford, she felt her body call out to him. When she looked at this young man Cooper, she felt nothing. He was a beautiful man, but she did not desire his touch. She did not desire to touch him. If she took up with him, as clearly the Lord intended, she would have to be with him sexually. She would have to do it. She could not imagine it, but she would have to do it as his wife. This beautiful man, why couldn't she desire him?

Oh, maybe this was not even the Lord! Maybe this was all in her head.

He was peering across the table at her with love. He had reached across and now he was holding her hand. She became aware of his scab picked raw. She was repulsed. She could not go through with it. He was beautiful, but he repulsed her. She would repulse him right back, and end this crazy thing.

"Cooper," she told him, "I am not twenty-five. I am not thirty. I am thirty-four years old."

"And as beautiful as a spring morning."

She set her face. "And I am pregnant."

Cooper squeezed her hand. "Yes. That is what Reverend Morrisohn told me."

Mamie became cold, very cold, starting with the hand holding his picked-scab hand and chilling all the way up her shoulders and spreading throughout the rest of her body and soul. Cooper had that handsome smile on his face again. She saw now that it was the smile of a damned fool.

"Reverend Morrisohn told you?"

Cooper whispered, "Nobody else has to know. What we do, we do in the name of the Lord."

Mamie was furious, but she hid it under a pleasant, ladylike smile. "Let's do it then."

You fool.

Don't Go Spilling My Fruit

So two weeks after Jefferson Cooper began to court Mamie Culpepper, they were wed—they did it in the name of the Lord and to keep her reputation clean.

Cooper was the natural choice to fix it.

He was not a man inclined to run wild with women, for the Lord had changed his heart on a lifeboat on the high seas. Furthermore, he was a loyal disciple of Buford Morrisohn, not a damned fool, as Mamie had called him in her heart. And it was Brother Morrisohn who had spoken to him about the fine church lady who would be brought down low because of a certain callous act—a fine church lady who was in desperate need of a fix, and a quick one.

Now Cooper, a man who had survived in the face of certain death, was not one to compromise the Commandments of the Lord regarding fornication and adultery—of course he would have preferred a virgin for a wife—but neither was he an automaton or a marionette who ascribed a literal and fixed translation to spiritual principles. In short, Cooper believed that we are all born in sin and shaped in iniquity, and no man should be another's judge. Should he who had taken a man's life look with scorn upon the face of a woman who, at the age of thirty-four, had yielded, after resisting it valiantly for years, to the spiteful sexual nature of sin and corruption?

Cooper had believed that the Lord would provide him a wife who was beautiful, which Mamie was, who was strong in the Lord, which Mamie was, and who was chaste, which Mamie, Brother Morrisohn had informed him, indeed was, despite the loss of her maidenhead.

Forced sexual engagement at the hands of the spiteful white teen Chet Harbaugh might have robbed her of her virginity, but not her virtue. Neither would it rob her of her place in their spiritual community, if Jefferson Cooper had any say in the matter.

As Brother Morrisohn had put it, "The boy found her alone and had his way with her. It is a hateful and ugly act."

She never spoke of the thing that the boy had done to her, and Cooper did not press the issue. It was a lady's prerogative to choose not to speak of such indelicate matters. She was a fine wife otherwise, and passionate, though a little unimaginative in the bedroom, which was just further indication of the intactness of her virtue.

She had a big, soft body that was a wonder to look upon. Her breasts were indeed the cassava melons that the Song of Solomon spoke about. Her wide hips were a delight to behold. Her skin was black and starless as the perfect night.

She knew her Bible, he had to admit, better than he did, and thus was a great assist in the penning of sermons. He would watch and listen as she expounded on Scripture and then he would recapitulate her energy and ideas when he preached.

She was neither frivolous nor lazy nor a nag and she was proud, though not of her beauty, as are some women, but proud of being a woman, a lady, and she was content to follow his lead, though he was young and she had been independent of husbandly leadership well into her midthirties. There was never a need to rebuke his Mamie or to remind her that the man is head of the house as Christ is head of the church. In fact, it was she who demanded that he be the man by letting him control all of the money they earned from their joint labors in the fields of fruit. She always reminded him to send money to his mother and siblings back in Jamaica; she was not jealous of his mother. She understood the love of a mother, having lost her own dear mother a few years earlier.

She always spoke with a gentle tenderness to him, a wifely deference; she always called him Mr. Cooper, or Cooper, in public and "husband" in private, even while making love. He found it amusing that she blushed when he called her baby or darling or lover. She preferred to be called wife, or Mrs. Cooper, but she was proud of their marriage and she cherished her wedding band, which had cost him a week's worth of unloading trucks for the Andersons.

She said that the ring was too good to wear because someone might try to steal it. She preferred to carry it in her purse or in her bosom wrapped in tissue paper. She was always pulling it out, showing it to her women friends, or in a moment of leisure setting it on the table and watching it with quiet sighs.

He liked to watch her come and go in that yellow dress and kerchief. She had a way of walking that demanded attention, especially now that the baby was beginning to show. He liked to watch the way men watched her, the men who had not been worthy of her, the men she had passed up on because they were not saved enough, the men who had passed up on her because she was too saved, the men who had allowed her to reach her thirties without a mate. Their nets had missed this great catch, but their missing out had allowed her to grow strong in the Lord. She was a woman easy to love and Cooper loved her with all his heart.

He decided that when the baby was born, he would love it too. He anticipated that he would have to ignore for a while the sly smiles and titters of the others who would make untoward suggestions about the baby's ancestry spelled out in its skin. But years later, he knew, the baby's complexion would not matter at all, for he himself was fair-skinned and thus many would simply come to assume that the mix of the child was that of his yellow skin with Mamie's black.

It was the Harbaugh boy who caused all the trouble.

Come citrus picking season, the boy would have that smirk on his face every time he came near Mamie. When he came near, Mamie would freeze up, like someone who had lost control of her limbs. Sometimes her basket of oranges would spill. At times like these, Cooper would go to his wife and put his arms around her and she would become calmer. The freckle-faced boy would stare at them with stupid fascination, then say something arrogant or vicious before driving off: "Watch it there, Sister Culpepper. Don't go wasting my oranges. Time's a passing and time is money. Pick 'em up. You help her there now, Reverend Cooper."

Then he would drive off, cackling. It angered Cooper to see his wife have to submit to this torture, never mind that the boy publicly disrespected their marriage by calling her Culpepper and him Cooper.

One day the boy came by, driving slowly past in his truck as he was wont to do, and Mamie spilled her oranges, and he shouted to her, "Watch it there, Sister Culpepper. Don't go spilling my fruit."

Had the boy driven off immediately things might have turned out better for everybody, but he did not. He waited there laughing. In fact, he stopped his truck. It sat there in park while he laughed.

Cooper, who as always was nearby, had heard the boy's words. This time he had said it different—"Don't go spilling my fruit"—which in the mind of a man steeped in the King James Version of the Bible was a far cry from "Don't go wasting my oranges."

The boy might as well have shouted to all the pickers that Mamie was carrying his seed, his fruit.

Cooper felt as though every eye among the pickers was upon him, accusing him of being less than a man to this good woman who had been so badly wronged, and as he felt their scorn burn into his back the Spirit of the Lord left him and he was filled with wrath. He should have prayed, but he did not. So the devil took good hold, and Cooper walked right up to Chet Harbaugh sitting in that old Ford.

Chet Harbaugh kept right on laughing. He didn't ask why the big picker preacher was standing in front of his car, the big picker preacher whose wife he figured was pregnant for old black Reverend Morrisohn. Chet just kept right on laughing as the big man reached inside the car with one hand and grabbed him by his thin neck and used the other hand to slap his face until there was much blood and pain and, finally, unconsciousness.

There was a smart picker there named Amos, who spent a lot of time at the altar because of his drinking and gambling, and he admired young Cooper who had prayed with him often, so he told two of the Mexicans to get in Chet's car and drive the boy back into town, but drive slow. "Tek him to a doctor," Amos told them, "but don't be too clear on what all happened. We got to give Cooper a fighting chance."

The Mexicans said "Sí," and the car began to roll slowly down the road.

Then Amos told Cooper, "You in trouble, boy. You need to get on out of here fast. I got my old car. Tek it. Go south first, cause they gonna be lookin for you to head north. All the roads'll be blocked. Stay down in Homestead for a few days, maybe a few weeks. Keep out of sight.

Don't talk too much to nobody. Then when the Klan done did its firs' run at you, the army'll be mad at 'em and they'll have to rest up on their roadblocks. That's when you want to head north. Then go fast and go far, boy. Go on up to Jacksonville at least. Go on up to Georgia if you can stand it. Stay up there for a couple months, then send for your wife and child."

Mamie began to cry.

Cooper shook his head. "Why can't I take her?"

"Boy, is you crazy?" said Amos. "You go running down to Home-stead with your wife, they'll know it's you for sure. They'll probably hurt her as bad as they hurt you, if the pain of seeing you strung up don't kill her dead first. She's carrying a child, boy! Now go on. Get on out of here. God love you, Cooper."

Old Amos embraced Cooper and passed him the keys to his car. Then Cooper embraced his wife. The sun was high in the sky. Shadows were short, the air was sweet smelling, and their tear-flavored kiss was the last one they would ever share.

He told her, "I love you, wife."

She told him, "I love you, Mr. Cooper."

And then he was gone.

The sheriff came first, poking his nose around, calling it investigating. He was in the employ of the Harbaughs as well as their second cousin. He was big and chinless and wore a sweat-stained cowboy hat. He slapped some of the young men around pretty good, but they each told him the same story: Cooper stole Old Amos's car and fled north.

The Klan came that very night, burning more than a dozen wooden houses, and beating several young men pointed out by Chet as hav-ing been in on it, but killing no one. This angered Chet, who walked around now with his head bandaged in white like a high priest of righteous wrath. Chet demanded blood and vengeance, but it was picking season. Every able body was needed to bring in the crop.

The baby came next.

They named her Isadore. Isadore Cooper. She was born early. By everybody's recollection it was only a six-and-a-half-month pregnancy, and there was some gossip about why that was.

Did Mamie and Cooper, two stalwarts of the Faithful, engage in sexual communion before marriage? .

What of the rumor that Cooper had slapped the Harbaugh boy senseless for offending Mamie? What of the rumor that the boy was the baby's father? How could that be when the baby was so dark?

How could the baby even be Cooper's and be so dark? Was not Cooper a fair-skinned man?

The people of Goulds gossiped themselves into a self-righteous ecstasy and concluded that all would be resolved when Cooper returned to retrieve Mamie and the child. They were eager to see how it would all come out.

But Cooper had been gone two months now, and there was no sign of him. Everyone felt that it was safe for him to return, if he was careful about it, and collect his wife and child because the Klan had found a boy about Cooper's height and complexion up around Fort Lauderdale and worked out its blood vengeance on him. This boy was a known thief and troublemaker, so he has not sorely missed by anyone, except for the white girl he had been shacked up with, and everybody breathed a sigh of relief that now Cooper had a fighting chance because the white sheets and blazing crosses weren't coming out at night anymore.

The gossips noted that these days Mamie rarely left home and never without company—her cousin Glovine, Glovine's husband the Reverend Morrisohn, her aunti the old midwife, and her infant child Isadore, over whom she doted. By all accounts Mamie was a good mother, but there was clearly a pall of sadness and worry hanging over her, and it had something to do with the child. Mamie seemed ever in a state of agitation.

Then there came a day when the word out on the street was that Cooper had snuck back into town the night before and vanished again before the white people had even awakened.

The evidence was plain before everybody's eyes. Old Amos's automobile was parked outside his shack again. Everyone assumed, then, that this meant Cooper had come and collected Mamie and the baby. But how did he transport them away if he had given back Amos's car? There were rumors of a mysterious bus and then some talk of a friend with a car who had driven down with Cooper. There was even talk of Reverend Morrisohn brokering a deal with Old Man Harbaugh so that all was made right and Cooper and Mamie need no longer fear harm from any white man.

This rumor held the most power and survived the longest because there were quite a few who could testify to having witnessed Reverend Morrisohn being present at Mamie's house on the night that Cooper had snuck back into town. The same would testify that the Reverend Morrisohn (sometimes without his wife) was often at Mamie's house late into the night.

The same would also testify that the facts are these. Cooper drove back into town on the night in question. He parked the car in front of Old Amos's clapboard house and went inside to say something to Old Amos. Perhaps goodbye. Perhaps thank you for saving my life. Fifteen minutes later, wearing a large hat to conceal his features, he emerged in seemingly good spirits from Amos's dwelling and walked with the old pep in his step down the dirt road to the seventh of eight similarly built shacks. He went inside. There was a shout, but not of joy. Then, a few minutes later, he emerged from the dwelling of his wife and walked due north and was never seen in these parts again.

The same would also testify that when Cooper emerged from the dwelling of his wife, she emerged from it also following behind him, frantically beating her breasts and pleading with him to come back. But Cooper did not look back. Had he looked back, he would have seen Reverend Morrisohn emerging from the dwelling as well, with the baby Isadore in his arms, sleeping peacefully, swaddled in her little blanket with only her dark face exposed to the night. Had he looked back, he would have seen Reverend Morrisohn put a hand on Mamie's shoulder and say something into her ear that made her head fall to her chest and made her sob uncontrollably and then follow him back into the house.

The same would also tell you that Cooper just kept heading north, on foot, in that big old hat he wore to conceal his features and his tears.

Sobbing miserably.

Why is Reverend Morrisohn in my wife's house at 2 in the morning? Why does my child look so much like him?

My Sister

My Dearest Sister,

I hope this letter finds you in the best of health and under the blessings and Grace of our Lord and Savior Jesus Christ.

I got this from a transcript of a guy who was interviewed on a talk show. I think you will find it interesting:

When I look at a beautiful woman, what do I see? I see that she is beautiful and that is all. I do not desire her. Now don't take this the wrong way. I am not saying that I don't desire women. I am not saying that I am gay. I am saying that I am thirty years old and I have been with women, as you call it, and I am no longer attracted to all that this implies. I see a woman and my sexual impulse is stifled by her husband, or her boyfriend, and her mortgage, her dying mother, her job, her children, her headaches, her allergies, her trip to the Bahamas that she is saving up for, her promotion at work, her speeding ticket—every complication in her life. That takes all of the sexiness out of it for me. I already have a wife with all of these things, so when I am in a bar and some hot number comes up to me, I don't care how hot she is, I begin to see all of these things instead of her sexy breasts or butt. We cannot separate women—people—from everything that they are. The idea of a one-night stand is great, but how realistic is that? Oh sure, it is a one-night stand, but then next week she is calling you at work. The sex and the sexiness are just an excuse to burden you with her complications. So then you have hookers, but they are lowlifes. You want to catch a disease? So then you have masturbation, but that is lonely. So then you stay faithful to your wife, not because you love her that much, but because you cannot afford any more complications—and your wife has complications, plenty of complications, enough for two lifetimes. But then something happens, something wonderful. You end up in bed with this teenage girl. You have discovered someone who has no complications at all. She is just a beautiful, loving, grateful, worshipful body next to you in the bed. If she has a boyfriend, he is some snot-nosed kid. No real complication there. If she has a job, it is not that important. She does not really need the money and it's not like she is going to work as a counter girl at the drugstore all of her life. So that's not a complication either—she will skip work to be with you. She has parents, and if they find out about you there will be trouble. But of course she won't tell them about you because that would be so immature and not grown-up on her part. Remember now, you are her secret affair, so she must keep you a secret if she is to feel grown-up. So parents, usually, are not a complication. She has school—but the hours are regular. So that's not a complication. In fact, that makes things better. It gives her something to occupy her time so she doesn't get on your nerves. She starts to pester or bore you, you remind her she has homework to do. Money. That's not a complication. If she needs money, it's small time—money for lunch or perfume or a hot-looking outfit. She is so grateful when you give it to her because she doesn't understand that it's not real money. Real money is the stuff that comes regular like a mortgage or car payment or insurance. Real money is stuff that comes big, like busted plumbing, a sudden illness, college loans, funeral expenses, a tax lien—if any of these things affect your teenage girl, she doesn't bother you with it because her parents take care of it. If she gets sick, her parents tote the bill. If her car breaks down, same thing. When you give her money, it's for fun stuff—a new purse, say—but not for complications. Her parents pay her tuition, room, and board. So that's why I *got in trouble with these girls. I bit off too much. If I had done ten or twenty of them, I would have been all right. But three hundred, I think maybe that was going too far. I got caught with my hand in the cookie jar. So now they're calling me a pedophile. Do I look like a pedophile to you? These girls aren't children—they are fifteen- and sixteen-year-old women who are as yet un-burdened with complications. But you have your laws, and the law is the law. And after I do my time, what do you think I'm going to do? Go back to grown women? I would have to be crazy. Of course, my girls are always going to be under eighteen, and I'll be careful not to get caught this time. You say it's a crime. I say it only makes good sense.*

Sound familiar?

Sincerely,
Harrison Franklin

p.s. No, our father never touched me. He was bad, but not that bad. Clearly, in your case, the seed does not fall far from the tree. Stop f---ing that boy. You're doing to him what Daddy did to you. How the children suffer when adults cross that line. The suffering never ends, Elaine. They carry the suf-fering to their graves.

HERE ENDETH THE TESTAMENT OF THE APOCRYPHA

V. Testament of Exile

Book of Ezekiel 4:13
And the Lord said, Even thus shall the children of Israel
eat their defiled bread among the Gentiles, whither I will drive them.

The Freshman

Jedediah Witherspoon, "Reverend Jed" as he was called, held court every day at noon in the Plaza of the Americas, a tree-lined public forum and major thoroughfare on the campus of the University of Florida, and as the students passed through he accosted them like a twentieth-century Samuel.

To a couple holding hands: "Your parents sent you here to make grades, not babies!"

To a long-haired man drinking beer from a paper bag: "God has a new weapon for dealing with the slothful—it's called Ronald Ray-gun. Zap! Zap!"

To the Krishnas serving vegetarian meals in the plaza and their potential recruits: "Heed not the false prophet! God is no cow!"

The reverend's doggedness, which reminded Elwyn of himself before he had sinned, never failed to attract a sizeable crowd. Unfortunately, many of the other students came only to make sport of his ministry. Some of them called him Big Black Jed.

One young man went so far as to wear blackface makeup and a suit similar to the reverend's, then, positioning himself a few feet to the left of the fiery evangelist, proceeded to shadow him throughout the sermon.

When Reverend Jed raised his Bible to heaven, the young man raised his.

When Reverend Jed fell to his knees to cry "Hosanna!" the young man knelt also, like a mime in training.

When Reverend Jed pointed at two men holding hands—"God has a new weapon for dealing with the sodomite!"—the crowd exploded with laughter, for his blackface twin had beaten him to the punch line.

"Ronald Ray-gun. Zap! Zap!" said the young man, aiming his forefinger.

Reverend Jed, set on edge from hours of fruitless evangelizing among the cackling throng, dropped his Bible and his pacifist stance and approached the boy.

Sensing the danger, Reverend Jed's daughter ran and thrust herself between the scrawny student and her father, a man of great height and girth, whose other nickname was "The Goliath of God."

A somber-faced young woman in white tennis shoes and a shapeless black dress, Sister Donna restrained Reverend Jed with a hand on his shoulder. "Daddy," she reminded, "other sheep need tending."

The Bible in his hand again, the angry black preacher barked after the boy—"The wicked flee when no man pursueth, but the righteous are bold as a lion!"—and he and his daughter went back to evangelizing and soliciting donations from the jeering, foolish throng.

"But now," lamented Elwyn, "I am numbered among the foolish."

Six weeks into his freshman year and already he had gone back twice to be with Sister Morrisohn. It seemed they couldn't spend enough time together.

Last trip, after he kissed his family goodbye and got into his car laden with clean laundry and Tupperware containers of his mother's fried chicken and homemade cookies, he drove north on the turnpike forty miles before suddenly crossing the median and making a U-turn.

When he got back to Sister Morrisohn, she fell into his arms crying, "Elwyn. Elwyn, my darling."

Peeling off her clothes.

And his.

Up before the morning sun, he stumbled into the bathroom, braced himself against the sink, peered into the mirror at his shameless sinner's face, his shameless erection.

He got back to Gainesville at 1:35 p.m., five minutes late to his calculus class, and as the professor lectured he slept facedown in his textbook and dreamt dreams of a sexual nature.

In Gainesville, Elwyn took care to avoid those who knew him as a Christian from back home. Upon their approach, he pedaled down many a wrong street and ducked into stores he had no intention of entering, looking, always looking, the other way. He was indeed a backslider. But, he reasoned, a backslider is less evil than a hypocrite.

Scripture says the hypocrite is a foul smell in the nostrils of God, but Christ is married to the backslider.

The word of God is the word of God.

* * *

"I am naked in bed with my fingers in my p---y. Come home. For just one day. Come see how it misses you."

"Too much schoolwork."

"You always have too much schoolwork."

"I was home two weeks ago."

"Do you love me?"

"I call you every night."

"A girl likes to hear her guy say it when he's so far away."

"Elaine . . ."

"Please."

"I love you," he told her, though he wished he did not mean it. Life would be so much easier if he did not mean it.

"I believe you, my love, but you're so far away."

Yes, he thought, but not far enough.

On the third floor of Rawlings Hall, everyone had a nickname.

Brain Dead was a sixth-year engineering major, who would never graduate until he passed his freshman composition classes. He couldn't string together two coherent sentences, he often omitted verbs, and a first grader could spell better. On the other hand, Brain Dead could calculate the square roots of complex equations in his head without use of pencil or calculator.

Brain Dead's best friend was a sunburned freshman, Squeak, who was named for his voice, which was indeed a squeak.

Squeak and Brain Dead taught Elwyn to play poker and he stayed up many nights defending his plastic tumbler of pennies from them. He was not enthusiastic about gambling, which he knew was a sin, but he was trying to fit in.

"Woe unto thee, thou backsliders!" Squeak squeaked, laying down a flush. He picked up the *Go Gators* cap they used as the pot for their penny-ante games, poured the coins out onto the table, and drew them to him with arms outstretched in mimicry of the great shepherd reclaiming his lost sheep. "Render unto Caesar that which is Caesar's."

"The rich just get richer," Brain Dead complained, downing a shot of Captain Morgan.

"That's right," Squeak squeaked with an arrogant nod. Squeak's father ran a Pepsi distributorship in Ann Arbor. They held their games in his private suite where even the resident assistant didn't enter without knocking first, which gave them enough time to hide the beer and rum under the bed.

Squeak passed Elwyn the deck. "It's your deal. What's your game, Preacher?"

"Preacher?" Elwyn had a confused look on his face. "Where'd you get that?"

"Aren't you a preacher, dude?"

"Not me."

"You're not a preacher?" the others chimed in: Brain Dead, A-T-O Joe, Punching-bag Brown, and Elwyn's roommate, whom everyone called Gypsy, not because he was a brilliant sophomore cellist with the university symphony who could be heard late at night practicing Franz Liszt's "Hungarian Rhapsody," but because he had inherited a pair of strangely protruding eyebrows and an olive complexion from his Syrian mother.

Elwyn laughed. "What would make you think I'm a preacher?"

They all seemed reluctant to speak, except for Squeak, the rich boy, who pointed out, "Things. Little things."

"Like what?" Elwyn, in his nervousness, sent his neatly stacked pennies flying with an elbow jerk. "What things?"

He did not go to church. He kept his Bible and tracts stashed in his briefcase. He took great care in the way he handled the letters he wrote weekly to Pastor, Sister Morrisohn, his grandmother, and his parents. No envelope was ever left unsealed so that its contents might be perused, *except* for Sister Morrisohn's, which were addressed to *Elaine* and mailed in lavender stationery covered flagrantly with flowers and hearts, evidence to all that he had a lover and was, therefore, worldly.

Perhaps I should let them read her most recent epistle, he smugly mused.

My Dearest Elwyn,

It has been a week since we made love, a week of the jitters. Do I love you, or am I horny? I'm up to a pack a day, and I'm sure your grandmother's on to me. In missionary circle Monday night, she announced, staring right at me, "I smell smoke, but I don't see the fire!" Will she always hate me? Brother Suggs proposed again. Smile. I love only you. I'm touching myself as I write this.

"Things like that," said Squeak, indicating the scattered pennies.

"Don't get upset, dude. It's just a nickname. Chill out," said Gypsy, the peacemaker. "Lay off him, Squeak."

Elwyn, laughing a fake, good-natured laugh, got down on his knees to collect his fallen pennies.

But Squeak kept at it: "You don't drink, you don't smoke, you don't curse, you don't get laid . . ."

Gilly Gorilla, the discus thrower, taught him to play table tennis, and then she ran up an impressive string of victories against him.

Sixty-six straight.

She taught him the rules of chess also, but in a few days he was playing her to a draw. Four draws in a row.

"Pretty soon I'll be beating you," he told her, not so modestly.

The hypercompetitive Gilly Gorilla smiled evilly. "You think so?"

The game was called "chess for beers": each chugged a beer from a six-pack, they played a game of speed chess, and the loser (Elwyn, two in a row) chugged the remaining four beers. It was the first and last time he ever imbibed strong drink, the first and last time he ever missed a day of class because of a hangover.

The Faithful do not drink alcohol, which is a sin.

Gilly Gorilla rolled him onto her lap and forced through his lips a mouthful of black coffee. He gagged when he tasted it and sat up, spitting. "How can people drink this mess?"

The Faithful do not drink coffee, which is a sin.

"What you need is more beer. Strange as it sounds, beer is the best cure for a hangover," she explained, pressing his head back down in her lap.

"Forgive me, Lord." His stomach still felt like someone had sanded it. "No more beer. Ever."

"And you call yourself a man."

"But really, what does drinking have to do with it? Samson never drank, and he was the strongest man in the world."

"Man?" Gilly Gorilla flexed her biceps impressively. "I am Samson."

"You're certainly more man than I am," Elwyn wisecracked.

She was strong and she wore a crew cut. Elwyn liked Gilly Gorilla, but the Faithful shunned homosexuality, which is a sin.

She grabbed him by the testicles and made him cry "uncle."

Punching-bag Brown, the only other black male on the third floor of

Rawlings Hall, often accompanied Elwyn to the piano room in the basement.

Punching-bag was a musical prodigy. Every time Elwyn got up, Punching-bag sat down and played almost note for note whatever Elwyn had been playing: Beethoven, Chopin, even impromptu gospel numbers that he made up.

"I never took a lesson in my life," he informed.

He had earned his nickname at an inner-city high school in Tampa, where he never won a fight against the thugs who harassed him daily. He had also never backed down from them even though his nose was twice broken and several teeth were knocked out.

"The pain isn't so bad," he explained, "and after a while, they've got to stop hitting you."

"Why fight if you can't win?"

"If you keep fighting, you always win. I graduate college next term. Most of them are in jail. Some of them are even dead."

"You have an incomparable ear for chords, Punching-bag. You have the courage of Daniel. You would make a great warrior for the Lord," Elwyn told him.

"Who says I'm not?" Punching-bag replied. "I'm Catholic."

The Faithful shun Catholics, who worship idols, which is a sin.

K-Sarah, the sunshine blonde, walked into the common lounge in a sleeveless blouse, a miniskirt, and heels. She slugged vodka straight from the bottle until she was drunk and fell asleep on the couch with her skinny limbs splayed every which way.

A-T-O Joe and Squeak, who had been watching, descended upon her.

Squeak lifted K-Sarah's blouse with a finger. "Jee-sus. I told you she wasn't wearing a bra. Check out the nippleage on these healthy danglers."

"She's out cold," said A-T-O Joe, with his hand on her knee. "Oh, grandmother, what nice legs you have."

"The better to wrap around your neck with, my dear," answered Squeak. "What a slut."

K-Sarah's pouty red lips parted and she snored.

It was 3 in the morning, and Elwyn and the perverts were the only ones left in the common lounge. They winked and made funny faces at him as they fondled the sleeping K-Sarah. He frowned his disapproval.

A-T-O Joe hoisted up her miniskirt, exposing her pristine underwear. "Oh, grandmother, what pretty panties you have."

"The better to pull down for you, my dear."

A-T-O Joe laughed, "Hehehe."

"Hehehe," answered Squeak, with his hand under her blouse.

Pouty-lipped K-Sarah snored contentedly.

The vodka bottle on the table beside her was half-empty. The vodka bottle was half-full. The word of God is the word of God. Elwyn got up and stepped over to them.

"Shusssh, don't wake her," Squeak told Elwyn. Then he turned to A-T-O Joe and said, "Hey, let's go get the cameras and take a few incriminating pictures. Hehehe."

A-T-O Joe sprang to his feet. "Hehehe. Great idea. Watch her for us till we get back, Preacher."

Elwyn lifted the slight K-Sarah and bore her away.

Behind him came, "F---king a**hole. Bring back our slut. Hehehe."

In her room he discovered black walls spangled with white stars, an autographed poster of Mr. Spock, a *Star Trek* floor mat spread before her bed. When he set her down on the bed, her eyes yawned opened.

"Preacher? Where is he?"

"Who?"

"The guy I was waiting for. The Alpha Pi guy." K-Sarah, a pre-med major, was what they called "easy." They had all witnessed it. She would meet a guy. They would talk. They would end up in her room. Then she would meet another guy. The Alpha Pi guy was after the tutor, after the senior English major, after the T.A., after the fat guy, after the old guy, after the quarterback. "His name is Jim."

Elwyn sat down beside her. "Maybe you should get some sleep. You're kind of drunk." He smoothed the hair off her forehead and tried to get her to lie down. He was careful where he placed his hands. He was a gentleman about it.

Tears were rolling from her eyes. He handed her tissue from her nightstand. She blew her nose and then dabbed at her eyes. "He never showed up."

"It's okay. Maybe he's not worth it."

"Maybe not. They never are," she slurred. She looked at her closed door. She looked at him. She looked at him with eyes that were drunk but inquiring. "What are you doing in my room, Preacher?"

He stammered embarrassedly, "You kind of fell asleep out there. You were kind of exposed. I brought you in so you could go to sleep."

"That was nice of you. How respectful you are."

"Thank you."

"You're welcome, Jim."

"No, I'm Elwyn."

"I know who you are, Preacher," she giggled. "I'm not that drunk. I know the difference between black and white. You're not the first black guy who's made a pass at me."

Elwyn raised his hands in alarm. "I would never do that. I swear."

"I'm just kidding. Can't you take a joke?" she laughed.

"It's not a very good joke."

"I think it is."

"I think you should go to sleep now. Goodnight." He got up to leave.

She waved her fingers. "Night night."

"Night night."

The drunk girl said, "But I can't sleep in these clothes."

Before he could stop her, she had flung off her blouse, kicked off her shoes, and unzipped her skirt.

He had seen enough.

He dashed to the door, but when she called to him, he turned.

His ears burned as she made another one of her not-so-funny jokes. It was kind of a request, or an invitation.

Elwyn answered, "No."

She said, "Why not? Because you're a preacher or because you're scared?"

But the glass was half-empty and half-full and the word of God is the word of God and her exposed bosom, though not as full as Sister Morrisohn's, was attractive in its own way, and God is a good God, God is a forgiving God, God knows that we are only human and he had never kissed any woman but Sister Morrisohn, and his breathing was shallow, every nerve in his body on fire for this Jezebel.

But he said, "You need to sleep. You're drunk."

"Que será, será," K-Sarah said, which was all she had learned, she claimed, in four years of high school Spanish.

He stood by the door, shamefaced.

She flashed her startling green eyes. "I'm drunk. But tomorrow night I'll be sober, Preacher."

She lay on the bed, her pert breasts pointing straight up to the star-spangled ceiling. He watched by the door until she was snoring. Then he drew a sheet over her body and left her room.

He prayed for forgiveness.

He did not pray for strength to resist temptation.

"Did you touch her?"

"No."

"Are you telling me the truth?"

"You know me."

"Do you like this girl?"

"No."

"Then why did you put yourself in that situation?"

"She was being taken advantage of by the worst kind of perverts. It was the Christian thing to do."

"And you didn't touch her."

"I told her to go to sleep . . . She's in there sleeping now, safe from those two fools."

"They know a harlot when they see one. Beware the daughters of Babylon."

"You are a daughter of Babylon."

"I'm not in the mood for your sarcasm."

"You're being silly."

"Don't try to play me for a fool. I'm not stupid. One day somebody's going to scoop you up. Somebody's going to marry you."

"Marriage isn't so bad. My mother and father are married." He laughed at his joke alone.

"Someday, I would like to marry again."

"Maybe someday you will."

"In the last year alone, I have turned down four proposals of marriage: Brother Whylie, Brother Meechum, Brother Gordon, and Brother Suggs."

"They're all anxious to get their hands on the Morrisohn treasure, no doubt."

"Brother Suggs has tried to place his hands on more than the treasure."

"Brother Suggs is toothless and can barely walk."

"But he knows what he wants. So do I. I want very much to marry you. There. I've said it."

Let her yap on. No way was he going to marry some old woman, no matter how much he loved her. But he knew that she knew he wouldn't say anything to hurt her either, which meant he wouldn't say anything at all.

"Am I so terribly old? Is being married to me such a horrible idea that you'd give up your religion to avoid it? Fornication is a sin. Marriage, even to an old thing like me, is not."

The trick was to let her say what she had to say. Let her get it out of her system.

"I was a good wife. Buford was older, but I never strayed. You don't know how much I loved him."

"He was a great man. I loved him too."

"But I know—and this is no trick to win points with you, Elwyn—but I know that if he were alive again and I was yet his wife, I would deceive even him to be with you. My love for you is that strong."

Offer no response. Let her get it out of her system. Let her talk it out.

"I am on my way to hell because I can't give you up, and you won't even consider the remotest possibility of marrying an old thing like me. You are the one for me. I want no other. I love you. God bless the day I f---ed you. I'm such an old thing."

"I don't see you as an *old thing*. But maybe I'm a young thing."

"Maybe you are. You're certainly ungrateful."

Like a lamp, she switched on, she switched off. He muttered to himself, "See? I should have just kept my big mouth shut."

"But you started this whole affair. It was you who wanted me. I was hot stuff. I remember the look on your face when you saw my p---y for the first time. When you first saw my breasts . . . when I pulled off my panties—all of it."

"Stop with that."

"The look on your face. You went crazy. You were like some kind of animal in a feeding frenzy. And my a**. You just loved my a**."

"Come on, now. Stop with that."

"Miss Star Trek is hot stuff now. Why don't you just go have your way with her? Go eat her p---y like I taught you."

"You are out of control."

"You used to hate eating p---y but I broke you in. It was me who did it. Now you love it."

"Elaine."

"Eat her! Go eat her! I give you permission!"

"I don't want that girl. I'm crazy to have even told you. I'll never tell you anything ever again."

"Aha! Now you're going to keep things from me. I'm down here, and you're up there. You think I'm stupid."

"What is wrong with you? I told you I'm not interested in her."

"You've done nothing but talk about her all night."

"It's you talking about her, not me."

Then she wept for two minutes. He held the phone listening. When she stopped, he said, "Are you okay, my love?"

"You better pray I don't run off with Brother Suggs, honey. A man with big feet like that has to have a huge d---k, right?"

"Wake up, Elaine. Earth to Elaine. Over."

"Honey. I like calling you honey. Honey, honey, milk and honey," she sang.

They hung up.

Elwyn went to bed thinking, So that explains it—she's drinking again.

That night, he was awakened by someone pounding on his door.

It was Gilly Gorilla.

"Preacher, get up! Something's happened to Quiet Fat Girl."

The most peculiar nickname in all of Rawlings Hall was Quiet Fat Girl.

The girl was, indeed, quiet and fat, but she probably had no idea that almost everyone in Rawlings referred to her as Quiet Fat Girl because, as far as they knew, no one in the dorm had ever actually spoken to her. No one even knew her real name, except perhaps for the women's resident assistant.

Her parents, they all assumed, were wealthy, because like Squeak on the men's side, Quiet Fat Girl lived without a roommate in one of the luxury suites. They only saw her for the few seconds it took her to get from her private suite to the main door, and from the main door back to her suite. If someone nodded to her, she nodded back. She never spoke a hello. And she was out of that door in a flash.

Elwyn opened his door.

Gilly Gorilla was gesturing wildly. Her housecoat hung unbuttoned, revealing the unnecessary brassiere over her mannish chest and the baggy white boxers. "Quiet Fat Girl's bleeding up my room. She might be dying."

"What happened?" asked his roommate Gypsy, appearing behind him.

"She knocked on my door bleeding and I took her inside." Gilly Gorilla pulled Elwyn by the arm. "Come on, Preacher. Hurry."

"Who? What?" said Gypsy, following them.

They raced down the hall to Gilly Gorilla's room, which was next door to Quiet Fat Girl's suite. A noisy crowd had gathered outside Gilly's door. A-T-O Joe's and Squeak's cameras clicked and flashed as they recorded the moment.

"Move out of the way!" Gilly Gorilla pushed through the crowd. "And give me that thing." She snatched A-T-O Joe's camera and hurled it like a discus. It hit the wall and exploded into parts, the film uncoiling like a serpent. Then she grabbed Squeak's, threw it to the ground, and stomped it to shards under her feet. "Take a picture of that!" she snarled.

Quiet Fat Girl, in her blood-soaked nightgown, lay on her side on Gilly Gorilla's Oriental throw rug, her arms hugging her waist.

Brain Dead said, "We should like maybe call an ambulance."

Brain Dead had the right idea, but Gilly Gorilla grabbed one side of Quiet Fat Girl and Elwyn grabbed the other and a few minutes later she was lying on the backseat of his old Mazda.

Gilly Gorilla sat in the back with her. Gypsy sat up front with him.

"It hurts," the girl said.

"We're almost there," soothed Gilly Gorilla. "Can't you go any faster, Preacher?"

"I'm going as fast as I can." They were on Archer Road. Shands Memorial Hospital was just over the next hill.

There came a sound from the back.

"Oh crap, she puked. It's a mess back here, Preacher."

"F---ing gross," gasped Gypsy. He pinched his nose and stuck his head out the window.

"I'm sorry," Quiet Fat Girl said. "I can't hold it back. Gaggh."

"It's a mess back here."

"Look what I did to your car. Gaggh."

Elwyn said, "Don't worry about the car. As long as you're all right."

"Gaggh. I did it again. Your poor car."

Elwyn glanced up in his rearview mirror. Quiet Fat Girl's head was on Gilly Gorilla's shoulder. They were both covered in vomit. "Stop worrying about the car. It's a car. What is your name?"

"Nicole . . . Watson."

"I'm going to say a prayer for you, Nicole." They roared over the top of the hill. The hospital was two blocks away. "No matter what happens, God still cares about you."

"Pray for me, Preacher. Pray."

Elwyn prayed for Nicole Watson, the quiet fat girl, who, doctors would later tell them, had actually been the quiet pregnant girl before she had thrown the infant down the garbage chute in the women's bathroom of Rawlings Hall. A vagrant would find the fetal corpse in a garbage dumpster two days later.

In a week, Nicole's belongings would vanish from her suite, and all that they would ever know about her they'd get from the local newspapers, which made Nicole's case front-page news for nearly a month. She was never charged with murder, for the baby had been stillborn.

Her father, however, was arrested for the part he played in originating the drama.

"Her own father!" said Gypsy, flinging down the newspaper. "And wouldn't you know he was one of my people. Greater f---ing Church of God."

Elwyn picked up the newspaper and put it in the wastepaper basket. "Don't make a hasty generalization. Not all preachers are like that."

"Find me a good one. They're all lechers."

"Not where I come from."

He was suddenly proud of his background. No one at the Church of Our Blessed Redeemer Who Walked Upon the Waters had ever molested a child. The Faithful protected their children.

"To the Faithful, children are sacred, for they are the future of our church. They are the hope of the world."

"You are amazing. How can you live with yourself?"

Gypsy went to his cello, which was leaned up against his desk, picked up the bow, and began to play "Amazing Grace."

Elwyn didn't suspect that Gypsy was being ironic. He found the music to be beautiful.

It occurred to him quite unexpectedly that he had been only sixteen when Sister Morrisohn and he first made love.

One could argue that she had molested him.

But no. That was different. What they had was different.

A single scented candle was burning, and the stars on the ceiling were treated to glow.

She was naked on the bed, one leg dangling over the edge, the other one doubled under her. He went to her and she pulled him down by the shoulders, her breath tingling warm against his neck.

"I'm not drunk tonight, see?"

"It's this kind of thing that sends a soul straight to hell."

"Preach it, brother. Preach it."

As they kissed, he felt his clothes becoming loosened on his body. Her hands knew their business. He was captivated by her agile, darting tongue.

They broke the kiss and she lay back on the bed. He climbed over her and felt the tug as she yanked down his pants. His shirt was already gone.

She said, "You're way cool, you know that? All you need is a sense of humor."

"What are you looking for, K-Sarah?"

"Whatever you happen to be right now."

She passed her hands over his chest. His hands gripped her slender bottom.

"Ooh," she said.

"Ooh," he said.

She was the right age. She was pretty. Her eyes glowed green as her glow in the dark stars.

Maybe he was scared. Maybe he was afraid of where this was going. It was going pretty fast, and he said, "What about the Alpha Pi guy?"

"Forget him. He's a loser. What about you, Preacher? What about you?"

K-Sarah grabbed him. As skinny as she was, she was strong enough to roll him over and climb on top. His erection was rock hard, but he was nervous. He was, frankly, scared. He had never been with anyone else. He looked down at his erection and saw it buck against her flat little stomach. She grabbed it with both hands and massaged it against the damp blond coil of her pubic hair.

He said to her, "If we get into something, you must promise not to see him anymore."

She rubbed his erection against her pubic hair. He took a deep breath. She rubbed the head of his erection against the moist lips of her sex. Ohmygod, he thought, I'm doing it. I'm really doing it.

She looked at him suspiciously. "Get into something?"

"A relationship," he explained. "We have to have rules. It kills me to see you dress so immodestly. And you must not drink or smoke anymore. Your body is the Temple of the living God. You've got to have standards."

"Are you like some kind of weirdo serial killer, Preacher?"

"What do you mean?"

"This is a joke. An example, at last, of your sense of humor."

"I want you to be my woman. You've got to have standards."

She released his erection and climbed off. When he came to her, she pointed to his clothes.

"Que será, será, Preacher."

"I don't think you understand—"

"I understand that you're very weird."

His mouth fell open. He just wanted to explain.

She saw the look and said, "It's all right. I still think you're cool, just a little bit weird."

She pecked him a sweet one on the cheek. "When I need prayer, I'll call you, okay? Prayer is important too."

Thus, she kicked him out of her room and out of her life.

And then the word, as it always does, spread quickly.

In the days that followed, everyone began to change toward him. They avoided him, or treated him with exaggerated deference when they couldn't avoid, crossing themselves and bowing. Stuff like that.

He was accused of Christianity, and there was no greater threat to the college student's hedonistic lifestyle than the love of God.

Even Gypsy thought him saved, his laughter winging up from the bottom bunk.

"You didn't boink K-Sarah? Everyone boinks K-Sarah. Even I boinked K-Sarah."

"I used to be a Christian," Elwyn confessed, "but I'm a backslider now."

"I hate preachers."

"But preachers preach the word of God—"

"My father thinks *he* is God!" Elwyn could hear the angry thunk, thunk from below, Gypsy punching his mattress. "He used to beat my thighs with a broom handle because I fell asleep in church. I was just a kid, but I was supposed to go to church seven, eight, nine times a week without falling asleep? Each time the church doors opened, there I was getting out of that f---ing Buick. How do you fight against God?"

Thunk, thunk, thunk.

"Gypsy?"

"My mother knew about his women. I'm sure everyone in the church knew about his f---ing women. But when I found someone, what happened? More broom handle. Whack, whack, whack."

Thunk, thunk, thunk.

"Sins of the flesh, he said. Whack, whack, whack."

Thunk, thunk, thunk.

"He called me a sodomite."

Elwyn watched as Gypsy got out of bed and paced back and forth in the dark.

"The worst part was that I loved him. I believed in him. I thought there was something wrong with me because he had chased this boy away from me. Now I realize he was the love of my life."

"A boy? I thought—"

"If you could think, Preacher, you'd curse God and die."

Gypsy lit a cigarette and opened the blinds. He sat in his bikini underwear with his feet propped up on his cello case. Smoking.

"Pray for me, Preacher, like you did for Quiet Fat Girl."

Elwyn put the pillow over his head. His roommate was a sodomite. Smoking was not permitted in the dorms. Elwyn particularly disliked smoking. The Faithful do not smoke, which is a sin.

"My prayer won't do any good," Elwyn said.

"Reverse hypocrisy. You're a sinner accused of Christianity." Somehow the whole situation had put her in a cheerful mood. "I find it all very amusing, don't you?"

"I don't think you'd laugh if you could see how messed up he is."

He glanced at Gypsy, asleep in his bikini underwear on the chair by his desk.

"He'll get over it. Children have a way of outgrowing bad fathers."

"I have a good father."

"Yes. Roscoe the Good. Elwyn the Lucky," she joked. "The only difference between my father and Gypsy's is that mine never set foot in church. Daddy was no Christian, but like Jesus, he sure did love the little children."

Amazingly her voice still had its cheer.

"My checkered past began so long ago I can't even remember it. I'd always been Daddy's girl, in a manner of speaking. I had his first baby at fourteen. The day they buried my mother, Daddy slipped a hand in my pants and told me from now on I would sleep in his bed. I was her replacement. So I cooked, cleaned, raised my little brother. I didn't sleep alone in a bed again until I was eighteen. A hospital bed. *That* baby didn't survive."

"Maybe it was a good thing . . . I mean, to have a baby with your own father."

"*Two* babies with my father. Harrison."

"Harrison?"

"But he doesn't know."

She cried for a half hour, then hung up, she said, to save on the long distance.

When she called back, Elwyn tried to comfort her, but she told him, "Things are the way they are and it will never change. Kids are defenseless from their parents. You expect your parents to not hurt you, but sometimes they do. The good thing is you get to grow up. You can outgrow a bad daddy. I love life now, thanks to Buford and you, my love. Your friend Gypsy will be all right. He's got to learn to start seeing himself for who he is, not for what his father says he is. You can't let people define you. You've got to define yourself. Otherwise you'll be a child all your life."

"Poor guy."

"Don't worry too much. He'll be all right. He's talented and smart. He'll find the right path. Just keep him at a safe distance."

"I sleep in my pajamas."

"Wise. And get out of Sodom first chance you get."

"He wouldn't try anything with me. I'm bigger than him."

"I'm sure you are bigger. Hmmm," she said. "It's amazing how in such a short time he's rubbed off so much on you—gambling, drinking, and now sodomy too, big boy."

"Ha. The way I put it on you, you of all people should know I am not gay."

"Not yet."

"What!"

"These gays, they prey on innocent minds like yours. You'll have an erection one night and he'll offer to help you out. It will feel good, but you'll feel guilty afterward, and he'll tell you that it's not you, it's him. He'll tell you that coming in his mouth is no different than masturbating."

"You make me so sick with your dirty talk. One minute you're playing with yourself over the phone, the next you're calling me a sissy. What kind of girlfriend are you? You should be nice to me."

"You sound like a sissy right now. You should hear yourself. What an impact this kid is having on you. Move out of there right away. Save yourself."

"Ha-ha, very funny. I'm straight. No one can make me into what I'm not."

"It happened to me."

"You're lying."

"No I'm not."

"Shut up."

"It's true."

"What are you saying?"

"I can't talk about it. I'm too ashamed. It is pure Sodom and Gomorrah, but believe me it did happen. Just like you, I thought I was strong enough to fight her off."

"Some woman raped you?"

"Seduced."

"Is that why you like oral sex so much?"

"Please stop being an idiot. It does not become you."

"Two women. It's so gross."

"Regrettable maybe, but gross, I don't know."

"You liked it . . . ?"

"I refuse to talk about it. Just drop it. Shut up. Stop harassing me about it. You won't listen to me anyhow. You think you know everything. I'm forty-four years old but you won't listen to me, so I'll let you learn the hard way," she said. "Seduction sneaks up on you, gay or straight. Having your body held feels good, Elwyn, gay or straight. We all want to be held. None of us wants to be alone. Loneliness is the worst . . . Elwyn?"

He did not answer.

"I've often thought how interesting it is to hear Christians, men, say they long to be touched by Jesus. It is strangely sexual, don't you think? They say they want to be held by Him, to be kissed by Him, to be touched by Him. I guess it makes sense. You were never held by your father when you were a child and feeling afraid or hurt? His touch comforted you just like your mother's did. It didn't matter that he was a man and she was a woman. It's called human contact and our bodies respond to it. It kind of works like that with sex too. You are between sleep and wake, and I touch you, and you become aroused. I bring you to orgasm and you turn around and discover that it was not mine, but a man's hand that had touched you. Your penis is just a piece of flesh that responds in a certain way to touch, just like your heart. Elwyn?"

He did not answer.

She said, "I have known of men, real men, tough guys, athletes and such, who will let a homosexual blow them or who will take the homosexual from behind. As long as they do not blow him or let him take them from behind, they feel that they themselves are not homosexual.

It happens all the time in prison. These men consider themselves to be straight. Elwyn. What do you think of a woman, a terribly weak and terribly lonely woman, who allows another woman to caress her and kiss her and to live with her for a while as a man and wife? Would you call a woman like that gay because she thought, for a time, that she was in love with a woman?"

He did not answer.

"Elwyn?"

He did not answer because he had hung up the phone.

"Never, ever, ever hang up on me, do you hear me? It is beyond rude. We need to have this out."

"You don't want me to have any friends at all. You don't want me to have any friends but you. You're choking me. You're strangling me. You make up these stories to control me. A Christian is not gay because he loves Jesus. And women should not lie together as man and wife. You're just rationalizing everything to justify satanic acts. You are of the devil. You are demon filled. You need prayer."

"You do have a sissy for a roommate."

"Goodnight, Elaine!"

"Have none of your other friends said anything about it? Two handsome, musically talented boys bunking in the same room. You like that word bunking, huh? Bunking. Bunking. Are you on the top *bunk* or the bottom *bunk*?"

"Goodnight, Jezebel. Sleep tight and alone. You need prayer."

"Bunking, bunking, bunking, bunking. Bunk me. Bunk me."

"I'm hanging up this phone."

"Don't you dare hang up on me, little boy!"

"Bye, Elaine."

"Aha, are you saying bye or *bi?*"

Elwyn hung up the phone again.

Elaine laughed herself to sleep.

She awoke the next morning drenched in tears.

He told them.

It was a horrible treachery, but Elwyn told. Sister Morrisohn had gotten to him. He had kept worrying that they would find out anyway and then think that maybe he was gay too. So he told them that Gypsy was gay.

But it backfired.

No one else would have Gypsy as a roommate now that they knew what he was, but neither would they accept Elwyn, the blabbermouth.

So they were stuck with each other.

Thus ostracized, Elwyn slipped back into old habits. He prayed publicly three times a day. He carried his Bible wherever he went. He handed out tracts feverishly. Here he was, a total backslider, striking up a friendship with the Reverend Jedediah Witherspoon, who was glad to have him join the Holy Roller team.

"I see the spirit of the Most High God emanating from you. To-gether, we shall do great things for the Lord, young man. I won't hold your faith against you."

Elwyn didn't hold Brother Witherspoon's faith against him either.

He was not a Holy Roller as were Reverend Jed and his daughter Donna, who was a first-year student at the nearby Santa Fe Community College, and he would never be. He was numbered among the Faith-ful for life, Praise God. But when the dark and evil world is closing in, Christians of whatever faith must band together. Plus, the nearest branch of the Church of Our Blessed Redeemer Who Walked Upon the Waters was a two-hour drive away in Jacksonville.

So now, while Reverend Jed preached at the Plaza of the Americas, Donna and Elwyn distributed tracts and Bibles and collected whatever money the students journeying to and from class were willing to give.

At the insistence of Donna, he started an interfaith Bible study group on Thursday nights in the bowling alley of the J. Wayne Reitz Student Union. Thursday was league night, which meant more souls to save.

On Wednesdays, Donna and Elwyn put on orange T-shirts that said *Gators for Christ!* and rode their bikes and handed out Bibles in Porter's Quarters, the two-and-a-half square miles of clapboard houses where the city's poorest lived in the shadow of crime and vice. They even entered the park where young men in enormous gold chains and expensive sneakers exchanged Ziploc bags of drugs for money, jewelry, and sex. They sang hymns and ministered to the young men, though not one of them that Elwyn knew of ever showed up at the Bible study he invited them to.

One morning there was a message etched on the last stall in the men's room: *GYPSY'S AIDS CLINIC.*

Missives of hate were slipped under their door nightly.

Faggot Go Home!!!
Wanted, tutor for Sodomy 101
UFagsSUCK!

Gypsy was excluded from the poker games in Squeak's suite. Only Punching-bag Brown remained loyal to him. They played duets from time to time in the piano room.

"I don't see what all the fuss is about. Gay or not, I still like him," Punching-bag said.

So did Elwyn. He had only been doing his Father's will when he exposed Gypsy as a homosexual.

Whenever Elwyn offered him a tract, Gypsy sucked his teeth and said derisively, "F---ing church mouse!"—as though it were entirely Elwyn's fault that everyone in Rawlings now called him Sweet Gypsy Rose.

Now they called Elwyn Reverend Gator.

One night, Gypsy came back to their room with his laundry, a black eye, and no attempt at explanation.

He got on the phone and Elwyn overheard him filing a police report for assault and battery.

He heard the names Michael Kraft and Joseph Manzetti—who were Squeak and A-T-O Joe.

The first week in November, Elwyn moved off campus and into the small bedroom at the back of the Witherspoon home. The rent was low ($75 a month) because he had agreed to give Donna piano lessons on Saturday afternoons.

He was not a Holy Roller, but since Reverend Jed and Donna had proven kind to him, Elwyn ignored Pastor's warning and attended Sunday services at the Holy Roller Tabernacle of Faith Gainesville Chapter with them. The real difference, he soon discovered, between the Holy Rollers and the Church of Our Blessed Redeemer Who Walked Upon the Waters was not so much the speaking in tongues, but the noise. The Rollers used tambourines and drums along with their piano and organ.

Then there was Donna, hands raised, eyes rolled up into her head, waiting for the spirit to descend. When it arrived, she tried to pull him along with her.

"Come on, Elwyn, let Him into your heart. He wants to use you."

Elwyn wouldn't budge from his seat. He wasn't into all of that showboating.

So off she would go, shouting, "Atallabula, Atallabula," dancing light-footed down the aisle.

They couldn't make him carry on like that. He was not a Holy Roller.

Donna grabbed his hand as they prayed at the start of a piano lesson one afternoon. She leaned against him, smelling of Ivory soap and strawberry jam on toast, which she ate constantly. God's food—bread and berries—is how she explained her sweet diet. She and her father were vegetarians. Elwyn thought she was going to kiss him when she pressed her cheek against his and said: "I want you to teach me my favorite song."

The hymnal was opened to page 39, "I Find No Fault in Him."

He shook his head. "You haven't progressed that far. It's only your fourth lesson."

"I have faith in you. You can teach me anything." She raised holy hands. "Atallabula, Atallabula, Sa Sa Sa, Atallabula," she chanted in that unknown tongue, which this time came from somewhere deep in her breast.

Donna was not exactly pretty, not exactly ugly. Her teeth, though uneven, were white and clean. Underneath her baggy dresses, from what he could see, was a lean, hard body. Her face was long and serious looking—she was no beauty—but when she smiled it was so genuine his heart melted. She was on fire for the Lord, and you couldn't want a better, more compassionate friend.

Elwyn found himself wondering what it would be like to lie with Donna on their wedding night.

It would be interesting. It would be blessed.

* * *

"Donna held my hand today."

"Two whole weeks. I'm surprised she waited so long to make her move, Reverend Gator. The question now is how you feel about her."

"I have to admit that there are some things about her that I like. She's a good Christian and one of the kindest people I know."

"Kiss my a**."

"In fact, I am happy and content to do mission work with her. With her, I do the Lord's work and I am happy. With you, I never do the Lord's work. It always ends up in bed because our relationship is vile and carnal. I have never had a sexual thought about Donna. She would make a good Christian wife—if I were interested in her, I mean."

Her voice came back without its usual cheer: "I should have guessed it would happen eventually. You're living in her house. If you were living in my house, they couldn't keep me off you. Reverend Witherspoon, that sly fox, is setting you up to be his son-in-law. Good Christian wife my a**."

"You're too cynical. The Witherspoons are the kindest people in the world and wholly devoted to the Lord's work."

"I am no stranger to the good Reverend Witherspoon, my dear un-informed Elwyn. He was famous, more like infamous, in the '60s. He had a big hippie church up somewhere in Colorado. Jesus freaks. They were for peace, love, and marijuana. He had a TV show that came on for a half hour each week, and a catch phrase: God has a new weapon for HOPE—it's called DOPE. He lived in a mansion. He got busted for fleecing his flock of a million dollars. He went to prison for tax evasion. Lost his mansion, his ministry, his money. Everything. Now he's a Holy Roller street-corner evangelist. Give me a break."

"I don't believe you."

"It was in the newspapers. Go look it up, college boy."

"I don't even care if you're right. I'm talking about what they are now. They are good people."

"They are looking for a husband."

"I told you, we're platonic!"

"She's eighteen and ugly, and she isn't going anywhere anytime soon. Then along comes you. Devout, talented, naïve. God has a new weapon for HOPE—it's called a BIG DOPE. Wake up, you big dope. If you want to leave me, then go ahead. But don't let some homely preacher's daughter set you up for a shotgun wedding. That would just be too clichéd."

"You are so paranoid. That was all in the past. They're in the church now."

"Just because they're in the church doesn't mean they're not human. Look at us. We are in the church."

She always brought up their affair when she couldn't get him to see the world as she saw it of late: that secretly everyone was selfish, evil, and crafty.

"You just can't face the facts. I'm growing up. I'm outgrowing you. I need to be with people my own age."

"Why do I waste my time trying to protect you? I should just let you marry that pit bull–looking, frigid, ugly, stupid, ignorant, bad-breath heifer."

"What would be so wrong with marrying Donna Witherspoon?"

"Monkey children."

"Goodnight to you."

"Don't you dare hang up on me!"

"You don't own me! I'll hang up when I feel like!"

"Elwyn, I am with child."

"Hehehe. Don't try that one on me. Talk about cliché. You're too old, Gran'ma. Hehehe."

"Don't call me that."

He laughed again. Squeak's laugh, hehehe.

She waited until he'd had his fun, and then she said, "Didn't I seem a little heavier to you when you visited last week? My mood swings? Don't you see how we've been fighting lately? That's not normal for us."

She paused to let it sink in. It sank in.

"You called me Gran'ma. What if I told you that in seven months you are going to be the father of Gran'ma's child?"

It sank in deep.

"Elwyn, I'm older than your mother! I can't wait to hear Pastor read from the prayer sheet, Pray that Elwyn and Sister Morrisohn's child be born healthy. Amen, amen. We screwed up big, Elwyn. I know the exact night it happened too. Remember that night? You just hate to wear a condom. You have too much faith in the pull-out. That is not proper birth control, young man. I knew one day it would happen. I warned you."

It sank in that his life was over.

"But I should have known better at my age. Oh the shame when everybody finds out."

This was the end. He was dead.

"We can't have an abortion because killing is a sin and we're Christians. You're going to be a father, Elwyn. I don't expect you to marry me because you're so young. But this poor baby . . . it'll be so alone . . . I'll be so alone . . . I don't blame you if you never want to see me again. You're a man. You were just doing what men do. My body was there, and you were a man. I'm not asking you to do the Christian thing. I'm a grown woman. I'll deal with it somehow."

He was dead. Dead. *Here lies Elwyn James Parker. 1963–1982. Died of childbirth.*

She shouted into the phone, "Where are you, Elwyn? Talk to me. We have to do something."

There was only one thing that they could do, as Christians, but what would his parents say about a daughter-in-law older than they were? And his grandmother, who had caught them in the act but spared them the humiliation of open confession—this would kill her, if she didn't kill them first.

"I don't know what to do."

"Time to grow up. Time to start acting like a man."

". . . Yes."

"Time to stop acting like you can just use people's bodies and not bear the consequences of your actions. This is what you get for using me."

". . . Yes."

"You must marry me."

". . . Yes . . . I know."

"You know?"

". . . I have to marry you."

"But you don't sound happy. This is our baby. We must not hate it. You will be happy with me. I will make you happy. I'll let you finish school. I'll pay for everything. You'll never have to worry about anything. Then when you finish college and come home to us, everything will be wonderful. Please don't hate me, my darling. Please don't hate our baby."

"I don't hate you or the baby. I hate myself. I got myself into this mess. Now I'm stuck with it. The wages of sin."

She gasped. "I am not the wages of your sin."

"Not you," he said. "The baby."

* * *

"Elwyn? Elwyn? I'm not pregnant," Sister Morrisohn said, cackling.

"What?"

"I'm not pregnant. But how do you feel? This is just how you're going to feel when Donna and the good reverend pull this same stunt on you. It's an old trick. It's how all the homely preachers' daughters find a husband."

He wiped a tear from his eye. "You are too much. I can't take anymore of you tonight. Bye."

"But my darling, I did it for your own good. Oh God, I love you, Elwyn. I am not the wages of your sin. Don't let Donna Witherspoon be the wages of your virtue. She's too ugly for you. She's setting you up—"

He put the phone down. He felt both anger and relief.

Mostly anger.

What he should have been feeling was sadness. But the sadness over this exchange wouldn't come for another nine years.

Nine years later, during a more somber exchange, he would have occasion to understand how much Sister Morrisohn really loved him and how much of her own happiness she had been willing to surrender to ensure his.

As it was, after Elwyn hung up that night, he went to bed feeling mostly anger.

Sister Morrisohn, for her part, had a sleepless night. In the morning, she arose and reread Harrison's letter. *Stop f---ing that boy.* Then she went to the Yellow Pages and looked up the number to the abortion clinic, called, and made the appointment.

At her breakfast table, she finished off a bottle of fine wine, and she wept terrifically.

* * *

So as not to yield to temptation, Elwyn spent the next few nights away from the Witherspoons in a hotel room. Then he formally moved out of the Witherspoon home on Saturday after he'd found a new place and an old roommate.

It surprised Gypsy.

It surprised Elwyn too, that he had asked and that Gypsy had accepted. But he had to grow up. He had to get out from under her control.

Then Gilly Gorilla, who had overheard the discussion, came between them. "The dorms suck big time. Would you kind gentlemen have room for a third?"

Now the rent would be split three ways.

God is good. God is so good.

Though he told her not to, Donna, in her shapeless black dress, insisted on helping with the move.

When everything was set down in the new place, he left Gypsy and Gilly Gorilla to finish up and he drove Donna back home and they got down on their knees and prayed together. They held hands during their prayer. Elwyn began to weep and Donna put her arm around him.

"What's the matter?" she asked. "You can tell me."

He told her about Sister Morrisohn. He told her everything. Donna began to weep. He held her. They kissed. Or rather, he kissed her. Donna the Holy Roller. Donna who spoke in tongues. He kissed Donna's tongue. Put his hand under her dress. Caressed her body. Her intact maidenhead. She cried into his lips.

It was a very good kiss. He apologized for it. The kiss. Apologized for everything. And the ugly girl arose, in her ugly black dress, and told him to leave.

He left.

She never spoke to him again after that, though they continued to see each other around campus. Whenever he saw her he would think, She is very beautiful but it is on the inside. She will make some Christian a great wife. How I wish it were me.

In the nearby town of Micanopy, they held their Christmas tryst.

Sister Morrisohn continued to smoke despite his objections, and she had him sneaking out of the room to buy her cigarettes.

The stranger approached him and said, "You're the Reverend Gator. Oh man, this is so cool. Dude, I seen you around. Would you pray for me? Man, do I need prayer."

Even in his big hat and dark glasses, they knew it was him. He laid holy hands against the forehead and prayed that the man's father survive open-heart surgery. The man thanked him and got into a car with a nervous blond woman who Elwyn doubted was his wife. By the time it occurred to Elwyn that the woman bore a striking resemblance to K-Sarah, the car had driven out of the parking lot.

He stepped in fresh chewing gum.

Angling his foot, he scraped most of it off on the edge of the side-walk. Nevertheless, it was a sticky walk back to their room, and when he got there he angrily tossed the cigarettes on the bed where Sister Morrisohn lay.

"Now what's your problem?" she asked, reaching for the pack. As she tore open the plastic wrap and tapped out a cigarette, she gestured for the ashtray, which he passed to her. She put the cigarette between her lips as she said, "I hope it's not Gypsy again."

He kicked off his gummed-up shoes. "You're not my mother."

She frowned with her eyes. "Maybe I was too harsh, but I was only trying to protect you from what I perceived as a potentially dangerous situation. You have no idea how wonderful you are. Everybody wants you." She lit her cigarette and exhaled smoke. "And get over it. It's not your problem anyway. It's not you beating on him. It's not you making his life miserable. It's his lifestyle. He chose to live like that."

Elwyn didn't respond. He went to where his kicked-off shoes had landed, collected them, and put them by the chair. He sat in the chair and removed his socks, each of which he tucked neatly into his shoes. Sister Morrisohn watched his fastidiousness with amusement. Her little neat freak. Cleanliness is next to Godliness.

"I don't hate gays. I hate their ways. I love some gays very much."

"Name one gay you love," he said glumly.

She winked and blew him a kiss. "Me."

He put his hands over his ears. "Liar. Stop messing with my head. You've never been with a woman."

She laughed and said, "Oh, Elwyn, give it a rest. You obsess over things too much. It's not your fault that Gypsy's that way. It's his choice."

"God made him that way."

She puffed mirthfully on her cigarette, launching little balloons of smoke that floated up and then disappeared into the ceiling. "It was his choice. God doesn't make you gay. Weakness makes you gay. I know from personal experience."

Elwyn shook his head at that, frowning, then said, "How do you know what God makes and what He doesn't? Are you God?"

She chuckled. "He sure has rubbed off on you. You sure do love you some Gypsy. You're better off without him. I'm not ashamed of having manipulated you to get you away from him. Leviticus 20:13. If a man also lie with mankind, as he lieth with a woman, both of them have

220 † JESUS BOY

committed an abomination: they shall surely be put to death; their blood shall be upon them—"

"You actually read the Bible? You actually read the Bible, then you drive all the way up here to put my penis in your mouth."

It didn't faze her. She said, "I like your penis in my mouth," and she kept right on puffing on her cigarette. Serenely. But Scripture is Scripture and Elwyn wanted so badly to hurt her.

"Leviticus 20:18," he said. "And if a man shall lie with a woman having her sickness—"

"Gross. Shut up!"

"—and shall uncover her nakedness; he hath discovered her fountain, and she hath uncovered the fountain of her blood: and both of them shall be cut off from among their people."

"Shut your fresh mouth. You are so gross. You are something else. That's not even in the Bible."

"Yes it is. It's the chapter you just quoted from. You should read the *whole* chapter before you try to quote Scripture with me."

"Arrogant little snot. I don't believe you."

"It's in there and we did do it. You let me uncover your fountain. You should be cut off. That's Bible. That's in there. Don't even try to act like you know the Bible better than me."

"Fresh-mouth boy. Sometimes the way you talk to me, you have no respect. There are some things that are private and should not be repeated. A girlfriend is supposed to be able to trust her boyfriend not to repeat certain things. You have a fresh mouth. You think you can talk to me any old way. You think you can just hurt me. You think I need you? I'm a grown woman. You think I don't have other options—"

"It's too cold in here." He reached up to the wall behind him and pushed the switch that controlled the air.

The cigarette bounced on her lip as she continued, "I never un-covered my fountain to you! I know the Bible just as well as you. It was something else that you would never understand, so don't even ask me about it. I was sick, I told you, but you were horny. We shouldn't have done it. But don't you go accusing me of uncovering my foun-tain, goddamn you. Not all blood is the same blood. It was something else."

"Okay. Calm down, Grandmother."

She fired, "And turn that air back up! I like it cold. I paid for the room. Put your socks back on if you don't like it. And don't call me Grandmother! What the hell is the matter with you?" She was shriek-ing. "I didn't drive all the way up here to fight with you!"

He was cowed.

He was cowed again by the fear that he would lose her. So why not lose her? She was ruining his life. Look at her smoking that cigarette. Cigarette smoking is a sin. It was all so confusing. There should be no cause for him to fear. He should want her to leave him. He got up and turned the air back up as she had commanded.

She was all his this week, this interminable week. Tomorrow was Christmas, and his parents, especially his mother, were upset that he was not at home to spend it with them. They little accepted his lame excuse: mission work.

His mother was refusing to take his calls.

"She still loves you. You know how women are," his father said. "Is it money? I've got a little savings account your mother doesn't know about— Oh why won't you come home for Christmas? It's Christmas, Elwyn."

He had no answer for his father.

Then there was the message on the answering machine left by his grandmother: "Is it just coincidence that you won't come home for the Lord's birthday, and Sister Morrisohn is supposedly spending it in Boston with her brother? I bet she's right there with you. That lying Jezebel. Beware the daughters of Babylon. If I could drive, I'd come up to Gainesville and check your mission work."

Not Gainesville, Gran'ma, Micanopy, a town not too far away, a town noted for its motels.

He shivered from the cold and said to Sister Morrisohn, "But it's really cold." He was supposed to be a man. Sex made you a man, didn't it? He felt like a little boy again with her.

"Put your sweater back on," she said, leering. She was better now. Like a light: switch on, switch off. She was patting the bed. "Or you can climb back under the sheets and do your duty."

"Is your fountain flowing again?"

"Don't piss me off, boy."

Obedience is better than sacrifice. The boy stripped to his shorts. The boy climbed back under the sheets. At least there was That. And That. And That. He put his open mouth against her neck. He thought happy thoughts. In vain.

"Okay, then, wait until I finish my cigarette," she said. "You're obviously not in the mood yet. I'll have to warm you up."

"Finish your cigarette," he grumbled. But it was a relief. Now at least he could get some sleep. He said to her, sarcastically, "Merry Christmas."

She began, "Merry Christ—" and got caught up in a fit of coughing. He let her cough some before patting her on the back. That helped a bit. Then he got her some water in a Dixie cup to drink. She said thanks afterward and lit another cigarette.

He sighed. He wanted a wife and children and happy friendships.

He wanted to be free. He had all the sex in the world he could want, but it was Christmas and he was missing his family.

He was still cold, so he embraced her, but there was no warmth in her body. He released her and pulled the sheets over his head, which helped only a little. She started coughing again. Let her cough.

Gypsy is indeed a sodomite, he thought, but I like him as much as I like Punching-bag and all of the other guys. She has no right to manipulate my feelings. This is America. I am free to like who I like. I like *her*, don't I? What could be worse than liking her? Some people are so ironic in their judgments of others. Some people are so quick to point fingers without looking at themselves first. The Lord said, He that is without sin, let him cast the first stone. She has some nerve to judge my feelings for Gypsy, she who admits to having sex with a lesbian—she who gave birth to her own brother.

She was still coughing. Her eyes were big. Fishlike. Let her cough. Let her cough until she croaks, he thought.

He hated the hell out of her at that moment. Who was she to be telling him what to do? Who was she to be controlling him? He was the man in this relationship, was he not? She should be taking orders from him. He was free to do what he wanted. He was free to do what he had already done. So why was he afraid to tell her about it? Why was he afraid to tell her that he had moved out of the Witherspoon's and into an apartment with his two new roommates, Gypsy and Gilly Gorilla?

She was coughing, and he drifted into sleep, thinking about how clever he was, thinking how he had gotten one over on her, and his sleep was bad, filled with images of hell and she was the devil and he was uncovering her fountain. He was drinking her fountain. Mouthfuls of red water. He was gulping it down. As she coughed.

When he woke up again, it was night, dark night with no lights on. She was lying on her side facing him, staring at him as she always seemed to do when she thought he wasn't looking. He would bet that she had memorized every part of his body.

She blushed because he had caught her looking. She started to turn away. He said to her, "Will you marry me?"

Water rolled out of her eyes.

He took her into his arms and said, "Will you? I mean this is stupid running around hiding like this. You're single. I'm single. I . . . I love you. I do. You make me crazy sometimes, but I love you."

She sobbed. "But—"

"I'm not ashamed of loving you. I want to marry you. Will you marry me?"

She crushed her body against his. She breathed the words yesyesyes against his face. They made love to break the bed. They made love to the break of day.

They made love like man and wife.

The Murky Jordan

Parking curbside on A1A was impossible.

This was Miami Beach, tourist season. Elwyn pulled into the parking garage of the Imperial Point Towers and pressed the secret code to raise the striped arm. The hymn playing on the car's cassette was "Stand by Me," and Sister Morrisohn was singing along with it.

"When I cross the murky Jordan, Lord, stand by me. Stand by me."

Elwyn said, "Stand by me."

Sister Morrisohn squeezed his hand. "Stand by us, Lord."

He felt a prick of fear—Yes, Lord, stand by us, stand by us now, please, as we are about to make this bold step. But when he looked down at her hand and saw the ring with the shiny stone on her finger, he regained his courage. It is the right thing to do, he told himself. The Lord is on our side this time.

He wheeled the car into an empty space and turned off the engine. He got out and opened her door like a good gentleman. He took her hands and bowed his head. He said a prayer out of force of habit. When he opened his eyes, hers were still closed. He kissed her and she opened her eyes. She wore her hair swept back. She wore a simple blue dress, the same color as his jacket. She was beautiful. He kissed her again, romantically this time.

"You're hungry," she observed.

"I'm hungry for you."

They got on the elevator and he pushed 12, his grandmother's floor.

As far as Elwyn knew, his grandmother was the only black person who lived in this Miami Beach condo. She resided there as a favor to Miss Fritz-Lev, who couldn't bear to part with her even after she had become too sickly with tired spells and diabetes to be much good as a maid. They had become friends, and Miss Fritz-Lev called Sister Cooper "Gran'ma," just like Elwyn did, and Sister Cooper called her "Miss Fritz" and referred to her as her "old lady"—even though technically this made no sense. Sister Cooper was actually five years older than Miss Fritz.

In the elevator, Elwyn prayed again, silently. He made sure that his lips weren't moving: Stand by me, Lord. Stand by me. He wanted to be strong for Sister Morrisohn, who was holding his hand. He didn't want her to know how it terrified him to face his grandmother.

The elevator stopped on 4. A well-groomed elderly couple got on. The woman wore a wine-colored dress that was tassel-tailed and stopped above the knees. The man wore a jacket of the same hue as the woman's dress with a white flower in his lapel. His slacks were sharply creased and his brown shoes shone from a recent polish. The man smiled stiffly. The woman said to Elwyn: "Nice jacket."

"Thank you." Well, it was a double-breasted, athletic cut after all.

"You going to the party on 10?" the woman asked Elwyn.

He debated answering her before he said, "Twelve."

"There's a party on 12?" She turned to her husband. "I don't know a party on 12. How many parties do they have in this place every night? This is a party condo now?" She turned again to Elwyn.

"Miss Fritz-Lev," he offered as explanation.

"Fritz-Lev?"

"Miriam Fritz-Lev," the husband said to his wife.

"Fritz-Lev's throwing a party too?"

The husband said to his wife, "No party. Don't you recognize him? This boy's the preacher lady's grandson."

The woman's eyes lit up. "I didn't recognize him. He's so big these days. How is the mother? How is the grandmother? Remember you would help your mother when you were small?" She measured how small with her hand to her waist. "He carried that vacuum by himself. This is the same boy, I can't believe it."

"A fine boy," said the husband, inspecting Sister Morrisohn unabashedly. He smiled at her—she returned it politely. Elwyn saw it and smiled too. My woman does look good, doesn't she?

The wife went on yammering: "Remember you cleaned for us when our lady was sick? It was the holidays. What was the year, Arny?"

"I don't remember the year," Arny said.

"It was a bad holiday that year. All the girls were sick." The elevator stopped on 10 and the door opened, but the woman didn't seem to notice. "Everybody sick. Nobody to clean. But your mother and your grandmother—"

"Here's the floor. Let's go." Arny took her arm, but she shrugged free. He threw his hands up and got off and she stood in the way to keep the door from closing.

"Your mother and your grandmother kept this place going. They worked for everyone who was sick. And they prayed. You could feel the caring in their hands. They put their hands on you and they prayed. People got better. And you trying to carry that vacuum. Ha-ha. I remember you. You were maybe three years old. How precious. You were this big."

She measured with her hand to show him how big he had been. "And now," she continued, smiling warmly as she backed out of the elevator, "you're all grown up." She nodded her approval at Sister Morrisohn. "All grown up," she repeated, with a sly wink, as the elevator doors closed.

It opened again on 12. They slowly walked down the brightly lit hallway to unit 12-G, holding hands. He could still feel her reluctance.

She had not supported the idea. Her plan was to go to Las Vegas and do it, then tell everyone they had done it. This visit to the condo was his idea—be up front about it and get Gran'ma's approval. If Gran'ma approves, no one will oppose us. It was crazy but exciting, and certainly more Christian than sneaking off to a city of sin to pledge their holy vows.

He knocked, and after a few minutes his grandmother opened the door. She was wearing a kerchief on her head and a gray housecoat. Her eyes grew large when she saw Sister Morrisohn with him, and she pushed up from her walker and seemed to stand up straighter.

"Gran'ma—" he began, but she cut him off.

"I see that ring on her finger." His grandmother shook her head sadly. "You all better come in and get this over with."

She moved aside and let them enter. They didn't go far. They stood a few feet from the door. He still held Sister Morrisohn's hand. The apartment was lit by fluorescent lights. Miss Fritz-Lev, a plump woman in a loose white blouse and old-lady shorts, sat on the couch in front of the TV with the phone pressed to her ear. One of the nighttime soap operas was on. *Dallas* or *Dynasty*, Elwyn wasn't sure which. Miss Fritz-Lev saw them and raised her fingers in greeting. They returned the wave and she went back to whoever it was she was talking to on the phone. Elwyn heard his grandmother say, "We'd better go in my bedroom. More private."

Elwyn led the way, still clutching Sister Morrisohn's hand. He knew this apartment well. He had practically grown up here in this condo, these rooms, where his grandmother had worked most of his life and now lived. Not much had changed over the years. There were the same crucifixes on the north and south walls. The furniture was still upholstered in royal-blue velvet. All around were the same pictures of Miss Fritz-Lev's boys as they were growing up, and now photos of her grandsons too. For years, Elwyn had worn the hand-me-down underwear of Billy, the youngest grandson, who was a sophomore at Berkeley now. Billy was a year older than Elwyn and had always been a few steps ahead of him. Elwyn doubted, however, that Billy had a serious lover he was about to marry. He had caught up to and surpassed Billy.

He led Sister Morrisohn into his grandmother's bedroom, which was tidy and clean with a large bed with a lacy cover and three wall shelves full of religious books and pamphlets. They sat down on the edge of the bed. They heard his grandmother huffing and her walker clacking and then her bulk appeared in the doorway. She came inside and closed the door behind her. There was a large wooden chair in the room, an antique-looking thing, with lion's paw legs and a velvet back. Elwyn's grandmother sat herself down in this chair, pushed her walker out of the way, and clasped her hands in her lap. She focused her attention on Sister Morrisohn, though her face did not seem angry this time, just very tired, like a woman who had been carrying a great burden.

She said, her dentures clicking, "Elaine Morrisohn, why are you doing this to me? You know I love this child. You know I would give my life for this child. Why did you have to go and pick him of all the handsome young boys at the church? Are you trying to kill me before my time, harlot?"

"Gran'ma," Elwyn warned.

But Sister Cooper would not acknowledge him. She kept her eyes on Sister Morrisohn. "I see that ring on your finger. Is that engagement or marriage? Please tell me that it's engagement. Please tell me there's still a chance to end this abomination."

Elwyn balled his fists and made as if to rise. "Gran'ma!"

But Sister Morrisohn put a hand on Elwyn's arm. "Don't be afraid of her. There's nothing that she can say."

Elwyn looked at Sister Morrisohn with love. Sister Morrisohn looked at Elwyn with love. Sister Cooper mumbled with disgust, "My God, she's got you whipped."

Sister Morrisohn put her hand on his face. She would not allow him to turn away. She would not allow him to be hurt by his grandmother's cruelty. And Elwyn looked at her. She was beautiful. He had made the right decision. He had never been so happy. He no longer feared his grandmother, whose dentures clucked forlornly in the background.

Sister Morrisohn said, "There is nothing that she can say. You know who I am. You know what I am. You know what I was. I've already told you everything I've done. I've held nothing back."

"Elaine."

"Kiss me."

He glanced at his grandmother nervously before kissing Sister Morrisohn on the lips. His grandmother closed her eyes and shook her head. But Sister Morrisohn was hungry. It surprised him, but he was still hungry too—even as he kissed her in front of his grandmother. He heard his grandmother beating her breasts. He heard his grandmother shout, "Stop it! Stop it now or get out of my house!"

If that's the way it must be, then that is the way it must be, but nothing was going to come between their love. Elwyn and Sister Morrisohn got up to leave.

As Elwyn passed her chair, his grandmother reached out and grabbed a handful of pants leg. "Please don't marry her."

Elwyn pulled away, and she was sobbing now and it touched him because he loved his grandmother. She clutched his hand desperately. He leaned down and caressed her face. "Really, I'm going to do it regardless, Gran'ma. Please try to be happy for us. All we want is your blessing."

"You will never get my blessing." She held him tight.

"Gran'ma, release me."

She closed her eyes and said, "Buford is your grandfather."

A Packet of Old Letters Bound by Red Ribbon

She told them to look under her bed for a lemon-colored sewing box. They looked until they found it. She told them to open the sewing box and search under the first shelf of needles and thimbles and colored patches of cloth and spools of thread for a packet of old letters bound by red ribbon. They found the packet of old letters under the first shelf and gave them to her. She frowned at them and said, "These are not for me. These are for her."

She passed the letters to Sister Morrisohn.

"Take them outside and read them." Elwyn's grandmother, her eyes still watery, pointed to the door. "Go outside. Read your letters, woman. I need to talk with my grandson in private. We won't be long. You all can do whatever you want after that. I promise you I won't interfere."

Elwyn and Sister Morrisohn touched hands. He told her, "Go, beloved. I'll be all right."

When Sister Morrisohn was outside and the door was closed, Elwyn's grandmother told him, "See, you think I'm just an old busybody getting all up in your business, but I'm not. I understand the feelings that a woman has for a man. I understand the feelings that a woman has for a man, because I had these same feelings once upon a time. Twice upon a time. I loved Private Cooper with all my heart, you know that, don't you? But long before Cooper, I loved Brother Morrisohn first and best."

He stood with his arms folded across his chest watching his grand-mother go through all of the motions of pain and anguish as she relayed her narrative.

"This is hard for me to tell you, child. I feel I can't keep back the tears. Private Cooper, now he was a good man. A real Christian. But he was not your real, blood grandfather. I was pregnant when I met him, but he was a good man. He loved me just as I was. He thought he was strong enough to bear it and he married me. But I lied to him about who Isa's daddy was. It destroyed him when he found out it was Buford. He loved Buford. He had trusted him. So he walked off and joined the war. What's worse was he knew I could never love him like I loved Buford. I know he still cared for me, he was such a good man. A finer young man I never met. That's why I kept his ring."

She took the ring out of her bosom and held it in her open palm.

"He sent me his picture from the war."

She looked with longing at the portrait of Private Cooper in his drab olive uniform that she kept in a standup gold frame on her desk.

"He sent me money. Despite all I had done, he was still trying to protect me from the shame. I didn't deserve a man like him. When he died, I got his army money and all the money he had from some prop-erty he had down in Jamaica. Such a good man. You see me crying? Old Gran'ma's crying hard for you, child. I know what it's like to love somebody who's wrong for you. Buford tried to take care of it the best way he could. He provided for Isa and me good enough, until I stopped being with him. I was trying to serve the Lord then with all my heart. He cut us off cold when I stopped being with him. I was a widow of this good man who had loved me despite my ways and had left me so much. I was touched by how he was still protecting and providing even from the grave. He didn't have to do any of that, but he was a Christian.

And what was I? I became ashamed to still be taking up with a married man. I should have confessed it all out loud, that would have taught Buford a lesson. But I was scared to lose my good name and position in the church. I tell you, Buford punished me and Isa because I stopped being with him. Is that Christian, to abandon your own child? But then later on when you were born, he had a change of heart. He was always sweet on you because you looked so much like him and he never had a son. He took care of you in his will, see? What do you think all that scholarship money is about?"

Elwyn's eyes were clouded with tears. "Brother Morrisohn was really my grandfather."

"Yes."

"And Beverly is my aunt."

"Your mother's sister. Your blood aunti."

"You never told her?"

"I never told her nor your mother. I'm the only one alive today that knows. And now you and that one out there." She indicated the door, beyond which Sister Morrisohn awaited.

Elwyn brushed back the tears. He found strength in his anger and he used it. "I don't believe you. I don't believe one word of it. You're a liar."

Her mouth fell open in shock to hear him talk to her this way. She said, "It's true. It's all true. I can't lie anymore. I got his love letters. He wrote me love letters long after your momma was born, while he was still being with me on the side. Talking about how he loved me and would always take care of his child Isadore. He wrote it all down, and I kept 'em. Elwyn, why are you crying?"

Elwyn was indeed crying now, and also from beyond the closed door there came a loud wail. The sharpness of Sister Morrisohn's cry made them both jump. Elwyn's grandmother turned her ear to the door from whence the mournful wail had come, and there was a look on her face that was almost a smile.

She said to Elwyn, "That sound, I think, means that she has opened her letters."

"Her letters?"

"My letters. The ones Buford wrote to me. The ones I kept."

He said weakly, "Gran'ma, you are an evil person."

His grandmother shook her old, gray head. "No, I'm not. I'm only human. Just like you. Just like her. Truth be told, I really like Elaine. I don't hate her. But the Bible says a man's not supposed to see his father's wife's nakedness." The look that was almost a smile became almost a smirk. "It's the word of God, and God's word cannot be challenged."

Elwyn closed his eyes and balled his fists in a gesture of hopelessness and futility and he said over and over, "Gran'ma, you're evil, you're evil. Gran'ma . . ."

She grunted. "We were meant to be together. It was the Lord's will. He promised that when Glovine died we would be together, but then that one out there came and took him from me."

"You are evil, Gran'ma, don't you see?"

She clucked her dentures and there was yet that half smile on her face. "I'm not evil, child. It's not me. It's Buford. He promised to marry me. He was supposed to be with me. But then when Glovine died, he broke his promise, he said I was too old, and he married that one out there. That skinny, little nothing. That high-yellow tramp. She's the devil. She's the evil one. But now she knows how it is. Ha-ha. Now she's learning her lesson. The Lord says you can't do wrong and get by. Listen to her out there. She's learning it now."

Elwyn wept as his grandmother turned her clucking dentures and her broad evil smile toward the closed door, beyond which they could still hear Sister Morrisohn's wailing.

In Their Tryst Room

Naked and weeping in their tryst room upstairs, she sat on the edge of the bed reading his letters.

"He was my husband."

She looked old to him. For the first time, she looked old to him. He had never seen her look like that before. It scared him.

He put a hand on her. She glanced up at him, holding the letters crushed to her chest.

She sobbed. "It's him. It's his handwriting. There's poetry in some of them. He wrote the same damned poems to me. Oh Buford. Oh Buford."

"It doesn't matter. It doesn't matter," he told her, taking the letters away, throwing them on the floor. "Nothing is going to keep us apart."

"I am your father's nakedness . . . your grandfather's . . . Leviticus 20:11 . . . the man that lieth with his father's wife hath uncovered his father's nakedness: both of them shall surely be put to death; their blood shall be upon them."

"He is not my father. He is my grandfather. And nothing can keep us apart."

She said to him, "Nothing?"

With courage, he confirmed it. "Nothing. Brother Morrisohn's dead and buried and we are alive."

"Oh Elwyn."

Then he fell upon her, and she upon him, and they made love again, desperately, in their tryst room upstairs, when he was still only eighteen and she was still only forty-four.

They were both so young and so innocent that they believed their own vows.

They believed them as powerfully and wholeheartedly as they believed the King James Version of the Bible, in which everything spoken was literally and perfectly true, and nothing was open for interpretation or debate.

Here Endeth the Testament of Exile

VI. TESTAMENT OF SONG

Book of Psalms 137
By the rivers of Babylon, there we sat down, yea, we wept,
when we remembered Zion. We hanged our harps upon the willows
in the midst thereof. For there they that carried us away captive
required of us a song; and they that wasted us required of us mirth,
saying, Sing us one of the songs of Zion. How shall we sing the Lord's song
in a strange land? If I forget thee, O Jerusalem, let my right hand forget her
cunning. If I do not remember thee, let my tongue cleave to the roof of
my mouth; if I prefer not Jerusalem above my chief joy.

Jackleg

The Old Combee Road Church in Lakeland, Florida, was universally referred to as the Big Church, for indeed it was the largest and most splendid edifice in the faith—nearly three thousand tithes-paying members in a cathedral designed to hold perhaps a thousand. Thus, the Big Church was too big. There were three separate morning services (10:00, 12:00, and 2:00) and alternate evening services on Monday and Tuesday nights, but even this was not enough. Youth hour and the lower-level Sunday school classes had to be held outside, with the children seated on the "foot" of the church, their backs erect—or under the movable canopy when the sun was too hot or when it rained. Sunday parking was a weekly spectacle. Two brethren, who were also officers from the Lakeland Municipal Police Department, were hired to direct traffic in and out of the parking lot and keep it flowing on Old Combee Road.

At the Big Church, standing-room only was yet the order of the day, and had been for the last decade, during which four proposals by the elders to build additional churches to counter the attendance problem had been rejected by the congregation. It seemed all the Faithful in Lakeland and the surrounding counties wanted to attend service at Old Combee Road, crowded or not, and nowhere else. And why shouldn't they? The Big Church, after all, was *the* church.

The Big Church was the headquarters of the Church of Our Blessed Redeemer Who Walked Upon the Waters and home to its governing minister and highest saint, Bishop Kirkaby Rogers, great-great-grandson of founder Reverend Dr. Cuthbert Rogers. The Big Church was where church doctrine was written. The Big Church was where the hymnals and tracts were printed and where the national, weekly, half hour radio program *Voice of the Shepherd* was recorded for broadcast. Ministers from all over the country came to be ordained here. The main campus of Bible College was its backyard.

The Big Church, then, was Mecca, but a Mecca with walls too elaborately designed to be expanded. So the beloved Bishop Kirkaby Rogers himself decreed that another church be established in the small community of Plant City about ten miles due west of Lakeland, and he hand-picked a twenty-one-year-old minister, Reverend Barry McGowan, to be its pastor. Reverend McGowan, a magnificent tenor, was voted "most charismatic" by his Bible College fellows, and charisma, Bishop Rogers believed, was essential when moving a goodly number (at least fifteen hundred, he prayed) of the flock from the Big Church to a renovated barn in Plant City.

So the young McGowans moved into the one-bedroom apartment next to the renovated-barn-turned-church and found that Bishop Rogers was right: the Old Combee Road congregation loved Barry, who set them on fire every Sunday for three weeks as guest speaker and featured soloist. The young minister knew his Scripture, and he was not long-winded: his sermons were pleasant and spiritually uplifting. And no one had ever sung "Grace That Is Greater Than All Our Sins" so perfectly. Heaven must sound like this young man.

The saints of Lakeland rejoiced and wept and cried—

Grace! Grace! God's Grace
Grace that will pardon and cleanse within
Grace! Grace! God's Grace
Grace that is greater than all our sins

And they came to the stone altar and threw themselves prostrate before the Maker.

Barry beamed, but Peachie, seated at the white piano, could feel that something was not right. These people smiled, but they kept asking about the baby. How old? How old? And you, Sister McGowan, only sixteen? You must have been an honor student to have finished high school so young, they said. You'll certainly do well.

With God's help, maybe. And Barry's singing. For their baby was indeed conceived out of wedlock and she had yet to complete high school, having just that week enrolled in night school. The confusing thing was that Bishop Rogers had chosen them fully aware of their "condition." Certainly, the most esteemed member of the church would not have selected them unless he thought they would be accepted by the saints of Lakeland.

Afterward, Bishop Rogers joined Barry at the fore of the pulpit. He extended his arms and shouted: "Saints! Saints! Reverend and Sister Barry McGowan. Don't you love them?" He clapped his hands, and the sound of applause in the Big Church was mighty like a storm. Bishop Rogers waited until there was quiet before he spoke into the microphone: "Those of you who live out near Plant City—Coronet Road, Jim Johnson Loop, Roseland Avenue, Mud Lake Road—you can join the McGowans for services every Sunday beginning next week. It's going to be a beautiful time in the Lord!"

Again the applause was great, but Peachie couldn't help thinking, They will not come.

And she was right.

Oh, the ushers were there, serious-faced, eight of them on loan from the Big Church, decked out in their black slacks and skirts, their white shirts and blouses. They stood at parade rest along the back wall, but once service began the doorway was quiet.

About sixty people occupied pews set to accommodate more than fifteen hundred. The young, vocal ones Peachie recognized as Barry's friends from Bible College, and the stiff ones with cameras she suspected were church officials who had come to gauge the success or failure of this bold new venture.

There was no choir that first Sunday, so Barry acted as minister of music as well as preacher and featured soloist. Between selections, he made wholesome jokes, at which the congregation laughed uproariously. To break the ice, he called on three friends from Bible College who were in the audience (Brothers Magellan, Philip, and Jackson) and got them to perform their version of "I'll Meet You in the Morning by the Bright Riverside."

Bless the Lord!

For Peachie, it was a joyous occasion that Sunday, in stark contrast to the lean weeks that followed. The lean years that followed. Another child that followed. The money problem that followed.

And Barry's delusions—that he was loved, that the people would eventually come.

Two and a half years later, in the early summer, the church still looked like an empty barn to Peachie, the eighteen-year-old mother of the church, as she played the piano for the couple dozen or so who showed up each Sunday.

Peachie had grown up over the two years. If she had stayed in school, she would have been a senior now getting ready to graduate. As it stood, she had not completed her night-school studies because of her duties as a mother of the children and as a mother of the church.

She had gained fifteen pounds, it looked good on her, and her lanky 5'9" frame didn't seem so lanky anymore. Her face and hips had become fuller. She still wore her hair in twin ponytails. It took her more than an hour to comb it back into submission, but sometimes she opened it up and let it flow about her head like a mane.

The hair was her hidden wildness. When it was open like that, she felt a freedom she did not possess in actuality. But there was a downside to it.

Barry would see her like this and rush to make ferocious and some-times satisfying love to her.

However, he feared this side of her too. Sometimes he would see her like this and call her the whore of Babylon and order her to comb it immediately.

That he called her a "whore," she believed, was highly ironic, but she had no proof, only her intuition.

"I figured it out," Peachie said one day as she combed her wild hair in front of the mirror. "They want you to sing gospel. They brought you up here to sing gospel. They brought you here to attract the black members of the Big Church."

"I'm an operatic tenor," Barry answered. "I don't sing boogie-woogie."

"It's not called boogie-woogie, it's called gospel. Everybody's sing-ing it. Stop being so old-fashioned. The church is changing. Welcome to the twentieth century. You hear what's happening on the radio. Your voice is so beautiful, better than Andraé Crouch—"

He shook his head and laughed at her. "You know that's not my thing."

"If you sing gospel, you'll appeal to that segment of the congrega-tion that likes gospel."

"The African American segment?" He watched her comb bob and pick into that wild growth of hair. "The black people? I don't want peo-ple to say I'm a minister of a black church. I minister to people of all colors."

"From the looks of our church," Peachie quipped, "you minister to people of no color."

"What did you say?" It was as simple as that. The simplest thing would set him off. He advanced on her with his hand raised.

"Please don't hit me, Barry," she said sardonically. She laughed at him as he came to her with his hand up. "Please don't hit me again, jackleg."

She said it without flinching. She turned her face to receive the blow. He brought his hand down hard against her face. It hurt, but not as bad as some of the others because he was eager to leave the house.

"See what you made me do?" he said, putting on his coat. "See what you made me do?"

"A**hole! Wife beater!" Peachie cursed hoarsely at him. He was so predictable. He was so hot to leave he couldn't even give her a proper beating. He must really be in love with this one this time. But she had no real proof, only her intuition.

He stormed out and slammed the door. She hollered after him, "Jackleg preacher!"

Peachie knew where he was going. She laughed some more. It was her freedom laugh. It was better than crying. She finished combing her hair and braided her twin ponytails. She dressed the children and took them across the street and left them with Miss Irma. As Peachie waited at the bus stop, she rubbed her swollen face and practiced the words she would say to him when she found him at the place where her intuition told her he had gone. "I want a divorce. Jackleg."

She grinned.

He hated that word, but it suited him so well.

Now she thought about what her mother and father would say. How they had warned her. How the Faithful would backbite. *Skinny, little nothing. Pregnant before she got married. Divorced before she turned twenty.* She cried then and couldn't stop even after the bus arrived.

She got off outside WCRX, the radio station that produced *Voice of the Shepherd*, and she prayed, for his sake, that Barry was inside where he worked part-time in the music room and sometimes guest deejayed during *Your Faithful Prayer Hour* with Sister Elizabeth Ling.

Peachie spoke with the security officer and the receptionist at the front desk, both of whom she knew from the Big Church. They were kind, but neither had seen Barry that morning. She thanked them and got on another bus that dropped her off about five blocks from the place where she knew he had gone. As she walked through the affluent neighborhood, she counted Cadillac, Mercedes, Cadillac, BMW. She would tell him: I want a divorce, Barry. It's been two years of hell.

Jackleg.

She lost her grin when she saw their old Toyota parked outside the sprawling two-story home of Elizabeth Ling, host of *Your Faithful Prayer Hour*. Now here was a whore of Babylon. Chinese slut.

Peachie knocked. She knocked for two hours. Peachie pounded. Then she "stole" their Toyota with her own key and drove to Brother Philip's house.

"I'm leaving Barry. I need money to get me and the kids back home. Today," she told him. "You said if I ever needed anything from you, all I had to do was ask. I'm asking now. I can't take this humiliation anymore. I found his car parked in front of her house."

"Yes. Sister Ling. Many of us know about it. Barry and Sister Ling have prayed about it. They're trying their best to stop. God will work it out in time," Brother Philip said.

"I want a divorce."

"I can't help you with this. Barry is my friend."

"I'm leaving him one way or the other." She began to cry again, and Brother Philip came and put his arms around her.

"Now," he said, massaging her back, "if you were my special friend, I might be compelled to help you out."

He put his tongue in her ear and she slapped him. "This is not the time for that."

"When is the time for us, Peachie?"

"Isn't that betraying Barry? You're no friend."

Brother Philip, who had been a star athlete in football, basketball, and track at Bible College, opened his shirt. His chest, like his shadowy cupid face, was smooth and hairless. He had a washboard-tight stomach. His skin was black as charcoal and he was twice as handsome as he was black. "Do you want the money or not, Peachie?"

"You're a pig."

At about 5, Barry walked into the apartment and slammed the door. "I don't know what you think you're trying to prove. You don't know what happened today. You're just jumping to conclusions. We were working on a record album. I swear it. There is nothing going on between me and Sister Ling."

"Yet no one answered that door for two hours. Yet you smell like a woman's perfume. Why don't you go pray over it some more, Jackleg, you and Sister Ling?" She pointed to the boxes of clothes, dishes, and toys for the boys, which she had packed and stacked against the wall. "As you can see, I've been busy."

"Where do you think you're going? You think you're going somewhere? You think you're going to take my children?"

"Then you can keep your damned children."

"Watch your mouth." He came at her with his hand raised.

Peachie stretched to her full height. "If you so much as lay a hand on me, Barry Sebastian-Bach McGowan, I'm going to tell everyone what you really are. I'll ruin you. I'll divorce you, I swear."

Barry slapped Peachie harder than he ever had. So hard she finally lost her smirk.

"Divorce?" he said, slapping her shocked mouth a second and third time until her neck hurt from the twisting. Her hands became claws and she went for his eyes. She came close, but he caught her and put her in a headlock and continued to slap her face.

"You can't divorce me. It's a sin. A woman shall not usurp authority over the man, 1 Timothy!"

"Thou shalt not commit adultery, Exodus 20!"

"Shut up!"

"Stop hitting me, a**hole!"

"Stop cursing!"

"A**hole! A**hole!"

He pushed her to the ground and began to kick her.

"My God, Barry! Stop hitting me. Stop hitting me. You're really hurting me."

"I'm your husband! I'm your husband!"

Barry was crying now too. He was only just sane enough to pull back when he realized he was kicking her in the stomach. He picked up one of her packed boxes and stormed into the bedroom with it. Peachie heard him in there ripping it open. Then it sounded like he was flinging things every which way. This is the sound, she said to herself, of a jackleg unpacking.

Peachie rolled over and thanked God she had left the boys with Miss Irma so they wouldn't have to witness this. She took one of the other packed boxes and slowly began to remove the things and set them back on the shelves where they belonged. Who was she fooling? She wasn't going anywhere. Not now. Not ever.

That night, when she was sure Barry was asleep, she snuck out of the bedroom and called Brother Philip from the church phone.

"I'm not going anywhere. I guess I'll have to give the money back."

He answered, "But it's yours. Please say you'll keep it, my darling."

"I'm giving it back. And I'm not your darling."

"Okay, Sister Peachie, whatever you say. But I have to tell you that you were wonderful. I'm your slave forever."

"Well, you're a slave without a master because it will never happen again, that's for sure." Then she conceded: "But you were wonderful too, Brother Philip."

She checked to make sure the silent barn was really a silent barn.

Then she cooed, "It's never been so good."

Mother of the Church

She had promised that it would not happen again.

It did happen again, every day for the next fifteen days, and that in-cluded two Sundays. They had to be creative on Sundays. They had to find a reason for Barry to be away from her, and Sister Ling proved the perfect enticement. Peachie would apologize for having accused him of infidelity, and to prove her sincerity she would say, "But you have time to practice now. I have perfect faith in you. Go see Sister Ling. Get in a few hours of practice before night service." Then, after he left, she would take the boys over to Miss Irma and wait for Brother Philip to arrive. She didn't want to call it a pattern, but she had to admit that its realness was reinforced by its regularity.

His lovemaking was ravenous. He would begin undressing her in the car. She would ascend the stairs to his loft with her bottom exposed and Brother Philip nipping at it. Sometimes he hurt her in his eagerness to fill her. She became accustomed to his power, his size. When he had spent, he would lie atop her and kiss every part of her face and neck, and soon she would feel him growing again. Most of their time together was spent loving, and she was happy with this arrangement, for it left her little time to consider the reckless nature of what she was doing, or to speculate about the stranger aspects of it.

On the fifteenth day, he took a phone call from his disabled mother in the middle of their loving. He doted over his mother. She had been ailing with the flu, and he had made her promise to call him every few hours until she was feeling better. It gave Peachie, naked in his bed, a few moments to consider her problem. She was in love with him. It was wrong what they were doing, but it was good to be in love again. She believed he felt the same toward her, but there were things about him that were troubling. For instance, the words he had spoken the first time he had undressed her: "I will only make love to Faithful women. They are natural like the Lord wants a woman to be—but you, you're almost bald. You don't use a razor, do you?"

She had said, "No. That's just the way God made me."

She recalled that he had then lowered his head and run his tongue over the fine hairs. And then sniffed them, frowning. She recalled, too, that the loving which followed had been spectacular. She was not so naïve as to believe anymore that she was the only Faithful woman who engaged in premarital, now extramarital, sex, but she could not get his words out of her head. And his mother. Sometimes he was a worse momma's boy than Barry.

But she loved him. She loved him as much as she used to love Barry, and that was a lot.

He hung up the phone after talking with his mother and came back to the bed. He had a vacant expression in his eyes.

"Now Momma knows about us," he said simply.

"Oh Lord."

"Momma does not approve."

"Lord, help us."

Brother Philip smiled. "But Momma will keep our secret."

"She's a good momma," Peachie said. "She loves her little boy."

The Holy Ghost Power in Me

There was no question about it. It was indeed perverse.

Their special thing was to show their naked backsides to the TV at 2:00 p.m. on Fridays.

They would wait until the *Holy Ghost Hour with Reverend Barry* came on, then drop their drawers, turn their butts to the TV screen, and moon Barry and Sister Ling as they sang the show's theme song, "Holy Ghost, Holy Ghost, Holy Ghost Power in Me," which Peachie had written, but got no credit for. Then Brother Philip would ride her from behind, doggy-style. They liked to imagine that Barry was watching their naked buttocks as they rocked and huffed to orgasm.

Sometimes they invoked his name.

Oh Barry, I'm doing your wife! Brother Philip would shout. I've got the Holy Ghost penis in her!

Or Peachie would say, Oh Barry, he's hitting my sweet spot again! I can feel his miracle healing!

Doing it during the show was the most fun they had together. The show never failed to fire them up, even when it was mentioned during church, like when Barry would announce to the congregation, which now numbered over one thousand, "Don't forget to support the show. Tune in on Fridays." Peachie would find Brother Philip's eyes in the audience and they would wink at each other to their dirty version of the catchy hymn she had written for Barry's show:

Tune in, my love.
Tune it in me.
How's the reception in there?
I feel it. I feel it. Don't touch that dial. I feel the Holy Ghost penis
moving deeply in me.

The years had flown by. If Peachie had gone to college, she would have been in her senior year now getting ready to graduate. She was twenty-two years old, and over the years she had gained another forty or so pounds. Barry found the weight disgusting. Well, of course, slant-eyed Sister Ling might weigh a hundred pounds soaking wet.

Brother Philip, on the other hand, thought the weight looked good on Peachie. It was a nice weight for her height. It made her once narrow behind a lot juicier and a lot more desirable.

"Lord knows, I like a juicy booty," he would say, slapping it. Pulling her panties down with his teeth.

They had been together almost four years behind Barry's back. It was true love, they were certain.

These days Barry was all about money. He had an accountant and a broker he met with weekly. He drove a Mercedes. He owned a car phone. He played golf at an exclusive club. Barry was making serious money now with the church, which had grown along with his record sales.

But he was in the middle of setting up his satellite network, and Peachie and Brother Philip both believed that when that came through he would be rich enough and brave enough to dump Peachie and marry Sister Ling. But from what Peachie had overheard, the satellite cable church was at least four years away from completion. So they had to wait. Or they could make their move *before* Barry.

It was a crazy idea, but they were so in love they kept thinking about it. They could break away now and start their life together, though they would be ostracized by the church. Everyone would hate them, the wife of the great young evangelist and his best friend. What a shame. Barry would be seen as a hero and they would be shunned by the Faithful.

"And where will we live?" Peachie wondered aloud on this particular Friday afternoon after making love with her big juicy butt exposed to her husband's televised presence.

"We can get a place. I have money. We'll make love all day."

"Where will we worship?"

"You are so small-minded." He whistled at the ceiling, shaking his head in disbelief. "There are other churches, you know?"

"We are the one true church."

"Literally, Peachie?"

"That's what I've always believed. You know how it is. Come on." She thought about it and laughed. "I mean, like, it would be weird at another church. Like what other churches could we go to?"

"Baptist."

"Too worldly."

"We're worldly." He pointed to the TV screen upon which the credits were rolling. Behind the credits were various still images from sacred events at the Church of Our Blessed Redeemer Who Walked Upon the Waters. Mostly they were of Barry and Sister Ling doing missionary work and singing, but some of them featured Peachie at the piano and others showed Brother Philip standing next to Barry. "We are worldly and carnal and perverse." Barry laughed and began kissing her. They were both still naked.

"Yes," she said hoarsely, kissing him back, "but Baptists smoke and drink."

"How about the Holy Rollers?" he suggested.

She snorted. "My mom would kill me."

"You've got to grow up. Step out on your own," he said, but she had that look on her face. No way, buddy. No Holy Rollers for me. "Really, though, it's not so bad. I used to date a Holy Roller girl."

"I don't want to hear about your Holy Roller girl."

"Church of God?"

"No."

"Church of Christ?"

"They don't even allow pianos in their church. I'm a musician. Sorry, my friend. Next."

He put his hand in hers. They sat naked on the floor on a blanket that they had spread for their carnal purposes. On the TV, the credits had finished rolling and now there was an appeal from the bishop for donations to the scholarship fund. The song in the background was "Count Your Many Blessings."

Brother Philip said to Peachie, "Seventh Day Adventist?"

Peachie sighed. "I like pork." She grabbed his penis. "I like pork a lot."

"Church of the First Born?"

"No."

"Church of the Holy Ghost?"

"No."

"I used to date a Church of the Holy Ghost girl."

She turned away from him. "You and your girls."

"Don't be mad at me, Peachie."

"You just don't understand."

"Let's make it about love."

"I have a husband."

"Do you believe in love?"

"I do. I still do," she said, looking dreamily into his dreamy eyes.

"Then that's all we need."

"We'll be alone. It'll be so difficult."

"Love will conquer all. Love will find a way."

"Will it?" She let him kiss her. She found the answer she needed in his kiss. Love *will* find a way, but there was the clock on the wall. "We have to go." She started packing up.

It was a Friday, their favorite day for loving because of the TV show, but also because they got to stay an extra hour together. He was a good man, this man she loved. She had no feelings for Barry anymore. Let him have his slim little Sister Ling. Barry was not half the man Brother Philip was. But they had better hurry, or she'd be late picking up the kids.

She watched him dress. His naked body was beautiful. She had memorized his body so that she would have it when he was not with her. She had memorized its feel. As they drove, she held his hand and watched his handsome profile. There was a place behind his ear that she loved to kiss because of the way he would scrunch up his nose. She kissed that place now. He scrunched up his nose. She put her hand in his lap and caressed his firm thighs. He responded with an erection that inflated his trousers. She had memorized his smell so that she would have it when he was not with her. Because of their schedules, they would not be able to get together for at least three days. She had to work on the church minutes and the bulletin and this week's Passage for Reflection. She had to practice with the adult choir. Easter was coming up and she had to meet with the Youth Cantata Committee. "I love

Friday, but I hate it too," she sighed. "Three whole days before I can be with you again." She unzipped his pants, leaned over, and put his penis in her mouth. She had memorized his taste so that she would have it when he was not with her.

They got to Miss Irma's too soon. They did not notice Barry's Mercedes parked across the street.

Brother Philip kissed her twice, once for loving him, once to seal their promise, and she got out of his car with reluctance as she always did and walked across the street to Miss Irma's, missing him so much already. Counting down the hours until she could love him again.

Before she could knock on the babysitter's door, Barry tapped her on the shoulder. "Leave the kids with the old lady. Let's just you and me go home for a few minutes to talk."

She turned to confront the angry mask that was his face. "Barry—"

"I saw you get out of his car."

But everything had been planned and timed so perfectly. How?

Barry answered the question she did not ask, "There was no show today. It was a repeat. I suspected for a long time, but I had to see for myself. Oh Peachie, why did you do this to me?"

His voice sounded pained, which surprised her. She thought that he would be happy. He had his Sister Ling. What did he care what she did? But this pain in his voice, it touched her. It was the Barry who was sick who she nursed back to health. It was the Barry who was broke whose side she had stood by. This was the Barry who had wept at the pain of rejection—wept real tears when she had turned him down that first time. But that Barry was dead and gone and had no right to show up here now. This Barry should be happy she was sleeping with his best friend.

Well, he found out before she was able to execute her plan. Okay.

So be it. Too bad. Now she had no choice. She would be forced to leave him earlier than planned. Some ugly days would come, she knew, but then it would all be over, and things could start to get better again. She would marry Brother Philip. It's what she wanted anyway.

But what would be left of her?

Barry was here now to take, and he would be righteous in his wrath. What would be left? Already his hand was raised. He would take and take, she knew. Would there be enough of her left for Brother Philip?

He grabbed a handful of her hair and twisted it until it hurt.

"Oh God, Barry, give me a chance to explain. Give me a chance to live. I deserve a chance to live."

He had her by the hair—she was forced to turn to face the blow that she saw coming. She closed her eyes and it broke against her cheek. She cried in her mind while she was still conscious, Don't take it all. I know you are angry. Leave a little bit for me and Brother Philip. It's not fair to take it all.

She saw the second blow coming. This one lifted her. She knew she would land against Miss Irma's door, and she braced herself, but there was no door. She fell through the opening and landed faceup on Miss Irma's carpet, which smelled of cigarettes and baby poop.

She heard her children screaming. She heard Miss Irma shouting for the police. She saw Barry's hands reaching for her. He lifted her like when he was loving her. There was a feeling of weightlessness. She felt herself flying through the air. There was the screaming pain as she landed on Miss Irma's glass coffee table. She felt the glass break against her face. She felt the glass bite into her face, into her breast near her heart.

Things were getting confused in her head. She loved this man, and he loved her, and she deserved to be beaten because she was a Christian. The harder he beat, the more she deserved it, Praise God, because Barry had never loved her so hard, thus sayeth the Lord, turn to page forty-seven in your hymnals.

But he was not supposed to take it all. That was not fair. He was supposed to leave her some.

Leave me some, you jackleg hypocrite!

She reached out blindly with her hand. If she could just get her hand on a shard of Miss Irma's broken glass table, she would show Barry how hard she could love him back. She would take and take, and leave nothing for Sister Ling. She would shove that glass shard right into his balls.

Barry loomed over her. She beat at him with her hand, but there was no shard of hard love in her hand, only the oozing warmth from her bleeding breasts.

She raised her empty hand to his face. She beat his face weakly. She stopped beating. She anointed his forehead with blood from her breasts. She drew the shape of the cross. Then she drew a smiley face next to the cross.

She said, "I bless you."

"What are you doing? You stupid woman."

"Don't take it all. Leave some for me, Jack."

"Jack?"

"Jackleg!"

"You won't get a penny from me, you harlot."

"I don't want your money. I just want you to leave. I just want love."

"You crazy woman." He put his hands behind her head and ran them down the length of her ponytails that once he had so loved. Still loved. He put his face against hers. "You crazy Peachie. My crazy girl."

His face felt so warm. He was not greedy anymore. He was not taking. He was even trying to give some back. He was the old Barry again. The generous Barry she had loved.

He said, "I wanted you to be happy."

She said, "I wanted to be happy with you."

"I failed to make you happy."

"I'm not happy with you."

"I don't know what happened to us. I don't know." He had blood in the shape of a cross and a smiley face on his forehead. He touched her face gently. "You were my girl."

She smiled at the smiley face. "You were my jackleg."

"Jackleg."

"My rich and famous jackleg. I'm proud of you. You're known all over the world."

"You never told me that before."

"You never listened before."

"You wanted me to sing boogie-woogie."

"I wanted you to sing whatever you wanted to sing, but I wanted you to sing it to me."

"You never told me that before."

"Try opening your ears. Try listening."

They held each other. Barry laughed. Peachie somehow managed a laugh. The boys were still crying. Miss Irma was on the phone with the police. And Peachie and Barry were laughing as a shadow fell over them.

Peachie and Barry looked up. It was Brother Philip looming over Barry's shoulder.

Barry sprang up with his fists clenched. Brother Philip got him in a bear hug. Barry punched Brother Philip in the stomach. They fell to the ground, rolling over what was left of the furniture in Miss Irma's living room, clawing at each other like tomcats.

Miss Irma and the children screamed.

Peachie, her eyes fixed on the battle, watched to see who would win.

Blood in the Pews

They did not fight. They did not talk about what had happened. They did not talk about what would happen next. Barry slept in the big bed in their bedroom. The apartment had been renovated over the years of success and money to include five bedrooms among other upscale chambers, but Peachie slept in the boys' room just in case. The next day was Sunday. At a quarter to 9, they heard a commotion coming through the walls. They opened the door to the renovated barn that was now their magnificent church, with a membership of 1,115 or so. Had they overslept? The place was already full. Every seat was taken up. They checked the clock. Service was scheduled to begin at 10, and it was not even 9 yet.

Barry threw on a suit and went out there. Peachie rushed to get the boys ready. She was running a comb through Junior's hair, when Barry came back in from out there and shut the door behind him. He looked badly shaken up. He seemed out of breath.

Peachie said, "What?"

Barry told her, "You tell me. Go out there and see for yourself."

She did not go out there because she still had on her sleeping clothes, but she stuck her head through the door. The church was full. It took her nearly half a minute to realize that everyone in the church was female—a church full of women, and they were not Faithful women.

She noted the straightened hair, the jewelry and makeup, some of them even in pants in the house of God.

Peachie had not read the newspaper headline that morning, *Televangelist Beats Wife as Babysitter, Children Look On.*

Neither had Barry.

They saw her and began to applaud. Some of them were saying, "Praise the Lord." Others were saying, "Come on out, Sister McGowan. Come on out."

Peachie went back inside and shut the door behind her. Junior was brushing his own hair now. Barry was staring at her bug-eyed. He said, "What do they want?"

She said, "They want me."

"For what?"

She shrugged and shook her head. "I have no idea."

She found a housecoat and threw it on over her sleeping things and she walked past Barry. He said, "You're going back out there?"

Peachie shrugged again. "To see what they want."

She went back out there in her housecoat and slippers and black eye and bandaged neck, and the applause started up again. She stood there for a few seconds, not sure what to do. What do these women want? Why are they clapping?

But then she started feeling embarrassed and she pulled the sash of her housecoat tighter. She wasn't used to applause anymore. Since they had come up here and built the church, all of the applause had been for him. This was like in the old days, but she wasn't used to it anymore.

And applause for what, she thought? Cheating on my husband?

These women are crazy. I am a harlot. In Bible days I would be stoned.

But the applause continued, and so did the chant: "Sister Peachie! Sister Peachie! Sister Peachie!"

So she sat down at the piano, for it is there that she had always felt most confident, and she positioned her hands over the keys. She played the first chords of "Amazing Grace," which was her favorite hymn. The women in the church seemed to like it too. She heard their voices now over the thunderous applause.

They were shouting, "Sister Peachie! Sister Peachie! Sister Peachie!" as she played the hymn. She played through her pain. She played through her self-hate. She played through her self-doubt and disillusionment. Her confidence came back. She heard the voice of God, and He was love.

She stopped playing just long enough to open her ponytails and free her wild hair.

The women in the renovated barn loved that even more. They shouted, "Play it! Play it!" and Peachie did. For the first time in a long time, she felt the Holy Ghost power her.

A half hour later, the adjoining door to their home opened and seven-year-old Barry Junior walked out and came to her. He was wearing his good suit and his hair was properly brushed and he put his mouth to her ear so that she could hear above the noise. He told her that he was hungry and asked if they could have eggs for breakfast today and he told her that his daddy could not make breakfast for them anymore because he had gotten in the car and driven off after saying he was never coming back.

Here Endeth the Testament of Song

VII. Testament of a Joyful Noise

Book of Psalms 117
O Praise the Lord, all ye nations: Praise Him, all ye people.
For His merciful kindness is great toward us; and the truth
of the Lord endureth for ever. Praise ye the Lord.

Senior Year

It was a Saturday afternoon.

Benny hung a left on Miami Gardens Drive and cruised the rest of the way to his father's home.

Miami Gardens was a much nicer neighborhood than Opa-Locka where he had grown up. The houses were larger here and so were the yards. There was the occasional glimpse of a pool in the backyard, the occasional glimpse of a white face. The neighborhood elementary school, Garden Grove, had no noticeable graffiti on its walls. The cars had less primer on them. Roscoe had done all right for a school bus driver.

Benny wheeled his Mercedes into Roscoe's driveway. Roscoe's house had a well-manicured lawn and an extra room built over the carport. From what Benny could see, there was no vehicle in the carport. He nodded his head and said, "I'm in luck."

He chuckled, thinking about what he was about to do. He got out of his car and went to their mailbox.

The letter was in a sealed envelope with the words *FOR ELWYN/ FROM BENNY* on the front.

After he put it in their mailbox, he went back to his car and glanced down at his Rolex. It was two minutes past 5. He would get back to his town house in time to have the teleconference with the Chilean bankers and still have time to shave and shower in preparation for his dinner with Marie, who was home on spring break from the University of Florida. She was in her junior year, one year behind Elwyn, the college senior who, Benny knew, was home on spring break too. Benny chuckled again and pulled out of the driveway.

"Time to make things happen," he said.

Exactly five minutes later, Isadore and Roscoe Parker pulled into their driveway.

Roscoe hadn't talked much on the way home. Isadore had gone on and on about a late-model Buick Regal she had heard that the church mechanic Brother Pendergast had recently taken into his shop. The owner was interested in selling, she had heard. From the way she spoke, Roscoe knew that she had more than just heard. She had most likely gone to the shop and looked at it. She had probably negotiated a price—a good price, knowing Isadore, who was shrewd when it came to matters of business and money. Now, he suspected, she was feeling him out to see if he had the money to make good on a deal she had already made. Money, money, money, everything was money. And what was so wrong with their old car? Roscoe prepared himself for a long night.

Isadore got out of the car, still talking about the Buick she had heard the owner was willing to sell, and took the mail from the mailbox. She thought at first that it was some junk mail thing for Elwyn, as all the credit card companies seemed to be courting him these days, but there was no stamp on it. She saw that it was from Patsy's boy and it was addressed in big letters to Elwyn. Isadore felt weak in the knees. She waited for Roscoe to bring in the few bags of groceries they had picked up. She read the name *Benny* again and water began to pour from her eyes.

When Roscoe came inside, he heard her sniffling, saw her heaving angrily in her seat. He went to her. "Beloved, what is it?"

She pushed him off and flung the envelope at his face, but it flapped off course and missed. The she jumped up and ran inside the bedroom and locked the door.

Roscoe looked down at the envelope on the floor and read the name *Benny* and said, "Oh Lord. Please Lord. Don't do this to me tonight."

He went to the bedroom door. He was angry with Benny. Why was he doing this? Roscoe had begged him specifically not to do this. Benny had always seemed like such a nice boy. Now he was deliberately trying to destroy his family. Why would he do this?

Roscoe wondered out loud how Jesus would react if His outside child had tried to sabotage His marriage. He didn't like the answer he was hearing in his head because it went contrary to his very justifiable anger: Jesus would have compassion, understanding, and forgiveness for Benny because Jesus would admit that He had screwed up Benny's life by being a knockabout, no-account bedhopper and creating this situation in the first place.

Roscoe tapped lightly on the door. "Beloved, we need to talk. And we need to talk right now. This thing has gone on too long, and something has got to be done about it. Maybe something can be worked out. I mean, the boys are both grown men now."

There were no words coming from the locked door, only loud sobbing.

Roscoe said, "Beloved, as the man of this house, I'm ordering you to open this door right now or I'm going to kick it down, you hear me?"

Then he heard laughter. She was laughing at him.

Roscoe went into the Florida room and sat in his overstuffed recliner, where it was customary for him to accept defeat.

But this one was a big one. This one was big.

Around 7, Elwyn came home from cleaning up the church grounds with the maintenance brethren, and he found Roscoe in his recliner with an envelope in his hands.

He found the house strangely quiet for a Saturday night. No one was eating. No one was praying. No one had turned on the lights, though the sun had just about set. He felt an ominous mood in the house. His mother was not in her usual places, bustling about, cooking or cleaning or fussing. He said to his father, "Mom home?"

"In her room."

"Is she sick?"

Roscoe handed him the envelope. "This came for you today." It was dark in the Florida room with the blinds drawn, a sharp contrast to Roscoe's white eyes and teeth when he spoke. "Remember, son, I love you."

Elwyn took the envelope into the bedroom and sat down on the bed with the lights off. Through the partially opened door, he watched the unmoving profile of his father in the Florida room. His thoughts turned dark.

Whatever was going on, he figured it had something to do with him.

And Sister Morrisohn.

He looked down at the letter in his hand. It had no stamp on it. It was not a credit card offer. He pondered again the darkness in his home and how it might be related to this letter to him from Benny.

Who was Benny?

He opened the envelope and found the note:

Dear Elwyn,

 You don't know me, but I am looking for someone to play piano at my upcoming wedding, and I hear that you are a great pianist. The wedding is in June, so we have a lot of time left to get together and work out the plans before the big day.

Elwyn smiled. As a college student, he could always use the few hundred dollars he earned from playing at weddings. But he still could not shake the bad feeling. He did not understand the darkness in his house.

He read the rest of the letter.

We need to get together . . . I would like to get to know you . . . I'm sure it's going to be great . . . blah, blah, blah . . . Here is my phone number . . .

Sincerely,
Your brother Benny

Nothing unusual there.

And then he read the closing again.

He thought nothing of it, and he stretched out on his bed. Later, he decided, after he had rested from his labor, he would drive up to Mary's house and take care of some private business. There was nothing like sex to relax one after a hard day's labor. He chuckled to himself and soon he fell asleep.

He awoke with a start and recalled the closing: *Your brother* Benny, not *Brother* Benny.

Elwyn knew then that he had to pray.

For years he had been hearing the rumors about some boy named, yes, Benny, but he had always dismissed them. Not *my* father, he would say. Not Roscoe. But his house was dark tonight and his mother was locked in her room and there was this letter.

Elwyn got out of bed and fell to his knees and clasped his hands before his face and cried out, "Lord, Lord, I beseech Thee, Oh Lord. Is there none righteous but Thee? They are all born in sin and shaped in iniquity. Lord. Lord. Lord. What do You want me to do? My heart is heavy. Is there none righteous? Tell me. Lord. Tell me."

The next day he arose from his knees with the sun, having prayed all night. He felt nothing, except the pain in his knees and the sadness in his heart for this wicked and adulterous generation.

"We are an abomination. The Lord should send down hellfire. If we were all wiped out, no one would miss us. We're not worth it. Faithful . . . the Faithful . . . we are anything but."

Later that day, he confronted his father and received terse, unambiguous answers to all of his questions.

After that, he did not speak to his father for close to a year.

I Must Tell Jesus

The evening still haunts my mind.

I still feel the oppressive summer heat on the back of my neck. I still see the Florida sky redden with the dying sun, then turn black and speckled with stars. I still see the enormous black tent under which were seated row after row of black people, and quite a few whites, dressed up for churching, the men in handsome suits and ties, the women in colorful dresses and stylish, often flamboyant hats. None of the women wore jewelry or pants as they did in some churches. None of the men wore dreadlocks or braids or sweat suits or athletic footwear or had tattoos or pierced ears or gold teeth. These were the Faithful, the ultrapure and true servants of God, and this was their tent meeting. It was the summer of 1986 and the place was Miami, Florida. There were about a thousand people in all gathered under that tent on the parking lot of the Orange Bowl. I was there to meet my brother Elwyn for the first time.

There was a tall man preaching that night, but I do not remember a thing he said. I do recall that he roared a lot and he bellowed. He kept repeating something, some sort of catch phrase, some comically exaggerated syllable that I had found humorous at the time, but I have since forgotten what it was. There was another man, also tall but with a smallish head, who sang several hymns. He was someone special, I know, because he had been introduced as some sort of TV star or performer. The Reverend Barry Somethingorother. I humbly admit that I cannot say I recall this singer with particular clarity either, though I do remember him better than the preacher because he was accompanied in his performance by my brother, for whom I had come to this revival meeting under the enormous black tent. I remember the man's voice. I remember that his voice was a good voice. He was a good tenor. But his talent paled in comparison to my brother's. It was June. My wedding was a week away. I had time off from work and wanted to get some good bonding in with my little brother before the big day.

There was originally another musician playing, a woman of some advanced age in a white dress and white shoes and a hat, also white, that made me think of those old-fashioned nurses' uniforms, but for this part of the service she yielded to Elwyn, who had recently returned home after finishing up college. Elwyn would accompany the tall man with the small head on a series of hymns—"specials," they were called in the bulletin they passed out. When my brother's name was called by the minister hosting the service, there were cries of "Amen" and "Praise the Lord" and the crowd became noticeably more excited.

He had told me to expect this, but even with that warning I was not prepared for what I witnessed that evening. He was their favorite, their returning hero, their hometown boy done gone up to college and come back home to make them all proud. They were saying praises for the tall man too, but I believe it was only to be polite because the tall man had been up on the pulpit all along, as he was also a minister of some sort, and it was only after Elwyn's name was called and he stood up that the assemblage began to titter with this special kind of joy. I heard many a voice say "That Elwyn can sure hit them keys" and "Elwyn's good" and "Elwyn plays like he's got thirty fingers." I tingled with pride and expectation.

He was dressed in black—black coat, pants, tie, and shoes. Even a black shirt. The only bright color on his person was the red flower that he wore in the lapel of his coat. The bright white open-top grand piano was off to the left of the stage, or pulpit, so I was afforded a side view of him when he sat down. When his pant leg moved, I saw that his socks were black too.

The first song was called "Yes, God Is Real," and the audience ate it up. They were on their feet waving, applauding, shouting "Hallelujah!" When the tenor's voice took him high on the chorus—"Yes, God is real/He's real in my soul"—Elwyn answered with a funky blues chord from the lower register that had them shout "Yes" and "Praise Him" and "That's all right now." When the tenor held a note, Elwyn syncopated the stretch with a seductive beat that had the audience rocking and stamping their feet in time until the stamping of the feet became like a bass drum, or a string bass—it was part of the music now.

By the end of the song, there was no one left seated. People—men in suits and women in expensive dresses and high heels—were hugging each other, hugging themselves, crying real tears, waving their hands to heaven, rocking back and forth, groaning, and moaning. While the small-headed singer was taking a bow (McGowan! The Reverend Mc-Gowan was his name!), Elwyn struck the keys again and they were into a song that I knew from my handful of days in church and Vacation Bible School. "I Must Tell Jesus."

If "Yes, God Is Real" made them dance, "I Must Tell Jesus" made them wail.

The chords he put in this song were richer and more mournful than I ever remembered them being. Heads were shaking. People were wailing long sad notes. Eyes were shut tight as lips moaned in call-and-response echo, "I must, Lord—I must tell you, Lord."

When they got to the chorus—"I must tell Jesus/I must tell Jesus/I cannot bear these burdens alone"—he slowed it down so that every chord would penetrate to the bone, every note would be felt, every note would cause a tremor within.

After it was over, he tried to get up and leave the piano and return to the relative anonymity of his seat in the pews, but they made him return. They had started back singing the song. He couldn't let them sing it unaccompanied, so he turned to the piano, and without even sitting down, played them into an almost sonorous wail of pain and lament. But this time he played them too hard. They asked for it, and they got it. His music set loose in them something that should have remained bound.

For the next half hour it was organized chaos. No one was singing the words of the hymn anymore—they were moaning it, murmuring it, groaning it—as he played it on and on, still standing, like a film clip I had once seen of Little Richard the rock and roll singer in concert. With endless variations of mournful chords and evocative runs and trills that penetrated the tendermost places in the heart and the soul, he played and they responded with an almost tormented wail.

The preachers had all left the pulpit and were going from person to person in the assemblage, laying their hands on the wailing people's foreheads and praying for them. It was magnificently moving. I was moved.

When service finally got back under control a half hour later, a kind woman loaned me her handkerchief and I wiped the water from my eyes.

I was relieved that I hadn't done something crazy like run up to the altar and gotten saved.

Sister Morrisohn and Sister Elwyn Parker

We met up after service.

"I am Benny."

He took my hand and said, "I know." Then he embraced me. He was about an inch taller than me and he laid his head against my neck and began to sob. We held each other for more than a minute.

Again I was moved. Again I felt the urge to do something crazy, something magnificently biblical, like kiss him on his neck and say, "Oh my brother, how have I missed thee."

When we got to Sister Morrisohn's house, I wasn't sure what to expect. I had encountered her at the tent meeting, where she had been noticeably avoiding serious eye contact with Elwyn through years of practice, I suppose. She had not, however, avoided eye contact with me. She was trying to tell me something with her eyes. Just after the meeting, while people gathered to gossip and embrace, and Elwyn, the star, before he had come to me, was surrounded by a sea of handshakers and neck huggers, his woman slid over to me and said in a hushed tone, "You didn't tell him about the airport, did you?"

"No. Should I have?"

Of course not. I had better sense than that. The first day I meet my brother I'm just going to up and tell him, By the way, I met your woman a few years back. Man, she's hot. She kissed me on the neck.

She was wearing an elegant, form-fitting white suit, with a jacket and skirt of the same material and a blouse of undulating white silk. She wore a stylish white hat, pinned to which (along the silk ribbon) was a red rose of the same variety that Elwyn wore in his lapel. Her unadorned black hair flowed down her back magnificently. She wore silver shoes. She was relieved when I told her I hadn't told him and she said hurriedly, "Thank God. He doesn't know we ever met. As his lover, I realize I should have told him, but I didn't. I figured if Roscoe hadn't told him about you then it wasn't my place to do so. He and Roscoe already have a funny relationship, but he gets so crazy when I keep things from him."

As well-dressed church people milled about us, I winked at the beautiful lady like I had that day at the airport and said, "So you're his lover, huh?"

She said, "Don't play with me, little boy," and brushed past me angrily.

I immediately regretted my joke. It was out of place. I worried how she would react to me when we met again later.

But when Elwyn and I got to her house, the atmosphere was, to my surprise and relief, relaxed. She greeted us at the door—I got a friendly handshake and a hug, he got a big shameless kiss on the lips—and she took us on a tour of the house, for my benefit. It was a nice house, though I cannot say that I remember much about it. I remember that it was big and that it was in Coral Gables and that it was less interesting than watching the interplay of those two frisky . . . teens. What made me happy was that they were accepting me into their little secret. After the brief tour, she went into the kitchen to bring us back drinks and pastries.

While she was away, Elwyn said to me, "What do you think of her?"

"She's beautiful."

He nodded, accepting the compliment. "Where do you know her from?"

It caught me off guard. I stammered. "I just met her."

"Please don't lie to me. I saw you talking to her at the tent."

I put a fist over my mouth and chewed on it. "Jesus, man, don't put me on the spot like that."

"You are my brother. We need to start acting like brothers."

"I don't want to get all mixed up in the middle of something like this, man. Don't do this to me. I just met you." My fist was still in my mouth. "Maybe you should ask her."

"You can rest assured that I will," he said without smiling.

"Jesus, man, I'm sorry. Don't do this to me."

He was still nodding his head as she walked back into the living room with our pastries and fruit punch. We had a pleasant conversation after that, though I cannot recall what about. My stomach was jumping from apprehension.

I must say, though, that he seemed happy in her presence and she seemed happy in his. Furthermore, I was struck dumb by the fact that the whole time we were there having this supposed conversation of introduction, she sat upon his lap.

The whole time.

She practically clung to his neck. A few times I swear to God I saw her caress his obvious erection and I was forced by modesty to look away. I focused my attention on the vase of long-stemmed red roses instead. It occurred to me that the rose in Elwyn's lapel had come from this very same bouquet. He had come here this evening, before the service at the tent meeting, and brought her the roses, and she had cut one and pinned it to his lapel and then pinned one to her hat so that they would appear in public in matching roses. How sweet. I was touched.

Before long, my stomach stopped jumping. I think that was right after they excused themselves and left me alone in the living room to head
into her bedroom, lock the door, and make scandalously loud love.

Now we were in my car, headed north to something and somewhere
else he wanted to show me. My brother Elwyn, piano player, Christian,
man of mystery.

It was well after midnight, and we were on I-95 approaching the
city of Pompano. We had been driving about an hour after leaving Sister Morrisohn's home. It had been a tearful goodbye for them. As it
always was, he informed.

The surprise trip into their bedroom had lasted about fifteen minutes. My ears told me that they had been trying to be quiet about their
lovemaking in there but had been horribly unsuccessful. Amazing. This
after bringing tears to my heathen eyes with his heartfelt piano playing at the revival meeting. My church boy brother and his much older
lover, it was all so very weird to me.

As we approached this other mysterious thing he had dragged me
all the way up to Pompano to see, I was yakking my head off in the car
from nervousness.

"It's like, my God, I have a brother! I'm actually ashamed of myself,
really. I don't know what held me back all these years—maybe because
I didn't want to get Roscoe in trouble. I don't usually let other people's
foolishness keep me from making the right choices in my life. If I had
done that, I never would have gone to college in Boston, believing that
I was too poor to afford it. Even worse, the love of my life and I would
never have gotten engaged, believing that my mother's flaky relationship with her father somehow made us kin and therefore our relationship incestuous and therefore off-limits."

At that, he turned his face toward me. For most of the drive, he had let me talk and talk, with grunts and nods and the occasional street direction being his only contribution to our conversation. But now he said, "So, you're saying that she's your sister."

"No," I explained. "She's the daughter of a man my mother used to live with."

His voice was flat, though his words indicated that he was genuinely interested. He said, "So, you're saying you used to have sex with her while your mom and this man lived together."

"No. We never had sex while they lived together. In fact, we still haven't had sex."

For a moment, his eyes grew wide as though he were going to exclaim something, but then he said in that same deflated voice, "That's good. Good for you. One should remain a virgin until the wedding night. You're a good Christian for that, or whatever. If people would live according to the principles in the Bible, Christian or not, they'd be better off. They're sound principles. I wish that I had been more . . . but she's a good girl and everything, right? You sound like you really love her. You must really love her to overcome . . . incest."

I squared my shoulders. "It's not incest. Marie isn't my sister. She isn't related to me. She's my future wife."

"She's your mother's husband's daughter. That makes her your sister."

"My mother never married her father."

"If your mother had married her father—make a left here, then go down to the next light—would you still be marrying her?"

"My mother and her father have gotten over it. They support us now. They're going to be at the wedding. You'll meet them. You'll see."

From his throat came an indignant sound, and then he retorted, "I must point out that you are avoiding the question, Benny. I don't mean to be argumentative. It is a meaningless point because you are going to do whatever it is you are going to do, and I am still going to play at your wedding because that is an agreement I made before I was made aware of your situation, but you must understand that from now on when I look at you two, I will see a man who married his sister. The biblical principle is simple, Benny. My mother's husband is my father—"

"But he was never my mother's hus—"

He raised his voice then and spoke sternly to me: "—and my mother's live-in lover of many years is my mother's husband in the eyes of the common law, right?"

"He is not her common-law husband."

"But if he had continued to date your mother, never marrying her, but simply continued to date her and live with her and she with him, you would have had some reluctance to marrying his daughter, no?"

"That is beside the point."

"Imagine the wonderful family dinners at which a man and his lover are parents of children who are also lovers."

"That's not how it was. We never had sex, I told you."

"You never had sex because you knew that it would be wrong to do so. Why else would you not have sex? You're not saved and sanctified. You're not born again. Turn left here." He pointed to a dark, narrow street. I made the turn. I noticed that the neighborhoods had begun to decline. There were young men hanging out on street corners in groups of three and four, smoking, talking boastfully loud, playing loud music. It reminded me of Opa-Locka where I had grown up. I would not say that my brother was smiling, exactly, but there was a certain smug triumph in the air around him as he spoke. He was lecturing me. Preaching to me. His arrogance was as tangible as the summer heat and just as oppressive. "Look at it another way," he said. "Your mother and this man get married, and then divorce, would you not feel some reluctance in marrying his daughter?"

I was tired of this conversation and I'm sure it showed on my face because his voice became suddenly light and cheerful.

"You don't have to answer. I don't know why I keep doing this to people. It's not my place to judge people, especially when they're better than me. You got your act together. Nobody needs to tell you what to do. You with your college degrees. Stop at the next house. The green one with the truck in the drive. That's her house."

I pulled up and parked alongside the sagging chain-link fence. "Whose house?"

"My wife's. She lives here with her mom and dad. We got married last month. We still haven't found a place."

Like Unto Ishmael, Like Unto Moses

We've still been carrying on," he said about Sister Morrisohn, "because old habits die hard, but really it ended for us like three years ago. We almost did it. We almost got married. This was back during my first year in college. We should have done it, Benny. We should have. I loved her. I proposed to her and everything. But then I went and told my grandmother. We were in a motel room in Micanopy when I asked her and she said yes, and I had to go and get my grandmother involved. I was so young. So naïve. So stupid. I wanted her blessings because she was the only one who knew what was going on, and she had kept it a secret for me, you know? Oh, what she revealed to me that day—it ruined my life.

"You see, what I didn't understand, what I didn't know, was that people who have lived before you, they may not be as educated as you, they may not be as accomplished as you, but you can never push past them because they were here before you. They know stuff. They have lived. They know stuff about you that you don't even know. This is their world, not yours. You just got here. You haven't earned the right to call it yours yet. You think you're hot stuff, but you're not—not with them. They were living and breathing and loving and leaving before you were even born. I mean, you take the book of Exodus and look at the story of Moses. You know the story of Moses? The Ten Commandments and all that. He was born a slave in Egypt, but only stayed a slave for three months. They were killing Hebrew boys in those days, and his mother, fearing for his life, floated him down the Nile, where he was found by Pharaoh's daughter. Now Pharaoh's daughter adopted the child as her son, but needed a midwife for him, so she sent a nearby slave (actually the babe's big sister) to fetch her a midwife, and the girl went and got for the job her own mother (the babe's own mother too). So now Moses grows up a prince in Egypt and soon he is next in line for the throne. Moses is a prince and his mother and his sister are his slaves, and the woman he thinks is his mother, Pharaoh's daughter, is actually his enemy, an Egyptian, but she does not tell him this because she loves him since she has raised him as her son. I used to think all that was fine. I used to think, Well, the Lord works in mysterious ways. It's God's will, I used to say. But now I see it a different way. What about Moses? What about him?

"Moses wakes up one morning and suddenly his mother is not his mother and his slaves are not his slaves. He's like walking around in his noble robes in a daze. He's saying, So if my mother's not who I think she is and I'm not who I think I am, then who are my people? Someone points out the slaves building the pyramids under the oppressive heat of the sun and the stinging lash of the Egyptian taskmasters. Them over there, this pointing someone says, them over there are your people. So now he finds himself face-to-face with this fact, I am not who I thought I was. No one is who I thought he was. I have to rethink everything. My friends are my enemies. My enemies are my friends. I have been lied to my whole life. My whole world is upside down. And I am new to this knowledge, but these others—they have known of this since forever. They have been lying to me about who I am. I did not know who I was, but they knew and they kept it from me. One minute I am a prince, grandson to the king, the next I am a Hebrew slave.

"It's not fair to Moses. It's not fair to have your whole world suddenly shift like that—from slave to mother. Some slave who is not related to you at all ends up being someone whose existence explains all that you are. Someone who knows more about you than you know about yourself. But that is what happens when you are dealing with people who were here before you were. You are not their equals. There is no way to have any kind of real relationship with them. You will always feel that there are things they aren't telling you—important things, life-and-death things. This is why the Bible says honor thy mother and thy father—honor them because you certainly can't befriend them. How can you befriend them when they know more about you than you know about yourself? It's too easy for them to manipulate you. You have no choice but to honor them. Even if you hate them, you have to honor them.

"My grandmother tells me that Brother Morrisohn is my grandfather. That's not fair. I lived all my life with him as some really nice guy, a great and honorable church elder, whom I admired. Not to mention now Sister Morrisohn is like my . . . step-grandmother. It's just not fair. What is she going to tell me next—that I am adopted? That my real name is Moses and she found me floating down the River Nile? This is why in the Bible there is all of that *who begat whom*. Chapter after chapter of begats. This way people can't lie to you, or keep things from you. This way it's written down for all to see, no matter who you are or what year you were born. Abraham begat Isaac who begat Jacob; therefore, Abraham is Jacob's grandfather and not just some old shepherd he might bump into at the watering hole.

"I mean like this thing with you and Elaine. Okay, so she met you before tonight. Years before. You won't tell me about it. She won't tell me about it. That's fine because it's only a *few* years ago. So I give it to her straight. I tell her, this is the kind of thing that drives a wedge between us, honey bun. You keep things from me. You treat me like a child—that's what it means to be a child, to not know things that everybody else knows. This is my brother, but you met him before tonight and you're lying to me. So we're making love and I'm shouting at her as I'm laying it on her hard and she's telling me this story about you and her and my father, *our* father, at the airport. How she mistook you for me. How she kissed you on the back of the neck. That story. Yeah, that one. So now I understand that she knew about you for like five years and did not tell me. She did not want to hurt my relationship with my father—our father, I should say. So she withheld knowledge about my own brother from me. She made that choice because she wanted to save my relationship with a weak and ineffectual parent. She made the choice to keep me in the dark about . . . *me*. She had the knowledge and manipulated it. But five years is only a *few* years ago. I was alive five years ago. I was of sound mind and body five years ago. I could just as easily have discovered you five years ago and not told her about it, so as far as this thing at the airport is concerned, she and I are on equal terms, sort of. But what if we go further back?

"What if while I was loving her tonight, while I was laying it on her good and she was trying not to scream because you were just beyond the door, I demanded that she go further back? Way back. Back to when you and I weren't even born yet, but to when we were in the womb. She is about our father's age. She is the age of our mothers. She was there. She was present while we were being conceived. She knew everybody because she was a member of the church back then. I asked, What do you know about Benny? What do you know of Patsy, Benny's mother? Well, says she, I don't want to tell you this. It is too hard to tell you this. Poor Benny, says she. I don't want to hurt him. Tell it, I demand of her.

Tell it! And I gave her a few hard thrusts from the hip, just the way she likes it.

"And she says, Well, Benny's mother Patsy and Roscoe and I were not saved back then. We were doing things that were not very Christian. We were all part of a group of young people who were wild and careless. Patsy was with Roscoe, they were a couple, and I was with another guy in the group—a white guy. We used to shoplift and whatnot. Patsy and Roscoe would go into the Woolworth's first. Because they were black, they would draw heat. Then my white boyfriend and I would go in. We were white—well, he was white, I only looked white if you didn't look too closely, but that was good enough—so nobody paid us much attention. While Roscoe and Patsy were drawing heat, my boyfriend and I would take things from the shelves and hide them in our clothes.

"This was a good plan that worked for many months. Eventually, however, we were caught. Buford and his dear wife Glovine bailed us all out and brought us to the church—all because of his daughter Beverly, who was part of our group from time to time, though we really didn't like her all that much. Patsy wasn't much on churching, so she played the game for a while and then stopped going as soon as she no longer needed Buford Morrisohn's legal help cleaning up her record. I broke up with my white boyfriend because I had my eyes on Buford, the rich old guy with the plump sickly wife. Roscoe, who was handsome as hell, settled down and started playing the dashing gentleman with some of the nice little girls at the church, including one Isadore Cooper—though he and Patsy were still an item. In fact, Isadore and Patsy found themselves with child at about the same time. This was a problem. *Pastor Buford Morrisohn, at the request of Mamie Cooper, visited with and counseled young Roscoe, after which Roscoe married Isadore and the marriage, as we all know, prospered.*

"I am one who believes, she continued, that Patsy lost her longtime boyfriend Roscoe Parker because Roscoe loved Isadore more. The man simply made a choice, and a sound one. There are those who believe that Patsy lost her man because she turned her back on the Faithful, who had done so much to help her with her legal problems. Her record is spotless now thanks to the church, but so is mine. So is Roscoe's. Again, she insisted, I do not hold with these people who believe the church had anything to do with Roscoe's choice. In fact, she said, the truth is that many of us were still behaving kindly toward Patsy when the child Benjamin Franklin Willett was born.

"He was baptized at the Church of Our Blessed Redeemer Who Walked Upon the Waters same as you, she informed me. Buford Morrisohn stood as his godfather and I, Elaine Franklin, now Morrisohn, stood as his godmother. My friend Patsy—my *best* friend Patsy—gave him my last name. It was only after the bad blood between Isadore and Patsy came to a boil that it was decided that all relations with Patsy and her son Benjamin Franklin would be cut off. The Faithful have known about Benny all along. Benny is not one of their discoveries, but one of their discards. He is like Ishmael, cast off into the wilderness with his mother. We got rid of him to save you, she informed me. And try as I might, Benny, after hearing that I could not continue my thrusting."

I Am One of the Faithful

I am one of the Faithful," I said to my brother.

"Were," my brother said to me.

"Elaine Morrisohn is my godmother."

"Was," he said to me. "She told me they had it annulled."

"You can have a godmothership . . . annulled?"

Elwyn put his hand on my shoulder. "See what I'm saying, brother? You can't trust people older than you."

At that point I was so low I was almost inclined to agree with him. "It's not old people you can't trust. It's you people. You *Faithful*. Why do you even call yourselves that? I can't believe you . . . you cast me off."

"It wasn't me. I was just a kid. And what are you complaining about? You did great. Look at you. College graduate. MBA. Businessman. You earn more money in one year than Roscoe makes in ten."

He indicated my car with a nod—the Mercedes.

"You're certainly doing better than me. You're doing better than I ever will," my brother said.

"That's not the point at all. I had no family growing up. I was alone. You don't understand. You'll never understand. I kept a scrapbook on you. I wanted to know everything about you. You were my brother. I had these fantasies about who you were. About what games we would play if we were together."

"Hey, man, take it easy."

"Why can't you understand this?"

"But I do understand," he said. "When I found out about you, after the anger, I kept filling in the blanks. I would go back and say, When I was here, Benny was there. When I was this, Benny was that. When I was in kindergarten, Benny was in kindergarten, like that."

"That's not exactly what I'm talking about, but, yeah, okay, stuff like that."

Elwyn looked at me. He was trying to see something in me. We were brothers, but would we ever be friends? *Could* we ever be friends?

He shook his head again and got out of the car. I got out of the car too, and after taking note of my uncertain surroundings, I set my alarm with a click of the remote on my keychain.

"Don't you worry," he assured, as we walked up the driveway to the front door of the house where his wife lived. "You and Marie will make it."

"I know we will," I said defiantly. I put my finger in his face. "Because I'm not one of you," I told him. "I love her. And she's not my sister."

Laughing, he reached the door and knocked on it. It was 2:15 in the morning. I felt weary and worn and sad, like the lines of the famous old hymn. Elwyn said to me, still smiling with mirth, "Well, I love Sister Morrisohn, and she's my grandfather's wife. And your ex-godmother."

He didn't have to add that, yet I was too worn out to fight with his arrogant butt anymore.

"But the thing that hurts me more than anything," he continued, his laughter waning, "is that now I know with a certainty that she and I can never be together. I can forgive her for Brother Morrisohn—she had no control over that. She did not know that he was my grandfather, but she always knew that Roscoe was my father."

"What are you saying?"

"She knew. Roscoe was her friend, and she became involved with his son. How would you feel if one of your childhood friends became involved with your child?"

"I see what you're saying."

"And furthermore, and worst of all, how do I know that she and Roscoe, back when they were young and they were friends, did not share more than a friendship?"

"Well, in light of all that has happened, she would have told you that."

"Maybe not."

"Well, you should have asked her. You *should* ask her."

"I could not." He shook his head sadly. "I cannot."

"So then it's over?"

"No. Never."

"But—"

"I love her. She will ever be mine."

The way he said it was so over-the-top ridiculous that I started to laugh, but I stopped when I saw that he was crying.

He tried to cover the tears by hiding his face in his shirt.

He sniffled and sobbed while I watched, uncertain what I should do. After a while I reached out and gave him a tentative hug.

After a while the tentative hug became a real hug.

Then we composed ourselves.

"Does Sister Morrisohn know that you're married?"

"She knows, and she hates me for it. She's been withholding the loving as punishment. Tonight is only the second time we've been together since I got married a month ago. We did it right after the wedding. We did it hard. I think she was trying to take me back from my wife or something. When that didn't work, she cut me off cold. But tonight was good. We're back together again. You know how it is."

"No," I said. "No. I don't know how it is."

He sighed. "Read your Bible. Most of the great men of God were in this same situation, but back then you could marry more than one woman. I understand now why that was."

Gone was the sensitive, weeping brother I had embraced mere moments ago, and standing in his place again was the original arrogant, vainglorious knucklehead, to whom I said, "Please tell me why that was, Elwyn. Please tell me why the *great men* of God could have three or more wives back then. Call me ignorant, but it sounds a bit sexist and chauvinistic to me. Polygamy?"

"I see you're being sarcastic," he replied with a smirk. "I'm not going to argue with a nonbeliever and his ungodly feminist ideas. The Bible is the Bible. A great man of God must marry for love and also to ensure the continuation of his line. Quite often the one you love is, for whatever reason, not capable, nor fit, to bear your children. In such cases, you must have more than one woman."

I looked at him, and I guess my jaw was hanging open or something, because the expression on his face told me that the one on my face was like someone having a conversation with a strange alien creature that had just dropped in from outer space, except that the strange alien creature had been living on this planet and behaving this way for like two thousand years while building great civilization after civilization and conquering lesser creatures and getting them to see things his way. So it was okay to have two women. Or three. What of adultery? Well, the Bible is the Bible. That was his explanation. This was my brother. I wanted to laugh at him or shoot him. I couldn't figure out which.

Then a mischievous grin spread across his face and he punched me playfully in the shoulder. "I'm just kidding you. I love Elaine Morrisohn with all my heart, okay? I wish I could marry her. I just wish. If I could marry her, I would never want for any other woman. I would never cheat on her. There is no one else in this world for me, but her," he said earnestly. "But this is the way it's got to be. I can't leave her. And I can't have her. I'm caught between a rock and a hard place."

I was relieved to hear him say that. I asked him, "Does your wife know about Sister Morrisohn?"

Elwyn put a finger to his lips and shushed me. "No way. You must really think I'm crazy."

He knocked on the door again, harder this time, and the lights went on inside the house. I heard chains being unhooked, bolts being slid. I heard an alarm being turned off with a series of coded beeps. The door finally swung open, and I saw for the first time his other woman, his young wife, my sister-in-law. She was very tall, about six feet, though not very *attractive*. There were big pink rollers in her hair that matched the big pink slippers on her feet.

She was at least six months pregnant.

Elwyn gave her a dry, unromantic peck on the cheek and put his arm around her, presenting her. "Benny, this is my wife Mary. Mary, this is my brother Benny. He's getting married next week. I'm going to play at his wedding, honey."

I leaned in for a hug and she extended her hand for a shake. We shook, said hi and hi, while trading polite, toothy smiles with each other. Then she and Elwyn went inside the house, and I got in my car and drove back down to my condo in Miami Beach.

HERE ENDETH THE TESTAMENT OF A JOYFUL NOISE

VIII. Testament of Fire and Lamentations

We may live in a tent or a cottage,
And die in seclusion alone;
But the Father Who seeth in secret,
Remembers each one of His own.
We shall shine as the stars of the morning,
With Jesus the Crucified One;
We shall rise to be like Him forever,
Eternally shine as the sun.
—Judson W. Van DeVenter, "We Shall Shine as the Stars"

The Leap

The Church of Our Blessed Redeemer Who Walked Upon the Waters was packed for the first night of the revival, with people squeezed so close together that chairs had to be brought from the nursery and the dining hall. Still there were many people standing along the back wall of the church.

And it was hot. A noisy fan labored in each corner, and the stained glass windows of the building were wide open, but the blanket of thick

July heat was not thrown off.

I wiped the sweat from my forehead with the tissue I kept in a box in the piano seat. I loosened my tie. As the pianist, I had my own fan, but trust me—this was not a good night for the central air to conk out.

Sharing the pulpit with Pastor were the Reverend Dr. Barry Mc-Gowan—Peachie's ex-husband—on break from his TV show at church headquarters in Lakeland; the Evangelist Rev'run Lewis from Tifton, Georgia, who had traveled to Miami by chauffeur-driven Winnebago to work his annual miracle; and a white minister who wore no tie.

When the musical portion of the service concluded, I only half listened as Rev'run pronounced sentence on this "weak and abominable generation" with his famous "Lake of Fire" sermon. I knew the sermon by heart. As far back as I could remember, Rev'run had been preaching the "Lake of Fire," his best sermon, on the first nights of his revivals, realizing, perhaps, that his audience would grow thinner and sleepier, and would carry less pocket change as the week advanced.

It was my job to remain alert, prepared to render inspirational accompaniment should Rev'run launch into song or melodious prayer. So I picked my teeth, wiped away sweat, fanned myself, yawned, and picked my teeth again without appearing irreverent or inattentive—a simple trick for me since I had been the church's pianist on and off for most of my life and consistently for the past five years since I had graduated college. The main thing on my mind that night was how I would pay this month's bills.

If I didn't get any sub work, I'd have to cut at least ten yards, which worked out to two yards a day—unless I planned to work weekends. My church paycheck, $200, would be cut on Friday, and I could steal another $150 from Visa. My MasterCard was maxed out. I would have to borrow the rest from my mother. Or Sister Morrisohn. Perhaps I should definitely cut a few yards on Saturday.

Rev'run was walnut-brown and fat. His head was bald, his lips beet-red. Tonight he wore a double-breasted suit woven from the finest mint-green polyester. His swollen midsection strained against the buttons. On the pinkie finger of each hand, he wore a gold ring on which was inscribed *The Holy Ghost Is with You* (his left hand) and *Behold the Son of God* (his right). The Church of Our Blessed Redeemer Who Walked Upon the Waters frowned upon jewelry, but we made an exception for Rev'run.

Pastor once explained, "Rev'run is a divine instrument of God. Let God alone hold him responsible for his eccentricities."

Rev'run preached rhythmically in a majestic baritone and punctuated his message by stomping a foot or pounding the lectern with a fist. When Rev'run ended a phrase or caught his breath, he grunted his trademark syllable, "AH," and the congregation echoed his cue with shouts of "My Lord," "Oh Lord," "Yes Lord," and "Amen."

Rev'run bellowed, "You say your hearts belong to Jesus-AH."

The Faithful cried, "My Lord."

"But y'all bearin the wrong kinda fruits-AH."

"Oh Lord."

"You say you're an apple tree-AH, but I see bananas on your branches-AH. You claim to be a Christian-AH, but I see malice in your heart for your brother-AH. You say you love the Lord-AH, but you spendin your time makin goo-goo eyes at your neighbor's wife-AH. All the vices known to man, you is doin 'em-AH. You smokin-AH, drinkin-AH, womanizin-AH. Some of you even manizin-AH. Stay with me now-AH. Yes! You sodomizin-AH. But you foolin yourself thinkin God ain't lookin-AH. But Oh-AH!—"

"My Lord."

"Oh-AH!"

"Oh Lord."

"Oh-AH!"

"Yes Lord."

"Oh-AH!"

"Amen."

"Hallelujah-AH!" he wailed, raising his large hands toward heaven. "I believe the poet when he says-AH, 'Vice is vice and vice versa-AH.' And let me tell you, brother-AH, and sister-AH, and mother-AH, and father-AH. You goin to the lake-AH—"

"My Lord."

"To the lake-AH!"

"Oh Lord."

"To the lake-AH!"

"Yes Lord."

"To the lake of fire-AH!"

"Amen."

"Hallelujah!" Rev'run shouted. He clapped his hands and laughed victoriously.

The congregation followed his lead. The Spirit was moving.

Sister Naylor screamed and fell to the floor—fainted dead away, except for her trembling legs. The ushers, clearing a path through the extra chairs and stools, rushed to Sister Naylor, threw the velvet shawl over her legs, and dragged her to the back of the church.

Deacons Arnold Blake and Trevor Miron, who had been feuding over money bet on a football game, who had sworn never again to share the same pew, who had come close to exchanging blows at last week's prayer meeting, found each other in the happy confusion and embraced, tears flying everywhere. It would take more than five dollars to lure them into the lake of fire.

Sister Elaine Morrisohn—president of the Missionary Society—rolled her gray eyes heavenward and entreated, "Try me, Lord. Try me."

I found her words sadly ironic, for I had indeed tried Sister Morrisohn, who had been my lover since I was sixteen. She had been my lover for . . . twelve years. I had been trying Sister Elaine Morrisohn for nearly half my life, and it was good.

Up on the pulpit, Pastor clapped his hands and commanded, "Heed the words of God's anointed. Heed his words."

The famous Christian entrepreneur and televangelist Reverend Dr. McGowan, a tall man with a small head, closed his eyes tightly, and soon tears were streaming. He stretched his arms around his torso and began to rock back and forth in his chair. He groaned, "God is good. God is so good."

Trapped in her web of dark senility, my old grandmother struggled to her feet and began to tell her life story in a loud, rasping voice. When she regained control of her mind, which happened only rarely, she apologized for having spoken out of turn and dropped back into her seat. A few minutes later she was up leaning on her walker again, saying: "My mother, being part Indian, never used a straightening comb in her life, but she had such pretty hair. Not like this old dry head I got from my father . . ."

"Try me, Lord," said Sister Morrisohn. "Try me."

"Heed the words of God's anointed," said Pastor.

"God is good. God is so good," said the Reverend Dr. McGowan.

The white minister was the only one who seemed to be as unaffected by the proceedings as I was.

Unlike the rest of the men, the white minister wore neither a tie nor a jacket, just a simple white shirt and a pair of black slacks, which weren't particularly well pressed. He sat with legs crossed in the plush throne-room chair, reading the advertising on his handheld cardboard fan. Sweat rolled off his pink face, soaking his shirt. He stared at the front of the fan—Martin Luther King Jr. and family in church. Moments later, he flipped to the back of the fan—the Brigg's Funeral Home. Then he flipped to the front again, and after that the back, and so on, only occasionally breaking the pattern to wipe away a lock of sandy brown hair that had fallen to the front of his face and obstructed his view.

Was it possible that in the whole building, I alone noticed the man spinning the fan from front to back, back to front?

Yet not even I was prepared for the leap.

The white minister hopped to his feet with a loud thuh-dump. He latched onto Rev'run's shoulder and slung the fat preaching man from Georgia into the famous entrepreneur and televangelist Reverend Dr. Barry Sebastian-Bach McGowan's lap.

All at once a hush fell over the church.

When the white man grabbed the microphone, deafening feedback squealed from the speakers. He was about to speak. We all leaned forward to hear what he would say. The white minister shouted into the microphone, "Sontalavala, Sontalavala, Ghila! Sontalavala!"

With that, he clapped a monstrous Bible to his chest and leapt from the five-foot-high pulpit without touching one of its seven steps, ran down the path those standing in the aisle quickly cleared for him, and sprinted through the stained glass doors of the church.

We heard a car door slam and an engine fire up outside. Then we heard his tires screeching out of earshot.

I looked around the church, and everyone was stunned mute except for my grandmother, who stood again and lost herself in the oratory of senility: "We had only one mule to cover all that dry, rocky soil, but we prayed to God, and God touched the hearts of our neighbors who lent us their horses, their mules, their strength, but still it wasn't enough. We had to pack up everything we owned in the world and move down to Miami . . ."

Pastor signaled for me to play a hymn, any hymn.

Rev'run and the Reverend Dr. McGowan, untangled at last, began chattering to each other:

"Was he with you?"

"I thought he came with you."

"He didn't come with me."

The entire church was buzzing by the time I hammered the first chords of "Just as I Am." When the church finally began singing, it was without enthusiasm. Then Pastor made a faint attempt at altar call.

"Jesus loves even you . . . so come up and get saved before it's too late. Amen."

When no one responded, Pastor announced that a meeting of the Brethren would immediately follow. Then he adjourned, forgetting to pass the collection plates.

While I had found service entertaining for a change, I did not stay for the Brethren's meeting. On my way out, I shook hands with the Faithful, who were polite but abrupt. They were still jittery from the "miracle," as they were now calling it.

I passed by mothers and children congregated on the cemented space around the flagpole. They marveled at God's power and pondered the role of the white minister.

Sister Morrisohn stopped me. "You played real nice tonight, Brother Parker. How's Sister Parker and little Benjamin?" She smiled knowingly. "We missed them in service tonight."

"Sister Parker isn't feeling too well tonight," I lied. My wife Mary was a Baptist, and she had grown to despise the Faithful, calling us a bunch of "dry heads." In our five years of marriage, she had attended maybe a handful of Sunday-morning services, a few weddings, a few funerals.

"Really?" said Sister Morrisohn. "What did you think of the beautiful witness of that white brother? Didn't it touch you?" She rolled her eyes.

Aha, I thought, she found it interesting too.

"Yes, Sister, the Spirit was really moving in him."

"Indeed." Then she added in a way that only I would understand: "The Spirit hasn't moved in me in a long time."

"I'm certain it won't move tonight," I said in a way that only she would understand.

We separated ourselves from the crowd of women. We stood a safe distance from each other. We were just two members of the Faithful, the pianist and the president of the Missionary Society, making small talk after church.

"Service ended early, Brother Parker." (There is an opportunity, she meant.)

"I've got to get up early for subbing tomorrow." (I don't feel like it, I fired back.)

"Liars too shall have their part in the lake of fire." (It's hard being alone, my love.)

"I need to look for some yards." (Don't make it any harder than what it already is, my love.)

"You need money?" (You need money?)

"I've got some things lined up. Some yards." (I always need money. Who are you kidding? But don't embarrass me by giving me any. I'm trying to save what little is left of my pride.)

"Don't be afraid to tell me if you need." (I love you, my darling. I would do anything for you.)

"I'm okay. Really I am." (My life is sh---.)

"I just miss you is all." She took my hand, a sister in the Lord shaking the hand of her brother in the Lord. "I guess I don't always know my place."

Sister Morrisohn walked away. I opened my hand to see what she had left in it: two fifties.

Now with ten yards and what I could get from Visa, I'd be but $300 in the hole. Things were looking up.

Of course, I had tarried too long on the church grounds, and now my godsons Elwyn Miron (eleven), Elwyn Jones (ten), and Buford Elwyn Gregory (nine) had surrounded my car, hailing, "Goddy Elwyn. Goddy Elwyn. Wait!"

I had missed Elwyn's (Jones) birthday party (deliberately). I handed him, painfully, one of the fifties. He took it with a reach-in hug, and then he and the other two in their clean little suits and their shiny shoes skipped away, celebrating with squeals of innocent laughter and prepubescent ideas of what to do with the money. The last words I heard were "Nikes" and "Nintendo."

When I got home, I had every intention of telling Mary and Benjamin about the white minister, but they were watching a sitcom on TV. Mary sat on the couch; four-and-a-half-year-old Benjamin sat Indian-style on the floor, his face about a foot from the screen.

I said, "What did I tell you about sitting so close to the screen? You'll ruin your eyes."

Mary said, "Move away from that screen, Benjamin."

I said, "You wait until now to tell him to move away from the TV? You had all night."

Mary said, "Sure I had all night. I always have all night. And all day.

You're never home. You don't have a job, but you're never home. And when you do come home, all you do is give orders."

Mary's skin was a dark olive, her head of curly hair jet-black. She was tall—two inches taller than me, about the height of K-Sarah—and thin with long, delicate hands and fingers. In that respect she reminded me of Peachie. Also like Peachie, she had thick eyebrows that ran together in the middle of her forehead. Mary's brown eyes, though, seemed sensuous and at the same time too large to be set against her small nose and mouth.

Her left eye squinted almost shut whenever she became angry.

I said, "What do you mean I don't have a job? I work hard. Who puts food on the table? Who pays the bills?"

"Your mom, your dad, your brother, your friends, your credit cards, and anyone else who is willing to give you a handout," Mary said, squinting.

"That's not true," I said. (It was true.)

"Oh yes, you tell everyone you're a college graduate. Top of your class, you brag. Oh yes, you preach the benefits of a liberal arts education, but where is your job?"

"I work hard."

"A substitute teacher one day. A yard man the next. The big money rolls in at the end of the month when that dry-headed church pays you. All together you make about six hundred a month. Rent alone is five hundred!"

"I work hard." (My life is sh--.)

Benjamin, a sensitive boy who got upset every time we fought, buried his face in his hands and began to cry in deep heaves until Mary scooped him up.

"You're not fooling anyone, Elwyn. You're a beggar. If I didn't have a part-time job at Sears, we'd starve," she said, carrying Benjamin into his bedroom.

When she walked back into the living room about ten minutes later, she too was crying. She dropped down into the couch beside me, rested her head on my shoulders, wrapped her thin, downy arms around my stomach, but I refused to even look at her. That she was sorry came as no surprise to me. We had been through this routine too many times. Why was she always sorry after she had shredded my confidence? Why didn't she just learn to watch her mouth?

Mary said, "You try, Elwyn. You really try. We're gonna make it." She touched my cheek with tenderness. "If I had gotten my degree, I could help you more."

I wondered how much better off we would be if Mary had, in fact, completed her undergraduate studies in anthropology.

"You should take off your shoes, honey. Here. I'll take them to the room for you."

Kneeling in front of me, she took off my shoes and socks, and kissed my feet playfully. When I did not respond, she swelled up to cry again, but for some reason she didn't. She rose with my shoes and headed for the bedroom.

I wanted her to feel guilty. Go ahead feel guilty for opening your big mouth again.

She stopped at the bedroom door and turned. She was going to try one last time. "There's a couple slices of pizza in the kitchen if you're hungry," she said pleasantly.

Again, I did not acknowledge.

She went into the bedroom and slammed the door.

I did not acknowledge that either.

I loosened my tie, took off my shirt and pants, folded them neatly, and then placed them on the coffee table. I stretched out on the couch. My legs dangled over the armrest. I fell asleep.

Around midnight, I awoke. An obnoxious salesman on a TV commercial was shouting: "I want to save, save—I mean save you money!"

There was something about his manner that reminded me of Rev'run.

I got up, turned off the TV, and went to bed. Mary fought me for my favorite pillow, which I found pressed between her legs. I thought she was awake, so I said, "Tonight a visiting minister grabbed the mike from Rev'run, spoke in tongues, and leapt off the pulpit."

But Mary was snoring.

Or perhaps she was simply refusing to acknowledge.

The next morning, two schools called asking for me to sub. The elementary school was about fifteen minutes away, but I chose to sub across town at the high school, not because it was where I had graduated many years ago, but because it was located in a neighborhood that had many overgrown yards. I would carry the lawnmower in my trunk and visit some of the houses during lunch hour to set up yard work for later that day and the rest of the week.

Mary wanted to make love, but I was still angry about the night before.

"The Bible says, Let not the sun set upon your wrath."

I snorted. Imagine that, a Baptist quoting Scripture with me. "I'm not angry anymore," I told her. "I don't want to be late for school, and I want to conserve my energy in case I get some yard work."

She was in one of her giddy, chatty moods. "When we first got married, we used to do it every night and every morning, and sometimes you'd pick me up at work and we'd go do it in the car parked behind the dumpsters."

"Did you iron my white shirt?"

She handed me the shirt, still gabbing: "And we'd do it and do it until our knees were shaky."

"There are still wrinkles in this shirt." I held it up. "I can't wear this."

She touched the shirt with a finger. "Those are creases. Now we do it maybe once a month. This month is almost over and we haven't done it yet."

"This is the shirt with the missing buttons."

"Are we going to do it or not?"

"Do what?"

"Divorce," she said. For a second, she eyed me. Then she smiled as though she had been joking. "I mean sex. Are we going to do it at all this month? A woman has needs. Don't you hear what I'm trying to tell you, Mr. Sexy?"

But she wasn't fooling me. Joke or no joke, divorce was on her mind too.

I had never loved Mary. I was nearly certain she had never loved me. As long as we had been together, we hardly knew each other.

Why did we ever get married?

It was my senior year at the University of Florida, just before Christmas break in a piano cubicle in the student union. I was practicing "Clair de Lune." She was passing by on her way to her dorm room, a large fries and a strawberry shake in either hand, when, she claimed, she heard the music and knocked on the door.

I opened it, of course, after peeping out and glimpsing the leggy, curvaceous thing standing there.

"The music was so lovely," said she, the chatty freshman, who reminded me distantly of Peachie, "I just had to see who was playing it."

"Only me," I said, marveling at her pretty legs.

"Your playing is gorgeous. It's wonderful. I used to take lessons as a kid, but I could never play like that. How do you learn to play like that? It must take years of practice. You're so talented. It's the greatest music I have ever heard."

I stood up. She sat down. She played "Chopsticks."

When she finished, she lifted her hands from the keys and looked to me for appraisal. "That's all I remember. I used to know a lot more songs than that, but I guess when you don't practice it goes away. I used to go to piano lessons every Friday, but then when my father lost his business and we moved to Pompano—"

"Your playing is just lovely. I liked it very much. Let's play it together."

So I sat down and we played it together. Thigh against thigh.

"I've seen you around the labs. You're a senior, a physics major."

"Math," I corrected.

"Oh, that's right. You helped my friend Trudy pass calculus, remember? I was there with her a few times. That's where I know you from. Do you remember me?"

She did look familiar. "You're Jeff Edwards's girlfriend. ROTC Jeff?"

"Yes," she said. "I mean no. We broke up. He was too religious and all that."

"I'm in his Bible study group."

"I didn't mean it in a negative way."

"Yes you did."

"Yes I did," she admitted. "He was too pushy. Are you pushy?"

"Not anymore." A few weeks earlier, during a trip home to Miami, I had spent almost all of my time with Sister Morrisohn and almost none of it with my parents. Selfishness. Who was I to judge people? "Salvation is for everyone and at the same time not for everyone, if you know what I mean. I'll read the Bible to you, but then I let you do what you want to do. People have to be who they are."

Her eyes were fixed on my face. "What do you want to do now?"

"Anything you want to do." I reached for her strawberry shake, sipped it up through the straw. She took it back and sipped up the rest. I think we kissed for the first time after that, or maybe we kissed when we got back to her dorm. One thing led to another. There was more talk of music and math. More kissing. That first time I saw her naked, what turned me on the most was the way she neatly folded her little bra and her little pastel-colored underpants and placed them on the desk next to her books. It was such a cute and innocent thing to do just before having a penis shoved into you. It quite turned me on. Even these days, when I'm having a hard time getting aroused by her, I'll look around the room to see where she has placed her neatly folded undies. She always does it, and it never fails to do the trick. To be honest, I remember liking her big, sensitive nipples very much too, though not so much anymore.

Other than Sister Morrisohn, Mary was the first woman I had ever slept with, so when she became pregnant, I didn't encourage abortion. I proposed to her. My reasoning was that marrying Mary would help me end my years-old affair with Sister Morrisohn, which was almost as spiritually taxing as it was intoxicating.

I loved being with Sister Morrisohn, but it was an impossible love. The age thing. The grandfather thing. The Roscoe thing. There were just too many barriers to overcome.

I told myself that I wanted to give her a chance to find true happiness with someone else. Yet I knew, somewhere deep inside, that I would never find true happiness without her.

Poor Mary, I would never love her (the undie thing, yes). Mary was just a convenience.

But divorce scared me. I would never be able to live on the little money leftover after child support. And what if she needed alimony? And I wanted to see Benjamin grow up. I was stuck.

So on the morning after the white minister leapt from the pulpit, I approached Mary from behind, one finger brushing the inside of her thigh.

"Ah, yes," said Mary as she became soft lips, clean skin.

"It truly has been awhile," I said, with forced breathiness.

"I love you, Elwyn. I love you."

"That's good to know," I said.

But as I sat naked on the bed watching her neatly fold and place her little panties, I didn't believe a word of it.

"I'm a sub," I said to the security guard, who was new and didn't recognize me.

"Lift your arms."

I lifted my arms and she passed a buzzing paddle under them, up and down my legs, in between them.

"Okay. You're clean."

Mr. Byrd, my old principal, saw me. "That's Elwyn Parker. He's a sub."

The security guard nodded at him. "He's clean."

I shook Mr. Byrd's hand as I always did when I subbed at Miami Gardens High, and he said the same thing he always said: "The bars, the armed guards, the metal detector, you'd think this was a prison. What year did you graduate, Parker?"

"1982."

"In 1982, we sent two students to Harvard, six to Princeton and MIT, twenty to Stanford, forty to the University of Florida and Florida

State, and nearly two hundred to Miami-Dade Junior College. Over 70 percent went on to some kind of higher learning that year."

"I remember," I said, though I wondered at Mr. Byrd's astonishing memory. Would he recite the same figures if one day I told him I had graduated in, say, 1981?

Mr. Byrd pointed at two girls in cutoff shorts, halter tops, and gold sprinkles in their hair, which matched their gaudy gold necklaces and bangles. One girl was pregnant. They were both casually smoking cigarettes. "Put those cigarettes out!" he ordered in that deep growl that still struck fear in the hearts of wayward students. And me.

The girls eyed him menacingly before dropping their cigarettes and stomping them out with four-inch heels. They pouted rudely and disappeared around the corner, no doubt to smoke again, or worse.

Mr. Byrd took a deep breath and tapped the pipe in his breast pocket.

I waited for him to say *But now*.

"But now," he said, "I'm lucky if 40 percent of the students even graduate. Luckier still if half of those who somehow graduate can read. Luckier still that one of them doesn't blow me away for confiscating her cigarettes."

"We can't give up on them."

"We can't give up on them. That's why I keep fighting. I've had offers to come to other schools. Plum, that's my wife, she practically begs me every night to go to a different school where it's safer, but this is where my heart is. I love this neighborhood. I love this school. You know I went here myself as a kid? Yes, we were the Red Devils back then," Mr. Byrd said with a sly laugh. He put a hand on my back and patted me. "Maybe you could come out here and preach to them, I don't know."

We both laughed good and hard at that, but for different reasons.

I had a difficult time believing in God anymore. I wasn't an atheist, but neither was I certain God paid much attention to me. Maybe He was punishing me. That would explain it. I was smart and educated and hadn't held a full-time job since graduating college.

Behold the wrath of God.

Then Mr. Byrd said, "It was sure easier breaking up illegal Bible studies in the cafeteria."

"It sure was."

At lunch, I quickly devoured the tuna sandwich and apple tart that Mary had packed for me. I crossed the street to the first of four overgrown yards on the block and knocked on the door. An elderly brown-skinned man opened up, and when I offered to cut his lawn, he explained that he couldn't afford the twenty dollars.

"Fifteen?"

He shook his head. "I live on a fixed income."

"Don't your neighbors complain about the way the yard has gotten away from you?"

"Neighbors?" I followed the roll of his eyes down the street to the ghastly paint jobs, barred windows, barred doors, derelict cars parked in the yards—sometimes on the lawn itself—hedges grown out in profuse disarray. The neighborhood had gone, as they say, to hell. The old man's yard was but an eyesore among eyesores. "Around here nobody cares," he said.

I persisted. "Twelve?"

"I just don't have the money."

"What can you afford?" There was some leeway; I was my own boss, after all.

"Six?"

"That's low, but I'll do it for six," I said, figuring I'd make up the loss on someone else's yard. The idea was to foster goodwill. Soon there would be talk of the nice man who cuts yards cheap. The whole neighborhood would improve, starting with the lawns.

"Young man, I can't lie to you. I need to buy half a gallon of milk with some of that money." Behind him was the open door of his home, and out came the smell of stale urine. His unbuttoned pants hanging low on his waist somehow managed to stay on. "Times are hard."

I walked down to the next house and had more success. The youngish Hispanic woman who came to the door in hot pants and slippers greeted me with an exhausted smile. A baby bawled behind her from somewhere inside.

"Yes, cut it please. God it grows fast in the summer."

"I'll be back after school."

"Hurry back. The kids can't even play outside in the yard."

No one answered at the third house, but a branch sagging low with mangoes caught my eye. I picked a fat yellow one and went on to the fourth house. No one answered there either.

I couldn't believe it. One house. Twenty lousy dollars. I was still in the hole. I bit the mango, and it turned out to be quite sweet, but too stringy. I had to suck hard to dislodge the fibers between my teeth. I was still in the hole. I would have to cut four houses tomorrow to get caught up.

After school, I mowed the Hispanic mother's yard, and she paid me with two tens; then she thought about it and passed me another dollar, a tip.

"Please," she said, "come back next week."

Then I pushed the lawnmower down to the old brown-skinned man's house and began mowing. After a while, he came out and looked on from his porch.

When I finished, he walked across his freshly cut lawn in his bare feet and handed me the six dollars: three crumpled bills and twelve shiny quarters. I gave back the quarters.

"Go buy your milk," I said.

"What?"

"Go buy your milk, sir. God bless you."

The old man nodded. "God bless you, son."

I stuck my head into room 323-H.

"Not you again," Peachie joked. "I'm better. Go home."

She was bandaged and hooked up to tubes. She spotted the roses and lit up.

"For me?" She pointed to a vase on the nightstand. "Put them there. Pretty. Are they scented?"

"They cost me fifteen dollars."

"Big money. We'll send them back if they're not scented." Her eyes were red. She was still having trouble sleeping.

I put the roses in the vase, then moved back and sat on the edge of her bed. "I came by to tell you something interesting," I said. "Something interesting happened at church last night."

"If it's about the Reverend Dr. McGowan, save your breath. I was married to the man. I could write a book. Stingy, pompous, impotent."

"You have two children," I reminded.

"I meant stingy, pompous, and ignorant."

I laughed. "It's not about Barry."

"Good."

"Although he is in town."

"The annual revival. I know. He called me. Can you believe it? He wanted to pray for me."

"I warned you about him."

"When you loved me."

"I still love you."

She looked at the flowers in the vase. "You came to propose?"

"If it would save you."

"You would marry a harlot?"

"Don't call yourself that. And yes, I would marry a harlot to save you."

"You're sweet, Elwyn. You're my best friend. I should have married you. What the hell did I ever see in Barry? If I had married you, we would have been so happy. We would have been so cute. I wouldn't be involved in a child custody case with a multimillionaire that I have no chance of winning and you wouldn't be involved with Sister Youknow-who. We would have been two happy, normal lovebirds."

"From what I've learned about life, being a lovebird is anything but normal. Too many obstacles to true love." I frowned at the tubes and bandages. "When are you getting out of here, girl?"

"My doctor is very mad at me." She whispered, "I almost killed my-self, you know? I have to learn to follow my diet properly. Take my shots. Eat right. I could go into shock again. But this thing with Barry and the kids, and not having money, I am so stressed out that this damned sugar diabetes, or hypoglycemia, or whatever the hell it is, is the last thing on my mind. It's an unfair disease. It shouldn't happen to young people."

"My grandmother has lived with it since she was forty and she's just hit four score plus three. You can beat it. You can live a normal life."

"My life is never going to be normal, Elwyn. This is just another problem to add to a long and growing list." Peachie glanced over at the flowers in the vase. "Maybe death wouldn't be so bad."

I suddenly realized what was going on. I leaned down to her ear and pleaded, "You promised me that you wouldn't try to take your life again. You promised me, Peachie. Why are you doing this?"

"You're wrong," she protested, "I just forgot my diet this time, that's all. I was stressed. This isn't like before."

"You swear?"

"I swear on the Bible."

"I love you, Peachie. You're my best friend in the whole world."

"Why?"

"Because you're pretty and you can sure play that piano. You're the prettiest girl in the whole grade-four Sunday school class."

She laughed at that. "And?"

"And I want my godsons to grow up with a mommy."

"And?"

"Because things are going to get better for you, and you're going to be so happy, and so rich, and I'm going to need to borrow some money. That's what friends are for."

"Well, in that case," she said, "I'll be careful and watch my diet from now on."

"And put a few dollars aside for me," I laughed.

But soon she was gone again. "Oh Elwyn, everything is so . . . dark. I have to work so hard to make ends meet, and he has all that money. I can't see my children. My children are gone. Nobody loves me. Only my mother loves me." The tears were rolling down her cheeks.

"Jesus loves you. I love you . . . What you're trying to do, it's the only sin that cannot be forgiven."

"That and blasphemy." She clutched my hand and forced some cheer into her voice. "Tell me more about what it would have been like being married to you."

"My Peachie."

"I know you are kind and brave and smart. But are you good in bed?"

"My sarcastic, little Peachie." I brushed away her tears.

And then we were kissing. It was not supposed to happen. It was not. But it was good. The smell of roses. The cool, clean hospital air. Her soft lips. I had wanted it for so long. It was the most . . . satisfying kiss I had ever had.

The most appropriate.

She opened her eyes. Her eyes were smiling. "What was that all about, Brother Elwyn?"

"I've wanted to do that forever."

"Did I kiss you, or did you kiss me?"

"You pulled me down."

"Your face was already down here."

We kissed again. It was even better this time.

I was going to say something—something profound and from the heart—but Peachie opened her mouth first and ruined it. "If you didn't have Sister Youknowwho, would you divorce your wife and marry me?"

I tried to break free, but she held my hand tight.

"Sister Youknowwho. Right? Right? It's too late for us now. We ruined it. We are what we are. We can't change that, right, Brother Elwyn?"

She would not let go. I could not pull away from her grasp. What did she want me to say? What could I say? I would not say it. That I loved Sister Morrisohn more now than I ever could have loved Peachie.

We struggled on. I would not say it.

She held my hand until a stern nurse walked in a few minutes later and ordered me out. "You're going to have to leave, sir. Visiting hours begin again at 6."

"He's my friend," Peachie pleaded.

The nurse was serious looking and big. She said, "You need to rest."

"Don't go, Elwyn."

"I'm going," I said, happy to have my hand back. I kissed Peachie, on the forehead this time, and got up from the bed.

"Wait, you had something to tell me about church."

"It's nothing. Something funny happened at the revival last night is all. I'll tell you about it next time."

"You forgot to pray for me," Peachie reminded.

I turned to the nurse, who still had me by the elbow, urging me out with her girth. A miracle, the big nurse relented and allowed a brief prayer, after which she pushed me out of the room and shut the door.

I tried to practice the hymns I would play that night, in B major, which was for me the most difficult key, but I could not concentrate because Mary was upset.

No doubt, it had made little sense telling her about the old man whose yard I had cut for free that day, but I was proud of my good deed, and one ought to tell one's good deeds to one's wife. Especially when one's wife considers one pathetic. Or maybe not.

Mary inexplicably lost her cool. She slammed things. She walked around the apartment muttering. When she picked up the phone, I overheard her tell someone that she was married to a fool who cut yards for three dollars a piece.

In quarters!

Then Mary tried to slam the piano door down on my fingers, but I was too fast.

"This is it, Elwyn," she said, pointing at me. "Find a job or lose your wife. This is the last time I'm telling you."

Not another ultimatum, I thought. Must it ever be this way: sex in the morning, fight at night?

As I was leaving for the second night of the revival, I noticed that Benjamin was again sitting too close to the TV. I didn't mention it to Mary.

At the Church of Our Blessed Redeemer Who Walked Upon the Waters, it was customary to honor a visiting evangelist by acting more penitent than usual.

During revivals in years past, droves of weeping backsliders had come to the altar at Rev'run's behest and begged God to have mercy on their reprehensible souls. They had openly reconciled themselves with their Maker, and Rev'run had left Miami convinced that he had wrought a miracle.

This year, a greater miracle had preempted Rev'run's. God had sent a white man to speak His message in unknown tongues.

On the second night of the revival, the church was more crowded than the previous night as anxious, heat-oppressed saints awaited another spectacle. They were only just tolerating Rev'run.

Knowing this, perhaps, the fat man from Tifton, Georgia, preached cautiously, vapidly, and utterly without appeal. He seemed almost embarrassed to utter his customary syllable, "AH"; halfway through the sermon, he abandoned it entirely. When he finished preaching, only the regulars ambled up to the altar and dutifully accepted the Lord.

You could see it in their faces: where was the white minister?

Pastor frowned at the meager substance in the collection plate and said, "Since we forgot to take up collection last night, let's pass the plates around an extra time tonight."

The plates went around again and returned with less money

than the first time. Pastor shook his head in distaste and clapped his hands.

"Saints! Saints," he scolded, "is this how we take care of God's servant who has traveled all the way from Georgia? I want you to dig a little deeper into your hearts and pocketbooks. I'll start it with the first dollar."

Magnanimously, Pastor tossed a dollar bill into a collection plate. The Reverend Dr. McGowan, with much ceremony, flipped in four quarters. The plates went around again but returned with mere small change glittering around Pastor's dollar bill.

The Reverend Dr. McGowan, in a noble gesture to save the day, stood up and wrote the church a check, which he announced was for a hundred dollars.

There was scattered applause, but then nothing.

Service ended early again.

Before I could make it to my car, Sister Morrisohn pulled me aside and put a check in my hand.

"You don't have to do this." I looked down at the check. It was three thousand dollars. "Holy cow. No way. It's too much. You don't have to."

"But I did."

I shook my head. "Elaine, I can't keep taking money from you without paying back. I can't. I don't feel like a man. I feel like I don't know what, but not a man."

"You're a man. Believe me, you are. A big man." She licked her lips playfully. But then she got serious. "I'm very proud of you. I know what you're all about. I know what you're trying to achieve. Things are hard now, but you'll get it one day. I believe in you. You can't see where you are because you're so young, but I see because I'm older and I've seen it before. This is a down time. This is nothing. You're doing all of the right things and life is going to turn around for you eventually. Things are going to happen to you so big, you're not going to even remember these hard times. You've just got to stick with it and never give up. This check is not pity, Elwyn. This check is not to insult your manhood. This check is an investment in someone who is worth investing in. I believe in you and I love you."

She touched my face with her hand.

And because I knew it was useless to fight, I followed Sister Morrisohn to a hotel on Biscayne Boulevard, and we rented a room for two hours.

A large bed and a big-screen TV (with two porno channels) were the main luxuries, but that was not the point. The hotel, we had learned over the years, was safer than her house. As president of the Missionary Society, Sister Morrisohn received too many unexpected drop-in visitors.

We lay with our nakedness draped in cool silk sheets and our heads propped up by extrasoft pillows. Room service had brought wine, of which I did not partake, of course. I looked around the room, but could not locate her panties and bra, for she was not a neat folder of undergarments like Mary—no, she was a flinger, a discarder, a tosser, a passionate ripper of undergarments. She was neither neat nor gentle with anything that got in the way of her lovemaking, but I didn't mind. I wanted to make love to her. She wanted to make love to me. She had ripped my drawers off with her teeth. I must admit that I had eaten through her underthings too. We asked the Spirit to move that night and It sure did.

I wasn't an atheist, but heaven just seemed so far away. Mind you, God was certainly a good idea: someone who siteth high and looketh low and guideth my feet wherever they go. A God could help me regain control of my life. I wouldn't have to cut yards for three dollars a pop, or play piano for people who had less faith than I did. I wouldn't have to borrow money to pay rent. I might even honor my wife.

But in the absence of God, there was the hotel on Biscayne Boulevard and Sister Morrisohn. At least I still lusted after my mistress.

"You're beautiful," I said. "When will you marry?"

"When my lover grows up."

"You've taken a lover?"

"And he's married."

"I hear he doesn't love his wife."

She turned her head. "Then why did you marry her?"

I did not answer. I could not answer.

"But since you brought it up, I think I should warn you that I would like to marry again before it's all over," she said.

"You will make some guy the luckiest man in the world."

"Some guy." Sister Morrisohn smiled weakly and lay back on the extrasoft pillow. I climbed over her. We were making love again.

"My darling," she said as our lips met. "My darling, my darling, my darling."

Afterward, while we rested in each other's arms safe in the knowledge that crazy as it was we each had someone to love, she traced my face with her hands. "And another thing," she said suddenly. "Who *was* that white minister last night?"

"Beloved woman, you always know where my mind is at," I replied, shaking my head. "I've been dying to talk to somebody about that."

"One crazy guy," she said as I kissed her.

"One crazy guy," we said as we came up for air.

The Spirit was moving again.

This Do in Remembrance of Me

Three days later, Sister Morrisohn was rushed to Jackson Memorial Hospital.

Elwyn found out about it from Brother Al, who found out from Sister McGowan, whose lawn he was mowing—and she found out from Peachie McGowan (still in the hospital), who was walking to the cafeteria when they brought the president of the Missionary Society in.

"It was terrible," Peachie said. "She was like clawing at her face. I tried to call you, but you were subbing. Mary didn't know which school. I didn't push it. I didn't want to let on, you know? But I had to get hold of you somehow, so I called my ex-mother-in-law, who knows everybody's whereabouts."

Brother Al said, "Well I told Sister McGowan you been cutting grass in the same neighborhood all week by your old school. So I just waited for school time to be over, and I knew where you'd be at. I knew you was cutting the Lattimore house. Sister McGowan said that Peachie said she heard one of the doctors say that she ain't never gonna make it out of the hospital again. It's real sad. She ain't even that old."

Mary Parker screamed, "All this time! I should have known! You nasty-a**ed motherf---ker! You pervert! You dog!"

She was a dangerous Mary when angry. She picked up heavy objects and launched them at velocities so high they disintegrated when they hit the walls.

"A woman older than your own momma!"

Elwyn ducked out of the way of his flying music trophies. Mary plucked his Buford Morrisohn Scholarship for the Outstanding College-Bound Christian plaque from the wall. The plaque had a glass and marble face, but it was oddly shaped and he misjudged its flight pattern, and it broke his ring finger before exploding into a million pieces on the floor. "Ouch. Ouch."

Then she was on him. They fought like cornered cats. They were both bleeding in the end, but he got the worst of it.

Their son Benjamin, sitting in front of the TV, cried and cried. The nice police officer said, "Sir, I think it's best you sleep somewhere else tonight. Do your parents or other relatives live in town? We could give you a ride there if you don't have transportation."

"I have a car."

"Then you should leave now. We'll wait to see that you go. It's best when these things can be resolved. If they can't be, then the law steps in," said the nice police officer while removing the shackles from Elwyn's wrists.

◦⊚◦

Chester Harbaugh and His Old-Time Fiddle Band

Chorus
I'm going away (going away)
Soon my love (soooon my love)
I'm going away (going away)

Where you can't come
(yooou can't come)

I'm going away (going away)
And that you know (thaaat you know)
My heart will stay (stay-yay-yay)
I love you so
(I looove you so)

Verse 1 (Chet and Lester)
When we were young (we were young)
We played together (played together)
When we grew up (we grew up)
We fell in love (so in lo-o-o-vvvvve)
We had a home (home, home, home)
A life we shared (Oh yeahhh)
But now I go (Oh-oh)
And you can't come

Serious fiddlin
Repeat chorus

Verse 2 (Just Lester with autoharp)
Each night I pray
To God above
That they will say
They've found a cure
(Chet Comes Back in; Chet, Lester, and autoharp take us home sweet)

For this thing inside (thing inside)
That's taking me (taking me)
To that dark place (d-a-a-ark place)
Where you can't come
(yooou can't come)

Serious fiddlin

I'm going away (going away)
To that dark place (d-a-a-ark place)
My heart will stay (stay-yay-yay)
I love you so
(I looove you so)

Keep on fiddlin
Fade out

I'll Meet You in the Morning

On November 4, Sister Morrisohn was released into the custody of her live-in lover.

She wanted to die at home.

Her brother Harrison came down. He was a tall man, skinny with sharp features, thinning hair, and skin so fair he could pass for white. He had a pained expression on his face when Elwyn and he met.

The lover.

And the brother, who knew not that he was a son.

The latter thought the former was "so young."

The former thought the latter was "overtly homosexual," which makes sense considering how vehemently she had claimed to despise them—she was quite clearly in denial.

Harrison nodded, smiling wanly, Elwyn put his hand on Harrison's back, and they walked into the room where she lay sleeping. They sat in chairs placed round her bed. They talked in whispers about small things and large. Though they had never met as adults, they knew of each other. She had told Elwyn about Harrison, whom Elwyn had remembered as that light-skinned guy who used to sit with her when he was a kid. She had told Harrison about Elwyn, whom Harrison remembered as the boy who played the piano.

The lover.

And the son, who knew himself only as her brother.

When Elwyn complained how tough it was to find work these days, Harrison offered him a job as a technical writer at his company, but he would have to move to Boston. Elwyn was a Miami boy, palm trees and porno shops, plain and simple, so thanks for the offer, but he would have to turn it down. They continued to speak in whispers. She was just barely holding on.

Harrison said, "See, getting work nowadays is about attitude. Show them a little spine in the interview. Sell yourself."

"Every job is a dead end. No one wants to hire you."

"Show a little spine. She doesn't know this, but I never finished grad school. And my undergraduate grades were piss poor. Yet I make six figures. You've got to be a fighter. Don't take no for an answer. You have to learn to deal with rejection. The surest path to success is learning to overcome rejection."

Sister Morrisohn made a small movement in the bed. She was awake, and she saw them together. Her men. Elwyn nudged Harrison, and Harrison kissed her on the forehead. She smiled as best she could under the circumstances.

The day nurse came into the room and said, "It's time for her medicine."

"Let me do it," Elwyn said. He got up, filled the syringe, as they had taught him at the hospital, and cleared the air bubbles. He steadied her arm and injected her, then asked, "Better?"

Her words were slurred. "Better," she said. "You should have been a nurse, that's what you should have been. You could still be a nurse." Then she closed her eyes again. These days she slept a lot.

"She's right. You are good at that," Harrison observed. Then he looked down at his mother, whom he believed to be his sister, but continued to speak to Elwyn. "A little spine. Show them a little spine and you'll do all right."

When Harrison finally went to bed, Elwyn remained at her side in his chair in her room. She was sleeping peacefully. He was overcome by sadness and began to weep, so he sang softly to stop the tears, which did not stop: *I must tell Jesus all of my troubles I cannot bear these burdens alone in my distress He kindly will help me He ever loves and cares for His own I must tell Jesus I must tell Jesus I cannot bear these burdens alone I must tell Jesus I must tell Jesus, Jesus can help me Jesus alone.*

She had been listening for some time. Her eyes were open. They were clear and alert, but the shadow of death was in them.

He said, "Don't die, my love."

She said, "I love you."

He said, "Don't die."

She said, "Soon I will be done with the troubles of this world."

"Don't die," he said.

"Will you meet me there?"

He was holding her hand. "I'll meet you there."

"Will you meet me in the morning by the bright riverside?"

"When all sorrow has drifted away."

"I'll be standing by the portals."

"With the gates open wide."

"At the end of life's long weary day."

"I'll meet you."

"In the morning. In the morning."

He was holding her weak and trembling hand. "With a how do you do."

"And we'll sit down. We'll sit down."

"By the river. By the river."

"And with laughter old acquaintance renew."

He was tightly holding her hand. They weren't singing it. They were speaking it. They weren't speaking it. They were meaning it. "You'll know me in the morning. In the morning," he said.

"By the smile that I'll wear," she answered, smiling as best she could so that he would recognize it in heaven when he saw her again.

"When I meet you. In the morning."

"In the morning."

"In the morning. In the city that's built foursquare."

"Built foursquare."

He tenderly wiped the sweat from her brow. "I will meet you there," he told her.

"Promise me."

He crossed his heart. Then he told her: "Don't die."

She inhaled a deep breath. After exhaling, she said, "I wish he had lived."

"Who?"

"Our baby."

"What baby?"

"I gave up our baby."

Her eyes had darkened again, and he could not tell whether she was speaking to him or to a dream.

"I gave up our baby because I loved you too much to use him against you. You remember him? His name was Elwyn. He had my eyes and your skin. He played the piano and I loved him and you would have loved him. He played the piano so well. You taught him to play. I will meet him. In the morning. By the river. I will know him by the smile. That he wears. You didn't uncover my fountain, it was . . . abortion."

"Elaine, please, you don't have to tell me this."

"Open confession . . . good for the soul."

"You don't have to."

" . . . I don't want to go to hell."

She felt herself drifting off to somewhere dark and sweet and restful and quiet, and it seemed so good and so easy to go, but she knew that he hated when she kept things from him, so she gathered what was left of her strength and put it in her breath and pushed her breath over her tongue so that she could tell him: "It was Beverly Morrisohn seduced me."

"No, Elaine. You don't have to tell me any of this."

"And your father . . ."

"No, Elaine, you don't have to tell me. Just be here with me. Just stay here. Don't go away. Please don't leave me."

"Your father . . . I know you wanted to ask . . . I know you could not ask . . . Roscoe and I . . . never . . . ever . . . were just friends . . . just good friends . . ."

"I love you, my darling. You don't have to tell me any of this."

And truly she didn't have to, because though he had come to learn it late, Elwyn, here by her side on her deathbed, was now aware that he loved her for everything that she was and meant to him and therefore he had to accept everything that had made her who she was. He had come to accept all the good that had happened to her as well as the bad, the known as well as the secret, for the end result was this good thing, this woman he loved, the only woman he loved. The only one he would ever love.

For her part, it felt so sweet to go, but she would not release her strength to the winds just yet, for there was one dominant thought in her heart: Elwyn must know. I will tell him now so that when he sees me by the river he will know me. He will know me by the smile that I wear. He will know me by the smile he put there.

Thus, she did tell him and he did listen. Her softly spoken, delicately accented words floated up to heaven to open the gates to where she would be going soon.

"I love you," she said.

"I love you."

"I want you . . . to know that . . . I love you . . . my darling."

Then she went to sleep again.

Elwyn observed that it was no normal sleep.

It was a troubled sleep.

They rushed her to the hospital again, but the angels had come to take her home. As Jacob wrestled with his angel, Sister Morrisohn wrestled with hers. She lasted until morning.

She left him in the morning.

At the funeral, Elwyn sat, despite the protest of all, as her next of kin. His mother, his father—they could not face his proud, defiant countenance. Harrison sat on one side of him. Benny, at Elwyn's request, sat on the other. It was the biggest funeral in the history of the church. All of the gossips were in attendance. Beverly Morrisohn was not. Mary Parker and Benjamin were not.

After the ceremony, Elwyn and Harrison went back to the big house in Coral Gables to set things in order. She left most of it, the complicated things, insurance, real estate, investments, to Harrison, her brother. She left a nice chunk for the church. For Elwyn, she left a big check, which was a nice chunk too, but it did not dispel his grief. Elwyn went upstairs to the tryst room and stared out the window they used to look through while making love. He uttered a stream of swear words.

On December 21, four days before Christmas, his marriage to Mary was officially dissolved. She got three-quarters of the big check that Sister Morrisohn had left him, despite the efforts of his attorney.

All in all, 1991 was the worst year of Elwyn's life.

The Years of Borning and Begats: The Faithful

1845–1875: Bessie, a Freedwoman (mother of Aunti and Momma).

1859–1949: Aunti (Glovine's mother), a.k.a. Aunty Hames, sometimes Aunty Hanes (given name of Red Annie, slave girl): daughter of slaves Bessie and Uncle Red Rufus of the Colonel Hanes Culpeppar Plantation, Jenkins, Georgia.

1870–1935: Momma (Mamie's mother; also Aunti's half sister), a.k.a. "Big" Mamie Culpepper: daughter of Freedwoman Bessie and Freedman Mr. Lonnie Culpepper (or Mr. Lundi? Culpepper) formerly of the Colonel Hanes Culpeppar Plantation, Jenkins, Georgia.

1884–1942: Sarai Mayfield, a.k.a. Momma Mayfield (Orphelia Mayfield's mother; also Elaine Morrisohn's grandmother).

1896–1963: Glovine Morrisohn (née Hames): Hames, alternate spelling of "Hanes" from the Colonel Hanes Culpeppar Plantation, Jenkins, Georgia.

1901–1979: Buford Vansen Morrisohn.

1904–1952: Orphelia Franklin (née Mayfield) (Elaine Morrisohn's mother).

1908–1993: Mamie Cooper (née Culpepper), a.k.a. "Little" Mamie Culpepper (Culpepper, a version of "Culpeppar" from the Colonel Hanes Culpeppar Plantation, Jenkins, Georgia).

1913–1972: Frank Lester Franklin (Elaine Morrisohn's father).

1922–1943: Jefferson Thomas Cooper.

1935– : Beverly Morrisohn: daughter of Glovine and Buford Morrisohn.

1937–1991: Elaine Morrisohn (née Franklin).

1941– : Roscoe Parker (Elwyn's father).

1942– : Isadore Parker (née Cooper) (Elwyn's mother): daughter of Mamie Cooper and Buford Morrisohn.

1950– : Harrison Franklin (Sister Morrisohn's brother/son).

1958– : Barry Sebastian-Bach McGowan.

1959– : E.C. Philip.

1963– : Benny Willett (Roscoe's son).

1963– : Elwyn Parker.

1963– : Peachie McGowan (née Gregory).

1964– : Marie Willett (née Pierre) (Benny's wife).

1968– : Mary Parker (née Peters) (Elwyn's ex-wife).

1986– : Benjamin James Parker: son of Elwyn Parker.

The Years of Borning and Begats: Founders of the Faith

177?–1840: Cuthbert Rogers (founding member of the Faith).

1780–1831: Elwyn James the Younger (founding member of the Faith).

1809–1901: Curtis Rogers (Patriarch of the Faith).

1819–1866: Sanders Q. Dunbar (Patriarch of the Holy Rollers): a good man, like Adam, led astray by his wife, the apostate and reveler Dorothea Lovell.

1835–1912: Dorothea Dunbar (née Lovell): the apostate and false Prophet (so-called Prophetess of the Holy Rollers).

1838–1901: Josiah "Josh" Johnson, Freedman (Black Elder of the Faith) (Elder brother of Mosiah and Kinew).

1838–1909: Sixto Smith, runaway (Black Elder of the Faith).

1840–1912: Hiram Kirkaby Rogers (Bishop of the Faith).

1840–1920: Mosiah Johnson, Freedman (Black Elder of the Faith) (also first Black Bishop of the Faith/Bishop of Black congregations only).

1841–1879: Kinew Johnson, Freedman (Black Elder of the Faith).

1870–1933: Elwyn James Rogers (Bishop of the Faith).

1902–1981: Paul Silas Rogers (Bishop of the Faith).

1935– : Kirkaby Cuthbert Rogers (Bishop of the Faith).

Favorite Hymns & Performances

Glovine Morrisohn. Hymns: "There Is a Fountain"; "When They Ring Those Golden Bells"; "How I Got Over." Professional Performance: The Five Blind Boys of Alabama—"I'm a Rolling." Local Performance: Sister McGowan on piano and vocals—"He Could Have Called Ten Thousand Angels."

Buford Vansen Morrisohn. Hymns: "Someday the Silver Cord Will Break"; "Come Ye Disconsolate"; "Remind Me, Dear Lord." Professional Performance: The Davis Sisters—"Remind Me, Dear Lord." Local Performance: Elwyn Parker—"Jesus Loves the Little Children," piano solo.

Mamie Cooper. Hymns: "In the Garden"; "When They Ring Those Golden Bells"; "Real, Real, Real, Jesus Is Real to Me." Professional Performance: Clara Ward—"How I Got Over." Local Performance: Elwyn Parker—"I Must Tell Jesus," piano and congregation.

Jefferson Thomas Cooper. Hymns: "Amazing Grace"; "I Surrender All"; "Highway to Heaven." Professional Performance: Paul Robeson—"I'm a Soldier." Local Performance: Mamie Culpepper—"Blessed Assurance," piano and voice.

Elaine Morrisohn. Hymns: "Amazing Grace"; "My Surrender"; "I'll Meet You in the Morning"; "Precious Memories." Professional Performance: Chester Harbaugh—"Whispering Hope"; Jim Reeves—"Whispering Hope"; Tennessee Ernie Ford—"Whispering Hope"; Blackwood Brothers, JD Sumner solo version—"He Bought My Soul at Calvary." Local Performance: Elwyn Parker—"I Must Tell Jesus"/"I Need Thee Every Hour," piano and congregation.

Roscoe Parker. Hymns: "Silent Night"; "Twelve Days of Christmas"; "The Blood Will Never Lose Its Power." Professional Performance: Andraé Crouch and the Disciples—"The Blood Will Never Lose Its Power." Local Performance: Elwyn Parker—"I Must Tell Jesus"/"I Need Thee Every Hour," piano and congregation.

Isadore Parker. Hymns: "There Is a Fountain"; "Power in the Blood"; "The Blood Will Never Lose Its Power." Professional Performance: Sister Rosetta Tharpe—"God's Mighty Hand." Local Performance: Elwyn Parker—"The Blood Will Never Lose Its Power," piano and youth choir.

Barry McGowan. Hymns: "The Holy City"; "Day Is Dying in the West"; "Twelve Gates unto the City, Hallelujah." Professional Performance: Joe Feeney—"The Holy City," from the *Lawrence Welk Christmas Special*; Statesmen Quartet, James "Big Chief" Wetherington bass solo—"Hide Me, Rock of Ages." Local Performance: Himself—"His Eye Is on the Sparrow," solo.

E.C. Philip. Hymns: "Hallelujah Chorus"; "Power in the Blood"; "The

Blood Will Never Lose Its Power." Professional Performance: The Hawaiians—"Down From His Glory." Local Performance: Peachie McGowan—"Yes, God Is Real," solo, piano, and congregation.

Benny Willett. Hymns: "Jesus Loves Me This I Know"; "Jesus Loves the Little Children"; "I Must Tell Jesus." Professional Performance: George Beverly Shea—"How Great Thou Art," Billy Graham TV Special. Local Performance: Elwyn Parker—"I Must Tell Jesus," piano and congregation.

Elwyn Parker. Hymns: "Lord Do It"; "My Surrender"; "Calling for Me"; "Someday the Silver Chord Will Break." Professional Performance: James Cleveland—"Peace Be Still." Local Performance: Peachie McGowan—"Yes, God Is Real," solo, piano, and adult choir.

Peachie McGowan. Hymns: "Amazing Grace"; "Lord Do It"; "My Surrender." Professional Performance: Mahalia Jackson—"How I Got Over." Local Performance: Elwyn Parker—"The Blood Will Never Lose Its Power," piano and youth choir.

The Years of Elwyn Parker and Sister Morrisohn

1937: Elaine Franklin is born.

1955: Elaine Franklin moves to Miami, Florida.

1962: The affair of Elaine Franklin and Beverly Morrisohn ends.

1963: Roscoe Parker marries Isadore Cooper.

1963: Elwyn Parker is born.

1963: Buford Morrisohn marries Elaine Franklin.

1968: Buford Morrisohn loans Roscoe Parker the downpayment for his house.

1971: Buford Morrisohn buys Elwyn a piano.

1976: Buford Morrisohn funds the Buford Morrisohn Scholarship for the Outstanding College-Bound Christian; names Elwyn Parker as its first recipient.

1979: Buford Morrisohn buys Elwyn a car.

1979: Buford Morrisohn dies.

1979: The affair of Elwyn Parker and Sister Morrisohn begins.

1980: Elywn Parker founds the Jesus Club.

1981: Elaine Morrisohn renames the upstairs guest bedroom the "tryst room" when skittish Elwyn finally agrees to try oral sex (in said room) and discovers that he likes it.

1982: Elwyn enters college.

1982: Sister Morrisohn aborts Elwyn's child.

1983: Elwyn and Sister Morrisohn break up.

1983: Elwyn and Sister Morrisohn make back up.

1983: Elwyn proposes to Sister Morrisohn.

1983: Elwyn takes back his proposal.

1986: Elwyn meets Benny.

1986: Elwyn graduates college.

1986: Elwyn marries Mary.

1986: Elwyn and Sister Morrisohn break up.

1986: Elwyn and Sister Morrisohn make back up.

1986: Elwyn's son Benjamin Parker is born.

1986: Sister Morrisohn endows the Benjamin Parker college trust fund.

1991: Elwyn moves in with Sister Morrisohn.

1991: Sister Morrisohn dies.

1991: The affair of Elwyn Parker and Elaine Morrisohn ends.

The Lord of Travel

The next customer is a real laydown.

She rides in on a bike. It's like she has *Scholarship Money* stamped on her forehead. I run in order to get to her before Curly or the Arab can.

"My name is Ida," she says, taking my hand.

I love the way you speak, Ida. Where are you from?

"I'm from New Jersey," she says.

New Jersey, I say.

This New Jersey joke runs through my brain—something about the Garbage State Bridge—but I can't remember the punch line. It's just as well. If I offend her, I'll have a harder time selling her the car. So I play up the tough Northerner thing.

Oh yes, the South sucks. Too slow. Not like up North, I say (although the farthest north I've ever been is Gainesville). Not like New Jersey. Only one thing would make a sane person leave New Jersey for a one-horse town like Miami. You're a student.

"Yes. U.M. How did you guess?"

Glasses, looking intelligent but stunning on your pretty face. You rode a bike. And I don't see your father, husband, or boyfriend. All independent women in this town are students or lawyers.

When Ida laughs, her teeth show even and white. Her laugh says she likes me, trusts me. I have sold myself well. If this keeps up, she's going to drive home in a brand-new clunker and they'll need a wheelbarrow to deliver my paycheck.

I run a hand over the shiny parts of the car and begin my spiel.

Beautiful finish, I say. One owner, I claim. Great gas mileage, I lie, for a car this size. Four-door convenience—just right for someone with a lot of friends. I myself took this baby to the beach last week (just don't tell my manager, ha-ha-ha), and girl, let me tell you how they envied me. A true classic, only ten thousand were made.

She notices a door handle is missing.

That little thing can be fixed, I say. Oh yes, we were going to fix that anyway. Don't you worry about that.

She runs a hand along the scratched-up left side.

And those scratches? We can paint those. Here, let me write it down. Scratches . . . Door handle . . . Anything else? Okay. Back tires, sideview mirror, dent in roof. Good, good. We'll take care of everything, really.

She turns to eye other cars on the lot. Resistance.

Ida, I say, touching her hand, making Honest Abe eye contact. Ida, for the kind of money you're looking to spend, this is the best buy in town. The absolutely best buy. True, I could show you something a bit nicer, a little cleaner, but you'd have to raise your sights. Over there, for instance—the red Mustang. Pretty, isn't it? I'd love to sell it to you, but you're talking at least four thousand dollars more. Can you do that?

"No."

I didn't think so. You see, Ida, I'm not the kind of guy who is going to rip off a young, attractive sister like yourself. Especially with you being in school. I was a student, and I know what it's like to live on a budget. Plus, you might become a lawyer one day and sue the hell out of me.

"That's right," she laughs.

I laugh.

Black people have to stick together, I say, opening the car door.

I take her for a test ride, and she begins to act more and more like a buyer. She adjusts her seat and the rearview mirror to her comfort. She fiddles with the radio. She plays with the knobs on the dashboard until she figures out the air conditioner. Cool air rushes out of the vents, humming. For my part, I am pleased that the car doesn't stall in neutral as it did the day before.

All the while I'm saying, Nice car, isn't it? Drives great, doesn't it? Air feels good, doesn't it?

And I watch her head nod in approval. I am putting Ida in a "yes" mood. After saying yes twenty times, it's hard to say no. Psychology.

Ida turns down a lonely street and punches the accelerator. The car belches forward, its ancient V-8 roaring mightily, *Out of my way! I am the Lord of Travel, master of the road!* Blue-gray smoke trails out of the exhaust pipes, but Ida doesn't notice. She is a woman in love with a car. She smiles all the way back to the lot.

We park.

Ida sucks in a deep breath. When she turns to face me, her smile is replaced by a look of false concern. She is about to pretend she is little interested in the car so that she can get a better deal from me. She will claim she can't afford it, say she needs to think about it, say she is considering other cars, say she wants her father, husband, boyfriend to look at it before she decides. She will try very hard to get the best possible deal, and she will fail utterly. However valiant be her fight, she is outmatched. You see, Ida is buying her first car; I sell them every day.

You felt good in that car, didn't you?

I nod my head. She nods hers.

It drove so sweetly, didn't it?

I nod my head. She nods hers.

If you could get a good deal on this car, you'd buy it, wouldn't you?

I nod my head. She nods hers—and then she shakes it, saying, "But I don't know how much it costs."

Ida, did I mention cost? Listen to me carefully. If I write a deal that you, IDA, feel is the best deal in the world on this wonderful car that you, IDA, are in love with, would you, IDA, buy the car and drive it home today?

I nod my head. She nods hers. "Yes, if you did all those things. Yes," Ida commits. Ida is a real laydown, the customer who buys it just the way you lay it out—no questions, no resistance, just an occasional burst of delighted giggling.

We go inside and she signs her name to various documents that give her title to the overpriced gas guzzler. She writes the dealership a check. I hand her the keys. She drives off.

Done deal.

The others come over and pat me on the back to hide their envy. They ask how much money I made.

Too much, I tell them.

The manager shakes my hand. Biggest sale of the month on a car he thought no one would sell, the Lord of Travel—a wreck on wheels, a bone mobile, a junker, a heap. And to sell it as though it were the best car on the lot! He mentions a bonus. What wouldn't he do for the guy who just bought him another month or two in his cushy job?

Then Ida returns.

I see her through the glass doors, walking briskly. She seems irritated. I suspect she is suffering from buyer's remorse, the headache buyers get when they drive off the lot and begin to realize that they didn't get such a sweet deal after all.

The others move away from me, eyebrows raised. Oh-oh, they think. Another sale gone sideways. Customer wants her money back.

I suspect they are right.

Ida says, "You forgot to give me one of those temporary tags."

(Praise God.)

No problem, I say. Wouldn't want you to get a ticket.

I make out the tag, the magic marker shaking in my grasp. I tape it to her rear windshield. I congratulate her again on her wise purchase, and she hugs me, of all things.

"I feel so independent now," she says.

The car coughs, rattles, emits black smoke, and finally starts. Ida smiles stupidly and drives off. She even waves goodbye.

Yes, a real laydown.

I go inside. I am a nervous wreck. My palms are sweating. I make for the bathroom but can't get past Curly and the Arab, who block my path.

Curly says, "Close call."

Never doubted it for a second, I say.

The Arab says, "I had a customer like that once. Easy sale. Full pop. A real laydown. He leaves the store, right? I'm celebrating when I get this phone call. It's raining and I had forgotten to show the guy how to work his wipers. So I explain it to him over the phone and we hang up. Half hour later, this guy shows up and he's pissed. The windshield wipers work fine, but the car stalls when he turns 'em on. Get it? So he can't drive in the rain. He can't have the wipers and the engine on at the same time."

Curly laughs. "I remember that car. Twenty-dollar paint job covered up all the rust. Came this close to selling it to a missionary when it conked out."

"That's the car, that's the car," says the Arab, who hates being interrupted. "So I tell this guy to bring the car back tomorrow so's the
mechanic can look at it. The wires are crossed or something. No. He
wants it done now or he wants his money back. We go back and forth
like this. But you know me. I finally tell him to make like Michael Jackson and *beat it!* He starts to cuss and scare off the other customers, and
he wants to sue . . ."

The Arab drones on. I hardly listen, but I nod in the right places. I
know this story. I've been involved in hundreds like it. As Curly winds
up to tell his version of the same tale, I steal away to the bathroom
where I dry my palms and forehead.

What is wrong with me?

Checking the mirror, I notice my tie hangs funny, and there is a
grimy spot where my gold tie pin would be if I had not hocked it. I need
a haircut. Once again I forgot to shave. Otherwise, I look great.

So what is wrong with me?

I am sweating. My stomach is jumping. Is it Ida? Is it guilt? No, I am
a salesman; I'm hardcore.

Awhile ago, I closed a phone deal with a local millionaire. Like
many wealthy people, he was above coming to the dealership, so I had
to go to his house to deliver the car and pick up the check. When he
saw that I was black, he revealed himself as a bigot. At his request, I sat
in the back during the test drive. When we returned to his home, he did
not offer me a seat. I stood while he read through the papers. He even
let fly a comment about the damned niggers and spics who are ruining
this country. I was unmoved. I told him I was offering him a great car at
a great price; he signed the papers and bought the car. I felt a burning
hatred for the man, but no guilt for selling him a car. Money is green
and silver and copper and gold, never black and white.

When I leave the bathroom, I find Ida waiting in the showroom. Behind her, through the glass walls, I see her car, the Lord of Travel. Its hood is popped open. Thick black smoke is billowing out of the oil pan, and water is spraying up from the radiator.

Well, Ida, I say, it's your car. You chose it. You paid for it.

"Yes, but you said . . ." she begins.

It's your car. You paid for it.

She considers this silently.

I wait for her to attack me, threaten to sue, or burst into tears. I've seen it all before. Instead she turns away from me and stares at her smoking car. *Great Deal* is still written on the front windshield in large red letters. The handlebar and front tire of her bike lean out of the half-closed trunk. I deny my need to help her; I must be firm. It is important that she understand it is *her* car polluting the air with smoke and rusty water. No deposit. No return.

When she does turn on me, she is well composed. "I'll stop payment on the check," she says.

It has already been cashed, I tell her.

At our dealership, we "hammer" checks. In other words, we send a runner to cash the check at the issuing bank as soon as we receive it. Ida's check was cashed before she had driven off the lot the first time.

"I'll call a lawyer," she says.

So will we, I say. Now let's see, you were eighteen when you read and then signed the buyer's order, right?

"I trusted you," she says.

You chose the car. You signed for it. Now, if you want our mechanic to look at it, just say so and I'll get him to check it out for you tomorrow. If not, you'd better call a towing company to haul it off our lot, or the manager will charge you fifty dollars per day for storage.

Ida wears a white coverall that hangs to midthigh, and a light breeze flaps the material around her chubby legs. Flap, flap, flap. Black and smooth is her skin, but at times the loose cloth around her shoulders shifts to reveal a frilly bra strap and the lighter flesh beneath it. Her hands balled into fists are useless on her hips. When her eyes fill up and turn red, I notice something else about Ida, something I didn't notice before.

I am surprised—disturbed by it.

"How much will your mechanic charge?" she asks.

If you're nice about it, nothing. Just parts and labor and taxes.

As though there is anything left to charge.

And I'll have Miguel, the lot boy, drive you home in his pickup. I don't want you riding that bike home. It's getting dark. Give me your keys.

Taking her keys, I touch her hand. I linger. I pull away.

As a car salesman, I meet many women I could happily fall in love with, but I usually realize this after I have sold them cars, and then it is too late. The smart ones never want to see me again. And the dumb ones, well, I don't call them back after sex. I just can't respect anyone dumb enough to get screwed twice by the same guy.

It isn't really a bad car, I say. Once we fix it up, you'll see you made a wise purchase.

"Okay," she says, "but promise me." Now she is on the verge of tears. I let her take my hand.

Trust me, I say.

"Promise me," she says.

Trust me.

I nod my head.

She nods hers.

"I do trust you," she says, my cold hand warm in both of hers. "You're not like the rest of them."

No, I'm not, I say.

What I notice is the amazing resemblance. They are sisters in sadness, Ida and Elaine, the one lost to me forever.

When Miguel returns and they pull off the lot, Ida waves at me. She actually waves at me and smiles, this woman.

And it comes back to me: Love. God is love.

It is late.

Outside, the lot boys are locking the doors on all the cars. The security guard, having already blocked off two of the entrances, waits at the third. He checks his watch.

Inside, I watch the Arab dramatize his defeat by throwing up his hands. His customer, a tall, thin man in a white shirt and dress slacks, rises from his chair. The man wears no watch.

"I'm leaving," the man says. "I would like my money and my driver's license back."

The Arab says, "I'll call the manager." He moves toward the man in the white shirt and dress slacks. "Maybe we can work something out." He touches the man's shoulder as though they are old friends, and the man shrinks away.

The man says in a firm voice: "Please, young man, retrieve my money and my license. I no longer wish to do business with you."

"Okay, okay," says the Arab, making his way to the tower, where Curly, the manager, and I are waiting. "Okay. Okay."

The Arab needs a "turn"—a fresh salesman to save the sale. This is quite a surprise, for the Arab is our best closer.

"He's a puke," the Arab mumbles. He falls heavily into a swivel chair and swivels. "He's not buying. Throw him out on his ass."

The manager counts the man's deposit, $450 in twenties and tens.

He picks up the man's license and turns to me and Curly. "There's still money on the table. Who wants to play manager?"

Curly and I say "I do" at the same time.

"He's a puke, I tell you," insists the Arab.

But Curly and I feel no pressure taking a turn from the dealership's top earner. If we close a deal that has slipped from the Arab's stubborn grasp, then we are super salesmen and we get half the money. If we don't close it, no problem—we weren't expected to anyway. We go home early.

"Give it to me," Curly says, "I haven't had a sale in two days."

Yes, I reply, but I haven't lost a sale in a week.

Big Curly puts himself between me and the manager. "You owe me one," he says to the manager. "I can close this guy. I do well with clean-cut guys."

But preachers are my specialty, I respond.

"A preacher," says my manager, handing me the money and the license: Hezekiah McBride, forty-five, safe driver, most likely a Holy Roller. "Go make us some more money."

"A puke," says the Arab.

I step down from the tower and walk toward Hezekiah McBride. Brother McBride. Pastor McBride. A man whose diction speaks of sterling credit and a Holy Bible with Concordance in his briefcase. The good Reverend McBride is not here to play games with heathen who calls God "Allah." He's here to buy a car, and I'm just the Sunday school dropout to sell it to him.

So I take my time. I check the tires on our showroom model. I take a side trip into an empty office and sit in the dark for thirty seconds. I come out and sip water from the fountain. I address Miguel, who is now pushing a dust mop over the showroom floor. I ask him if he is certain all the cars outside are locked up. When he informs me they are, I say "Good" in my most authoritarian baritone and then sip from the fountain again.

I take my time not because I'm afraid of Hezekiah McBride, but because I have his license and his money, which he won't leave without. A power game. The longer a buyer stays in the store—no matter how badly you treat him—the more likely it is he will buy.

Hezekiah McBride demands his money and license as soon as I arrive, ignoring my palm extended for an introductory shake; I hand everything over but position myself at the exit of the half-office so that he cannot leave without pushing past me impolitely. He fumbles to replace his license and money in his fat wallet. In the process, he drops two twenties; I pick them up, hand them to him.

"Thanks," he says.

Hezekiah McBride, because he is a man of God, hopes to conceal his anger. I shall use this against him.

Hezekiah, I say, I could hear your voice way up in the management tower, and, well, we've been having some trouble with him.

I point in the general direction of the Arab.

"That young man is a liar and a thief," he says. "He lied about what he was going to give me for my trade-in until I got ready to sign the papers."

Did he now?

"He said he'd give me a thousand, but then he added the cost of air and tires and rust proofing to the new car, raising its price by $750."

In effect, paying you $250 for your trade-in.

"Two hundred fifty dollars."

I frown. I pick up the buyer's order.

Is this the deal?

"Yes."

Trading in a '74 Eldorado. Moderate condition . . .

"Good condition," he corrects. "It just had a paint job."

. . . Some rust. Missing grille. Bald tires. Forty-two thousand miles.

"Two hundred forty-two thousand," he says. "It went over twice."

Thanks for being so honest.

"Mine is not a deceitful tongue."

I lower the buyer's order. I look him straight in the eye.

I appreciate that, Hezekiah. If more people were honest, selling cars would certainly be a lot more enjoyable. You'd be surprised what sort of junk I pay top dollar for.

He says, "No one can fool you. You're a car salesman."

So many years in church, I say, has made me an easy mark for the false tongue.

"Really? What faith are you?"

I say, It's against policy for me to discuss religion at work.

I could've said, My faith is money—though it didn't used to be.

Even now, on Sundays, when I'm not slamming customers or stealing the commission from some ignorant green pea, I might visit the Church of Our Blessed Redeemer Who Walked Upon the Waters to check on the Faithful. I arrive late, take a seat in the back, of course, sing as loud as anybody else—without use of a hymnal—the songs I've known since childhood, and then leave as soon as the musical portion ends. I like music. I can pick a tune on the piano with the best of them, but I have no time for sermons anymore and no faith, except for the green kind, since Elaine passed.

One day I left my wife and my child and my God for her. It was long overdue. She was hospitalized. No cancer. No heart disease. No high blood pressure whirling out of control. An embolism—whatever that is—in her brain. And then in my heart.

"Love," she said. The green, electric mountains became hills, then smaller hills, and then they flattened against the horizon.

The blip-blip became a sigh.

"What?" I said, leaning close to her ear.

"God is love," she said. And then she died, even though I held her hand. She was only fifty-four years old.

"You wouldn't be a Holy Roller, would you?" Hezekiah McBride asks.

Are you?

With his thumbs, he pulls his pants up higher than his waist. "I'm pastor of the Greater Miami Holy Rollers' Tabernacle of Faith."

Beaming, I shake his hand.

I lie, I'm a Holy Roller too!

"Really? I've never seen you in service. Where do you worship?"

I'm not local.

"Kendall, Goulds, Homestead . . . ?"

Yes, Goulds.

(Wherever that is.)

"Pastor Jeroboam, right?"

Yes. (I guess.)

"Well," he says, "you must come up to Greater Miami next week. We're having a tent meeting, and believe me, brother, you don't want to miss the Reverend Jedediah Witherspoon. He's a dynamic speaker come all the way down from Gainesville."

Reverend Jedediah Witherspoon, I echo. I know him well. (He hates me. So does his daughter.)

"What a wonderful testimony he has. He had it all in the '60s, but then because of sin—"

He lost it all. His mansion, his money, his TV show. He spent some time in prison. But now his ministry up there at that University of Florida has come back strong. I wonder if his daughter Donna is going to be there with him. She has a wonderful testimony too.

"You even know his daughter. Well this is something," he says. "To meet a brother at a car dealership."

He made some preachers, He made some salesmen, I say.

"Amen."

I tell you what I'm going to do for you, Pastor McBride. I'm going to simplify this deal. How much do you really think your trade-in is worth?

He knits his brow. "About $800."

A '74 Eldorado with no tires, no grille, and serious rust?

"Five hundred?"

Pastor, it's got over 200,000 miles.

"Three hundred?"

A hundred fifty dollars tops, I say.

"That's no deal. The other guy offered me more."

On paper he did. But when you figured it out . . .

He sighs.

What about this? What if I buy the car from you? What if I give you the $150 in cash? Real money. It's more than these heathens are going to give you when they finish writing it up on paper.

"Cash? Can you do that?" he says.

Yes, I'll buy the car myself. I need something to putter around town in. You can add what I give you to your down payment and get a cheaper monthly rate. And we don't have to let the dealership know. This is between brothers.

"Amen to that," he says. And Hezekiah McBride, without my asking him to, sits down and once again pulls out his $450 in tens and twenties; I reach into my wallet and pull out the "biscuit"—the $150 that the dealership gives me for just such occasions.

I give the biscuit to Hezekiah, and he gives it back to me with his down payment. Now he's happy with the deal.

So am I.

Perhaps if Pastor Hezekiah McBride had earned a useless bachelor's degree in mathematics like I did, he'd realize that biscuit or not, I just snatched his trade-in for a hundred dollars less than the Arab was offering him.

"You are on a roll, my friend," says the Arab.

We could've made more money if you hadn't been so transparent.

"Like you're hurtin for money," Curly says, "after the mint you made on that black girl."

I shouldn't have buried her, I say. It's her first car.

"So?"

She rode in on a bike.

"Don't worry about it," says my manager. "With the money you made, you can afford to take her out to a fancy dinner. Wine her, dine her, take her to bed. I did it a hundred times when I was in sales."

The Arab says, "Best lovers are customers."

Curly says, "Ever notice how when a customer forces a great deal out of you, I mean practically steals the best car on the lot, this same jerk customer—instead of being satisfied—always returns again and again to complain about everything? But you rip a customer off, bury the sucker like you did that black girl today—and guess what? That customer never bothers you again. If anything, a sucker like that refers other suckers to you."

She's not a sucker, I counter.

"No offense," says the Arab, "but you know young black women are the easiest sell. Young black women, then young black men, then young white women, young white men, and like that all the way up to the toughest sell, old white men."

So where do sand-niggers like yourself fit in?

"Hey!" exclaims the Arab.

Are kikes on that list?

"Wait a minute," says Curly, rising to his feet—Curly whose paternal grandfather survived Treblinka.

I turn to my manager, but he is a peckerwood with the power to fire me.

He smiles. "Take it easy," he says, putting a hand on my shoulder.

"You've gone overboard," says Curly. "You wouldn't like it if I called you the N-word."

"I thought we were friends," says the Arab.

Forgive me, I say. You are my friend. You are all my friends. I'm just under a lot of pressure.

"But you made so much money," say the Arab, Curly, and my manager.

Yes, I did, I say.

But maybe money isn't everything.

I pull up to my parents' house, where I live in a room over their garage. A light is on in the living room, and through the verticals I make out my mother, my father, and my ex-wife Mary, who I know is there to ask me in a most displeasing fashion why child support payments haven't been received in two months, so I back up and out of the driveway.

I drive a two-seater tonight, my reward for burying Ida and bamboozling Pastor Hezekiah McBride. The odometer reads 25—a virgin. The smell is Windex and Lysol and something lemony. Then the car smells like smoke too, when I light a cigarette. I'm trying to quit. I take two, three, four drags and I crumple the cigarette into the ashtray. Then I chew a piece of Juicy Fruit, wad it up, and stick it in the ashtray as a little something for the new owners to find—let them know I was here first. I ride the clutch. I make the tires squeal when I round corners. I pull onto the lonely expressway, pretend it is the autobahn, crank it up to 120.

As usual, I end up in that bad section of town where Peachie, my oldest and dearest friend, lives. My car is eyed by two lanky young men with heads shaved except for on the top where there is a profusion of short, tight braids tied together with rubber bands. I get out of the car. I do not bother to lock the doors. It ain't my car. What do I care?

Inside, Peachie lights cherry incense. She goes into the bedroom and comes out in a see-through slip. We fall onto the couch and grope each other until it is obvious nothing more is going to happen tonight. For some reason, my stud machine is stuck in neutral.

I light a cigarette.

Peachie rolls off my lap and sits up, scratching her bare ass. "I thought you quit smoking." She makes a prune face and fans the fumes away from her, gets up, and mounts her exercise bicycle set up in the middle of the small living room—THE AMAZING CENTRO-CYCLE, LOSE TEN POUNDS IN TEN DAYS (actual weight loss may vary from user to user).

She begins to pedal. "Smoking is going to give you cancer."

The spirit is willing, but the flesh is weak.

I take a final puff and mash the cigarette into the bright red ceramic elephant-fending-off-tiger-attack ashtray on her coffee table.

"You're the only one who ever uses that," she observes.

I get up and reach for Peachie again.

She covers her breasts with the see-through slip and shoos me away.

"Don't start the engine if you don't want to drive," she quips, pedaling faster. "So talk."

My life is shit.

"Not your life," she says. Pedal. Pedal. "Your job. Just quit your shitty job."

It's not that easy. I love my shitty job. It's great getting paid to play mind games on people.

"It must be, because they certainly don't pay you much. Your ex-wife is hounding you for child support. When was the last time she let you see your son? And look at you—a car salesman who can't afford a car. You're a college graduate, isn't that what they call irony?" Pedal. Pedal.

Peachie, my once-skinny Peachie, weighs close to two hundred pounds. But she manages the restaurant now. She's moving out of this dump at the end of the month. In a year, she'll apply for a franchise, and she'll get it. She's that good at what she does. I have faith in her.

It beats preaching, I say.

"Who're you kidding? Preachers make plenty of money. Barry is a millionaire ten times over. And I know from experience that they get laid a lot too. Should I mention Barry again?"

It's just a joke, I say.

"The joke is that as old as you are, you still live with your parents."

Thanks for cheering me up, Peachie. I feel so good I could just kill myself. Praise the Lord for friends like you.

"That'll teach you to withhold sex from me. You know how snippy I am when I don't get my quota."

Look, if you're serious about it, I'll come over on the weekend. I'll help you pack and we can do some et cetera.

"No way, stud. The kids are coming over. We're going up to Disney World."

You've really gotten your life together, Peachie. I'm proud of you. I envy you.

"All I had to do was figure out that the Lord wasn't going to help Peachie until Peachie helped Peachie. The solution was on the inside all the time."

I wish I could get my life together. Everything I touch seems to turn to crap. I have no luck. Everybody seems to be doing great, but me. You—you're my friend and all; I mean, I'm not jealous of your success, but I do have a college degree.

"And I don't. And yet things are working out for me."

See what I'm saying? Right. I'm thirty. I live with my parents. I'm a car salesman.

"Yes." The big wheel on the bike is turning faster now. Pedal. Pedal. "Maybe you should accept the Lord again."

Give me a break.

"It might help," she laughs. "Maybe God is mad at you for turning your back on Him. Get saved and see what happens. I'm saved."

No offense, Peachie, but what kind of saved woman—

"Don't go getting into my sex life, boy, or you won't get any more of this sweet thing ever again." She rubs her round little tummy suggestively. "My private groove is my private groove. I pay my tithes. I give to the poor. I say my prayers at night. I'm saved. I want to go to heaven when I die. God stays out of my sex life."

What! But that's not saved, Peachie. That's not saved like it was when we were growing up. That's so worldly. So secular. God's people have to be apart. They have to be different. Christians these days—I don't understand them at all. They go to parties, they drink, they have premarital sex, they wear the fashions of the world. Even the music. These days you can't tell the difference between a church song and hip-hop.

Peachie is pedaling. Peachie is ignoring me. Finally, after I have finished my venting, she says into the silence, "So who has rendered you impotent this time? A secretary, a fry cook, a bag lady—"

Bag ladies don't buy cars.

"A maid, a postal clerk, a stripper? Strippers buy cars, don't they?"

Yes. I've had a few strippers.

"A ditch digger, a cop, a paralegal . . . ?"

A student, I say.

"Aha! Seduction of the innocent. That's your specialty. Have you slept with her yet?"

No. But I think there may be something more to it this time.

"You?" She gets off the bike, wipes the sweat from her brow with the hem of the slip. Peachie's a big woman now. But her body looks real nice with the extra pounds. Real nice. "Give me a break."

Really. I regret ripping her off.

"Regret? Not you." Now Peachie mimics me: "I feel no guilt. I'm a salesman. I'm hardcore. I've got a hard-on for hard cash."

The student reminds me of Elaine.

Peachie opens her lips and sucks in air. Now she says in a soft voice, "In what way?"

It's in the way she cries, she reminds me. I ripped her off, threw it in her face, and yet she doesn't hate me.

"Turning the other cheek," Peachie says. "So much like Christ."

Not funny, Sister McGowan.

"I couldn't resist. Why did you rip her off?"

Blinded by greed, I guess.

"It's not greed if they don't pay you shit. Blinded by stupidity most likely." Peachie kisses me on the forehead. "Go after her."

Yeah. I'm thinking the same thing.

"And make amends."

I no longer subscribe to the concept of guilt. It is not by your works that ye are saved, Peachie. But I'm thinking the same thing.

"And get out of the car business. It's taking your soul."

I no longer subscribe to the concept of a soul or a God, Peachie, but I'm thinking the same thing.

Peachie slaps my mouth playfully. "Liar, liar, liar. You're just as much a Christian as you've ever been."

What proof do you have that this is so?

"Your life, in fact, is shit, but you're still able to love."

I think about this for a few moments, then I say, Good answer, Peachie. Good answer.

"God is love," Peachie says. "God is here with us right now."

So here I am the next morning, fighting with Lou the service writer. First he tells me the Lord of Travel is going to have to wait its turn in line. The mechanics won't get to it until late tomorrow. They won't finish it until late the day after that. It's going to cost at least $400.

Four bills? I know you can fix it for less than four bills, I say. The car is for my mother, Lou. I'm sure you can do it for less than four bills, and don't give me that crap about waiting in line. We work together, Lou.

Lou says, "What can I do? I don't own the business. I don't make the rules."

I know, I know. But remember, Lou, I covered for you on that tires and batteries thing, and all I asked for was a measly twenty when I could've asked for fifty or a hundred. Remember, Lou, one hand washes the other.

Lou remembers the tires and batteries thing. "I'll see what I can do," he says, "for your mother."

At 1 p.m., Lou calls me.

I run to the service area and pay my "mother's" tab, fifty dollars in cash, which I hand Lou and which he puts in his wallet.

The Lord of Travel does not emit smoke nor spray water anymore, but I notice it pulls too much to the left. When it runs, I can hear its belts grinding. It stalls, once in a while, in idle. I worry about the brakes, which are slow to respond. I take it back to Lou, who is not happy to see me but smiles anyway.

My mother says the car needs a tune-up, new belts, a new battery, new brake shoes, I tell him. She travels out of town a lot and wants to feel secure on the road. By the way, she was wondering if you could check the alignment and, if it's not too much trouble, throw a couple tires in the trunk. The ones in back are just about worn out.

"Your mother is a thief," Lou says.

And she needs it by 5 . . . today.

"My God."

It's just a little favor, Lou.

He whispers, "Okay. But after this, no more. We're even."

Sure, Lou.

"No. To hell with that. Now you owe me."

I'll take care of you, I say. I know a few people who could use a dis-counted set of tires, no questions asked.

They finish the Lord of Travel just after 4 p.m. I take it for a test drive, and I am impressed. Lou had them put over a thousand dollars worth of parts and labor into the car in less than seven hours. And all for fifty dollars and a smile! The car wasn't so bad after all. It just needed to have a few specific parts repaired.

I take it across the street to the Amoco station where I fill it with gas using the dealership's credit card. Then I slide Miguel five dollars, and he washes and waxes it until I can see my reflection—I am framed in a shave, a haircut, a new tie. I'm not so bad either.

Curly pats me on the back. "Lookin good. I hope the sex is worth all this."

I'm not after sex this time.

"Is she rich?" asks the Arab.

It's not like that. This is my last day.

"Yeah?" says the Arab. "Where you headed this time? Buick? Isuzu? Honda?" He reads something in my expression that is not there. "Aha, so big-bonus Mike over at Honda got your attention again."

Curly says, "It's not a bad idea. They pay 30 percent after the tenth car."

"Thirty percent?" says the Arab. "Really?" He licks his lips, looks at me.

I have no idea, I say. I'm not going to Honda. I'm not going anywhere. One good deed for this woman and then I'm gone. I'm getting out of the business.

"Out of the business? No way," says the Arab. "Once a car salesman, always a car salesman. It's like religion."

"What will you do for money?" asks Curly.

Anything but this. I'll flip hamburgers. I'll paint houses. I need a real job. I'll sell Amway.

"No way," says the Arab. "You'll never quit."

"And why would you want to quit?" adds Curly. I am sandwiched between them. A determined hand on each of my shoulders keeps me from moving. "Why quit after you made so much money? Is it this girl?"

Of course. It's always a girl.

* * *

When Ida arrives, she does so in a car driven by a large, hairy man whose face is a mask of hatefulness. As the car rolls by, she points to me and the angry man gives me a look that leaves no doubt he wants to hurt me, so I toss Miguel the keys and run inside the showroom.

Take care of her, I say. Tell her I'm in a meeting and can't be disturbed.

Inside I watch, hidden behind the Arab, who always carries a can of Mace, and big Curly, who was on his college wrestling team before he flunked out.

Ida and the man park next to the Lord of Travel. They get out and slam their doors. The man runs his hands over the car. He seems pleased with what he discovers, and his expression softens somewhat. He looks at Ida, who shrugs her shoulders. She grabs the keys from Miguel, and she and the large man hop into the Lord of Travel and spin off for a test drive. Nearly an hour later, they return. The large man gets into his car and drives away without a word to Ida.

Ida stands beside the Lord of Travel, perplexed. I walk out to meet her.

"He likes the car," she says. "He had one like it when he was younger."

(Probably the same one.)

I told you it was a nice car, I say. You see, I am a nice guy. I had them fix it up for you and everything. And I paid for it out of my own pocket.

"I bet you did."

I really did.

"But you overcharged me for it in the first place."

I tried to get you the best deal I could.

"I bet you did."

I really did.

"Doesn't matter. If he says it's a nice car, it's a nice car."

He's your . . . mechanic?

"My boyfriend."

Lucky guy, I say.

"He came to get my money back. And, if necessary," she says, her eyes narrowing to slits, "to beat the hell out of you."

Lucky me, I think. But I know she would never let him hurt me, this hairy man she claims is her boyfriend. She brought him because she knows what I am capable of, and she wanted a fair fight this time. Smart.

Ida is beautiful. I want to hear her say that I'm not like the rest of them. I want another hug. I want to love her.

So I say, Well you got yourself a nice car, though, didn't you?

I nod my head. She nods hers.

All your friends will be impressed, won't they?

I nod my head. She nods hers.

And, I add, you made a new friend, didn't you?

I nod my head and extend my hand, but she only looks at me and laughs.

She says, "It never ends with you people, does it?"

No, I answer. I'm not like that anymore. I quit. I really did.

"Lucky you," she says, and then she gets into the refurbished Lord of Travel and drives away, leaving me standing there with my hand extended.

I think, God is love, God is love, God is love.

I am so choked up that the Arab almost beats me to the next customer who pulls up on the lot. But I can tell by the cut of the man's double-breasted jacket and his confident, purposeful stride that he's on a mission. That he's a preacher. The poor Arab doesn't have a chance.

I move so fast I must have wings.

HERE ENDETH THE TESTAMENT OF FIRE AND LAMENTATIONS

HERE ENDETH THE ENTIRE TESTAMENTS OF THE FAITHFUL OF THE CHURCH OF OUR BLESSED REDEEMER WHO WALKED UPON THE WATERS

HERE ENDETH THE CAUTION AND THE TALE

Amen